THE BL...

...read

...the war

she was an Assis... ...at the Treasury, and then worked with UNRRA in London, Belgium and Austria. She held a studentship in Philosophy at Newnham College, Cambridge, and then in 1948 she returned to Oxford, where she became a Fellow of St Anne's College. Until her death in February 1999, she lived with her husband, the teacher and critic John Bayley, in Oxford. Awarded the CBE in 1976, Iris Murdoch was made a DBE in the 1987 New Year's Honours List. In the 1997 PEN Awards she received the Gold Pen for Distinguished Service to Literature.

Following her writing debut in 1954 with *Under the Net*, Iris Murdoch wrote twenty-six novels, including the Booker Prize-winning *The Sea, The Sea* (1978). Other literary awards she received include the James Tait Black Memorial Prize for *The Black Prince* (1973) and the Whitbread Prize for *The Sacred and Profane Love Machine* (1974). Her works of philosophy include *Sartre: Romantic Rationalist* (1953), *Metaphysics as a Guide to Morals* (1992) and *Existentialists and Mystics* (1997). She wrote several plays including *The Italian Girl* (with James Saunders) and *The Black Prince*, adapted from her novel of the same name.

ALSO BY IRIS MURDOCH

Fiction

Under the Net
The Flight from the Enchanter
The Sandcastle
The Bell
A Severed Head
An Unofficial Rose
The Unicorn
The Italian Girl
The Red and the Green
The Time of the Angels
The Nice and the Good
Bruno's Dream
A Fairly Honourable Defeat
An Accidental Man
The Sacred and Profane Love Machine
A Word Child
Henry and Cato
The Sea, The Sea
Nuns and Soldiers
The Philosopher's Pupil
The Good Apprentice
The Book and the Brotherhood
The Message to the Planet
The Green Knight
Jackson's Dilemma
Something Special

Non-Fiction

Sartre: Romantic Rationalist
Acastos: Two Platonic Dialogues
Metaphysics as a Guide to Morals
Existentialists and Mystics

IRIS MURDOCH

The Black Prince

WITH AN INTRODUCTION BY
Candia McWilliam

VINTAGE BOOKS
London

Published by Vintage 2006

13 15 17 19 20 18 16 14

Copyright © Iris Murdoch 1973
Introduction copyright © Candia McWilliams 1999

First published in Great Britain in 1973 by
Chatto & Windus

Vintage
Random House, 20 Vauxhall Bridge Road,
London SW1V 2SA

www.randomhouse.co.uk/vintage

Addresses for companies within The Random House Group Limited
can be found at:
www.randomhouse.co.uk/offices.htm

The Random House Group Limited Reg. No. 954009

A CIP catalogue record for this book
is available from the British Library

ISBN 9780099283997 (from Jan 2007)
ISBN 0099283999

The Random House Group Limited makes every effort to ensure
that the papers used in its books are made from trees that have been
legally sourced from well-managed and credibly certified forests.
Our paper procurement policy can be found at:
www.randomhouse.co.uk/paper.htm

Printed and bound in Great Britain by
Cox & Wyman Ltd, Reading, Berkshire

To *Ernesto De Marchi*

INTRODUCTION

There are two great portraits of the author of *The Black Prince*. One is by her husband, John Bayley; the memoir entitled simply *Iris* that gives with his customary inordinate subtlety an account of her personality as it revealed itself in her last cruelly shaded years, a personality irreducibly good allied to an intellect and an imagination that were, in the long creative years before Alzheimer's disease encroached, well up to the problems of evil. The other great portrait is in paint and it is by Tom Phillips. Dame Iris, child-faced, wearing a shirt as blue as the faded-cotton-colour Canterbury bells that decorate the brief idyll of *The Black Prince*'s hero and his love, is before another painting; *The Flaying of Marsyas*, by Titian.

Apollo flays Marsyas who has dared rival his own art. Bradley Pearson, the 'author' of *The Black Prince*, may or may not in this book do something similar. Certainly there is a climatic murder, certainly its victim is an artist in a medium where Pearson believes himself pre-eminent. They are both writers, of two types to which their inventor did not belong. Bradley Pearson is a blocked exquisite paralysed by distaste and the chafe of time against staled potential. Arnold Baffin is younger and unafraid of the worst sort of broad thought and sweeping style. His is prolific, and successful. Among his titles are: *The Precious Labyrinth; The Gauntlets of Power; Tobias and the Fallen Angel; A Banner with a Strange Device; Essays of a Seeker; A Skull on Fire; A Clash of Symbols; Hollows in the Sky; The Glass Sword; Mysticism and Literature; The Maid and the Magus; The Pierced Chalice; Inside a Snow Crystal*.

It might be instructive at this point to turn for aesthetic reassurance to the list at the front of this book of Dame Iris's own *œuvre*. Assuredly she is teasing herself with this adroit and creepy list. Perusal of her own numinous but concrete titles, however, reassures. The jokes in her cod-list are pleasingly broad and spot-on, too. Only look in the special interest zones of the *Times Literary Supplement* to find those dispirit-ingly clever symbols clashing.

There are aspects of her art, to be found in each of her novels, that undoubtedly are gauche, implausible, even laughable. Their effect is paradoxical. Save in her very last, already fogged and struggling, novels, the curlicues, the foregrounded emblems, the impossible names, the mystery of how many of her protagonists make their living and so on, all serve to intensify the essence of the very particular world that is

I

contained in her fiction. Unrealistic some things may be, but the effect of the novels is to convey to us reality, unfolded, shaking out light and air from between its newly perceived and freed layers.

As quite a young child, reading a *Broons* annual (the Broons are a huge family of Glaswegians who have adventures and are published in a finely drawn cartoon series published to this day by D. C. Thompson) on the floor of the house of friends of my parents, I heard an adult say that she wished 'Iris Murdoch would not write her adjectives in threes.' So I watched out for this habit when I began to read her, and it is true, she favours a triplet. Occasionally there are bravura groups of four or five adjectives in an asyndetonic queue ('She was looking at me in the cool north indigo duskiness of the room with such a humble pleading diffident rueful tender look on her face . . .'). The effect of her stylistic idiosyncrasies is, curiously, not to impress the reader with the author's wrought technique, but to soothe them with her strength, the rough virtuous sense that her art is coming through the conduit of her work without the strain or sift of over-refinement.

Her work has a want of perfectedness that is respectful of a number of things holy to this artist and philosopher, who wrote, 'God does not and cannot exist. But what led us to conceive of him does exist and is constantly experienced and pictured. That is it is real as an idea, and also incarnate in knowledge and work and love.' Her shifts and raggedness are inclusive, her rich but not taut-polished and buttoned prose respectful of created perfection, as a wilfully smudged hubris-evading line of tragic verse or mosque-decoration might be.

The Black Prince tells us a story, which we must turn inside out, or handle and shape in shocked retrospect. It is not simply a trick, or it would not repay persistent re-reading. Although you remember the course the book in fact takes, you are bound at some point to wish existential freedom upon the characters in order that they may arrange things in another way. That is to say, her characters in this novel, preposterous as their names, situations or verbal tics may be, live.

She has also given us, in Bradley Pearson, an awful man to whom we nonetheless, and often in spite of ourselves, wish good things to happen. This flatters and surprises the reader. We are more used to find the base in ourselves. Bradley is vain, unspontaneous, cold, pompous, self-justifying, disloyal, heartless and mean. He is one in a number of frozen intellectual ingrates with dusty selfish ways of whom Dame Iris was, in Oxford, very possibly able to make a fair study.

Bradley has been married, to Christian, who, for good measure, he discovers to be Jewish well after their marriage is over. In itself implausible in a characteristically Murdochian way, the off-keyness and unintimacy however convey an atmosphere of peculiar profound uncertainty and unknowability that is consummated by the novel's end. Christian is rich and handsome and desirable. By the end of the book, in another flight of divergence from the likely, she is a considerable force in what is referred to as *haute couture*.

I have always relished this novelist on clothes; vatic, hieratic, Shakespearean, *travesti*, Mannerist, fairytale, seven league, old masterly, heraldic, the garments come from her head, transformative and magical and extravagant as *haute couture* itself (though she will treat a humble mac to the same glow), with no nod to the unfledged stuffs dependent from hangers most of us keep in our cupboards. Creative energy, a kind of exalted drive, and a quality perhaps most closely definable as innocence keep Dame Iris's descriptions of clothing, as of children and the young, from being at odds with her great themes, or, simply, beyond belief.

The young person who loses ideas and desire in *The Black Prince* is Julian Baffin, so called for Julian of Norwich. Julian is the daughter of Bradley Pearson's younger friend and more successful rival, Arnold Baffin, married to Rachel, a soft-bodied redhead in middle age whom her husband believes, at the beginning of the book, he may have murdered. By the book's end we see how the plot, like a bulb, held itself within its replete beginning. 'Coming events do cast shadows', as Pearson says.

Julian Baffin is as ambiguous to look at as is her name, and she, crucially, dresses as the hero of the play by which she is possessed, *Hamlet*, at one of the plot's crises. At other times she recalls a timid deer, a lion, a fox. She is the herald of romance and also of danger. Our view of her good faith fluctuates. Is she manipulative or innocent, delinquent and destructive or just young; and is not to be young to be all of the foregoing? As in other novels by Iris Murdoch, the vocabulary of the young is touchingly unmimetic; very few young women of the Seventies, when Julian Baffin came to be and, presumably, is living, used the words 'absurd' or 'I say'. Yet these idioms roost quite easily in the branches of Iris Murdoch's stout yet airy novels. Perhaps it is to do with her lack of false dignity as an artist, the absence of a constructed personality lying against the grain of her nature, which is shiningly conveyed in her husband's account of the failure of her mental dismantling to reveal ugly layers of being.

Between Bradley and Christian, Arnold and Rachel and Julian, various forms of what represents itself as love are played out, complicated by the incrudescence of Bradley's pathetic deserted sister Priscilla and Christian's feckless doctor brother Francis, needed when he can be of use and otherwise horribly overlooked until he at last, with dingy furtive self-indulgence, brings about a death. Inattention as *de facto* murder cannot be unusual. Here it shows up what fancied itself hidden, as the glare of death will. One of the pleasures of the panoptic novel as Iris Murdoch gives it to us is the unsadistic but merciless exposure of illusion, untruth, infatuation. As she has Bradley Pearson say, 'What is ugly and undignified is hardest of all, harder that wickedness, to soften into a mutually acceptable past.'

And again, though he falls – or does he? the plot's ambiguity is watertight – far short of what he says, 'Art is concerned not just primarily but absolutely with truth. It is another name for truth.'

The Black Prince, then, is full of plot, of types – one might say characters – of love and of meditations upon art. It is, as is usual in the works of this writer, fantastically generous with ideas. At one point Bradley Pearson says to Julian, 'Shakespeare, by the sheer intensity of his own meditation upon the problem of his identity has produced a new language, a special rhetoric of consciousness.' Glancingly, in a conversation that is a courtship too, we look into the peopled thickets of a mind that prefigures Harold Bloom's (to me attractive) contentions. This long, satisfying and playful novel displays in its flower a mind at ease with what is concrete and what is not, and has forged a medium in which they are bound together in a creation that may be without a presiding single God but is saturated with what arouses the impulse to awe.

Throughout the book, I was arrested by beautiful writing of a very particular sort, arriving, as it were, unbidden, at ease, without announcing itself, almost swelling from the prose. Perhaps I may single out two examples. The first is when Bradley, having drunk a quantity of sherry in Bristol after a visit to his sister's unfaithful husband, thinks, 'There is . . . some hard-won calm when we see the world very detailed and very close; as close and vivid as the newly painted funnels of ships on a sunny evening.' The other tackles time and identity: 'The division of one day from the next must be one of the most profound peculiarities of life on this planet. It is, on the whole, a merciful arrangement. We are not condemned to sustained flights of being, but are constantly refreshed by little holidays from ourselves. We are intermittent creatures, always falling to little ends and rising to new little beginnings. Our soon-tired consciousness is meted out in chapters, and that the world will look quite different tomorrow is, both for our comfort and our discomfort, usually true. How marvellously too night matches sleep, sweet image of it, so neatly apportioned to our need. Angels must wonder at these beings who fall so regularly out of awareness into a fantasm-infested dark. How our frail identities survive these chasms no philosopher has ever been able to explain.'

Big, ostentatiously erudite and busily informative novels with an informing metaphor have enjoyed much success at this end of the century; stories with the stimulation of action and the roughage of fact. They can at their worst debase the novel, affording little place to thought or poetry, masquerading as teacher while in fact performing as distraction from the profound. It is the angelic genius of Iris Murdoch to interinanimate thought and feeling, not to set them in blocks against one another, but to fold them together and in so doing to trounce these nutritious tomes with her innocent, ruthless winged human flight of mind.

CANDIA MCWILLIAM
1999

Contents

Editor's Foreword

I am in more than one way responsible for the work that follows. The author of it, my friend Bradley Pearson, has placed the arrangements for publication in my hands. In this humble mechanical sense it is through my agency that these pages now reach the public. I am also the 'dear friend' (and such) who is referred to and at times addressed in the book. I am not however an actor in the drama which Pearson recounts. My friendship with Bradley Pearson dates from a time in our lives posterior to the events here narrated. This has been a time of tribulation when we needed and happily found in each other the blessings of friendship. I can say indeed with confidence that were it not for the encouragement and sympathy which I was able to give to Bradley, this story would probably have remained untold. Those who cry out the truth to an indifferent world too often weary, fall silent, or come to doubt their own wit. Without my help this could have been so with Bradley Pearson. He needed someone to believe him and someone to believe in him. He found me, his *alter ego*, at the time needful.

What follows is in its essence as well as in its contour a love story. I mean that it is deeply as well as superficially so. Man's creative struggle, his search for wisdom and truth, is a love story. What follows is ambiguous and sometimes tortuously told. Man's searchings and his strugglings are ambiguous and vowed to hidden ways. Those who live by that dark light will understand. And yet: what can be simpler than a tale of love and more charming? That art gives charm to terrible things is perhaps its glory, perhaps its curse. Art is a doom. It has been the doom of Bradley Pearson. And in a quite different way it is my own.

My task as editor has been a simple one. Perhaps I should

9

more justly describe myself as – what? A sort of impresario?
A clown or harlequin figure who parades before the curtain,
then draws it solemnly back? I have reserved for myself the last
word of all, the final assessment or summing up. Yet I would
with better grace appear as Bradley's fool than as his judge. It
may be that in some sense I am both. Why this tale had to be
written will appear, in more senses than one, within the tale. But
there is after all no mystery. Every artist is an unhappy lover.
And unhappy lovers want to tell their story.

P. A. Loxias
Editor

Bradley Pearson's Foreword

Although several years have now passed since the events recorded in this fable, I shall in telling it adopt the modern technique of narration, allowing the narrating consciousness to pass like a light along its series of present moments, aware of the past, unaware of what is to come. I shall, that is, inhabit my past self and, for the ordinary purposes of story-telling, speak only with the apprehensions of that time, a time in many ways so different from the present. So for example I shall say, 'I am fifty-eight years old', as I then was. And I shall judge people, inadequately, perhaps even unjustly, as I then judged them, and not in the light of any later wisdom. That wisdom however, as I trust that I truly think it to be, will not be absent from the story. It will to some extent, in fact it must, 'irradiate' it. A work of art is as good as its creator. It cannot be more so. Nor, such as he in this case is, can it be less. The virtues have secret names: they are, so difficult of access, secret things. Everything that is worthy is secret. I will not attempt to describe or name that which I have learnt within the disciplined simplicity of my life as it has latterly been lived. I hope that I am a wiser and more charitable man now than I was then – I am certainly a happier man – and that the light of wisdom falling upon a fool can reveal, together with folly, the austere outline of truth. I have already by implication described this 'reportage' as a work of art. I do not of course by this mean a work of fantasy. All art deals with the absurd and aims at the simple. Good art speaks truth, indeed *is* truth, perhaps the only truth. I have endeavoured in what follows to be wisely artful and artfully wise, and to tell truth as I understand it, not only concerning the superficial and 'exciting' aspects of this drama, but also concerning what lies deeper.

I am aware that people often have completely distorted general ideas of what they are like. Men truly manifest themselves in the long patterns of their acts, and not in any nutshell of self-theory. This is supremely true of the artist, who appears, however much he may imagine that he hides, in the revealed extension of his work. And so am I too here exhibited, whose pitiful instinct is alas still for a concealment quite at odds with my trade. Under this cautionary rubric I shall however now attempt a general description of myself. And now I am speaking, as I explained, in the *persona* of the self of several years ago, the often inglorious 'hero' of the tale that follows. I am fifty-eight years old. I am a writer. 'A writer' is indeed the simplest and also the most accurate general description of me. In so far as I am also a psychologist, an amateur philosopher, a student of human affairs, I am so because these things are a part of being the kind of writer that I am. I have always been a seeker. And my seeking has taken the form of that attempt to tell truth of which I have just spoken. I have, I hope and I believe, kept my gift pure. This means, among other things, that I have never been a successful writer. I have never tried to please at the expense of truth. I have known, for long periods, the torture of life without self-expression. The most potent and sacred command which can be laid upon any artist is the command: wait. Art has its martyrs, not least those who have preserved their silence. There are, I hazard, saints of art who have simply waited mutely all their lives rather than profane the purity of a single page with anything less than what is perfectly appropriate and beautiful, that is to say, with anything less than what is true.

As is well known, I have published very little. I say 'as is well known', relying here for my fame upon publicity deriving from my adventures outside the purlieus of art. My name is not unknown, but this alas is not because I am a writer. As a writer I have reached and doubtless will reach only a perceptive few. The paradox perhaps of my whole life, and it is an absurdity upon which I do not cease to meditate, is that the dramatic story which follows, so unlike the rest of my work, may well prove to be my only 'best seller'. There are undoubtedly here the elements of crude drama, the 'fabulous' events which simple people love to hear of. And indeed I have had, in this connection, my own good share of being 'front page news'.

12

I will not attempt to describe my publications. They were, in the context to which I alluded above, much talked *of*, though not I fear read. I published a precocious novel at the age of twenty-five. I published another novel, or quasi-novel, at the age of forty. I have also emitted a small book of 'texts' or 'studies', I would not exactly call it a work of philosophy. (*Pensées* perhaps.) Time has not been given me in which to become a philosopher, and this I but in part regret. Only stories and magic really endure. How tiny one's area of understanding is art teaches one perhaps better than philosophy. There is a kind of despair involved in creation which I am sure any artist knows all about. In art, as in morality, great things go by the board because at the crucial moment we blink our eyes. When is the crucial moment? Greatness is to recognize it and be able to hold it and to extend it. But for most of us the space between 'dreaming on things to come' and 'it is too late, it is all over' is too tiny to enter. And so we let each thing go, thinking vaguely that it will always be given to us to try again. Thus works of art, and thus whole lives of men, are spoilt by blinking and moving quickly on. I often found that I had ideas for stories, but by the time I had thought them out in detail they seemed to me hardly worth writing, as if I had already 'done' them: not because they were bad, but because they already belonged to the past and I had lost interest. My thoughts were soon stale to me. Some things I ruined by starting them too soon. Others by thinking them so intensely in my head that they were over before they began. Projects would change in a second from hazy uncommitted dreams into unsalvageable ancient history. Whole novels existed only in their titles. The three slim volumes which have emerged from this wrack may seem a meagre foundation upon which to rest the sacred claim of being 'a writer'. But in fact (I feel inclined to say 'of course') my faith in myself in this respect, my sense of the absoluteness of this destiny, this even doom, has never weakened or wavered. I have 'waited', not always with patience, but, in recent years at least, with an increasing confidence. I have felt ever behind the veil of the future that a great achievement was hidden still. Let those smile who have endured as long. And if it should turn out that this small story about myself is all that my destiny is for, is the crown after all of my expectation, shall I feel myself cheated?

Not cheated surely, for against that darkness one is bereft of rights. No man has the right to exercise divine power. All that one can do is to wait, to try, to wait again. The elementary need to render a truthful account of what has been so universally falsified and misrepresented is the ordinary motive for this enterprise: and to tell of a wonder which has thus far remained secret. Because I am an artist this story takes the form of a work of art. May it be worthy of those deeper motives which it also owns.

I shall describe myself a little more. My parents kept a shop. This is important, though not as important as Francis Marloe thinks, and certainly not in the way that he thinks. I mention Francis first of any of my 'players' not because he is the most important: Francis is not important at all and has no deep connection with the course of these events. He is a subsidiary, a sidesman, in the story as I fear he is generally in life. Poor Francis will never be the hero of anything. He would make an excellent fifth wheel to any coach. But I make him as it were the mascot of the tale, partly because in a purely mechanical sense he opens it, and if on a certain day he had not, and so on, I might never, and so on. There is another paradox. One must constantly meditate upon the absurdities of chance, a subject even more edifying than the subject of death. Partly too I give a special place to Francis because he is, of the main actors in this drama, probably the only one who believes that I am not a liar. My gratitude to you, Francis Marloe, if you are still among the living and should chance to see these words. That another, later, believed me has proved of infinitely greater value. But you were *then* the only one who saw and understood. Across the aeons of time which have passed since that tragedy, I salute you, Francis.

My parents kept a shop, a sort of paper shop, down in Croydon. The shop sold daily papers and magazines, writing paper and so on, and horrible 'gifts'. My sister Priscilla and I lived in this shop. We did in fact often have our tea there, and I have a 'memory' of sleeping under the counter. But the shop was the house and the mythical domain of our childhood. Some fortunate children have a garden, a landscape, as the 'local habitation' of their early years. We had the shop: its drawers, its shelves, its

14

smells, its endless empty cardboard boxes, its particular dirt. It was a shabby unsuccessful shop. Our parents were shabby unsuccessful people. They both died when I was in my twenties, my father first, my mother not long after. My mother lived to see my first book published. She was proud of me. My mother filled me with exasperation and shame but I loved her. (Be quiet Francis Marloe.) My father I simply disliked. Or perhaps I have forgotten my affection for him. One can forget love, as you will perceive that I shortly find out.

I will not go on about the shop. I still dream about it at least once a week. Francis Marloe thought this very significant when I told him once. But Francis belongs to that sad crew of semi-educated theorizers who prefer any general blunted 'symbolic' explanation to the horror of confronting a unique human history. Francis wanted to 'explain' me. In my moment of fame, a number of other and much cleverer people attempted this also. But any human person is infinitely more complex than this type of explanation. By 'infinitely' (or should I say 'almost infinitely'? Alas I am no philosopher) I mean that there are not only more details, but more kinds of details with more kinds of relations than these diminishers can dream of. You might as well try to 'explain' a Michelangelo on a piece of graph paper. Only art explains, and that cannot itself be explained. We and art are made for each other, and where that bond fails human life fails. Only this analogy holds, only this mirror shows a just image. Of course we have an 'unconscious mind' and this is partly what my book is about. But there is no general chart of that lost continent. Certainly not a 'scientific' one.

My life, until the drama which brought it so significantly to a climax, had been an uneventful one. Some people might call it dull. In fact, if one can use that rather beautiful and pungent word in an almost non-emotive sense, my life had been sublimely dull, a great dull life. I was married, then ceased to be married, as I shall tell. I am childless. I suffer from intermittent stomach troubles and insomnia. I have usually lived alone. After my wife, and also before her, there were women about whom I shall not speak since they are irrelevant and unimportant. Sometimes I saw myself as an ageing Don Juan, but the majority of my conquests belonged to the world of fantasy. I wished in after years when it seemed too late to start that I had kept a diary. One's capacity to forget absolutely is immense. And this would have been some sort of monument with an almost guaranteeable value. A sort of Seducer's Diary with metaphysical reflections might have been an ideal literary form for me, I have often thought. But the years are spent and gone to oblivion that might have filled it. So much for women. On the whole I have been cheerful, a solitary but not unsociable, sometimes unhappy, often melancholy. (Cheerfulness and melancholy are not incompatible.) I have had few intimate friends. (I could not I think be 'friends' with a woman.) This book is in fact the story of an 'intimate friendship'. I found good friends, though not intimate ones ('pals' you might call them) through my office work. I do not speak of those years 'at the office'; nor do I speak of those friends, not out of ingratitude, but partly for aesthetic reasons, since they do not figure in the tale, and also out of delicacy since they may no longer wish to be associated with me. Alone of these old 'pals' I mention Hartbourne, because he seems such a typical denizen of my great years of dullness, and so can conveniently represent the others; and also because he did at last misguidedly, but with sincere and friendly intent, involve himself in my fate. I should say that 'the office' was the office of the Inland Revenue, and that I have been for most of my official working life an Inspector of Taxes.

I am not, then, proposing to describe my life as a 'taxman'. For some reason which I cannot fully understand the profession of 'taxman', like the profession of 'dentist', seems to excite laughter. But this laughter is, I suspect, uneasy. Both taxman and dentist only too readily image forth the deeper horrors of human life: that we must pay, perhaps ruinously, for our pleasures, that our resources are lent, not given, and that our most irreplaceable faculties decay even as they grow. And in an immediate sense, what makes a man more obsessively miserable than income tax or the toothache? No doubt this accounts for the defensive covertly hostile mockery with which one is greeted when confessing to either of these trades. I used to think however that no one but fools like Francis Marloe actually believed that tax inspectors chose their profession out of secret sadism. I cannot think of anyone less sadistic than myself. I am gentle to timidity. Yet latterly even my quiet and respectable calling has been used as evidence against me.

When this story starts – and I will not much longer delay its inception – I had already retired, at an earlier age than is usual, from the tax office. I worked as an Inspector of Taxes because I had to earn a living which I knew I should never earn as a writer. I retired when I had at last saved enough money to assure myself a modest annuity. I have lived, as I say, until latterly, without drama, but with unfailing purpose. I looked forward to and I toiled for my freedom to devote all my time to writing. Yet on the other hand, I did manage to write, and without more than occasional repining, during my years of bondage, and I would not, as some unsatisfied writers do, blame my lack of productivity upon my lack of time. I have been on the whole a lucky man. And I would say that even now. Perhaps especially I would say it now.

The shock of leaving the office was greater than I had anticipated. Hartbourne warned me that it would be so. I did not believe him. Perhaps I am, more than I realized, a creature of routine. Perhaps too, with scarcely pardonable stupidity, I imagined that inspiration would come with freedom. I did not expect the complete withdrawal of my gift. In the years before, I worked steadily. That is, I wrote steadily and I destroyed steadily. I will not say how many pages I have destroyed, the number is immense. There was pride in this as well as sorrow. Sometimes I felt at a (terrible phrase) dead end. But I never despaired of excellence. Hope and faith and absolute *devotion* kept me plodding onward, ageing, living alone with my emotions. And at least I found that I could always write something.

But when I had given up the tax office and could sit at my desk at home every morning and think any thoughts I pleased, I found I had no thoughts at all. This too I suffered with my bitterest patience. I waited. I tried to develop a new routine: monotony, out of which value springs. I waited, I listened. I live, as I shall explain soon at more length, in a noisy part of London, a seedy region that was once genteel. I suppose I have myself, together with my neighbourhood, made my pilgrimage away from gentility. Noise, which had never distressed me before, began to do so. For the first time in my life I urgently wanted silence.

Of course, as might be pointed out with barbed humour, I had always in a sense been a devotee of silence. Arnold Baffin once said something like this to me, laughing, and hurt me. Three short books in forty years of sustained literary effort is not exactly garrulity. And indeed if I understand anything that is precious, I did understand how important it was to keep one's mouth shut until the right moment even if this meant a totally voiceless life. Writing is like getting married. One should never commit oneself until one is amazed at one's luck. I hate, in any context, an intemperate flux of words. Contrary to what is modishly thought, the negative is stronger than the positive and its master. What I needed now however was literal silence.

So I decided for a time to leave London, and at once began to feel closer to my hidden treasure. My decision taken, my confidence returned, and I felt that latent biding power which is the artist's true grace. I decided to rent a cottage for the summer beside the sea. I had never in all my life had enough of the sea. I had never lived with it, never lived in a lonely place with only the sound of waves, which is no sound but the murmur of silence itself. In this connection I must mention too a not altogether rational idea which I had nourished more or less vaguely for a long time: the notion that before I could achieve greatness as a writer I would have to pass through some *ordeal*. For this ordeal I had waited in vain. Even total war (I was never in uniform) failed to ruffle my life. I seemed doomed to quietness. And it could be a measure of this quietness, and of the gentle timidity of which I have spoken, that a summer spent out of London could even for a second present itself to me as a trial! Of course for a man like myself, conventional, nervous, puritanical, the slave of habit, such a departure could reasonably be thought of as an adventure, a daring and unpredictable move. Or did I know by intuition that wonderful and terrible things were really imminent at last, trembling into being just behind the curtain of the future? My searching eye was caught by the advertisement: a seaside cottage at a modest rent. Its name was *Patara*. I had made the necessary arrangements and was just about to depart when Francis Marloe as the messenger of fate knocked upon my door. I did eventually get to Patara, but what happened there did not include anything that I had expected.

As I now read this Foreword through I see how meagrely it conveys me. How little perhaps can words convey except in the hands of a genius. Though I am a creative person, I am a puritan rather than an aesthete. I know that human life is horrible. I know that it is utterly unlike art. I have no religion except my own task of being. Conventional religions are dream stuff. Always a world of fear and horror lies but a millimetre away. Any man, even the greatest, can be broken in a moment and has no refuge. Any theory which denies this is a lie. For myself, I have no theories. True politics is simply the drying of tears and the endless fight for freedom. Without freedom there is no art and no truth. I revere great artists and the men who say no to tyrants.

It remains to record a dedication. There is of course one for whom this book was written whom I cannot name here. With a full heart, to witness duty, not to show my wit, I dedicate the work which you inspired and made possible to you, my dearest friend, my comrade and my teacher, with a gratitude which only you can measure. I know you will forgive its many faults, as you have always with a percipient mercy condoned the equally numerous shortcomings of its author.

Bradley Pearson

Now follows BRADLEY PEARSON'S STORY which is entitled:

The Black Prince

A Celebration of Love

Part One

It might be most dramatically effective to begin the tale at the moment when Arnold Baffin rang me up and said, 'Bradley, could you come round here please, I think that I have just killed my wife.' A deeper pattern however suggests Francis Marloe as the first speaker, the page or house-maid (these images would appeal to him) who, some half an hour before Arnold's momentous telephone call, initiates the action. For the news which Francis brought me forms the frame, or counterpoint, or outward packaging of what happened then and later in the drama of Arnold Baffin. There are indeed many places where I could start. I might start with Rachel's tears, or Priscilla's. There is much shedding of tears in this story. In a complex explanation any order may seem arbitrary. Where after all does anything begin? That three of the four starting points I have mentioned were causally independent of each other suggests speculations, doubtless of the most irrational kind, upon the mystery of human fate.

As I have explained, I was about to leave London. It was a raw damp cold afternoon in May. The wind carried no flowery smells, but rather laid a moist healthless humour upon the flesh which it then attempted to flay. I had my suitcases ready and was about to telephone for a taxi, had in fact already lifted the phone, when I experienced that nervous urge to delay departure, to sit down and reflect, which I am told the Russians have elevated into a ritual. I replaced the instrument and went back into my crowded little Victorian sitting-room and sat down. The result of this manoeuvre was that I was immediately aching with anxiety about a number of arrangements which I had already checked ten times over. Had I got enough sleeping pills? Had I packed the belladonna mixture? Had I packed my notebooks? I can only write in a certain kind of notebook with the lines a certain distance apart. I ran back into the hall. I found the notebooks and the pills and the belladonna of course, but by now the suitcases were half unpacked again and my heart was beating violently.

I lived then and had long lived in a ground-floor flat in a small shabby pretty court of terrace houses in North Soho, not far from the Post Office Tower, an area of perpetual seedy brouhaha. I preferred this genteel metropolitan poverty to the styleless surburban affluence favoured by the Baffins. My 'rooms' were all at the back. My bedroom looked on to dustbins and a fire escape. My sitting-room on to a plain brick wall caked with muck. The sitting-room, half a room really (the other half, stripped and degraded, was the bedroom) had wooden panels of that powdery dignified shade of green which can only be achieved by about fifty years of fading. This place I had crammed with too much furniture, with Victorian and oriental bric-à-brac, with tiny heterogeneous *objets d'art*, little cushions, inlaid trays, velvet cloths, antimacassars even, lace even. I amass rather than collect. I am also meticulously tidy though resigned to dust. A sunless and cosy womb my flat was, with a highly wrought interior and no outside. Only from the front door of the house, which was not my front door, could one squint up at sky over tall buildings and see above the serene austere erection of the Post Office Tower.

So it was that I deliberately delayed my departure. What if I had not done so? I was proposing to disappear for the whole summer, to a place incidentally which I had never seen but had adopted blind. I had not told Arnold where I was going. I had mystified him. Why I wonder? Out of some sort of obscure spite? Mystery always bulks larger. I had told him with a firm vagueness that I should be travelling abroad, no address. Why these lies? I suppose I did it partly to surprise him. I was a man who never went anywhere. Perhaps I felt it was time I gave Arnold a surprise. Neither had I informed my sister Priscilla that I was leaving London. There was nothing odd in that. She lived in Bristol with a husband whom I found distasteful. Suppose I had left the house before Francis Marloe knocked on the door? Suppose the tram had arrived at the tram stop and taken Prinzip away before the Archduke's car came round the corner?

I repacked the suitcases and transferred to my pocket, for re-reading in the train, the third version of my review of Arnold's latest novel. As a one-book-a-year man Arnold Baffin, the prolific popular novelist, is never long out of the public eye. I have had differences of opinion with Arnold about his writing. Sometimes in a close friendship, where important matters are concerned, people agree to differ and, in that area, fall silent. So, for a time, it had been with us. Artists are touchy folk. I had, however, after a superficial glance at his latest book, found things in it which I liked, and I had agreed to review it for a Sunday paper. I rarely wrote reviews, being in fact rarely asked to. I felt that this tribute would be some amends to Arnold for former criticisms which he had perhaps resented. Then on reading the novel with more care I decided regretfully that I detested it just as much as I detested its numerous *confrères*, and I found myself writing a review which was in effect a general attack upon Arnold's whole *œuvre*. What to do? I did not want to offend the editor: one does sometimes want to see oneself in print. And should not a critic simply speak out fearlessly? On the other hand Arnold was an old friend.

Then the front door bell (already too long delayed by my rambling narrative) rang.

The person who stood outside (within the front door of the house, but without my subsidiary front door) was strange to me. He seemed to be trembling, perhaps from the recent attentions of the wind, perhaps from nerves or alcohol. He wore a very old blue raincoat and a stringy fawn scarf of the throttling variety. He was stout (the raincoat failed to button) and not tall, with copious greyish longish frizzy hair and a round face and a slightly hooked nose and big very red lips and eyes set very close together. He looked, I later thought, rather like a caricature of a bear. Real bears, I believe, have eyes rather wide apart, but caricatured bears usually have close eyes, possibly to indicate bad temper or cunning. I did not like the look of him at all. Something significantly ill-omened which I could not yet define emanated from him. And I could smell him from where he stood.

Perhaps I might pause here yet again for a moment to describe myself. I am thin and tall, just over six feet, fairish and not yet bald, with light fine silky rather faded straight hair. I have a bland diffident nervous sensitive face and thin lips and blue eyes. I do not wear glasses. I look considerably younger than my age.

The smelly person on the doorstep began talking at once very fast, saying things which I could not hear. I am a trifle deaf.

'I am sorry, I cannot hear what you are saying, what do you want, speak up, please, I cannot hear you.'

'She's back,' I heard him say.

'What? Who's back? I do not understand you.'

'Christian's back. He's dead. She's back.'

'*Christian.*'

This was the name, not pronounced now in my presence for very many years, of my former wife.

I opened the door wider and the person on the step, whom I now recognized, slipped, or dodged, into the flat. I retreated into the sitting-room, he following.

'You don't remember me.'

'Yes, I do.'

'I'm Francis Marloe, you know, your brother-in-law.'

'Yes, yes –'

'As was, that is. I thought you should know. She's a widow, he left her everything, she's back in London, back in your old place –'

'Did she send you?'

'Here? Well, not exactly –'

'Did she or didn't she?'

'Well, no, I just heard through the lawyer. She's back in your old place! God!'

'I see no need for you to come –'

'So she's written you? I wondered if she'd have written you.'

'Of course she hasn't written to me!'

'I thought of course you'd want to see her –'

'I don't want to see her! I cannot think of anyone I less want to see or hear of!'

I shall not attempt here to describe my marriage. Some impression of it will doubtless emerge. For the present story, its general nature rather than its detail is important. It was not a success. At first I saw her as a life-bringer. Then I saw her as a death-bringer. Some women are like that. There is a sort of energy which seems to reveal the world: then one day you find you are being devoured. Fellow victims will know what I mean. Possibly I am a natural bachelor. Christian was certainly a natural flirt. Sheer silliness can be attractive in a woman. I was, of course, attracted. She was, I suppose, a rather 'sexy' woman. Some people thought me lucky. She brought, what I detest, disorder into my life. She was a great maker of scenes. In the end I detested her. Five years of marriage seemed to have convinced both of us of the utter impossibility of this state. However, shortly after our divorce Christian married a rich unlettered American called Evandale, went to live in Illinois, and as far as I was concerned disappeared forever.

There is nothing quite like the dead dull feel of a failed marriage. Nor is there anything like one's hatred for an ex-spouse. (How can such a person *dare* to be happy?) I cannot credit those who speak of 'friendship' in such a context. I lived for years with a sense of things irrevocably soiled and spoiled, it could give suddenly such a sad feel to the world sometimes. I could not liberate myself from her mind. This had nothing to do with love. Those who have suffered this sort of bondage will understand. Some people are just 'diminishers' and 'spoilers' for others. I suppose almost everybody diminishes someone. A saint would be nobody's spoiler. Most of one's acquaintances however can be blessedly forgotten when not present. Out of sight out of mind is a charter of human survival. Not so Christian, she was ubiquitous: her consciousness was rapacious, her thoughts could damage, passing like noxious rays through space and time. Her remarks were memorable. Only good old America cured her for me in the end. I put her away with a tedious man in a tedious and very distant town and was able to feel that she had died. What a relief.

Francis Marloe was another matter. Neither he nor his thoughts had ever been important to me, nor as far as I could see to anyone. He was Christian's younger brother, treated by her with indulgent contempt. He never married. After lengthy trying he qualified as a doctor, but was soon struck off the register for some irregularity in the prescription of drugs. I learnt later with abhorrence that he had set up in business as a self-styled 'psycho-analyst'. Later still I heard he had taken to drink. If I had been told that he had committed suicide I should have heard the news without either concern or surprise. I was not pleased to see him again. He had in fact altered almost beyond recognition. He had been a slim tripping blond-haloed faun. Now he looked coarse, fat, red-faced, pathetic, slightly wild, slightly sinister, perhaps a little mad. He had always been very stupid. However at that moment I was not concerned about Mr Francis Marloe, but about the absolutely terrifying news which he had brought me.

'I am surprised that you felt it your business to come here. It was an impertinence. I don't want to know anything about my ex-wife. I finished with that business long ago.'

'Now don't be cross,' said Francis, pursing up his red lips with a fawning kissing sort of movement which I remembered with loathing. 'Please don't be cross with me, Brad.'

'And don't call me "Brad". I'm catching a train.'

'I won't keep you for a moment, I'll just explain, I've been thinking – yes, I'll make it snappy, just please listen to me, *please*, I beseech you – Look, it's this, you see you're the first person Chris will be looking up in London –'

'*What?*'

'She'll come straight to you, I bet, I intuit it –'

'Are you completely mad? Don't you know how – I can't discuss this – There can be no possible communication, this was utterly finished with years ago.'

'No, Brad, you see –'

'Don't call me "Brad"!'

'All right, all right, Bradley, sorry, please don't be cross, surely you know Chris, she cared awfully for you, she really cared, much more than for old Evans, she'll come to you, even if it's only out of curiosity –'

'I won't be here,' I said. This suddenly sounded horribly plausible. Perhaps there is a deep malign streak in all of us. Christian certainly had more than her share of sheer malignancy. She might indeed almost instinctively come to me, out of curiosity, out of malice, as cats are said to jump on to the laps of cat-haters. One does feel a certain curiosity about an ex-spouse, a desire doubtless that they should have suffered remorse and disappointment. One only wants bad news. One wants to gloat. Christian would yearn to satisfy herself of my wretchedness.

Francis was going on, 'She'll want to show off, she's rich now you see, sort of merry widow style, she'll want to show off to her old friends, anybody would, oh yes, she'll be sniffing after you, you'll see, and –'

'I'm not interested,' I cried, 'I'm not *interested*!'

'You are interested, you know. Why if ever I saw an interested look on a bloke's face –'

'Has she got children?'

'There you are, you *are*. No, she hasn't. Now I've always liked you, Brad, and wanted to see you again, I've always admired you, I read your book –'

'Which book?'

'I forget its name. It was great. Maybe you wondered why I didn't turn up –'

'No!'

'Well, I was bashful, felt I was small fry like, but now with Christian turning up it's – You see, I'm in debt up to the neck, have to keep changing my digs and that – Now Chris sort of paid me off you might say some time back, and I thought that if you and Chris were likely to get together again –'

'You mean you want me to intercede for you?'

'Sort of, sort of –'

'Oh God!' I said, 'Get out, will you?' The idea of my prising money out of Christian for her delinquent brother struck me as unusually lunatic even for Francis.

'And, you know, I was knocked when I heard she was back, it's a shock, it changes a lot of things, I wanted to come and chew it over with somebody, for human interest like, and you were natural – I say, is there any drink in the house?'

'Just go, will you please.'

'I intuit she'll want you, want to impress you and that – We broke down in letters, you see, I was always wanting money, and then she got a lawyer to stop me writing to her – But now it's like a new start, if you could just sort of ease me in, bring me along like –'

'You want me to pose as your friend?'

'But we could be friends, Brad – Look, is there anything to drink in the house?'

'No.'

The telephone began to ring.

'Go away please,' I said, 'and stay away.'

'Bradley, have a heart –'

'Out!'

He stood before me with that air of revolting humility. I threw open the sitting-room door and the door of the flat. I picked up the telephone in the hall.

Arnold Baffin's voice was on the wire. He spoke quietly, rather slowly. 'Bradley, could you come round here please – I think that I may have just killed Rachel.'

I said immediately, quietly too but in emotion, 'Arnold, don't be silly. Don't be *silly*!'

'Could you come round at once please.' His voice sounded like a recorded announcement.

I said, 'Have you called a doctor?'

A moment's pause. 'No.'

'Well, do so!'

'I'll – explain – Could you come round at once –'

'Arnold,' I said, 'you can't have killed her – You're talking nonsense – You can't have –'

A moment's pause. 'Maybe.' His voice was toneless as if calm. A matter doubtless of severe shock.

'What happened – ?'

'Bradley, could you –'

'Yes,' I said, 'I'll come round at once. I'll get a taxi.' I replaced the receiver.

It may be relevant to record that my first general feeling on hearing what Arnold had to say was one of curious joy. Before the reader sets me down as a monster of callousness let him look into his own heart. Such reactions are not after all so abnormal and may be said in that minimal sense at least to be almost excusable. We naturally take in the catastrophes of our friends a pleasure which genuinely does not preclude friendship. This is partly but not entirely because we enjoy being empowered as helpers. The unexpected or inappropriate catastrophe is especially piquant. I was very attached to both Arnold and Rachel. But there is a natural tribal hostility between the married and the unmarried. I cannot stand the shows so often quite instinctively put on by married people to insinuate that they are not only more fortunate but in some way more moral than you are. Moreover to help their case the unmarried person often naïvely assumes that all marriages are happy unless shown to be otherwise. The Baffin marriage had always seemed pretty sound. This sudden vignette of home life set the ideas in a turmoil.

Still rosy with the rush of blood which Arnold's words had occasioned, and also, I should make clear (there is no contradiction), very alarmed and upset, I turned round and saw Francis, whose existence I had forgotten.

'Anything the matter?' said Francis.

'No.'

'I heard you say something about a doctor.'

'The wife of a friend of mine has had an accident. She fell. I'm just going over.'

'Shall I come too?' said Francis. 'I might be useful. After all, I am still a doctor in the eyes of God.'

I thought for a moment and said, 'All right.' We got a taxi.

I pause here to say another word or two about my protégé Arnold Baffin. I am anxious (this is not just a phrase, I feel *anxiety*) about the clarity and justice of my presentation of Arnold, since this story is, from a salient point of view, the story of my relations with Arnold and the astounding climax to which these relations led. I 'discovered' Arnold, a considerably younger man, when I was already modestly established as a writer, and he, recently out of college, was just finishing his first novel. I had by then 'got rid of' my wife and was experiencing one of those 'fresh starts' which I have so often hoped would lead on to achievement. He was a schoolmaster, having lately graduated in English literature at the university of Reading. We met at a meeting. He coyly confessed his novel. I expressed polite interest. He sent me the almost completed typescript. (This was, of course,

Tobias and the Fallen Angel. Still, I think, his best work.) I thought the piece had some merits and I helped him to find a publisher for it. I also reviewed it quite favourably when it came out. Thus began one of the most, commercially speaking, successful of recent literary careers. Arnold at once, contrary as it happens to my advice, gave up his job as a teacher and devoted himself to 'writing'. He wrote easily, producing every year a book which pleased the public taste. Wealth, fame followed.

It has been suggested, especially in the light of more recent events, that I envied Arnold's success as a writer. I would like at once and categorically to deny this. I sometimes envied his freedom to write at a time when I was tied to my desk. But I did not in general feel envy of Arnold Baffin for one very simple reason: it seemed to me that he achieved success at the expense of merit. As his discoverer and patron I felt from the start identified with his activities. And I felt, rather, distress that a promising young writer should have laid aside true ambition and settled so quickly into a popular mould. I respected his industry and I admired his 'career'. He had many gifts other than purely literary ones. I did not, however, much like his books. Tact readily supervened however and, as I have said, we soon instinctively avoided certain topics of conversation.

I was present at Arnold's marriage to Rachel. (I am speaking of a time which is now getting on for twenty-five years ago.) And after this for many years I used to have lunch with the Baffins every Sunday, and would usually see Arnold at least once during the week as well. It was like a family relationship. At one time Arnold even used to refer to me as his 'spiritual father'. The close regularity of these customs ceased after Arnold made a remark, which I will not retail here, about my work. Friendship survived however. It became even, in test and in tribulation, rather more intense, certainly more complicated. I will not go so far as to say that Arnold and I were obsessed with each other. But we were certainly of abiding mutual interest. I felt that the Baffins needed me. I felt, in relation to them, like a tutelary deity. Arnold was always grateful, even devoted, though there is no doubt that he feared my criticisms. He had perhaps, as he increasingly embraced literary mediocrity, a very similar critic inside his own breast. Often one identifies with what would otherwise prove a menace. Dislike of another's work is a deep source of enmity in artists. We are a vain crew and can be irrevocably estranged by criticism. It is a tribute to Arnold and myself, two demonic men, that we ingeniously preserved, for whatever reason, our affection for each other.

I should make clear that Arnold was not in any crude sense 'spoilt' by success. He was no tax-dodger with a yacht and a house in Malta. (We sometimes laughingly discussed tax-avoidance, but never tax-evasion.) He lived in a fairly large, but not immodest, suburban villa in a 'good class' housing estate in Ealing. His domestic life was, even to an irritating extent, lacking in style. It was not that he put on an act of being 'the ordinary chap'. In some way he *was* 'the ordinary chap', and eschewed the vision which might, for better as well as worse, have made a very different use of his money. I never knew Arnold to purchase any object of beauty. He was indeed quite deficient in visual taste, though he was rather aggressively fond of music. As to his person, he continued to look like a schoolmaster, dressed shapelessly, and retained a raw shy boyish appearance. It never occurred to him to play 'the famous writer'. Or perhaps intelligence, of which he had plenty, suggested this way of playing it. He wore steel rimmed specs, behind which his eyes were a very pale bluish-green, rather striking. His nose was pointed, his face always rather greasy, but healthy looking. There was a general lack of colour. Something of an albino? He was accounted, and perhaps was, good-looking. He was always combing his hair.

Arnold stared at me and pointed mutely at Francis. We were standing in the hall. Arnold looked unlike himself, his face waxy, his hair jagged, his eyes without glasses crazed and vague. There was a red mark like a Chinese character upon his cheek.

'This is Dr Marloe. Dr Marloe – Arnold Baffin. Dr Marloe happened to be with me when you rang up about your wife's *accident*.' I stressed the last word.

'Doctor,' said Arnold. 'Yes, you see – she –'

'She fell?' I suggested.

'Yes. Is he – is this chap a – medical doctor?'

'Yes,' I said. 'A friend of mine.' This untruth at least conveyed important information.

'Are you *the* Arnold Baffin?' said Francis.

'Yes, he is,' I said.

'I say, I do admire your books – I've read –'

'What's the situation?' I said to Arnold. I thought he looked as if he was drunk, and immediately after I could smell drink.

Arnold, making some sort of effort, said slowly, 'She locked herself into our bedroom. After it – happened – She was bleeding a lot – I thought – I don't quite know what – the injury was – At any rate – At any rate –' He stopped.

'Go on, Arnold. Look, you'd better sit down. Hadn't he better sit down?'

'Arnold Baffin,' said Francis, to himself.

Arnold leaned back against the hall stand. He leaned his head back into a coat that was hanging there, closed his eyes for a moment, and then went on. 'Sorry. You see. She was sort of crying and wailing in there for a time. I mean in the bedroom. Now it's all quiet and she doesn't answer at all. I'm afraid she may be unconscious or –'

'Can't you break open the door?'

'I tried to, I *tried* to, but the chisel, the – outside woodwork just broke away and I couldn't get any –'

'Sit down, Arnold, for Christ's sake.' I pushed him on to a chair.

'And you can't see through the keyhole because the key –'

'She's probably just upset and won't answer out of – you know –'

'Yes,' he said. 'I didn't want to – If it's all a – I don't know quite what – You go and try, Bradley –'

'Where's your chisel?'

'Up there. But it's a small one. I can't find –'

'Well, you two stay here,' I said. 'I'll just go up and see what's going on. I bet you anything – Arnold, stay here and *sit down*!'

I stood outside the bedroom door, which had been mildly disfigured by Arnold's efforts. A lot of paint had flaked off and

32

lay like white pearls upon the fawn carpet. The chisel lay there too. I tried the handle and called, 'Rachel. It's Bradley. Rachel!'

Silence.

'I'll get a hammer,' I could hear Arnold, invisible, saying downstairs.

'Rachel, Rachel, please answer –' The real panic had got inside me now. I pressed all my weight on the door. It was solid and well made. 'Rachel!'

Silence.

I hurled myself at the door, shouting, 'Rachel!' Then I stopped, and listened very carefully.

There was a tiny sound from within, a sort of little creeping mouse-like sound. I said, 'Oh let her be all right, let her be all right.'

More creeping. Then very softly in a scarcely audible whisper. 'Bradley.'

'Rachel, Rachel, are you all right?'

Silence. Creeping. Then a little hissing sigh. 'Yes.'

I shouted to the others, 'She's all right! She's all right!'

I heard them saying something behind me on the stairs. 'Rachel, let me in, can you? Let me in.'

There was a scuffling sound, then Rachel's voice, breathy and low down, close against the door, 'You come in. Not anyone else.'

I heard the key turn in the lock and I pushed quickly into the room catching a glimpse of Arnold who was standing on the stairs with Francis behind him a little lower down. I saw the two faces very clearly, like faces in a crucifixion crowd which represent the painter and his friend. Arnold's face was distorted into a sort of sneer of anguish. Francis's was bright with malign curiosity. Suitable expressions for a crucifixion. Inside I nearly fell over Rachel who was sitting on the floor. She was moaning softly now, trying frantically to turn the key again in the lock. I turned it for her and then sat down on the floor beside her.

Since Rachel Baffin is one of the main actors, in a crucial sense perhaps the main actor, in my drama I should like now to pause briefly to describe her. I had known her for over twenty years, almost as long as I had known Arnold, yet at the time that

I speak of I did not really, as I later realized, know her well. There was a sort of vagueness. Some women, in fact in my experience many women, have a sort of 'abstract' quality about them. Is this a real sex difference? Perhaps this quality is really just unselfishness. (In this respect, you know where you are with men!) In Rachel's case it was certainly not lack of intelligence. There was a vagueness which womanly affection and the custom of my quasi-family friendship with the Baffins did not dispel, even increased. Of course men play roles, but women play roles too, blanker ones. They have, in the play of life, fewer good lines. This may be to make a mystery of what had simpler causes. Rachel was an intelligent woman married to a famous man: and instinctively such a woman behaves as a function of her husband, she reflects, as it were, all the light on to him. Her 'blankness' repelled even curiosity. One does not expect such a woman to have ambition: whereas Arnold and I were both, in quite different ways, tormented, perhaps even defined, by ambition. Rachel was (in a way in which one would never think this of a man) a 'good specimen', a 'good sort'. One relied on her. There she was. She looked (then) just like a big handsome sweet contented woman, the efficient wife of a well-known charmer. She was a large, smooth-faced, slightly freckled, reddish-blonde person, with straightish gingery wiry hair and a pale complexion, a bit tall for a woman and generally on a larger scale physically than her husband. She had been putting on weight and some might have called her fat. She was always busy, often with charities and mild left-wing politics. (Arnold cared nothing for politics.) She was an excellent 'housewife', and often referred to herself by this title.

'Rachel, are you all right?'

There was a darkening reddish bruise under one eye and the eye was narrowed, though this was hard to see because the eyelids of both eyes were so grossly red and swollen with weeping. Her upper lip was also swollen on one side. There were traces of blood on her neck and on her dress. Her hair was tangled and looked darker as if wet; perhaps it was literally wet with the flow of her tears. She was panting now, almost gasping. She had undone the front of her dress and I could see some white lace of her brassière and a plump pallor of flesh bulging above. She had been crying so much that her face was almost unrecognizably puffed up, all wet and shiny and hot to look at. She started now to cry again, pulling away from my convulsive sympathetic gesture and plucking at the collar of the dress in a distraught way.

'Rachel, are you hurt? I've got a doctor here –'

She began awkwardly to get up, again pushing away my assisting hand. I got a whiff of alcohol from her panting breath. She knelt upon her dress and I heard it tear. Then she half ran half fell across the room to the disordered bed, where she flopped on her back, tugging at the bedclothes, ineffectually because she was half lying on them, then covering her face with both hands and crying in an appalling wailing manner, lying with her feet wide apart in a graceless self-absorption of grief.

'Rachel, please control yourself. Drink some water.' The sound of that abandoned weeping was scarcely bearable, and something far too intense to be called embarrassment, yet of that quality, made me both reluctant and anxious to look at her. A woman's crying can sicken one with fright and guilt, and this was terrible crying.

Arnold outside shouted, 'Please let me in, please, please –'

'Stop it, Rachel,' I said. 'I can't bear this. Stop it. I'm going to open the door.'

'No, no,' she whispered, a sort of voiceless whine. 'Not Arnold, not –' Was she still afraid of him?

'I'm going to let the doctor in,' I said.

'No, no.'

I opened the door and placed my hand on Arnold's chest. 'Go in and look at her,' I said to Francis. 'There's some blood.'

Arnold began to call out, 'Let me see you, please, darling, don't be angry, oh please –'

I pushed him back towards the head of the stairs. Francis went inside and locked the door again, whether out of delicacy or professional caution.

Arnold sat down on the stairs and began to moan. 'Oh dear, oh dear, oh dear –' My awkward appalled embarrassment mingled now with a horrible fascinated interest. Arnold, beyond caring about what impression he made, was running his hands again and again through his hair. 'Oh I am a bloody fool, I am a bloody fool –'

I said, 'Steady on. What happened exactly?'

'Where are the scissors?' shouted Francis from within.

'Top drawer dressing-table,' Arnold shouted back. 'Christ, what does he want scissors for? Is he going to operate or something?'

'What happened? Look, better move down a bit.'

I pushed Arnold and he hobbled stooping, holding the banisters, past the turn of the stair, and sat on the lowest step, holding his head in his hands and staring at the zig-zag design of the hall carpet. The hall was always a bit dim because of the stained glass in the door. I went down past him and sat on a chair, feeling very odd, upset, excited.

'Oh Christ, oh Christ. Do you think she'll forgive me?'

'Of course. What – ?'

'It all started with such a damn silly argument about one of my books. Oh God, why is one so stupid – we just went on arguing, neither of us would stop at all – We don't usually discuss my work, I mean Rachel thinks it's fine, there's nothing to discuss. Only sometimes if she's not feeling very well or something she picks on a thing in a book and says it refers to her, or that it's a picture of something we did or found or something together. Well, you know I don't draw from life like that, all my stuff is imagined, only Rachel suddenly thinks she spots something which she says is hurtful or spoiling or insulting or something, it's like a sudden persecution complex, it upsets her terribly. Most of one's friends are dying to be in one's books, they see themselves everywhere, but Rachel hates it if I even mention somewhere we've been together, she says it spoils it and so on. Anyway, oh Christ, Bradley, what a bloody fool I am – Anyway this started up with this sort of tiff and then she said something hurtful about my writing in general, she said, well never mind – Anyway we started rowing and I suppose I said some pretty critical things about her, just to defend myself, and we'd been drinking brandy after lunch – We don't usually drink much, but when we started to fight we just went on and on drinking, it was crazy. Then she got terribly angry and lost control and screamed at me, and I hate that. I sort of pushed her to stop her screaming and she clawed my face, see, she made quite a mark on me, God, it still hurts. I felt quite frightened and I just hit her to make her stop. I can't stand screaming and noise and anger, and they are frightening. She was yelling like a fury and saying awful things about my work and I just hit her with my hand to stop the hysterics, but she went on coming at me and coming at me, and then I picked up the poker from the fireplace just to hold it between us as a barrier, and just at that moment she jerked her head, she was dancing round me like a wild animal, and she jerked her head down and met the poker with a most ghastly crack – oh God – Of course I didn't mean to hit her, I mean I didn't hit her – And then she went down on the floor and she was so bloody quiet lying there with her eyes closed, I wasn't sure she hadn't stopped breathing – Well, I was in a complete panic and I got a jug of water and poured it over her and she just lay there and I was frantic – And then when I went to get some more water she jumped up and ran upstairs to the bedroom and locked herself in – Then she wouldn't open, wouldn't answer – I didn't know if she was shamming and it was spite or if she was really ill or what, so you see I didn't know what to do – Oh Christ, I didn't mean to hit her –'

There were sounds upstairs, the unlocking of a door, and we both jumped up. Francis, leaning down, said, 'She's OK.' His shabby blue suit was covered with dampish reddish silky siftings, which in a moment I recognized as Rachel's hair, which he must have clipped in order to examine her head. I saw his extremely dirty hand grasping the white banister.

'Thank God,' said Arnold. 'Do you know, I think she may have been shamming all the time. Anyway, thank God. What should – ?'

'There's nothing seriously wrong. She's got a very nasty lump on her head and she's a bit in shock. Could be a touch of concussion. Keep her in bed and keep the room dark. Aspirins, any of her usual sedatives, hot water bottles, hot drinks, I mean tea and that. Better let her see her own doctor. She'll soon be herself again.'

'Oh thank you so much, Doctor,' said Arnold. 'So she's all right, thank heaven.'

'She wants to see you,' said Francis to me. We had all moved back up to the landing.

Arnold began again calling, 'My darling, please –'

'I'll deal,' I said. I half opened the bedroom door, which was unlocked.

'Only Bradley. Only Bradley.' The voice, still almost inaudible, was firmer.

'Oh Christ. This is awful. I've had enough –' said Arnold. 'Darling –'

'You go down and give yourself another drink,' I told him.

'I wouldn't mind a drink,' said Francis.

'Oh don't be angry with me, darling –'

'Could you chuck out my mac,' said Francis. 'I left it in there on the floor.'

I went in and threw the macintosh out and closed the door again. I heard retreating steps as Arnold and Francis went away down the stairs.

'Lock the door, please.'

I locked it.

Francis had pulled the curtains and there was a sort of thick pink twilight in the room. The evening sun, now palely shining, made the big floppy flowers on the chintz curtains glow in a melancholy way. The room had the rather sinister tedium which some bedrooms have, a sort of weary banality which is a reminder of death. A dressing-table can be a terrible thing. The Baffins had placed theirs in the window where it obstructed the light and presented its ugly back to the road. The plate glass 'table' surface was dusty and covered with cosmetic tubes and bottles and balls of hair. The chest of drawers had all its drawers gaping, spewing pink underwear and shoulder straps. The bed was chaotic, violent, the green artificial silk coverlet swooping down on one side and the sheets and blankets creased up into a messy mass, like an old face. There was a warm intimate embarrassing smell of sweat and face powder. The whole room breathed the flat horror of genuine mortality, dull and spiritless and final.

I do not know why I thought then so promptly and prophetically of death. Perhaps it was because Rachel, half under the bedclothes, had covered her face with the sheet.

Her feet, with glossy high-heeled shoes on, protruded from under the green coverlet. I said timidly, almost as if making conversation and to establish a *rapport*, 'Here, let me take your shoes off.'

She remained stiff while, with some difficulty, I pulled off both shoes. I felt the soft warmth of the damp brown stockinged foot. A pungent sour odour joined the vapid smell of the room. I wiped my hands on my trousers.

'Better get properly into bed. Look, I'll straighten out your bedclothes a bit.'

She shifted slightly, removing the sheet from her face, and even lifting her legs so that I could pull out a blanket from under them. I arranged her a little bit, pulling the blankets up and turning the sheet back over them. She had stopped crying and was stroking the bruise on her face. The bruise seemed bluer, creeping round the eye socket, and the eye itself was reduced to a watery slit. She lay there, her moist disfigured mouth slightly open, staring at the ceiling.

'I'll fill you a hot water bottle, shall I?'

I found a hot water bottle and filled it from the hot tap in the wash basin. Its soiled woolly cover smelt of sweat and sleep. I got it a bit wet on the outside, but it felt quite warm. I lifted the sheet and blanket and thrust it in beside her thigh.

'Rachel, aspirins? These are aspirins, aren't they?'

'No, thank you.'

'Do you good.'

'No.'

'You'll be all right, the doctor said so.'

She sighed very deeply and flopped her hand back on to the bed, lying now with both hands symmetrically by her side, palms upward, like a limp disentombed Christ figure, still bearing the marks of ill-treatment. Tufts of cut hair adhered to the dried blood on the bosom of her blue dress. She said in a hollow louder voice, 'This is so awful, so awful, so awful.'

'You'll be all right, Rachel, the doctor says –'

39

'I feel so utterly – defeated. I shall – die of shame.'

'Nonsense, Rachel. It's just one of those things.'

'And he asks you round – to see it all.'

'Rachel, he was shaking like a leaf, he thought you were unconscious in here, he was terrified.'

'I shall never forgive him. Be my witness now. I shall never forgive him. Never, never, never. Not if he were to kneel at my feet for twenty years. A woman does not forgive this ever. She won't save a man at the end. If he were drowning, I'd watch.'

'Rachel, you don't mean this. Please don't talk in this awful sort of theatrical way. Of course you'll forgive him. I'm sure there were faults on both sides. After all you hit him too, you put your monogram on his cheek.'

'Ach –' Her exclamation expressed harsh, almost vulgar, disgust. 'Never,' she said, 'never, never. Oh I am – so unhappy –' The whimpering and the spilling tears began again. Her face was flaming hot.

'Stop, please. You must rest. Do take some aspirins. Try to sleep a little. I'll get you some tea, would you like that?'

'Sleep! With my mind in this state! He has sent me to hell. He has taken my whole life from me. He has spoilt the world. I am as clever as he is. He has just blocked me off from everything. I can't work, I can't think, I can't be, because of him. His stuff crawls over everything, he takes away all my things and turns them into his things. I've never been myself or lived my own life at all. I've always been afraid of him, that's what it comes to. All men despise all women really. All women fear all men really. Men are physically stronger, that's what it comes to, that what's behind it all. Of course they're bullies, they can end any argument. Ask any poor woman in the slums, she knows. He has given me a black eye, like any common brawler, any drunken husband like you hear of in the courts. He has hit me before, oh this isn't the first time by any means. He didn't know it, I never told him, but the first time he hit me our marriage came to an end. And he talks about me to other women, I know he does, he confides in other women and discusses me with them. They all admire him so and flatter him so. He has taken away my life from me and spoilt it, breaking every little piece of it, like the breaking of every bone in one's body, every little thing ruined and spoilt and taken away.'

'Rachel, don't, don't, don't, I won't listen, you don't mean any of this rigmarole. Don't say such things to me. You'll regret it later.'

'I'm just as clever as he is. He wouldn't let me take a job. I obeyed him, I've always obeyed him. I haven't any private things. He owns the world. It's all his, his, his. I won't save him at the end. I'll watch him drown. I'll watch him burn.'

'You don't mean it, Rachel. Better not say it.'

'And I won't forgive you either for having seen me like this with my face bruised to pieces and heard me talk horridly like this. I'll smile at you again but I won't forgive you in my heart.'

'Rachel, Rachel, you are upsetting me so!'

'And now you'll go downstairs and talk about me vilely to him. I know how men talk.'

'No, no –'

'I fill you with disgust. A broken whimpering middle-aged woman.'

'No –'

'Ach –' Again the horrible sound of aggressive violent disgust. 'Go away now, leave me please. Leave me alone with my thoughts and my torture and my punishment. I shall cry all night, all night. Sorry, Bradley. Tell Arnold I'm going to rest now. Tell him not to come near me again today. Tomorrow I will try to be as usual. There will be no recriminations, no reproaches, nothing. How can I reproach him? He will become angry again, he will frighten me again. Better to be a slave. Tell him I will be as usual tomorrow. Of course he knows that, he won't worry, he's feeling better already. Only let me not see him today.'

'All right, I'll tell him. Don't be cross with me, Rachel. It's not my fault.'

'Oh, go away.'

'Shall I get you some tea? The doctor said tea.'

'Go away.'

I went out of the room and closed the door quietly behind me. I heard a soft bound and then the key turning in the lock. I went down the stairs feeling very shaken and, yes, she had been right, disgusted.

It had become darker, the sun no longer shining, and the interior of the house seemed brown and chill. I made my way to the drawing-room at the back of the house where Arnold and Francis were talking. An electric fire and a lamp had been turned on. I noticed broken glass, broken china, a stain on the carpet. The drawing-room was a big over-patterned room with a lot of pseudo-tapestries and bad modern lithographs. Arnold's two big stereo loud-speakers, covered with a sort of fawn gauze, took up a lot of the space. Beyond glass doors and a veranda was the equally fussy garden, horribly green in the sunless oppressive light, where a great many birds were singing competitive nonsense lyrics in the small decorative suburban trees.

Arnold jumped up and began to make for the door, but I stopped him. 'She says she doesn't want to be visited again today. She says tomorrow she'll be as usual. She says she'll go to sleep now.'

Arnold sat down again. He said, 'Yes, better for her to sleep for a while. Oh my God, that's a relief. Let her rest a while. I'll expect she'll come down for supper in an hour or two. I'll make her something nice, give her a surprise. God, I do feel relieved.'

I felt I ought to check his relief a little. 'All the same, it was a very nasty accident.' I hoped Arnold had not been making his confession to Francis.

'Yes. But she'll come down, I'm sure she will. She's very buoyant. I'll let her rest now of course. The doctor says it's not – Have a drink, Bradley.'

'Thanks, sherry.' I thought, he has no conception of what he has done, of what she looks like now, of what she feels like now. No doubt he has never tried to read her thoughts. Maybe that way survival lay. Always to ignore the details of one's misdeeds. Or was I quite wrong? Perhaps already, having made her outcry, she had become quiet. Perhaps she would come down for supper and enjoy the delicacy which her husband had prepared. A marriage is a very secret place.

'All's well that ends well,' said Arnold. 'I'm sorry to have involved you both.' No doubt he was sorry. If he had not lost his nerve he could have kept the whole thing secret, he was probably thinking now. However, as Rachel had conjectured, he seemed to have largely recovered his composure. He was sitting very upright, holding his glass carefully in both hands, one leg crossed over the other and a small well-shod foot rhythmically signalling. Everything about Arnold was neat and small, though he was of average height. He had a small well-shaped head, small ears, a small mouth such as a girl would have liked to own, and ridiculously small feet. He had put on his steel-rimmed glasses and his face had resumed its healthy greasy look. His pointed nose probed the atmosphere, his eyes glinted towards me, diffidently. He had combed his pale lank hair.

Obviously the next thing was to get rid of Francis. Francis had put his macintosh on again, probably out of some instinctive self-defence rather than because of any intention of departing. He was helping himself to more whisky. He had pushed his frizzy hair back behind his ears, and his close dark bear's eyes peered inquisitively at me, at Arnold. He looked pleased with himself. Perhaps the unexpected renewal of his priestly function, however momentary and unimpressive, had cheered him, given him a little whiff of power. His eager interested look and the sudden sickening memory of his news made me feel intense annoyance. I now regretted having let him accompany me. His having met Arnold could have some undesirable consequence. On principle I usually avoid introducing my friends and acquaintances to each other. It is not that one fears treachery, though of course one does. What human fear is deeper? But endless little unnecessary troubles usually result from such introductions. And Francis, though a wreck and not to be accounted a serious danger, had always, with the natural talent for it of a failed person, been a trouble-maker. His gratuitous mission this very day had been typical. I wanted him out of the house. I also wanted to talk to Arnold, who was clearly in a talkative, excited, almost euphoric mood. Perhaps I had been wrong to speak of composure. It was more a matter of shock plus whisky.

Without sitting down I said to Francis, 'We needn't keep you now. Thanks for coming.'

Francis did not want to go. 'I was glad to help. Shall I go up and have a peep at her?'

'She won't see you. Thanks for coming.' I opened the sitting-room door.

'Don't go, Doctor,' said Arnold. Perhaps he wanted male support, to surround himself with men. Perhaps they had been having an interesting conversation. Arnold had something of the coarseness and the *camaraderie* of the *homme moyen sensuel*. This too could be a help in marriage. Arnold's glass struck his lower teeth with a slight clack. He had probably drunk a good deal since coming downstairs.

'Good-bye,' I said meaningfully to Francis.

'I'm so grateful, Doctor,' said Arnold. 'Do I owe you anything?'

'You owe him nothing,' I said.

Francis looked wistful. He had risen, recognizing the futility of resistance, taking his orders from me.

'About what we were talking about before,' he said to me conspiratorially at the door. 'When you see Christian –'

'I won't.'

'Anyway, here's my address.'

'I won't need it.' I led him through the hall. 'Good-bye. Thanks.' I shut the front door behind him and returned to Arnold. We sat, both of us crouching a little over the electric fire. I felt very limp and, in a blank sort of way, frightened.

'You are very firm with your friends,' said Arnold.

'He's not a friend.'

'I thought you said –'

'Oh never mind him. Do you really think Rachel will come down to supper?'

'Yes, I do. This is just a matter of experience. She never sulks for long after a thing like this, not if I lose my temper. She's kind to me then. It's if I keep quiet she goes on and on. Not that we make a habit of scraps like this. But we sometimes both explode and then it's all over at once, clears the air. We're very close to each other. These rows aren't real warfare, they're an aspect of love. This may be hard for an outsider to understand –'

'I suppose usually there aren't outsiders around.'

'Quite. You do believe me, don't you, Bradley – It's rather important that you should. I'm not just defending myself. It's true. We both shout but there's no real danger. Understand?'

'Yes,' I said, reserving my judgement.

'Did she say anything about me?'

'Only about not wanting to see you today. And about being as usual tomorrow and everything forgiven and forgotten.' There seemed no point in retailing Rachel's eloquence to her husband. Anyway, what did it mean?

'She's such a good person, very forgiving, very kind. I'll leave her be for the moment. She'll soon pity me and come down. We never let the sun go down upon our wrath. It's fake wrath anyway. You do understand, Bradley?'

'Yes.'

'Look,' said Arnold, 'my hand's trembling. Look at the glass shaking about. It's quite involuntary. Isn't that odd?'

'You'd better get your own doctor tomorrow.'

'Oh, I think I shall be better tomorrow.'

'To see her, you fool.'

'Well, maybe. But she's very resilient. Anyway, she's not badly hurt, I got that quite clear. Oh thank God, thank God, thank God – I just misunderstood that scene with the poker. She was shamming, furious. I don't blame her. We're a couple of fools. She really isn't badly hurt, Bradley. The doctor explained. Christ, do you think I'm some sort of monster?'

'No. Do you mind if I tidy things up a bit?' I set a stool upright. I began to stoop around the room with a wastepaper basket, picking up broken glass and china, mementoes of the battle which now seemed so unreal, impossible. One casualty was a red-eyed china rabbit which I knew Rachel was very fond of. Who had broken that? Probably Rachel.

'Rachel and I are very happily married,' said Arnold.

'Yes, I'm sure.' He was probably right. They probably were. I sat down again, feeling very tired.

'Of course we argue sometimes. Marriage is a long journey at close quarters. Of course nerves get frayed. Every married person is a Jekyll and Hyde, they've got to be. You mayn't think it, but Rachel is a bit of a nagger. Her voice goes on and on and on sometimes. At least it has lately, I suppose it's her age. You wouldn't believe it, but she can go on for an hour saying the same thing over and over again.'

'Women like to talk.'

'This isn't talk. I mean that she repeats the same sentence over and over and over again.'

'You mean literally? She ought to see a psychiatrist.'

'No, no, no, that shows you simply haven't the faintest idea – It sounds like insanity but in fact she's perfectly sane. Half an hour later she's singing and making the supper. That's how it is, and I know it and she knows it. Married people live on inductions.'

'What sort of sentence does she repeat, saying what? Give me an example.'

'No. You wouldn't understand. It would sound awful when it isn't. She gets an idea and runs it for a while. For instance that I discuss her with other women.'

'You're not sort of – Are you?'

'You mean running around? No, of course not. Christ, I'm a model husband. Rachel knows that perfectly well. I always tell her the truth, she knows I don't have affairs. Well, I have had, but I told her, and that was ages ago. Why shouldn't I talk to other women, we're not Victorians! I have to have friends and talk freely to them, I can't give way on a point like that. And where it would make one mad with resentment one mustn't give way, one oughtn't to. Anyway, she doesn't really expect it, it's all dotty. Why shouldn't I talk about her sometimes? It would look jolly funny if she was a banned subject. It's always open kind sympathetic talk, I wouldn't say anything I wouldn't want her to hear. I don't mind her talking about me to her friends. Christ, one isn't sacred, and of course she does talk, she has lots of friends, she's not cloistered. She says she's wasted her talents, but that's not true, there are hundreds of kinds of self-expression, one doesn't have to be a bloody artist. She's intelligent, she could have been a secretary or something if she'd wanted to, but does she really want that? Of course not. It's a sort of empty complaint, and she knows it, it's just a kind of momentary annoyance with me. She does all sorts of interesting things, she's on endless committees, involved in campaigns for this and that, she knows all sorts of people, members of parliament, far grander people than me! She's not a frustrated person –'

'It's just a mood,' I said. 'Women have moods.' The agonized voice I had heard upstairs already seemed remote. Then it occurred to me that I was doing just what she had predicted.

'I know,' said Arnold. 'I'm sorry, Bradley, I'm getting over-excited and talking stupidly. It's sort of shock and relief, you know. I'm probably being unfair to Rachel, and it isn't as bad as it sounds, in fact it isn't bad at all. One must make allowances. At the age she's reached women always become a little bit odd. It passes, I imagine. I suppose they sort of review their lives. There must be a sense of loss, a feeling of the final parting with youth. A tendency to be hysterical isn't too uncommon, I suppose.' He added, 'She's a very feminine woman. There's a toughness in them. She's marvellous, actually.'

There was the sound of a lavatory flushing upstairs. Arnold moved to rise, then fell back. He said, 'There you are. She'll be down. I won't bother her just yet. I'm sorry I troubled you, Bradley, there was no reason, I just stupidly panicked.'

I thought, he will soon feel resentment against me because of this. I said, 'Naturally I won't mention this business to anyone.'

Arnold, looking a little annoyed, said, 'Do what you like. I'm not asking you to be discreet. More sherry? Why did you chuck that doctor chap out so, if I may say so, churlishly?'

'I wanted to talk to you.'

'What was all that he was saying to you just at the end?'

'Oh, nothing.'

'He said something about "Christian". Was he talking about your ex-wife? Wasn't that her name? Pity I never met her, but you got rid of her so early on.'

'I'd better go. Rachel will be coming down for the reconciliation scene.'

'Not for another hour, I reckon.'

'I suppose that's one of those skilled inductions you married people live by. All the same –'

'Don't be evasive, Bradley. *Was* he talking about your once wife?'

'Yes. He's her brother.'

'Really? Your ex-wife's brother. How fascinating. I wish I'd known, I'd have looked him over more carefully. Are you being reconciled or something?'

'No.'

'Oh come on, something's happening.'

'You love happenings, don't you. She's coming back to London. She's a widow now. It's nothing to do with me.'

'Why not? Aren't you going to see her?'

'Why the hell should I? I don't like her.'

'You are picturesque, Bradley. And so dignified! After all these years. I'd be dying with curiosity. I must say, I'd love to meet your ex-wife. I can never quite see you as a married man.'

'Me neither.'

'So that doctor fellow is her brother. Well, well.'

'He's not a doctor.'

'What do you mean? You said he was.'

'He was struck off the register.'

'Ex-wife, ex-doctor. How interesting. What was he struck off for?'

'I don't know. Something to do with drugs.'

'But what to do with drugs? What did he do exactly?'

'I don't know!' I said, beginning to be exasperated in a familiar way. 'I'm not interested. I never liked him. He's some sort of scoundrel. By the way, I hope to God you didn't talk to him about what really happened tonight. I just told him there'd been an accident.'

'Well, what really happened wasn't very – I daresay he guessed –'

'I hope not! He's capable of blackmailing you.'

'That man? Oh no!'

'Anyway, he disappeared out of my life long ago, thank God.'

'But now he's back. Bradley, you *are* censorious, you know.'

'I disapprove of some things, oddly enough.'

'Disapproving of things is all right. But you mustn't disapprove of people. It cuts you off.'

'I want to be cut off from people like Marloe. Being a real

person oneself is a matter of setting up limits and drawing lines and saying no. I don't want to be a nebulous bit of ectoplasm straying around in other people's lives. That sort of vague sympathy with everybody precludes any real understanding of anybody.'

'The sympathy needn't be vague –'

'And it precludes any real loyalty to anybody.'

'One must know the details. Justice, after all –'

'I detest chatter and gossip. One must hold one's tongue. Even sometimes just *not think* about people. Real thoughts come out of silence.'

'Bradley, not that, please. *Listen!* I was saying justice demands details. You say you aren't interested in why he was struck off the register. You ought to be! You say he's some sort of scoundrel. I'd like to be told what sort. You obviously don't know.'

Making a strong effort to check my exasperation I said, 'I was glad to get rid of my wife and he went too. Can't you understand that? It seems simple enough to me.'

'I rather liked him. I asked him to come and see us.'

'Oh Christ!'

'But, Bradley, you mustn't reject people, you mustn't just write them off. You must be curious about them. Curiosity is a kind of charity.'

'I don't think curiosity is a kind of charity. I think it's a kind of malice.'

'That's what makes a writer, knowing the details.'

'It may make your kind of writer. It doesn't make mine.'

'Here we go again,' said Arnold.

'Why pile up a jumble of "details"? When you start really imagining something you have to forget the details anyhow, they just get in the way. Art isn't the reproduction of oddments out of life.'

'I never said it was!' said Arnold. 'I don't draw direct from life.'

'Your wife thinks you do.'

'Oh that. Oh God.'

'Inquisitive chatter and cataloguing of things one's spotted isn't art.'

'Of course it isn't –'

'Vague romantic myth isn't art either. Art is imagination. Imagination changes, fuses. Without imagination you have stupid details on one side and empty dreams on the other.'

'Bradley, I know you –'

'Art isn't chat plus fantasy. Art comes out of endless restraint and silence.'

'If the silence is endless there isn't any art! It's people without creative gifts who say that more means worse!'

'One should only complete something when one feels one's bloody privileged to have it at all. Those who only do what's easy will never be rewarded by –'

'Nonsense. I write whether I feel like it or not. I complete things whether I think they're perfect or not. Anything else is hypocrisy. I have no muse. That's what being a professional writer is.'

'Then thank God I'm not one.'

'You're such an agonizer, Bradley. You romanticize art. You're a masochist about it, you want to suffer, you want to feel that your inability to create is continuously significant.'

'It is continuously significant.'

'Oh come, be humbler, let cheerfulness break in! I can't think why you worry so. Thinking of yourself as a "writer" is part of your trouble. Why not just think of yourself as someone who very occasionally writes something, who may in the future write something? Why make a life drama out of it?'

'I don't think of myself as a writer, not like that. I know you do. You're all "writer". I don't see myself in that way. I think of myself as an artist, that is as a dedicated person. And of course it's a life drama. Are you suggesting that I'm some sort of amateur?'

'No, no –'

'Because if you are –'

'Bradley, please let's not have this silly old quarrel again, I don't feel strong enough.'

'All right. Sorry. Sorry.'

'You get so worked up and flowery! You sound as if you were quoting something all the time!'

I felt a sizzling warmth in my coat pocket wherein I had thrust the folded manuscript of my review of Arnold's novel. Arnold Baffin's work was a congeries of amusing anecdotes loosely garbled into 'racy stories' with the help of half-baked unmeditated symbolism. The dark powers of imagination were conspicuous by their absence. Arnold Baffin wrote too much, too fast. Arnold Baffin was really just a talented journalist.

'Let's start up our Sundays again,' said Arnold. 'I so much enjoyed our talks. We must just keep out of those old rat runs. We're both like mechanical toys when certain subjects are mentioned, we go whirring off. Come to lunch next Sunday, why not?'

'I doubt if Rachel will want to see me next Sunday.'

'Why ever not?'

'Anyway I'm going abroad.'

'Of course, I'd forgotten. Where are you going to?'

'Italy. I haven't made detailed plans yet.'

'Well, you aren't going at once, are you? Come next Sunday. And let us know where you'll be in Italy. We're going there too, we might meet.'

'I'll ring up. Better go now, Arnold.'

'All right. Thanks. And don't worry about us. You know.'

He seemed ready to let me go now. In fact we were both of us exhausted.

He waved me off and closed the door quickly. By the time I reached the front gate I could hear his gramophone. He must have hared straight back into the drawing-room and put on a record, like a man racing for his fix. It sounded like Stravinsky or something. The action and the sound set my teeth on edge. I am, I fear, one of those who, according to Shakespeare, are 'fit for treasons, stratagems and spoils'.

It was now, I was surprised to see from my watch, nearly eight o'clock in the evening. The sun was shining again, though a part of the sky was covered with dark metallic cloud which had been drawn across it like a curtain. There was a rather lurid light, such as these early summer evenings can produce, when a clear but strengthless sun shines at the approach of night. I noticed green leaves in the suburban gardens outlined with an awful clarity. The feathered songsters were still pouring forth their nonsense.

I felt very tired and a little muzzy and weak at the knees with fear and shock. A mixture of emotions raged. Partly, I still felt something of the sheer unholy excitement which I had experienced initially at the thought of a friend (especially this one) in trouble. I felt too that, as far as the trouble was concerned, I had acquitted myself quite well. However it was also possible that I might have to pay the penalty for this. Both Arnold and Rachel might resent my role and wish to punish me for it. This was a particularly irritating anxiety to develop just as I was proposing to go away and forget all about Arnold for a time. It was alarming to find myself suddenly so bound up by exasperation, irritation, affection. I resented and feared these ligatures. I wondered if I should not now delay my departure until after Sunday. On Sunday I could test the atmosphere, estimate the damage, make some sort of peace. *Then* I could depart in a suitable state of indifference. That they would both resent me as a witness seemed inevitable. However in so far as they were both decent rational people I could expect from them a conscious effort to inhibit resentment. This seemed a reason to see them again soon so as to allow them to make their effort before the thing became historically fixed. On the other hand I had, in that lurid evening light, a superstitious feeling that if I did not make my escape before Sunday something would grab me. I even wondered if I should take a taxi (one passed me at that moment), go back to my flat, pick up my luggage, and go straight on to the station, catching whatever train I could, even if it meant waiting there until the following morning. But this was obviously an absurd idea.

Connected now with my nagging anxiety about what the Baffins were going to think of me was the huge problem of Christian. Yet was it a problem? If Francis had not so intolerably turned up would I have felt my ex-wife's return to London to be any concern of mine? There was no reason why we should ever meet by accident. And if she should call on me I could politely tell her to go away. Would this be worse than an annoyance? I was not sure. Francis had certainly raised ghosts, was himself a spectre of a particularly nasty kind. And why had I been such a perfect lunatic as to introduce him into the Baffin household? It was the worst thing that I could have done. And I knew prophetically that it was the sort of stupid action which could madden me with remorse. Of course Arnold had immediately latched on to Francis. Arnold was a natural latcher-on. And now that he had learnt the fascinating news that Francis was my ex-brother-in-law and an unfrocked doctor he would be sure to pursue the acquaintance. That must not happen. I wondered if I could decently just ask him not to. I decided that, although undignified, that was perhaps the best and simplest thing to do. The prompt and absolute excision of Francis from my life was a necessity. Arnold would understand: all too well, but I was after all fairly used to running the gauntlet of Arnold's understanding.

I then began to wonder what on earth was happening now back at the Baffins' house? Was Rachel still lying like a disfigured corpse staring at the ceiling, while Arnold sat in the drawing-room drinking whisky and listening to *The Firebird*? Perhaps Rachel had drawn the sheet over her face again in that appalling way. Or was it all quite different? Arnold was kneeling outside the door begging her to let him in, weeping and accusing himself. Or else, Rachel, who had been listening for my departure, had come quietly down the stairs and into her husband's arms. Perhaps now they were in the kitchen together, cooking the supper and opening a special bottle of wine to celebrate. What a mystery a marriage was. What a strange and violent world, the world of matrimony. I was glad to be outside it. The idea of it filled me with a sort of queasy pity. I felt at that moment so 'curious', in just Arnold's sense of the word, that I almost turned back to snoop around the house and find out what had happened. But of course such an action was not in my character.

By this time I was not far from the underground station, and I had decided to commit no follies. There was no question of rushing out of London that night. I would make my way quietly homeward, eat a sandwich in my local pub, and go early to bed. I had had a hard evening, and this was one of the moments at which I felt myself no longer young. Tomorrow I would decide whatever by then seemed still to need decision, such as whether I should postpone my departure until after Sunday. I felt with some relief that at any rate today's little dramas were now over. There was however one still to come.

I had crossed the main road and entered the little shopping street that led to the station. The evening had darkened though the pale lurid sun was still shining. Some of the shops had switched their lights on. There was a shadowy light, not exactly twilight, but an uncertain vivid yet hazy illumination, wherein people walked like spirits, bathed in light and not revealed. The rather dream-like atmosphere was intensified, I suppose, by my own tiredness, by having drunk alcohol, by having eaten nothing. In this mood of rather doom-ridden spiritual lassitude I noticed with only a little surprise and interest the figure upon the other side of the road of a young man who was behaving rather oddly. He was standing upon the kerb and strewing flowers upon the roadway, as if casting them into a river. My first thought was that he was the adherent of some Hindu sect, not then uncommon in London, and that he was performing some religious rite. A few people paused to look at him, but Londoners were by now so accustomed to 'weirdies' of all kinds that his ritual aroused little interest.

The young fellow appeared to be chanting some sort of repetitive litany. I now saw that what he was strewing was not so much flowers as white petals. Where had I seen just such petals lately? The fragments of white paint which the violence of Arnold's chisel had dislodged from the bedroom door. And the white petals were being cast, not at random, but in relation to the regular and constant passage of motor cars. As a car approached the young chap would take a handful of petals out of a bag and cast them into the path of the car, uttering the while his rhythmic chant. Then the frail whitenesses would race about, caught in the car's motion, dash madly under the wheels, follow the whirlwind of the car's wake, and dissipate themselves further along the road: so that the casting away of the petals seemed like a sacrifice or act of destruction, since that which was offered was being so instantly consumed and made to vanish.

The young man was slim, dressed in dark narrow trousers,

a sort of dark velvet or corduroy jacket and a white shirt. He had a thickish mane of slightly wavy brown hair which grew well down on to his neck. I had paused and had been watching him for some moments and was about to set off again towards the station when, with one of those switches of *gestalt* which can be so unnerving, I realized that the light had deceived me and that this was in fact no young man but a girl. In the next moment I further realized that it was a girl whom I knew. It was Julian Baffin, Arnold and Rachel's teenage daughter and only child. (So named, I need hardly explain, after Julian of Norwich.)

I describe Julian here as teenage because that was how I still thought of her, though at this period she was I suppose in her earliest twenties. Arnold had been a young father. I had felt a modest avuncular interest in the fairy-like little girl. (I had never wanted children of my own. Many artists do not.) With the approach of puberty however she lost her looks and developed an awkward sulky aggressive attitude to the world in general which considerably diminished her charm. She was always fretting and complaining, and her little face, as it hardened into adult lines, grew discontented and secretive. That was as I recalled her. I had not in fact seen her for some while. Her parents adored her, yet were at the same time disappointed in her. They had wanted a boy. They had both assumed, as parents do, that Julian would be clever, but this appeared not to be the case. Julian took a long time growing up, she took little part in the self-conscious tribalism of the 'teenage' world, and still preferred dressing her dolls to dressing herself at an age when most girls are beginning, even pardonably, to interest themselves in war paint.

Not notably successful in exams and certainly not in the least bookish, Julian had left school at sixteen. She had spent a year in France, more at Arnold's insistence than out of her own sense of adventure, or so it had seemed to me at the time. She returned from France unimpressed by that country and speaking very bad French which she promptly forgot, and went on to a typist's training course. Fledged as a typist she took a job in the 'typing pool' at a Government office. When she was about nineteen she decided that she was a painter, and Arnold eagerly wangled her into an art school, which she left after a year. After that she had entered a teachers' training college somewhere in the Midlands where she had been, I think, for a year or perhaps two when I saw her on that evening strewing the white petals in the path of the oncoming motor cars.

Only now I realized, with yet another shift of *gestalt*, that the whirling white blobs were not petals at all, but fragments of paper. The wind of a passing vehicle carried one of these fragments right to my feet and I picked it up. It was part of a hand-written document whereon I could decipher, amid scrawl, the word 'love'. Perhaps this eccentric ceremonial had indeed some sort of religious purpose? I crossed the road and began to walk along the pavement behind Julian. I wanted to hear what it was that she was chanting, and would not have been surprised to find that it was in an unknown tongue. As I came close to her the murmured words sounded like the same constantly repeated phrase. *There's no telling? Masquerading? Are you ailing? He's compelling?*

'Hello, Bradley.'

Owing to her absence at college and the demise of our Sundays I had not seen Julian for nearly a year, and before that indeed infrequently. I found her older, the face still sulky but with more of a brooding expression, suggestive of the occurrence of thought. She had a rather bad complexion, or perhaps it was just that Arnold's 'greasy' look looked less healthy on a woman. She never used make-up. She had watery-blue eyes, not the flecked hazel-brown of her mother's, nor did her secretive and dog-like face repeat Rachel's large bland freckled features. Her thick undulating mane, which had no trace of red, was streakily fair with that dark blonde colour which is almost suggestive of green. Even at close quarters she still slightly resembled a boy, tallish, dour, who had just cut himself in a premature attempt to shave his first whisker. I did not mind the dourness. I dislike girls who are skittish.

'Hello, Julian. Whatever are you doing?'

'Have you been to see Daddy?'

'Yes.' I reflected that it was just as well Julian was out this evening.

'Good. I thought you'd quarrelled.'

'Certainly not!'

'You don't come any more.'

'I do. Only you're away.'

'Not now. I'm doing teaching practice in London. What was happening when you left?'

'Where? At home? Oh – nothing special –'

'They were quarrelling so I left the house. Have they calmed down?'

'Yes, of course –'

'Don't you think they quarrel more than they used to?'

'No, I – How smart you are, Julian. Quite a dandy.'

'I'm so glad you've come, I was just thinking about you. I wanted to ask you something, I was going to write –'

'Julian, what are you doing, with all that paper you're scattering?'

'It's an exorcism. These are love letters.'

'Love letters?'

'From my ex-boy-friend.'

I remembered that Arnold had mentioned rather unenthusiastically a 'hairy swain', an art student or something.

'Have you parted company?'

'Yes. I've torn them into the smallest possible pieces. When I've got rid of them all I'll be free. Here goes the last, I think.'

Taking from her neck the receptacle rather like a nose-bag which had contained the dismembered missives she turned it inside out. A few more white petals flew with the passing wind and were gone.

'But what were you saying, you were chanting something, a spell or such.'

' "Oscar Belling".'

'What?'

'That was his name. Look, I'm using the past tense! It's all over!'

'Did you abandon him or did he –?'

'I'd rather not talk about it. Bradley, I wanted to ask you something.'

It was quite dark now, a bluish night gauzed over by the yellow street lamps, and reminding me irrelevantly of Rachel's reddish golden hair adhering to the front of Francis's shabby blue suit. We walked slowly along the street.

'Look, Bradley, it's this. I've decided to be a writer.'

My heart sank. 'That's fine.'

'And I want you to help me.'

'It's not easy to help someone to be a writer, it may not even be possible.'

'The thing is, I don't want to be a writer like Daddy, I want to be a writer like you.'

My heart warmed to the girl. But my answer had to be ironical. 'My dear Julian, don't emulate me! I constantly try and hardly ever succeed!'

'That's just it. Daddy writes too much, don't you think? He hardly ever revises. He writes something, then he "gets rid of it" by publishing it, I've heard him actually say that, and then he writes something else. He's always in such a hurry, it's neurotic. I see no point in being an artist unless you try all the time to be perfect.'

I wondered if these were the views of the late Oscar Belling. 'It's a long hard road, Julian, if that's what you believe.'

'Well, it's what *you* believe, and I admire you for it, I've always admired you, Bradley. But the point is this, will you teach me?'

My heart sank again. 'What do you mean, Julian?'

'Two things really. I've been thinking about it. I know I'm not educated and I know I'm immature. And this teachers' training place is hopeless. I want you to give me a reading list. All the great books I ought to read, but only the *great* ones and the *hard* ones. I don't want to waste my time with small stuff. I haven't *got* much time left now. And I'll read the books and we could discuss them. You could give me sort of tutorials on them. And then, the second thing, I'd like to write things for you, short stories perhaps, or anything you felt I *should* write, and you'd criticize what I'd written. You see, I want to be really taken in hand. I think one should pay so much attention to technique, don't you? Like learning to draw before you paint. Do please say you'll take me on. It needn't take much of your time, not more than a couple of hours or so in a week, and it would absolutely change my life.'

I knew of course that it was just a matter of choosing a way of getting out of this gracefully. Julian was already grieving over the wasted years and regretting that she had not much time left. My grief and my regret were a rather different matter. I could not spare her a couple of hours a week. How dare she ask for my precious hours? In any case, the child's suggestion appalled and embarrassed me. It was not just the display of youthful insensibility. It was the sadly misplaced nature of her ambition. There was little doubt that Julian's fate was to be typist, teacher, housewife, without starring in any role.

I said, 'I think it's a very good idea and of course I'd like to help, and I do so agree with you about technique – Only just now I'm going to be abroad for a while.'

'Oh, where? I could visit you. I'm quite free now because my school has measles.'

'I shall be travelling.'

'But, Bradley, please, couldn't you just start me off before you go? Then we could have something to discuss when you come back. Please at least send me a book list, and I'll read the books and have a story written too by the time you come home again. Please. I want you to be my tutor. You're the only sort of possible real teacher in my life.'

'Well, all right, I might think about some books for you. But I'm no creative-writing guru, I can't give time to – What sort of books do you mean, anyway? Like the *Iliad*, the *Divine Comedy*, or like *Sons and Lovers*, *Mrs Dalloway* –'

'Oh *Iliad*, *Divine Comedy*, please. That's marvellous! That's just it! The big stuff!'

'And you don't mind poetry, prose – ?'

'Oh, no, not poetry. I can't read poetry very well. I'm keeping poetry for later on.'

'The *Iliad* and the *Divine Comedy* are poems.'

'Well, yes, of course they are, but I'd be reading them in a prose translation.'

'So that disposes of that difficulty.'

'You will write to me then, Bradley? I'm so terribly grateful. I'll say good-bye to you here because I must look in this shop.'

We had stopped rather abruptly a little short of the station outside the illuminated window of a shoe shop. High summer boots of various colours made out of a sort of lace occupied the front of the window. Slightly put out by the brusqueness of my dismissal I could not think of anything suitable to say. I saluted vaguely and said 'Ta-ta', an expression which I do not think I have ever used before or since.

'Ta-ta,' said Julian, as if this were a sort of code. Then she turned to face the lighted window and began examining the boots.

I crossed the road and reached the station entrance and looked back. She was leaning forward now with her hands on her knees, her thick hair and her brow and nose goldened by the bright light. I thought how aptly some painter, not Mr Belling, could have used her as a model for an allegory of Vanity. I watched, as one might watch a fox, for some minutes, but she did not go away or even move.

My dear Arnold, I wrote.

It was the following morning, and I was sitting at the little marquetry table in my sitting-room. I have not described this important room adequately yet. It has a powdery faded brooding inward quality, strongly smelling, perhaps literally, of the past. (Not dry rot so much as something like face powder.) It was also rather stubby, being truncated by the wall of my bedroom, which curtailed its former spread, so that the green panelling aforementioned clothed only three sides of the room. This false proportion sometimes made it feel, especially at night, as if it were part of a ship, or perhaps a first class railway carriage of the sort one might have found upon the Trans-Siberian railway about 1910. The round marquetry table stood in the centre. (Often this had a potted plant upon it, but I had just given away the current incumbent to the laundry lady.) Against the walls variously: a tiny velvet armchair with what Hartbourne, who was too stout to sit in it, called 'frilly drawers'; two frail-legged lyreback chairs (Victorian copies) with *petit-point* embroidery

60

seats, various (one with a sailing swan, the other with tiger lilies); a tall but rather narrow mahogany bureau bookcase (most of my books live on simple shelves in the bedroom); a red, black and gold lacquered display cabinet in the Chinese style, Victorian; a mahogany night-table with tray top, badly stained, possibly eighteenth century; a satinwood Pembroke table, also stained; a walnut hanging corner cupboard with curved doors. Then: drawn up against the table with me sitting on it, a curvaceous 'conversation chair', with upholstered arms and a greasy balding seat of red velvet. On the floor, a carpet with large amber roses on a black ground. Before the fireplace, a black woolly rug simulating a bear. Upon it a blowsy chintz armchair (Hartbourne size, usually known as 'his' chair) needing a new cover. The wide-shelved chimney piece was made of a dark slatey blue-grey marble, and the cave of the grate beneath was framed by a design of black cast-iron rose garlands, complete with veined leaves and thorns. Pictures, all tiny, hung mainly upon the 'false' wall, since I could not bring myself to pierce the wood, and the existing hooks upon the panelling were too high for my taste. Small oils these were, in thick gilt frames, of little girls with cats, little boys with dogs, cats upon cushions, flowers, the innocent heart-warming trivia of our strong and sentimental forebears. There were two little elegant northern beach scenes, and, in an oval frame, an eighteenth-century drawing of a girl with loose hair, waiting. Upon the chimney piece and in the red, black and gold lacquered display cabinet stood the little items, china cups and figures, snuff boxes, ivories, small oriental bronzes, modest stuff, some of which I may describe later since two at least of these objects play a role in the story.

Earlier that morning Hartbourne had telephoned. Unaware that I was about to depart, he had suggested luncheon. We had been long accustomed to lunch together when I was at the office, and had continued this custom during my retirement. I was at that moment still undecided about whether or not to delay my departure in order to consolidate my peace with the Baffins on Sunday. I gave Hartbourne an evasive reply, saying I would ring back, but in fact his call prompted me to decide. I resolved to go. If I stayed until Sunday I would be caught back into the idle

61

casual pattern of my London life, of whose ordinariness poor Hartbourne was a symbol. This was everything that I wanted to be done with, the relaxed banality of life without goals. And I was upset to find how really reluctant I was to leave my little flat. It was as if I was almost frightened. Spasms of prophetic home-sickness pierced me as I rearranged the china and dusted it with my handkerchief, obsessive visions of burglaries and desecrations. After a dream on the previous night I had hidden several of the more valuable things: hence the need to rearrange the others. The stupid thought that they would stand here silently on guard during my absence almost brought tears into my eyes. Exasperated with myself I decided to leave later that morning, catching an earlier train than the one I had aimed at yesterday.

Yes, it was time to move. I had felt, during recent months, sometimes boredom, sometimes despair, as I struggled with a nebulous work which seemed now a *nouvelle*, now a vast novel, wherein a hero not unlike myself pursued, amid ghostly incidents, a series of reflections about life and art. The trouble was that the dark blaze, whose absence I had deplored in Arnold's work, was absent here as well. I could not fire and fuse these thoughts, these people, into a whole thing. I wanted to produce a sort of statement which might be called my philosophy. But I also wanted to embody this in a story, perhaps in an allegory, something with a form as pliant and as hard as my cast-iron garland of roses. But I could not do it. My people were shadows, my thoughts were epigrams. However I felt, as we artists can feel, the proximity of enlightenment. And I was sure that if I went away now into loneliness, right away from the associations of tedium and failure, I would soon be rewarded. So it was in this mood that I decided to set forth, leaving my darling burrow for a countryside which I had never visited, and a cottage which I had never seen.

However it was necessary first to settle certain things by letter. I am, I must confess, an obsessive and superstitious letter-writer. When I am troubled I will write any long letter rather than make a telephone call. This is perhaps because I invest letters with magical power. To desiderate something in a letter is, I often irrationally feel, tantamount to bringing it about. A letter is a barrier, a reprieve, a charm against the world, an almost infallible method of acting at a distance. (And, it must be admitted, of passing the buck.) It is a way of bidding time to stop. I decided that it was quite unnecessary to visit the Baffins on Sunday. I could achieve all that I wanted by a letter. So I wrote:

My dear Arnold,

I hope that you and Rachel have forgiven me for yesterday. Although summoned I was nevertheless an intruder. You will understand me and I need exclaim no more on that point. One does not want witnesses of one's trouble however ephemeral it may be. The outsider cannot understand and his very thoughts are an impertinence. I write to say that I have no thoughts, except for my affection for you and Rachel and my certainty that all is well with you. I have never been an adherent of your brand of curiosity! And I hope that at least here you will see the charm of this lowering of the gaze! I say this in the gentlest way, and not as a reminder of our perennial argument.

I also write to ask you, as briefly as possible, a favour. You were of course interested to meet Francis Marloe, who by the weirdest accident was with me when you telephoned. You spoke of meeting him again. Please do not do so. If you reflect you will see how hurtful to me any such association would be. I do not propose to have anything to do with my former wife and I do not want any connection to exist between her world, whatever that may turn out to be, and the things of my own which are dear to me. It would of course be characteristic of you to feel 'interested' in probing in this region, but please be kind enough to an old friend not to do so.

Let me take this chance to say that in spite of all differences our friendship is very precious to me. As you will remember, I have made you my literary executor. Could there be a greater sign of trust? However, let us hope that talk of wills is premature. I am just now leaving London and will be away for some time. I hope I shall be able to write. I feel that a most crucial period in my life lies ahead. Give my fondest love to Rachel. I thank you both for your consistent cordiality to a solitary man; and I rely upon you absolutely in the matter of F.M.

With all affectionate and friendly wishes,

Yours ever
Bradley

By the time I had finished writing this letter I found that I was sweating. Writing to Arnold always, for some reason, provoked emotion: and in this case there was superadded the memory

63

of a scene of violence, which, in spite of my bland words, I knew the chemistry of friendship would take long to assimilate. What is ugly and undignified is hardest of all, harder than wickedness, to soften into a mutually acceptable past. We forgive those who have seen us vile sooner than those who have seen us humiliated. I felt a still unresolved deep 'shock' about it all; and although I had been sincere in telling Arnold that I was not 'curious', I knew that this was not, for me either, the end of the matter.

Refilling my pen, I began to write another letter, which ran as follows:

My dear Julian,

it was kind of you to ask my advice about books and writing. I am afraid I cannot offer to teach you to write. I have not the time, and such teaching is, I surmise, impossible anyway. Let me just say a word about books. I think you should read the *Iliad* and the *Odyssey* in any un-varnished translation. (If pressed for time, omit the *Odyssey*.) These are the greatest literary works in the world, where huge conceptions are refined into simplicity. I think perhaps you should leave Dante until later. The *Commedia* presents many points of difficulty and needs, as Homer does not, a commentary. In fact, if not read in Italian, this great work seems not only incomprehensible, but repulsive. You should, I feel, relax your embargo upon poetry sufficiently to accommodate the better known plays of Shakespeare! How fortunate we are to have English as our native tongue! Familiarity and excitement should carry you easily through these works. Forget that they are 'poetry' and just enjoy them. The rest of my reading list consists simply of the greatest English and Russian novels of the nineteenth century. (If you are not sure which these are, ask your father: I think he can be trusted to tell you!)

Give yourself to these great works of art. They suffice for a lifetime. Do not worry too much about writing. Art is a gratuitous and usually thankless activity and at your age it is more important to enjoy it than to practise it. If you do decide to write anything, keep in mind what you yourself said about perfection. The most important thing a writer must learn to do is to tear up what he has written. Art is concerned not just primarily but absolutely with truth. It is another name for truth. The artist is learning a special language in which to reveal truth. If you write, write from the heart, yet carefully, objectively. Never pose. Write little things which you think are true. Then you may sometimes find that they are beautiful as well.

64

My very good wishes to you, and thank you for wanting to know what I thought!

Yours
Bradley

After I had finished this letter and after some reflection and fumbling and excursions to the chimney piece and the display cabinet, I began a further letter which went thus:

Dear Marloe,

    as I hope I made clear to you, your visit was not only unwelcome but entirely without point, since I do not propose under any circumstances to communicate with my former wife. Any further attempt at an approach, whether by letter or in person, will be met by absolute rejection. However, now that you appreciate my attitude I imagine that you will be kind and wise enough to leave me alone. I was grateful for your help *chez* Mr and Mrs Baffin. I should tell you, in case you had any thoughts of pursuing an acquaintance with them, that I have asked them not to receive you, and they will not receive you.

Yours sincerely,
Bradley Pearson

Francis had, on his departure on the previous evening, contrived to thrust into my pocket his address and telephone number written upon a slip of paper. I copied the address on to the envelope and threw the paper into the wastepaper basket.

I then sat and twiddled for a bit longer, watching the creeping line of sun turning the crusty surface of the wall opposite from brown to blond. Then I fell to writing again.

Dear Mrs Evandale,

    it has been brought to my attention that you are in London. This letter is to say that I do not under any conceivable circumstances wish to hear from you or to see you. It may seem contradictory to send you a letter to say this. But I thought it possible that some sort of curiosity or morbid interest might lead you to 'look me up'. Kindly do not do so. I have no desire to see you and no interest in hearing about you. I see no reason why our paths should cross, and I should be grateful for the continuance of our total non-communication. Please do not imagine from this letter that I have in this long interim been speculating about you. I have not. I have forgotten you completely. I would not be concerned about you now were it not for an impertinent visit which I have received from your brother. I have asked him to spare me any further visits, and I hope that you will see to it that he does not again appear on my doorstep as your self-styled emissary. I would appreciate it if you would take this letter as saying exactly what it appears to say and nothing else. There is nothing of a cordial or forward-looking import to be read 'between the lines'. My act of writing to you does not betoken excitement or interest. As my wife you were unpleasant to me, cruel to me, destructive to me. I do not think that I speak too strongly. I was profoundly relieved to be free of you and I do not like you. Or rather I do not like my memory of you. I scarcely even now conceive of you as existing except as a nastiness conjured up by your brother. This miasma will soon pass and be replaced by the previous state of oblivion. I trust that you will not interfere with this process by any manifestation. I should, to be finally frank, be thoroughly angered by any 'approach' on your part, and I am sure that you would wish to avoid a distressing scene. I derive consolation from the thought that since your memories of me are doubtless just as disagreeable as my memories of you, you are unlikely to desire a meeting.

Yours sincerely,
Bradley Pearson

PS I should add that I am today leaving London and tomorrow leaving England. I shall be staying away for some time and may even settle abroad.

When I had finished writing this letter I was not only sweating, I was trembling and panting and my heart was beating viciously. What emotion had so invaded me? Fear? It is sometimes curiously difficult to name the emotion from which one suffers. The naming of it is sometimes unimportant, sometimes crucial. Hatred?

I looked at my watch and found that in the composition of the letter a long time had passed. It was now too late to catch the morning train. No doubt the afternoon train would be better in any case. Trains induce such terrible anxiety. They image the possibility of total and irrevocable failure. They are also dirty, rackety, packed with strangers, an object lesson in the foul contingency of life: the talkative fellow-traveller, the possibility of children.

I re-read the letter which I had written to Christian and reflected upon it. I had produced it out of some sort of immediate need for self-expression or self-defence, a magical warding-off movement, such as I have explained that I naturally indulge in as a letter-writer. However a letter, as I have at times to my own cost forgotten, is not only a piece of self-expression; it is also statement, suggestion, persuasion, command, and its sheer effectiveness in these respects needs to be objectively estimated. What effect would this letter have upon Christian? It now seemed possible that the effect would be the exact reverse of what I desired. This letter, with its reference to a 'distressing scene', would excite her. She would see behind it some quite other communication. She would come round in a taxi. Besides, the letter was full of genuine contradictions. If I was settling abroad why send it anyway? Perhaps it would be more effective simply to send a line saying 'Do not communicate with me'? Or else nothing at all? The trouble was that by now I felt so worried about Christian and so polluted by a sense of connection with her that it was a psychological necessity to send some sort of missive simply as an exorcism. To pass the time I wrote the envelope: our old address. Of course the lease had been in her name. What an investment.

I decided that I would send off the letter to Francis and postpone deciding what sort of communication, if any, to send to Christian. I also decided that it was now a matter of urgency to get out of the house and down to the station, where I could have lunch and await the afternoon train at leisure. It was just as well the earlier train had been safely missed. I have sometimes had the unpleasant experience, arriving very early for a train, of finding myself catching its predecessor with a minute to spare. Thrusting the letter to Christian into my pocket I found my fingers touching the review of Arnold's novel. Here was another unsolved problem. Although I was well able to consider refraining from doing so, I knew that I also felt very anxious to publish. Why? Yes, I must get away and think all these matters out.

My suitcases were in the hall where I had left them yesterday. I put on my macintosh. I went into the bathroom. This bathroom was of the kind which no amount of caring for could make other than sordid. Vari-coloured slivers of soap, such as I cannot normally bear to throw away, were lying about in the basin and in the bath. With a sudden act of will I collected them all and flushed them down the lavatory. As I stood there, dazed with this success, the front door bell suddenly began to ring and ring.

At this point it is necessary for me to give some account of my sister Priscilla, who is about to appear upon the scene.

Priscilla is six years younger than me. She left school early. So indeed did I. I am an educated and cultivated person through my own zeal, efforts, and talents. Priscilla had no zeal and talents and made no efforts. She was spoilt by my mother whom she resembled. I think women, perhaps unconsciously, convey to female children a deep sense of their own discontent. My mother, though not too unhappily married, had a continued grudge against the world. This may have originated in, or been aggravated by, a sense of having married 'beneath' her, though not exactly in a social sense. My mother had been a 'beauty' and had had many suitors. I suspect she felt later in life, as she grew old behind the counter, that if she had played her cards otherwise she could have made a much better bargain in life. Priscilla, though she made in commercial and even in social terms a more advantageous buy, followed somewhat the same pattern. Priscilla, though not as pretty as my mother, had been a good-looking girl, and was admired in the circle of pert half-baked under-educated youths who constituted her 'social life'. But Priscilla, egged on by her mother, had ambitions, and was in no hurry to settle with one of these unprepossessing candidates.

I myself had left school at fifteen and become a boy clerk in a Government department. I was living away from home and devoting all my spare time to my education and to my writing. I had been fond of Priscilla when we were children, but was now, and deliberately, cut off from her and from my parents. It was clear that my family could not understand or share my interests and I drew away. Priscilla, entirely unskilled, she could not even type, was working in what she termed a 'fashion house', a wholesale establishment of the 'rag trade' in Croydon. She was, I imagine, some sort of very junior assistant or clerk. The idea of 'fashion' seems a little to have turned her head: perhaps my mother was concerned in this too. Priscilla began to lard herself with make-up and haunt the hairdresser and was always buying new clothes which made her look like a guy. Her pretensions and her extravagance were, I believe, the cause of quarrels between my parents. Meanwhile I myself had other interests and was suffering the anxiety of those who know at an early age that they have not had the education which they deserve.

To cut a long story short, Priscilla really got quite 'above herself', dressing and behaving 'grandly', and did eventually satisfy her ambition of penetrating into some slightly 'better' social circles than those which she had frequented at first. I suspect that she and my mother actually planned a 'campaign' to better Priscilla's lot. Priscilla went to tennis parties, indulged in amateur dramatics, went to charity dances. She and my mother invented for her quite a little 'season'. Only Priscilla's season went on and on. She could not make up her mind to marry. Or perhaps her present beaux, in spite of the bold face which Priscilla and my mother jointly presented to the world, felt that after all poor Priscilla was not a very good match. Perhaps there was after all a smell of shop. Then, doubtless as a result of working so hard on her season, she lost her job, and made no attempt to obtain another. She stayed at home, fell vaguely ill, and had what would now I suppose be called a nervous breakdown.

By the time she recovered she was getting on into her twenties and had lost some of her first good looks. She talked at that time of becoming a 'model' (a 'mannequin'), but so far as I know made no serious attempt to do so. What she did become, virtually, and not to put too fine a point upon it, was a tart. I do not mean that she stood around in the road, but she moved in a world of business men, golf club bar proppers and night-club hounds, who certainly regarded her in this light. I did not want to know anything about this; possibly I ought to have been more concerned. I was upset and annoyed when my father once approached the subject, and although I could see that he had been made utterly miserable, I resolutely refused to discuss it. I never said anything to my mother, who always defended Priscilla and pretended, or deceived herself into believing, that all was well. I was by this time already involved with Christian, and I had other matters on my mind.

Priscilla met Roger Saxe, who ultimately became her husband, somewhere in that golf club whisky bibbing fandango. I first heard of Roger's existence when I learnt that Priscilla was pregnant. There seemed to be no question of marriage. And Roger, it appeared, was willing to pay half of the abortion bill, but demanded that the family should pay the other half. This piece of pure caddishness was my first introduction to my future brother-in-law. He was in fact reasonably well off. My father and I put up the money between us and Priscilla had her operation. This illegal and thoroughly sordid drama upset my poor father very much indeed. He was a puritan very like myself, and he was a timid law-abiding man. He felt ashamed and frightened. He was already ill, became iller, and never recovered. My mother, a very unhappy woman, dedicated herself now to getting Priscilla married off soon somehow to somebody or anybody. Then, we never quite knew how or why, about a year after the operation Priscilla got married to Roger.

I will not attempt a lengthy description of Roger. He too will appear in the story in due course. I did not like Roger. Roger did not like me. He always referred to himself as a 'public school boy', which I suppose he had been. He had a little education, and a great deal of 'air', a 'plummy' voice and a misleadingly distinguished appearance. As his copious crown of hair became peppery and then grey he began to resemble a soldier. (He had once done some army service, I think in the Pay Corps.) He held himself like a military man and alleged that his friends nicknamed him 'the brigadier'. He cultivated the crude joking manners of a junior officers' mess. He worked in fact in a bank, about which he made as much mystery as possible. He drank and laughed too much.

Married to such a man it was not likely that my sister would be very happy, nor was she. With a pathetic and touching loyalty, and even courage, she kept up appearances. She was house-proud: and there was eventually quite a handsome house, or 'maisonette', in the 'better part' of Bristol, with fine cutlery and glasses and the things which women prize. There were 'dinner parties' and a big car. It was a long way from Croydon. I suspected that they lived beyond their means and that Roger was often in financial difficulties, but Priscilla never actually said so. They both very much wanted children, but were unable to produce any. Once when drunk Roger hinted that Priscilla's 'operation' had done some fatal damage. I did not want to know. I could see that Priscilla was unhappy, her life was boring and empty, and Roger was not a rewarding companion. I did not however want to know about this either. I rarely visited them. I occasionally gave Priscilla lunch in London. We talked of trivialities.

I opened the door, and there was Priscilla. I knew immediately that something must be wrong. Priscilla knew that I detested *ad hoc* arrangements. Our luncheon 'dates' were usually fixed by letter weeks in advance.

She was smartly dressed in a navy blue 'jersey' coat and skirt, looking pale and tense, unsmiling. She had retained her looks into middle age, though she had put on weight and looked a good deal less 'glossy', now resembling a 'career woman': the female counterpart perhaps of Roger's specious 'military look'. Her well-cut ungaudy clothes, deliberately 'classic' and quite unlike the lurid plumage of her youth, looked a bit like uniform, the effect being counteracted, however, by the vulgar 'costume jewellery' with which she always loaded herself. She dyed her hair a discreet gold and wore it kempt and wavy. Her face was not a weak one, somewhat resembling mine only without the 'cagy' sensitive look. Her eyes were narrowed by short sight, and her thin lips were brightly painted.

She said nothing in reply to my surprised greeting, marched past me into the sitting-room, selected one of the lyreback chairs, pulled it away from the wall, sat down upon it and dissolved into desperate tears.

'Priscilla, Priscilla, what *is* it, what's happened? Oh, you are upsetting me so!'

After a while the weeping subsided into a series of long sighing sobs. She sat inspecting the streaks of honey-brown make-up which had come off on to her paper handkerchief.

'Priscilla, what *is* it?'

'I've left Roger.'

I felt blank dismay, instant fear for myself. I did not want to be involved in any mess of Priscilla's. I did not even want to have to be sorry for Priscilla. Then I thought, of course there is exaggeration, misconception.

'Don't be silly, Priscilla. Now do calm yourself please. Of course you haven't left Roger. You've had a tiff –'

'Could I have some whisky?'

'I don't keep whisky. I think there's a little medium-sweet sherry.'

'Well, can I have some?'

I went to the walnut hanging cupboard and poured her a glass of brown sherry. 'Here.'

'Bradley, it's been awful, awful, awful. I've been living trapped inside a bad dream, my life has become a bad dream, the kind that makes you shout out.'

'Priscilla, listen. I'm just on the point of leaving London. I can't change my plans. If you like I can give you lunch and then put you on the Bristol train.'

'I tell you I've left Roger.'

'Nonsense.'

'I think I'll go to bed if you don't mind.'

'To *bed*?'

She got up abruptly, pushed out of the door banging herself against the lintel, and went into the spare bedroom. She came out again, cannoning into me, when she saw that the bed was not made up. She went into my bedroom, sat on the bed, threw her handbag violently into a corner, kicked off her shoes and dragged off her jacket. Uttering a low moan she began to undo her skirt.

'Priscilla!'

'I'm going to lie down. I've been up all night. Could you bring my glass of sherry, please?'

I fetched it.

Priscilla got her skirt off, seemingly tearing it in the process. With a flash of pink petticoat she got herself between the sheets and lay there shuddering, staring in front of her with big blank suffering eyes.

I pulled up a chair and sat down beside her.

'Bradley, my marriage is over. I think my life is probably over. What a poor affair it has been.'

72

'Priscilla, don't talk so –'

'Roger has become a devil. Some sort of devil. Or else he's mad.'

'You know I never thought much of Roger –'

'I've been so unhappy for years, so unhappy –'

'I know –'

'I don't understand how a human being can be so unhappy all the time and still be alive.'

'I'm so sorry –'

'But lately it's been sort of pure intense hell, he's been sort of willing my death, oh I can't explain, and he tried to poison me and I woke in the night and he was standing by my bed looking so terrible as if he was just making up his mind to strangle me.'

'Priscilla, this is pure fantasy, you mustn't –'

'Of course he's off after other women, he must be, though I wouldn't mind really if he didn't hate me. Living with someone who hates you is – it drives you mad – He's so often away in funny ways, says he's late at the office and when I ring up he isn't there. I spend so much time just wondering where he is – And he goes to conferences, I suppose there are conferences, once I rang up and – He can do anything he likes and I'm so lonely, oh so lonely – And I put up with it because there was nothing else to do –'

'Priscilla, there's still nothing else to do.'

'How can you say that to me, how can you. This cold hatred and wanting to kill me and poison me –'

'Priscilla, calm yourself. You can't leave Roger. It doesn't make sense. Of course you're unhappy, all married people are unhappy, but you can't just launch yourself on the world at fifty whatever you are now –'

'Fifty-two. Oh God, oh God –'

'Stop it. Stop that noise, please. Now dry yourself up and I'll take you back to Paddington in a taxi. I'm going to the country. You can't stay here.'

'And I left all my jewels behind and some of them are quite valuable, and now he won't let me have them out of spite. Oh why was I such a fool! I just ran out of the house late last night, we'd been quarrelling for hours and hours and I couldn't stand it any more. I just ran out, I didn't even take my coat, and I went to the station and I thought he'd come after me to the station, but he didn't. Of course he's been trying to drive me to run away and then say it's my fault. And I waited at the station for hours and it was so cold and I felt as if I was going mad through sheer misery. Oh he's been so awful to me, so vile and frightening – Sometimes he'd just go on and on and on saying "I hate you, I hate you, I hate you" –'

'All spouses are murmuring that to each other all the time. It's the fundamental litany of marriage.'

' "I hate you, I hate you –" '

'I think you were saying that, Priscilla, not him. I think –'

'And I left all my jewels behind and my mink stole, and Roger took all the money out of our joint account –'

'Priscilla, brace up. Look, I'll give you ten minutes. Just rest quietly, and then put your togs on again and we'll leave together.'

'Bradley – oh my God I'm so wretched, I'm choking with it – I made a home for him – I haven't got anything else – I cared so much about that house, I made all the curtains myself – I loved all the things – I hadn't anything else to love – and now it's all gone – all my life has been taken away from me – I'll destroy myself – I'll tear myself to pieces –'

'Stop, please. I'm not doing you any good by listening to your complaints. You're in a thoroughly nervous silly state. Women of your age often are. You're simply not rational, Priscilla. I daresay Roger has been tiresome, he's a very selfish man, but you'll just have to forgive him. Women just have to put up with selfish men, it's their lot. You can't leave him, there isn't anywhere else for you to go.'

'I'll destroy myself.'

'Now make an effort. Get control of yourself. I'm not being heartless. It's for your own good. I'll leave you now and finish packing my own bags.'

She was sobbing again, not touching her face, letting the tears flow down. She looked so pitiful and ugly, I reached across and pulled the curtain a little. Her swollen face, the scene in the dim light, reminded me of Rachel.

'Oh I left all my jewels behind, my diamanté set and my jade brooch and my amber ear-rings and the little rings, and my crystal and lapis necklace, and my mink stole –'

I closed the door and went back to the sitting-room and closed the sitting-room door. I felt very shaken. I cannot stand un-bridled displays of emotion and women's stupid tears. And I was suddenly deeply frightened by the possibility of having my sister on my hands. I simply did not love her enough to be of any use to her, and it seemed wiser to make this plain at once.

I waited for about ten minutes, trying to calm and clear my mind, and then went back to the bedroom door. I did not really expect that Priscilla would have got dressed and be ready to leave. I did not know what to do. I felt fear and disgust at the idea of 'mental breakdown', the semi-deliberate refusal to go on organizing one's life which is regarded with such tolerance in these days. I peered into the room. Priscilla was lying in a sort of abandoned attitude on her side, having half kicked off the bedclothes. Her mouth was wet and wide open. A plump stock-inged leg stuck rather awkwardly out of the bed, surmounted by yellowish suspenders and a piece of mottled thigh. The graceless awkwardness of the position suggested a dummy which had fallen over. She said in a heavy slightly whimpering voice, 'I've just eaten all my sleeping pills.'

'What! Priscilla! No!'

'I've eaten them.' She was holding an empty bottle in her hand.

'You're not serious! How many?'

'I told you my life was ruined. You went away and shut the door. Go away now and shut the door. It isn't your fault. Just leave me in peace. Go away and catch your train. Let me sleep at last. I've had misery enough in my life. You said there was nowhere to go to. There is death to go to. I've had misery enough in my life.' The bottle fell to the floor.

I picked it up. The label meant nothing to me. I made a sort of dart at Priscilla, trying stupidly to pull the bedclothes up over her, but one of her legs was on top of them. I ran out of the room.

In the hall I ran to and fro, starting off back to the bedroom, then running towards the flat door, then back to the telephone. As I reached the telephone it began to ring, and I picked it up.

There were the rapid pips of the 'pay tone', and then a click – Arnold's voice said, 'Bradley, Rachel and I are just in town for lunch, we're just round the corner, and we wondered if we could persuade you to join us. Darling, would you like to talk to Bradley?'

Rachel's voice said, 'Bradley, my dear, we both felt –'

I said, 'Priscilla's just eaten all her sleeping pills.'

'What? Who?'

'Priscilla. My sister, just taken bottle sleeping pills – I – get hospital –'

'What's that, Bradley? I can't hear. Bradley, don't ring off, we –'

'Priscilla's taken her sleeping – Sorry, I must ring – get doctor – sorry, sorry –'

I jammed the phone down, then lifted it again and could still hear Rachel's voice saying 'anything we can do?' I banged it back, ran to the bedroom door, ran back again, lifted the phone, put it down, began to pull the telephone books out of the shelves where they live inside a converted mahogany commode. The telephone books slewed all over the floor. The front door bell rang.

I ran to the door and opened it. It was Francis Marloe.

I said, 'Thank God you've come, my sister has just eaten a bottle full of sleeping pills.'

'Where's the bottle?' said Francis. 'How many were in it?'

'God, how do I know – The bottle – God, I had it in my hand a moment ago – Christ, where is it –'

'When did she take them?'

'Just now.'

'Have you telephoned a hospital?'

'No, I –'

'Where is she –'

'In there.'

'Find the bottle and telephone the Middlesex Hospital. Ask for Casualty.'

'Oh Christ, where is the bloody bottle – I had it in my hand –'

The door bell rang again. I opened it. Arnold, Rachel, and Julian were standing outside the door. They were neat and smartly dressed, Julian in a sort of flowered smock looking about twelve. They appeared like a family advertising corn flakes or insurance, except that Rachel had a bruise under one eye.

76

'Bradley, can we –'

'Help me find the bottle, I had the bottle she took, I put it down somewhere –'

A cry came out of the bedroom. Francis called, 'Brad, could –' Rachel said, 'Let me.' She went into the bedroom.

'What's this about a *bottle*?' said Arnold.

'I can't read the blasted telephone number. Can you read the number?'

'I always said you needed glasses.'

Rachel ran out of the bedroom into the kitchen. I could hear Priscilla's voice saying, 'Leave me *alone*, leave me *alone*.'

'Arnold, could you telephone the hospital and I'll look for the – I must have taken it into the –'

I ran into the sitting-room and was surprised to see a girl there. I got an impression of freshly laundered dress, freshly laundered girl, girl on a visit. She was examining the little bronzes in the lacquered display cabinet. She stopped doing this and watched me with polite curiosity while I started hurling cushions about. 'What are you looking for, Bradley?'

'Bottle. Sleeping pills. See what kind.'

Arnold was telephoning.

Francis called out. I ran to the bedroom. Rachel was mopping the floor. There was a vile smell. Priscilla was sitting on the side of the bed sobbing. Her petticoat with pink daisies on it was hitched up round her waist, rather tight silken knickers cut into her thigh, making the mottled flesh bulge.

Francis, talking quickly, excited, said, 'She was sick – I didn't really – it'll help – but a stomach pump –'

Julian said, 'Is this it?' Without entering she thrust a hand round the door.

Francis took the bottle. 'Oh that stuff – That's not –'

'Ambulance coming,' called Arnold.

'She can't do herself much harm with that. Need to take an awful lot. It makes one sick actually, that was why –'

'Priscilla, do stop crying. You'll be all right.'

'Leave me *alone*!'

'Keep her warm,' said Francis.

'Leave me alone, I hate you all.'

'She isn't herself,' I said.

'Get her into bed properly, snuggled down a bit,' said Francis.

'I'll make some tea,' said Rachel.

They retired and the door shut. I tried again to pull the bed-clothes back, but Priscilla was sitting on them.

She jumped up, savagely pulled the blankets back, then crashed on to the bed. She pulled the clothes violently over her, hiding her head. I could hear her mumbling underneath, 'Ashamed, oh ashamed – Showing me to all those people – I want to *die*, I want to *die* –' She began sobbing.

I sat down beside her and looked at my watch. It was after twelve. No one had thought to pull the curtains back and the room was still twilit. There was a horrible smell. I patted the heaving mass of blankets. Only a little of her hair was visible, with a dirty line of grey at the roots of the gold. Her hair was dry and brittle, more like some synthetic fibre than like human hair. I felt disgust and helpless pity and a prowling desire to vomit. I sat for a time patting her with the awkward ineffectual gesture of a small child trying to pat an animal. I could not make out what forms I was touching. I wondered if I should firmly pull off the covers and take her hand, but when I plucked at the blankets she burrowed deeper and even her hair disappeared.

Rachel called, 'The ambulance has come.'

I said to Francis, 'Could you deal with this?' I went out into the hall, past where Francis was talking to the ambulance men, and went into the sitting-room.

Julian, looking like one of my pieces of china, was back in her place by the display cabinet. Rachel was lying sprawled in an armchair with a rather odd smile on her face. Rachel said, 'She'll be all right?'

'Yes.'

Julian said, 'Bradley, I wonder if I could buy this off you?'

'What?'

'This little thing. I wonder if I could buy it? Would you sell it to me?'

Rachel said, 'Julian, don't be so tiresome.'

Julian was holding in her hand one of the little Chinese bronzes, a piece which I had had for many years. A water buffalo

78

with lowered head and exquisitely wrinkled neck bears upon his back an aristocratic lady of delicate loveliness with a many-folded dress and high elaborate hair.

'I wonder if – ?'

Rachel said, 'Julian, you can't ask people to sell you their belongings!'

'Keep it, keep it,' I said.

'Bradley, you mustn't let her –'

'No, I'll buy it –'

'Of course you can't buy it! Keep it!' I sat down. 'Where's Arnold?'

'Oh thank you! Why, here's a letter addressed to Dad, and one for me. May I take them?'

'Yes, yes. Where's Arnold?'

'He's gone to the pub,' said Rachel, smiling a little more broadly.

'She felt it wasn't quite the moment,' said Julian.

'Who felt?'

'He's gone to the pub with Christian.'

'WITH CHRISTIAN?'

'Your ex-wife arrived,' said Rachel, smiling. 'Arnold explained that your sister had just attempted suicide. Your ex-wife felt it was not the moment for a reunion. She retired from the scene and Arnold escorted her. I don't know where to exactly. "To the pub" were his words.'

I ran out of the room. Men were coming in with a stretcher. I ran out of the house.

Perhaps at this point in my story, my dear friend, I may be allowed to pause and speak to you directly. Of course the whole of what I write here, and perhaps somehow unconsciously my whole *œuvre*, has been a communication addressed to you. But this direct speaking is a kind of relief, it eases some pressure upon the heart and upon the intelligence. There is an element of confession. It is a relief to be able to stand back, even to admit failure, and to admit it in a context where such an admission has no element of falsity. When the believer, fortunate man, asks God to forgive not only the sins he can remember, but also the sins he cannot remember, and, more touching still, the sins he cannot even recognize, so benighted is he, as sins at all, the sense of liberation and subsequent calm must be tremendous. So now in writing for you, and now in offering that writing to you, my penetrating critic, I feel a calmness, a sense of having done my best, and an acceptance of your perception of the frailty of my achievement. There are moments, I know, when I must seem to you like a sort of monomaniac, a man brimming over with delusions of grandeur. Perhaps any artist must be such a maniac, one who feels that he is God. Any artist must sometimes be filled with an intense pleasure in his work, a sense of its radiant merit, a vision of it as excelling. This is not a matter of comparisons in any ordinary sense. Most artists pay little attention to their contemporaries. Those who nourish them belong to the past. Only the vulgar are anxious when hearing others praised. One's sense of one's own excellence is uninvidious, imprecise, probably healthy, perhaps essential. Equally important is that humility, that sense of unavoidable limitation, which the artist must also feel when he sees, huge behind his own puny effort, the glimmering shade of perfection.

It is not my intention to accompany this book with a commentary upon it of equal length. The 'story' shall never be long kept in abeyance. The luxury of addressing you directly is the fulfilment of a desire which is itself one of the subjects of the book. In our long discussions of the form this work should take you confirmed the legitimacy of this 'device', though what comes so from the heart deserves perhaps a warmer name: this indulgence, let us say, of an irrepressible lyricism, an involuntary expression of love. My book is about art. It is also, in its humble way, a work of art: an 'art object', as the jargon has it; and may perhaps be permitted, now and then, to cast a look upon itself. Art (as I observed to young Julian) is the telling of truth, and is the only available method for the telling of certain truths. Yet how almost impossibly difficult it is not to let the marvels of the instrument itself interfere with the task to which it is dedicated. There are those who will only praise an absolute simplicity, and for whom the song-bird utterance of the so-called primitive is the measure of all, as if truth ceases to be when it is not stammered. And there are of course divinely cunning simplicities in the works of those whom I hardly dare to name, since they are so near to gods. (Gods one does not name.) But though it may always be well to attempt simplification, it is not always possible to avoid at least an elegant complexity. And then one asks, how can this also be 'true'? Is the real like this, *is* it this? Of course, as you have so often pointed out, we may attempt to attain truth through irony. (An angel might make of this a concise definition of the limits of human understanding.) Almost any tale of our doings is comic. We are bottomlessly comic to each other. Even the most adored and beloved person is comic to his lover. The novel is a comic form. Language is a comic form, and makes jokes in its sleep. God, if He existed, would laugh at His creation. Yet it is also the case that life is horrible, without metaphysical sense, wrecked by chance, pain and the close prospect of death. Out of this is born irony, our dangerous and necessary tool.

Irony is a form of 'tact' (witty word). It is our tactful sense of proportion in the selection of forms for the embodying of beauty. Beauty is present when truth has found an apt form. It is impossible finally to separate these ideas. Yet there are points at which by a sort of momentary artificiality we can offer a diagnosis. This again is, that which amuses logicians, something which is a case of itself. How can one describe a human being 'justly'? How can one describe oneself? With what an air of false coy humility, with what an assumed confiding simplicity one sets about it! 'I am a puritan' and so on. Faugh! How can these statements not be false? Even 'I am tall' has a context. How the angels must laugh and sigh. Yet what can one do but try to lodge one's vision somehow inside this layered stuff of ironic sensibility, which, if I were a fictitious character, would be that much deeper and denser? How prejudiced is this image of Arnold, how superficial this picture of Priscilla! Emotions cloud the view, and so far from isolating the particular, draw generality and even theory in their train. When I write of Arnold my pen shakes with resentment, love, remorse, and fear. It is as if I were building a barrier against him composed of words, hiding myself behind a mound of words. We defend ourselves by descriptions and tame the world by generalizing. What does he fear? is usually the key to the artist's mind. Art is so often a barrier. (Is this true even of the greatest art, I wonder?) So art becomes not communication but mystification. When I think of my sister I feel pity, annoyance, guilt . disgust and it is in the 'light' of these that I present her, crippled and diminished by my perception itself. How can I correct these faults, my dear friend and comrade? Priscilla was a brave woman. She endured unhappiness grimly, with dignity. She sat alone in the mornings manicuring her nails while tears came into her eyes for her wasted life.

My mother was very important to me. I loved her, but always with a kind of anguish. I feared loss and death to an extent I think unusual in a child. Later I sensed with profound distress the hopeless lack of understanding which existed between my parents. They could not 'see' each other at all. My father, with whom I increasingly identified myself, was nervous, timid, upright, conventional, and quite without the grosser forms of vanity. He avoided crossing my mother, but he patently disapproved of her 'worldliness' and detested the 'social scene' into which she and Priscilla were constantly attempting to penetrate. His dislike of this 'scene' was also compounded with a simple sense of inadequacy. He was afraid of making some undignified mistake, revelatory of lack of eduction, such as the mispronunciation of some well-known name. I shared, as I grew up, my father's disapproval and his anxiety. One reason perhaps why I so passionately desired education for myself was that I saw how unhappy the lack of it had made him. I felt for my misguided mother pain and shame which did not diminish but qualified my love. I was mortally afraid of anyone seeing her as absurd or pathetic, a defeated snob. And later still, after her death, I transferred many of these feelings to Priscilla.

Of course I never loved Priscilla in the way that I loved my mother. But I felt identified with her and vulnerable through her. I often felt ashamed of her. In fact Priscilla could have made a worse marriage. As I have said, I did not care for Roger. I could never, apart from anything else, forgive him for humiliating my father at the time of Priscilla's 'operation'. However, as the years went by, there was a kind of fairly solid ordinariness about that 'maisonette' in Bristol, with its expensive kitchen equipment and its horrible modern cutlery, and the imitation 'bar' in the corner of the drawing-room. Even the stupider vanities of the modern world can have a kind of innocence, a sort of anchoring steadying quality. They are poor substitutes for art, thought and holiness, but they are substitutes and perhaps some light may fall upon them. House-pride may have contributed, at times, towards the saving of my sister, towards the saving of many women.

However pride and 'grim courage' were not now the order of the day. Priscilla, with whom I was conversing, had by this time more or less convinced me that she really did mean to leave her husband and had in fact left him. Her distress at this catastrophe took a certain obsessive form. 'Oh why was I such a fool as to leave my jewels behind!' she repeated again and again and again.

It was the day after her exploit with the sleeping pills. The ambulance had taken her to the hospital from which she had been discharged on the same afternoon. She was brought back to my flat and went to bed. She was still in bed, in my bed, the time being about ten-thirty in the morning. The sun was shining. The Post Office Tower glittered with newly minted detail.

I had of course failed to find Arnold and Christian. Looking for someone is, as psychologists have observed, perceptually peculiar, in that the world is suddenly organized as a basis upon which the absence of what is sought is bodied forth in a ghostly manner. The familiar streets about my house, never fully to recover from this haunting, were filled with non-apparitions of the pair, fleeing, laughing, mocking, overwhelmingly real and yet invisible. Other pairs simulated them and made them vanish, the air was smoky with them. But it was too good a joke, too good a *coup*, for Arnold to risk my spoiling its perfection. By now they were somewhere else, not in the Fitzroy or the Marquis or the Wheatsheaf or the Black Horse, but somewhere else: and the white ghosts of them blew into my eyes, like white petals, like white flakes of paint, like the scraps of paper which the hieratic boy had cast out upon the river of the roadway, images of beauty and cruelty and fear.

When I returned to the house it was empty, the door of my flat wide open. I sat down in the sitting-room, upon the 'conversation' chair, and felt for a while pure fear, dread in its most classical and awful form. Arnold's 'joke' was too obscenely good not to be taken as a portent: it was the visible part of some huge invisible horror. I sat there for a while panting at it, too sick even to try to analyse my distress. Then I began to notice that something was wrong with the room, something was missing. At last I pinpointed the absence of the bronze water-buffalo lady, one of my favourite pieces, and recalled with annoyance that I had given it to Julian. How had that happened? This too was a portent, the vanishing object which preludes the vaporization of Aladdin's palace. Then as I began finally to wonder where my sister was and how she was getting on Rachel rang up to say that Priscilla had been discharged and was on the way back.

Lying horribly awake that night I decided that the matter of Christian and Arnold was simple. It had to be simple: it was either simplicity or insanity. If Arnold 'made friends' with Christian I would simply drop him. In spite of having solved this problem I could not sleep however. I kept following series of coloured images which, like the compartments of a swing door, simply led me round and landed me back again in the aching wide-awake world. When I slept at last I was humiliated in my dreams.

'Well, why did you rush away in such a hurry? If, as you say, you decided ages ago to leave Roger, why didn't you pack a suitcase and go off in a taxi some morning when he was at the office, in an orderly manner?'

'I don't think one leaves one's husband like that,' said Priscilla.

'That's how sensible girls leave their husbands.'

The telephone rings.

'Hello, Pearson. Hartbourne here.'

'Oh, hello –'

'I wondered if we could have lunch on Tuesday.'

'Sorry, I'm not sure, my sister's here – I'll ring you back –'

Tuesday? My whole concept of the future had crumpled.

Through the open door of the bedroom as I laid the phone to rest I could see Priscilla wearing my red and white striped pyjamas, flopped in a deliberately uncomfortable position, her arms spread wide like a puppet, still steadily crying. The horror of the world seen without charm. Priscilla's woebegone tearful face was crumpled and old. Had she ever really resembled my mother? Two hard deep lines ran down on either side of her blubbering mouth. Beyond the runnels of the tears the dry yellow make-up revealed the enlarged pores of her skin. She had not washed since her arrival.

'Oh Priscilla, stop it, do. Try to be a bit brave at least.'

'I know I've lost my looks –'

'As if that mattered!'

'So you think I look horrible, you think –'

'I don't! Please, Priscilla –'

'Roger hated the sight of me, he said so. And I used to cry in front of him, I'd sit and cry for hours with sheer misery, sitting there in front of him, and he'd just go on reading the paper.'

'You make me feel quite sorry for him!'

'And he tried to poison me once, it tasted so horrible and he just watched and wouldn't eat any himself.'

'That's just nonsense, Priscilla.'

'Oh Bradley, if only we hadn't killed that child –'

She had already been on to this subject at some length.

'Oh Bradley, if only we'd kept the child – But how was I to know I wouldn't be able to have another one – That child, that one child, to think that it existed, it cried out for life, and we killed it deliberately. It was all Roger's fault, he insisted that we get rid of it, he didn't want to marry me, we killed it, the special one, the only one, my dear little child –'

'Oh do stop, Priscilla. It would be twenty now and on drugs, the bane of your life.' I have never desired children myself and can scarcely understand this desire in others.

'Twenty – a grown-up son – someone to love – to look after me – Oh Bradley, you don't know how I have yearned day and night for that child. He would have made all the difference to Roger and me. I think Roger began to hate me when he found I couldn't have children. And it was all his fault anyway. He found that rotten doctor. Oh it's so unjust, so unjust –'

'Of course it's unjust. Life is unjust. Do stop whining and try to be practical. You can't stay here. I can't support you. Anyway, I'm going away.'

'I'll get a job.'

'Priscilla, be realistic, who would employ you?'

'I'll have to.'

'You're a woman over fifty, with no education and no skill. You're unemployable.'

'You're so *unkind* –'

The telephone rings again.

The oily ingratiating tones of Mr Francis Marloe.

'Oh Brad, please forgive me, but I thought I'd just give a tinkle to ask how Priscilla is.'

'She's fine.'

'Oh good. Oh Brad, I just thought I'd tell you the hospital psych said better not leave her alone you know.'

'Rachel told me yesterday.'

'And Brad, listen, don't be cross, about Christian –'

I bang the telephone down.

'You know,' Priscilla was saying as I re-entered the room, 'Mummy would have left Dad if she could have afforded it, she told me so when she was dying.'

'I don't want to know things like that.'

'You and Dad made me feel so ashamed and inferior in the old days, you were both so cruel to me and Mum, Mum was so unhappy –'

'Either you must return to Roger or you must make some definite financial arrangement with him. It's nothing to do with me. You've got to face up to things.'

'Bradley, please, will you go and see Roger – ?'

'No, I will not!'

'Oh God, if only I'd taken my jewels with me, they mean so

much to me, I saved up to buy them, and the mink stole. And there's two silver goblets on my dressing table and a little box made of malachite –'

'Priscilla, don't be childish. You can get these things later.'

'No, I can't. Roger will have sold them out of spite. The only consolation I had was buying things. If I bought some pretty thing it cheered me up for a while and I could save out of the housekeeping money and it cheered me up a little bit. I got my diamanté set and I got a crystal and lapis necklace which was quite expensive and –'

'Why hasn't Roger telephoned? He must know you're here.'

'He's too proud and hurt. Oh you know in a way I feel so sorry for Roger, he's been so miserable, shouting at me or else not talking at all, he must be so terribly unhappy inside himself, really wrecked and mentally broken somehow. Sometimes I've felt he must be going mad. How can anyone go on living like that, being so unkind and not caring any more? He wouldn't let me cook for him any more and he wouldn't let me into his room and I know he never made his bed and his clothes were filthy, and smelt and sometimes he didn't even shave, I thought he'd lose his job. Perhaps he has lost his job and didn't dare to tell me. And now it must be even worse. I kept the house a bit tidy though it was hard to when he so obviously didn't care. Now he's all alone in that filthy pigsty, not eating, not caring –'

'I thought he was surrounded by women.'

'Oh there must have been women, but such awful women, so sordid, just wanting his money and getting drunk, all like Roger was before I married him, such an empty materialistic world – Oh I am so sorry for him, he's made such a hell all round himself and now there he is in the middle of it having a sort of breakdown and the place full of unwashed dishes –'

'Well, why don't you go home and wash up!'

'Bradley, please would you go to Bristol –'

'It sounds to me as if you're dying to go back to the man –'

'Please would you go and get my jewels, I'll give you the key.'

'Oh do stop going on about your jewels. They're all right. They're legally yours anyway. A wife owns her own jewellery.'

'The law isn't anything. Oh I do want them so, they're the only things I've got, I haven't got anything else, I haven't anything else in the world, I feel they're calling out to me – And the little ornaments, that stripey vase –'

'Priscilla dear, do stop raving.'

'Bradley, please, please go to Bristol for me. He won't have had time to sell them yet, he won't have thought of it. Besides, he probably imagines I'm coming back. They're all still in their places. I'll give you the key of the house and you can go in when he's at the office and just get those few things, it will be quite easy and it will make such a difference to my mind, and then I'll do anything you like, oh it will make such a difference –'

The front door bell rang at this point. I got up. I felt stupidly upset. I made a sort of caressing gesture to Priscilla and left the room, closing the door. I went to the front door of the flat and opened it.

Arnold Baffin was outside. We moved into the sitting-room, smoothly, like dancers.

Arnold's face, with any emotion, tended to become uniformly pink, as if a pink light had been switched on to it. He was flushed so now, his pale eyes behind his glasses expressing a sort of nervous solicitude. He patted my shoulder, or dabbed at it with the quick gesture of one playing 'tig'.

'How is she?'

'Much better. You and Rachel were so kind.'

'Rachel was. Bradley, you're not angry with me, are you –'

'What is there to be angry about?'

'You know – they did tell you – that I went off with Christian?'

'I don't want to hear about Mrs Evandale,' I said.

'You are angry. Oh Christ.'

'I am NOT angry! I just don't – want to – know –'

'I didn't intend this, it just happened.'

'All right! So that's that!'

'But I can't pretend it didn't happen, can I? Bradley, I've got to talk to you about it – just to make you stop blaming me – I'm not a fool – after all I'm a novelist, damn it! – I know how complicated –'

'I don't see what being a novelist has to do with it or why you have to drag that in –'

'I only mean I understand how you feel –'

'I don't think you do. I can see you're excited. It must have amused you very much to be the reception committee for my ex-wife. Naturally you want to talk about it. I am telling you not to.'

'But Bradley, she's a phenomenon.'

'I am not interested in phenomena.'

'My dear Bradley, you *must* be curious, you must be. If I were you I'd be dying with curiosity. There's hurt pride, I suppose, and –'

'There's no question of hurt pride. *I* left *her*.'

'Well, resentment or something, I know time doesn't heal. That's the silliest idea of all. But God, I'd be so curious. I'd want to see what she'd become, what she was like. Of course she sounds like an American now –'

'I don't want to know!'

'You never gave me any idea of her. To listen to you talk –'

'Arnold, since you're such a clever novelist and so full of human psychology, please understand that this is dangerous ground. If you want to imperil our friendship go ahead. I can't forbid you to be acquainted with Mrs Evandale. But you must never mention her name to me. This could be the end of our friendship, and I mean it.'

'Our friendship is a tough plant, Bradley. Look, I just refuse to pretend that this thing hasn't happened, and I don't think you ought to either. I know people can be awful dooms for each other –'

'Precisely.'

'But sometimes if you face a thing it becomes tolerable. You ought to face this, and anyway, you've got to, she's here and she's determined to see you, she's absolutely mad with interest, you can't avoid her. And you know, she is a most enormously nice person –'

'I think that is the stupidest thing I have ever heard you say.'

'All right, I know what you mean. But since you still feel so emotional about her –'

'I don't!'

'Bradley, be sincere.'

'Will you stop tormenting me – I might have known you'd come round here with that air of triumph –'

'I don't feel any triumph. What is there to triumph about?'

'You've met her, you've discussed me, you think she's "a most enormously nice person" –'

'Bradley, don't shout. I –'

The telephone rings again.

I go and lift the receiver.

'Brad! I say, is that really you? Guess who this is!'

I put the telephone down, settling it carefully back on to its stand.

I went back into the sitting-room and sat down. 'That was her.'

'You've gone quite white. You're not going to faint, are you? Can I get you something? Please forgive me for talking so stupidly. Is she hanging on?'

'No. I put the thing – down –'

The telephone rings again. I do nothing.

'Bradley, let me talk to her.'

'No.'

I get to the telephone just after Arnold has lifted the receiver. I bang it back on to the rest.

'Bradley, don't you see, you've got to deal with this, you can't shirk it, you can't. She'll come round in a taxi.'

The telephone rings again. I lift it up and hold it a little way off. Christian's voice, even with the American tang, is recognizable. The years drop away. 'Brad, do listen, please. I'm round at the flat, you know, our old place. Why won't you come round? I've got some Scotch. Brad, please don't just bang the phone down, don't be mean. Come round and see me. I do so want to take a look at you. I'll be here all day, till five o'clock anyway.'

I put the telephone down.

'She wants me to go and see her.'

'You've got to, you've got to, it's your fate!'

'I'm not going.'

The telephone rings again. I take it off and lay it down on the table. It bubbles remotely. Priscilla calls in a shrill voice, 'Bradley!'

'Don't touch that,' I said to Arnold, pointing at the telephone. I went in to Priscilla.

'Is that Arnold Baffin out there?' She was sitting on the side of the bed. I saw with surprise that she had put on her blouse and

90

skirt and was putting some thick yellowish-pinkish muck on to her
nose.

'Yes.'

'I think I'll come out to see him. I want to thank him.'

'As you like. Look, Priscilla, I'm going to be away for an hour
or two. Will you be all right? I'll come back at lunch-time, maybe a bit late. I'll ask Arnold to stay with you.'

'You will come back soon?'

'Yes, yes.'

I ran in to Arnold. 'Could you stay with Priscilla? The doctor
said she shouldn't be left alone.'

Arnold looked displeased. 'I suppose I can stay. Is there any
drink? I wanted to talk to you about Rachel, actually, and about
that funny letter you wrote me. Where are you off to?'

'I'm going to see Christian.'

Marriage is a curious institution, as I have already remarked.
I cannot quite see how it can be possible. People who boast of
happy marriages are, I submit, usually self-deceivers, if not
actually liars. The human soul is not framed for continued proximity, and the result of this enforced neighbourhood is often an
appalling loneliness for which the rules of the game forbid
assuagement. There is nothing like the bootless solitude of those
who are caged together. Those outside the cage can, to their own
taste, satisfy their need for society by more or less organized
dashes in the direction of other human beings. But the unit of
two can scarcely communicate with others, and is fortunate, as
the years go by, if it can communicate within itself. Or is this the
sour envious view of the failed husband? I speak now of course of
ordinary 'successful' marriages. Where the unit of two is a
machine of mutual hatred there is hell in a pure form. I left
Christian before our hell was quite perfected. I saw very clearly
what it would be like.

Of course I was 'in love' with Christian when I married her,

91

and I felt that I was lucky to get her. She was a showy pretty woman. Her parents were in business. She even had a little money of her own. My mother was impressed, slightly intimidated; Priscilla too. Later, when I imagined I knew more about 'love', I decided that my feeling about Christian was 'just' overwhelming sexual attraction, plus a curious element of obsession. It was as if I had known Christian as a real woman in some previous incarnation, and were now reliving, perhaps as a punishment, some doomed perverted spiritual pattern. (I suspect there are many such couples.) Or as if she had died long before and come back to me as a demon lover. Demon lovers are always relentless, however kind in life. And it was sometimes as if I could 'remember' Christian's kindness, though all now was spite and demonry. It was not that she was usually, though she was sometimes, grossly cruel. She was a spoiler, a needler, an underminer, a diminisher, simply by instinct. And I was Siamese-twinned to her mind. We reeled about joined together at the head.

The reason why, after swearing that I would not see her, I changed my mind and rushed to her was simply this. I realized quite suddenly that I would now be in torment until I had seen her and *settled* that she had no more power over me. Witch she might be, but surely not for me any more. And this was of course made much more obviously necessary by Arnold's having, by this vile chance, 'got in on her'. I think his describing her as 'an enormously nice person' had some cosmic effect on me. So she had got out of my mind and was walking about? Arnold had seen her with innocent eyes. Why did this threaten me so terribly? By going to see her myself I would be able to 'dilute' the power of her meeting with Arnold. But I did not think all this out immediately. I acted on instinct, wanting to know the worst.

The little street in Notting Hill where we had lived in our more recent previous existence had become a good deal lusher since those days. I had, of course, avoided it always. I saw now as I ran along the pavement that the houses had been glossily painted, blue, yellow, dusty pink, the doors had fancy knockers, the windows cast iron decorations, false shutters, window boxes. I had dismissed the taxi at the corner as I did not want Christian to see me before I saw her.

The sudden recrudescence of the far past makes one dizzy even when there are no ugly features involved. There seemed to be no oxygen in the street. I ran, I ran. She opened the door.

I think I would not have recognized her at once. She looked slimmer and taller. She had been a bunchy sensuous frilly woman. Now she looked more austere, certainly older, also smarter, wearing a simple dress of mousy light-brown tweed and a chain belt. Her hair, which used to be waved, was straight, thick, long-ish, faintly undulating, and dyed, I suppose, to a reddish brown. Her face was more bony, a little wrinkled, the faintest wizening effect as on an apple, not unpleasant. The long liquidy brown eyes had not aged or dimmed. She looked competent and distinguished, like the manager of an international cosmetic firm.

The expression of her face as she opened the door is hard to describe. Mainly she was excited, almost to the point of idiotic laughter, but attempting to appear calm. I think she must have seen me first through the window. She did in fact laugh, in a suppressed burp of merriment as I came in, and exclaimed something, perhaps 'Jesus!' I could feel my own face twisted and flattened as if under a nylon stocking mask. We got into the sitting-room which was mercifully dark. It seemed to look very much as it had used to look. Huge emotions like gauze curtains made the place breathless, perhaps actually made it dark. One cannot at the time name these (hate? fear?), only later can one press them away and give them names. There was a moment of stillness. Then she moved towards me. I thought, rightly or wrongly, that she was going to touch me, and I moved back towards the window, behind an armchair. She laughed, in a sort of crazy wail like a bird. I saw her uncontrolled laughing face like a grotesque ancient mask. Now she looked old.

She had turned her back on me and was fiddling in a cupboard.

'Oh Jesus, I shall get the giggles. Have a drink, Bradley. Scotch? I guess we need something. I hope you're going to be nice to me. What a horrid letter you wrote me.'

'Letter?'

'There was a letter addressed to me in your sitting-room. Arnold gave it to me. Here, take this and stop trembling.'

'No, thank you.'

'God, I'm trembling too. Thank heavens Arnold rang up and said you were coming. I might have fainted otherwise. Are we glad to see each other?'

The voice was faintly steadily American. Now that I could see her more distinctly among the dark blurry browns and blues of the room I realized how handsome she had become. The old terrible nervy vitality had been shaped by a mature elegance into an air of authority. How had a woman without education managed to do that to herself in a little town in the Middle West of America?

The room was almost the same. It represented and recalled a much earlier me, a younger and yet unformed taste: wicker-work, wool-embroidered cushions, blurry lithographs, hand-thrown pottery with purple glazes, hand-woven curtains of flecked mauve linen, straw matting on the floor. A calm pretty insipid place. I had created that room years and years and years ago. I had wept in it. I had screamed in it.

'Relax, Brad. You're just meeting an old friend, aren't you? You were quite excited in your letter. Nothing to be excited about. How's Priscilla?'

'All right.'

'Your ma still alive?'

'No.'

'Unwind, man. I'd forgotten what a bean pole you are. Maybe you got thinner. Your hair's thinner but it's not grey is it, I can't see. You always did look a bit like Don Quixote. You don't look too bad. I thought you might be an old man all bald and shambling. How do I look? Jesus, what a time interval, isn't it.'

'Yes.'

'Drink, won't you, it'll loosen your tongue. Do you know something, I'm glad to see you! I looked forward to you on the ship. But I guess I'm glad to see everything just now, I get a buzz from the whole world just now, everything's bright and beautiful. Do you know I did a course in Zen Buddhism? I guess I must be enlightened, everything's so glorious! I thought poor old Evans would never get on with the departure scene, I prayed every day for that man to die, he was a sick man. Now I wake up every morning and remember it's really true and I close my eyes again and I'm in heaven. Not a very holy attitude is it, but it's nature,

94

and at my age at least you can be sincere. Are you shocked, am I awful? Yes, I think I am glad to see you, I think it's fun. God, I just want to laugh and laugh, isn't that odd?'

The coarse style was new, transatlantic in origin I assumed, though I had imagined her life there as very genteel. The way she used her body and eyes was not new, was however more conscious, as if taken up into the amused ironical *persona* of an older and more elegant woman. The older woman flirts with a self-controlled awareness which can make her assaults much more deadly than the blind rushes of the young. And here was a woman for whom to be conscious was to flirt. Her 'attack' now was hard to describe, it was so generalized throughout her being, but there was a steady emanation of pressure, generated by slight swaying movements, the angle of the head, the darting of the eyes, the trembling of the mouth. Expressions such as 'ogling' would be far too crude to suggest these lures. The effect was of watching an athlete or a dancer whose quality is evident even in what appears to be complete repose. There was invitation which was also mockery, even brilliant self-mockery, conveyed in her poses. When she was young there had been simpering, involuntary silliness, in her coquetry. This was quite gone. She had mastered her instrument. Perhaps it was all that Zen Buddhism.

As I looked at her I felt that old fear of a misunderstanding which amounted to an invasion, a taking over of my thoughts. I tried to stare at her and to be cold, to find a controlled tone of voice which was hard and calm. I spoke.

'I came to see you simply because I thought that you would annoy me until I did. I meant what I said in my letter. It was not "excited", it was just a statement. I do not want and will not tolerate any renewal of our acquaintance. And now that you have satisfied your curiosity by looking at me and had your laugh will you please understand that I want to hear no more of you. I say this just in case you might conceive it to be "fun" to pester me. I would be grateful if you would keep away from me, and keep away from my friends too.'

'Oh come on, Brad, you don't own your friends. Are you jealous already?'

The jibe brought back the past, her adroit determination to retain every advantage, to have every last word. I felt myself blushing with anger and distress. I must not enter into argument with this woman. I decided to repeat my statement quietly and then go. 'Please leave me alone. I do not like you or want to see you. Why should I? It sickens me that you are back in London. Be kind enough to leave me absolutely alone from now on.'

'I feel pretty sick too, do you know? I feel all kind of moved and touched. I thought about you out there, Brad. We did make a mess of things, didn't we. We got so across each other, it spoilt the world in a way. I talked about you with my guru. I thought of writing to you –'

'Good-bye.'

'Don't go, Brad, please. There's so much I want to talk to you about, not just about the old days but about life, you know. You're my only friend in London, I'm so out of touch. You know I bought the upper flat here, now I own the whole house. Evans thought it was a good investment. Poor old Evans, God rest his soul, he was a real bit of all-American stodge, though he understood business all right. I amused myself getting educated, or I'd have died of boredom. Remember how we used to dream of buying the upper flat? I'm having the builders in next week. I thought you might help me to decide some things. Don't go, Bradley, tell me about yourself. How many books have you published?'

'Three.'

'Only three? Gosh, I thought you'd be a real author by now.'

'I am a real author.'

'We had a literary chap from England at our Women Writers' Guild, I asked about you but he hadn't heard of you. I did some writing myself, I wrote some short stories. You're not still at the old Tax grind, are you?'

'I've just retired.'

'You aren't sixty-five, are you, Brad? My memory's packed up. How old are you?'

'Fifty-eight. I retired in order to write.'

'I just hate to think how old I am. You should have got out years ago. You've given your life to that old Tax office, haven't you? You ought to have been a wanderer, a real Don Quixote, that would have given you subjects. Birds can't sing in cages. Thank the Lord I'm out of mine. I feel so happy I'm quite crazed.

I've never stopped laughing since old Evans died, poor old sod. Did you know he was a Christian Scientist? He shouted for a doctor when he got ill all the same, he got in a real panic. And they were organizing prayers for him and he hid the dope when they came round! There's a lot in Christian Science actually, I think I'm a bit of a Christian Scientist myself. Do you know anything about it?'

'No.'

'Poor old Evans. There was a sort of kindness in him, a sort of gentleness, but he was so mortally dull he nearly killed me. At least you were never dull. Do you know that I'm a rich woman now, really quite rich, proper rich? Oh Bradley, to be able to tell you that, it's good, it's good! I'm going to have a new life, Bradley. I'm going to hear the trumpets blowing in my life.'

'*Good-bye.*'

'I'm going to be happy and to make other people happy. GO AWAY!'

The last command was, I almost instantly grasped, addressed not to me but to someone behind me who was standing just outside the window, which gave directly on to the pavement. I half turned and saw Francis Marloe standing outside. He was leaning forward to peer in through the glass, his eyebrows raised and a bland submissive smile upon his face. When he could discern us he put his hands together in an attitude of prayer.

Christian jerked her hand in a gesture of dismissal, and then distorted her face into a simulated snarl. Francis moved his hands apart gracefully, spreading the palms, and then leaned further forward and flattened his nose and cheeks against the glass.

'Come upstairs. Quick.'

I followed her up the narrow stairs and into the front bedroom. This room had changed. Upon a bright pink carpet everything was black and shiny and modern. Christian flung open the window. Something flew out and landed with a clatter in the road. Coming nearer I saw that it was a stripey sponge bag. Out of it tumbled an electric shaver and a toothbrush. Francis scrambled for them quickly, then stood, consciously pathetic, his little close eyes blinking upward, his small mouth still pursed in a humble smile.

'And your milk chocolate. Look out. No, I won't, I'll give it to Brad. Brad, you still like milk chocolate, don't you. See, I'm giving your milk chocolate to Bradley.' She thrust the packet at me. I laid it on the bed. 'I'm not being heartless, it's just that he's been at me the whole time since I got back, he imagines I'll play mother and support him! God, he's a real Welfare State layabout, like what the Americans think all the English are. Look at him now, what a clown! I gave him money, but he wants to move in and hang up his hat. He climbed in the kitchen window when I was out and I came back and found him in bed! Wow! Look who's here now!'

Another figure had appeared down below, Arnold Baffin. He was speaking to Francis.

'Hey, Arnold!' Arnold looked up and waved and moved towards the front door. She ran away down the stairs again with clacking heels and I heard the door open. Laughter.

Francis was still standing in the gutter holding his electric razor and his toothbrush. He looked towards the door, then looked up at me. He spread his arms, then dropped them at his sides in a gesture of mock despair. I threw the packet of milk chocolate out of the window. I did not wait to see him pick it up. I went slowly down the stairs. Arnold and Christian were just inside the sitting-room door, both talking.

I said to Arnold, 'You left Priscilla.'

'Bradley, I'm *sorry*,' said Arnold. 'Priscilla attacked me.'

'Attacked you?'

'I was telling her about you, Christian. Bradley, you never told her Christian was back, she was quite bothered. Anyway, I was telling her about you, you needn't look like that, it was all most flattering, when she suddenly threw a sort of fit and jumped on me and locked her arms round my neck –'

Christian went into wild laughter.

'Maybe I ought to have stuck it out somehow, but it was all – well, I won't go into ungentlemanly details – I was just thinking it would be best for both of us if I cleared out when Rachel turned up. She didn't know I was there, she was after you, Bradley. So I hopped it and left her holding the baby. You see, Priscilla wound her arms quite tightly round my neck and I couldn't even sort of talk to her – Perhaps it was very ungallant –

98

I'm terribly sorry, Bradley – What would you have done, I mean *mutatis mutandis* –'

'You funny man, you,' said Christian. 'You're quite excited! I don't believe it was like that at all! And what were you saying about me, you don't know anything about me! Does he, Brad? You know, Brad, this man makes me laugh.'

'You make me laugh too!' said Arnold.

They both began to laugh. The hilarious excitement which Christian had been holding in check throughout our interview burst wildly forth. She laughed, wailing, gasping for breath, leaning back against the door with tears spilling from her eyes. Arnold laughed too, without control, hands hanging, head back, mouth gaping, eyes closed. They swayed. They roared.

I went straight on past them out of the door and began to walk quickly down the street. Francis Marloe ran after me. 'Brad, I say, could I talk to you a minute?'

I ignored him and he fell away. As I reached the corner of the road he shouted after me, 'Brad! Thanks for the chocolate!'

The next thing was that I was in Bristol.

Priscilla's endless lament about her jewels had at last conquered my resistance. With many misgivings and some disgust about my mission I had agreed to go to Bristol, let myself into their house at a time when Roger would be at the bank, and collect the longed-for baubles. Priscilla had then made out a long list of things, including some quite large ornaments and many articles of clothing, which she wanted me to rescue for her. I had reduced the list considerably. I was not at all sure of the legal position. I presumed that a runaway wife could be said to own her own clothes. I had told Priscilla that the jewellery was 'hers', but even of this I was not certain. I was definitely not going to remove any larger household items. As it was, I had engaged to bring away, besides the jewellery and the mink stole, a number of other things, to wit: a coat and skirt, a cocktail dress, three cashmere jerseys, two blouses, two pairs of shoes, a bundle of underwear, a blue and white striped china urn, a marble statuette of some Greek goddess, two silver goblets, a small malachite box, a painted Florentine work box, an enamel picture of a lady picking apples, and a Wedgwood teapot.

Priscilla had been much relieved when I had agreed to go and fetch these objects, to which she seemed to attach an almost magical significance. It was agreed that after their abstraction Roger should be formally asked to pack up and send the rest of her clothes. Priscilla did not imagine that he would impound these, once her jewels were saved. She kept saying that Roger might sell her 'precious things' out of spite, and on reflection I felt that this was indeed possible. I had hoped that my really, all things considered, very kind offer of a salvage operation would cheer Priscilla up. But once this source of anxiety was alleviated, she started up again an almost continuous rigmarole of remorse and misery, about the lost child, about her age, about her personal appearance, about her husband's unkindness, about her ruined useless life. Uncontrolled remorse, devoid of conscience or judgement, is very unattractive. I felt shame for my sister at this time and would gladly have kept her hidden away. However someone had to be with her and Rachel, who had heard a good deal of these repinings on the previous day, agreed, dutifully but without enthusiasm, to stay with Priscilla during my Bristol journey, provided I returned as early as possible on the same day.

The telephone rang in the empty house. It was office hours, afternoon. I was looking at my well-shaven upper lip in the telephone box mirror, and thinking about Christian. What these thoughts were I will explain later. I could still hear that demonic laughter. A few minutes later, feeling nervous and unhappy and very like a burglar, I was thrusting the key into the lock and pressing gently upon the door. I had brought two large suitcases with me, which I put down in the hall. There was something unexpected which I had perceived as soon as I crossed the threshold, but I could not at once think what it was. Then I realized that it was a strong fresh smell of furniture polish.

Priscilla had so much conveyed the desolation of the house. No one had made the beds for weeks. She had given up washing dishes. The char had left of course. Roger had taken a savage satisfaction in increasing the mess and blaming her for it. Roger broke things deliberately. Priscilla would not clear them up. Roger found a plate with mouldy food upon it. He smashed the plate upon the ground in front of Priscilla in the hall. There it lay, with the pieces of broken plate and the muck spread upon the carpet. Priscilla had passed by with vacant eyes. But the scene as I came through the door was so different that I thought for a moment that I must be in the wrong house. There was a quite conspicuous air of cleanliness and order. The white woodwork shone, the Wilton carpet glowed. There were even flowers, huge red and white peonies, in a big brass jug on the oak chest. The chest had been polished. The jug had been polished.

Upstairs the same rather weird cleanliness and order prevailed. The beds had been made with hospitaline accuracy. There was not a speck of dust anywhere. A clock ticked quietly. It felt eerie, like the *Marie Celeste*. I gazed out into the garden at a sleek lawn and irises in flower. The sun was shining brightly but a little coolly. Roger must have cut the grass since Priscilla's departure. I went to the long lower drawer of the chest of drawers where Priscilla said she kept her jewel case. I dragged the drawer open, but there was nothing in it but clothes. I jumbled them up, then searched other drawers there and in the bathroom. I opened the wardrobe. There was no sign of a jewel case or of the mink stole. Nor could I see upon the dressing-table the silver goblets or the malachite box which were supposed to be there. I felt very upset and ran into the other rooms. One room was simply full of Priscilla's clothes, lying on the bed, on chairs, on the floor, looking so bright and gay and odd. On my rounds I saw the blue and white striped china urn, which was considerably larger than Priscilla had suggested, and picked it up. As I stood at a loss upon the landing, holding the urn, I heard a sound below me and a voice said, 'Hello, it's me.'

I came slowly down the stairs. Roger was standing in the hall. When he saw me his mouth opened and his eyebrows went up. He was looking healthy and distinguished, wearing a well-cut grey sports jacket. His grey-brown hair was brushed back over his head in a neat dome. I put the vase down carefully on the chest beside the brass jug with the peonies.

'I came to get Priscilla's jewellery and stuff.'

'Is Priscilla with you?'

'No.'

'She isn't coming back, is she?'

'No.'

'Thank God. Come in here. Have a drink.' Roger's voice was prissy and plummy, rather loud, a pseudo-varsity voice, a public relations voice, a public-speaking cad's voice. We went into the 'lounge'. (A lounge lizard's voice.) Here too all was neat, there were flowers. The sun was shining.

'I want my sister's jewels.'

'Won't you drink? Mind if I do?'

'I want my sister's jewels.'

'I'm awfully sorry, but I don't think I can let you have them. You see, I don't know how valuable they are, and until –'

'And her mink stole.'

'Ditto.'

'Where are they?'

'Elsewhere. Look, Bradley, we needn't fight, need we?'

'I want the jewels and the mink and that vase I brought down and an enamel picture of –'

'Oh God. You know Priscilla's a mental case?'

'If she is, you made her one.'

'Please. I can't help Priscilla any more. I would if I could. Honestly, it's been such hell. She cleared out, after all.'

'You drove her out.' I saw Priscilla's little marble statuette on the chimney piece. It looked like Aphrodite. Miserable pity for my sister possessed me. She wanted her little things about her, they might console her. There was not much else left.

'It's no fun being in the house with a hysterical ageing woman. I did try. She got violent. And she stopped cleaning, the place was a wreck.'

'I don't want to talk to you. I want the stuff.'

'Everything valuable is in the bank. I thought Priscilla might raid the place. She can have her clothes, only for Christ's sake don't encourage her to fetch them in person. In fact I'd be jolly glad to have her clothes out of the house. But the rest I regard as *sub judice*.'

'Her jewels are her property.'

'No, they're not. She got them by skimping on the housekeeping. I starved to get those jewels. She didn't consult me, of course. But my God now I'm going to regard them as an investment, *my* investment. And the bloody mink. All right, don't start to shout, I'll be just to Priscilla, I'll make her an allowance, but I'm not in any mood for giving her expensive presents. I've got to know where I stand financially. She can't just cream off the valuables. She cleared out of her own accord. She must take the consequences.'

I felt incoherent humiliation and rage. 'You deliberately drove her out. She says you tried to poison her –'

'I just put an overdose of salt and mustard into her stew. It must have tasted awful. I sat and watched her trying to eat it. Little pictures out of hell. You've just no idea. I see you've brought two suitcases. I'll put out some of her clothes for you.'

'You took all the money out of the joint account –'

'Well, it was my money, wasn't it? There wasn't any other source of income! She kept drawing it out without telling me and buying clothes. She went mad over buying clothes. There's a room upstairs full of them, never worn. She simply wasted my money. Please let's not fight. After all you're a man, you can understand, you won't start to scream about it. She's a crazy disappointed woman and as cruel as a demon. We both wanted a child. She tricked me into marriage. I only married her because I wanted a child.'

'What are you talking about? You insisted on the abortion.'

'She wanted the abortion. I didn't know what I wanted. Then when the child was gone I felt awful about it. Then Priscilla told me she was pregnant again. That was your mother's idea. It wasn't true. I married her because I couldn't bear to lose a second child. And there was no child.'

'Oh God.' I went over to the chimney piece and picked up the marble statuette.

'Leave that alone, please,' said Roger. 'This isn't an antique shop.'

As I put it down there was a step in the hall and a beautiful young girl came in through the door. She was dressed in a mauve canvas jerkin and white slacks, tousled and casual like a girl on a yacht, her dark brown hair gilded. Her face glowed with something more exalted and inward than mere good health and sunshine. She looked about twenty. She was carrying a shopping bag which she put down in the doorway.

I felt utter confusion. Had there been a child after all? Was this she?

Roger leapt up and ran to her, his face relaxed and beaming, his eyes looking larger, more luminous, wider apart. He kissed her on the lips, then held her for a moment, staring at her, smiling and astounded. He gave a short 'Oh!' of amazed satisfaction, then turned to me. 'This is Marigold. She's my mistress.'

'It hasn't taken you long to install one.'

'Darling, this is Priscilla's brother. We'd better tell him, hadn't we, darling?'

'Yes, of course, darling,' said the girl gravely, pushing back her tousled hair and leaning up against Roger. 'We must tell him everything.' She had a light West Country accent and I could now see that she was older than twenty.

'Marigold and I have been together for years. Marigold was my secretary. We've been half living together for years and years. We never let Priscilla know.'

'We didn't want to hurt her,' said Marigold. 'We carried the burden ourselves. It was hard to know what to do for the best. It has been a terrible time.'

'It's over now,' said Roger. 'Thank God it's over.' They were holding hands.

I felt hatred and horror of this sudden cameo of happiness. I ignored the girl and said to Roger, 'I can see that living with a girl who could be your daughter must be more fun than observing the marriage vows with an elderly woman.'

'I am thirty,' said Marigold. 'And Roger and I love each other.'

' "For richer or poorer, in sickness and in health." Just when she was most in need of help you drove my sister out of her home.'

'I didn't!'

'You did!'

'Marigold is pregnant,' said Roger.

'How can you tell me that,' I said, 'with that air of vile satisfaction. Am I supposed to be pleased because you've fathered another bastard? Are you so proud of being an adulterer? I regard you both as wicked, an old man and a young girl, and if you only knew how ugly and pathetic you look, pawing each other and making a vulgar display of how pleased you are with yourselves for having got rid of my sister – You're like a pair of murderers –'

They moved apart. Marigold sat down, looking up at her lover with a dazed glowing stare. 'We didn't do this deliberately,' said Roger. 'It just happened. We can't help it if we're happy. At least we're acting rightly now, we've stopped lying anyway. We want you to tell Priscilla, to explain everything. God, that will be a relief. Won't it, darling?'

'We've hated telling lies, we really have, haven't we, darling?' said Marigold. 'We've both been living a lie for years.'

'Marigold had a little flat – I used to visit her – it was a miserable situation.'

'Now it's all dropped away and – oh just to be able to speak the truth, it's – We've been so sorry for poor Priscilla –'

'If you could only see yourselves,' I said, 'if you could only see yourselves – Now if you will kindly hand over Priscilla's jewellery –'

'Sorry,' said Roger. 'I explained.'

'She wanted the jewels, the mink, that statuette thing, that striped urn, some enamel picture –'

'I bought that statuette thing. It stays here. And I happen to like that enamel picture. These aren't just *her* things. Can't you see we can't start dividing things up now? There's money involved. She ran off and left the stuff, she can wait! You can have her clothes though. You could put a lot into those suitcases you brought.'

'I'll pack them, shall I?' said Marigold. She ran out of the room.

'You will tell Priscilla, won't you?' said Roger. 'It'll be such a relief to my mind. I'm such a coward. I've kept putting off breaking it to her.'

'When your girl friend got pregnant you deliberately drove your wife away.'

'It wasn't a plan! We were just muddling along, we were bloody miserable. We'd waited and waited –'

'Hoping she'd die, I suppose. I'm surprised you didn't murder her.'

'We had to have the child,' said Roger. 'That child's important and I'm going to act fairly by it. It has some rights, I should think! We had to have our happiness at last and have it fully and truthfully. I want Marigold to be my wife. Priscilla was never happy with me.'

'Have you thought about what's going to happen to Priscilla now and what her existence will be like? You've taken her life, now you discard her.'

'Well, she's taken my life too. She's taken years and years from me when I might have been happy and living in the open!'

'Oh go to hell!' I said. I went out into the hall where Marigold was kneeling, surrounded by an ocean of silks and tweeds and pink underwear. Most of it looked entirely new.

'Where's the mink?'

'I explained, Bradley.'

'Oh you should be ashamed,' I said. 'Look at you both. You are wicked people. You should be so ashamed.'

They looked at me with distress, concern for me, looked ruefully at each other. I could not touch them. It was as if their happiness had made them into saints. I wanted to scratch and tear them. But they were invulnerable, in bliss.

I said, 'I'm not going to wait while you pack these cases.' I could not bear to see the girl shaking out Priscilla's things and folding them neatly. 'You can send them on to my flat.'

'Yes, yes, we'll do that, won't we, darling,' said Marigold. 'There's a trunk upstairs –'

'You will tell her, won't you,' said Roger. 'Tell her as gently as you can. Make it clear though. You can tell her Marigold is pregnant. There's no way back now.'

'You've seen to that.'

'You must take her something now,' said Marigold, kneeling, her bland face glowing with the tender benevolence of real felicity. 'Darling, shouldn't we send her that statuette, or – ?'

'No. I like that thing.'

'Well then that striped vase, didn't she want that?'

'This is my house too,' said Roger. 'I made it. These things have their places.'

'Oh darling, *please* let Priscilla have that vase, just to please me!'

'Oh all right, darling – What a tender-hearted little muggins it is!'

'I'll pack it up carefully.'

'Don't think I'm the devil incarnate, Bradley old man. Of course I'm not a holy character, I'm just an ordinary chap, I doubt if you'll find an ordinarier. You must understand that I've had a rough time. It's been pure hell running two lives, and Priscilla's been awful to me for so long, she's really hated me, she hasn't said a kind or gentle thing to me for years –'

Marigold came back with a bulky parcel. I took it from her and opened the front door. The outside world looked dazzling, as if I had been in the dark. I stepped outside and looked back at them. They were swaying together, shoulder to shoulder, hand in hand. They could not check two radiant smiles. I wanted to spit upon the doorstep but my mouth was dry.

I was drinking light golden sherry in a bar and staring at the red, black and white funnel of a ship which was standing out against a hazy sky of intense blue. The funnel was very clear, very there, filled to the brim with colour and being. The sky was crazily infinite and huge, curtain behind curtain of gauzy granules of pure blue.

Later on they were shooting pigeons and the funnel was blue and white, the blue confounded with the sky, the white hung in space like a great cylinder of crinkly paper or like a kite in a picture. Kites have always meant a lot to me. What an image of our condition, the distant high thing, the sensitive pull, the feel of the cord, its invisibility, its length, the fear of loss. I do not usually get drunk. Bristol is the sherry city. Excellent cheap sherry, light and clean, is drawn out of huge dark wooden barrels. I was feeling, for a time, almost mad with defeat.

They were shooting pigeons. What an image of our condition, loud report, the poor flopping bundle upon the ground, trying helplessly, desperately, vainly to rise again. Through tears I saw the stricken birds tumbling over and over down the sloping roofs of warehouses. I saw and heard their sudden weight, their pitiful surrender to gravity. How hardening to the heart it must be to do this thing: to change an innocent soaring being into a bundle of struggling rags and pain. I was looking at a ship's funnel and it was yellow and black against a sky of tingling lucid green. Life is horrible, horrible, horrible, said the philosopher. When I realized that I had missed the train I rang the number of my London flat and got no reply.

'All things work together for good for those who love God,' said Saint Paul. Possibly: but what is it to love God? I have never seen this happening. There is, my dear friend and mentor, some hard-won calm when we see the world very detailed and very close: as close and as vivid as the newly painted funnels of ships on a sunny evening. But the dark and the ugly is not washed away, this too is seen, and the horror of the world is part of the world. There is no triumph of good, and if there were it would not be a triumph of good. There is no drying of tears or obliteration of the sufferings of the innocent and of those who have undergone crippling injustice in their lives. I tell you, my dear, what you know better and more deeply than I can ever know it. Even as I write these words, which should be lucid and filled with glowing colour, I feel the very darkness of my own personality invading my pen. Only perhaps in the ink of this darkness can this writing properly be written? It is not really possible to write like an angel, though some of our near-gods by heaven-inspired trickery sometimes seem to do it.

I felt, after leaving Roger and his Marigold, a humiliated misery which made me almost hysterical with anger. I saw, for this time, with perfect clarity how unjust and how unkind life had been to my sister. I felt a frenzy of remorse because I had not somehow imposed my will upon Roger and really made him suffer. I felt so unhappy and ashamed because I had not brought away even the few little pieces of consolation which she had, really with such humility, wanted: the 'diamanté set', the crystal and lapis necklace, the amber ear-rings. I had not got the mink stole, not even the little marble statuette of Aphrodite or the enamel picture of the lady picking apples. Poor Priscilla, I thought, poor poor Priscilla, with a pity for which I deserved no credit since I was simply feeling sorry for myself. Of course I 'put myself out' for Priscilla, and did it without any hesitation, because one has to do what one has to do. That human beings can acquire a small area of unquestioned obligations may be one of the few things that saves them: saves them from the bestiality and thoughtless night which lies only a millimetre away from the most civilized of our specimens. However if one examines closely some such case of 'duty', the petty achievement of some ordinary individual, it turns out to be no glorious thing, not the turning back by reason or godhead of the flood of natural evil, but simply a special operation of self-love, devised perhaps even by Nature herself who has, or she could not survive in her polycephalic creation, many different and even incompatible moods. We care absolutely about that with which we can identify ourselves. A saint would identify himself with everything. Only there are, so my wise friend tells me, no saints.

I identified myself with Priscilla for simple old mechanical reasons. If Priscilla had been an acquaintance for whom I cared as little as I cared for my sister not only would I not have lifted a finger for her, I would not even have retained the story of her sufferings in my head for a matter of minutes. As it was, I was humiliated and defeated in her humiliation and defeat. I tasted injustice and the special horror of seeing its perpetrators flourish. How frequent and how bitter is this aspect of human wretchedness. The wicked prosper in front of our eyes and go on and on and on prospering. What a blessing it must have been once to be able to believe in hell. A great and deep human consolation was lost to us when that ancient and respectable belief faded from our minds. Yet there was more offence even than that, something profoundly ugly and repulsive to me: that vision of Roger with his grey hair and his genial pseudo-distinguished air of an ageing worldly man, holding a girl who could be his daughter, a girl unused, unmarked and fresh. That particular juxtaposition of youth and age offends, and, I felt, offends rightly.

Later on the empty lighted street was like a theatre set. The black wall at the end of it was a ship's hull. The stone of the quay and the steel of the hull touched each other and I sat upon the stone and leaned my head against the hollow steel. I was in a shop lying under the counter with a woman, and all the shelves were cages containing dead animals which I had forgotten to feed. Ships are compartmental and hollow, ships are like women. The steel vibrated and sang, sang of the predatory women, Christian, Marigold, my mother: the destroyers. I saw the masts and sails of great clippers against a dark sky. Later I sat in Temple Meads station and howled inside myself, suffering the torments of the wicked under those pitiless vaults. Why had no one answered the telephone? A train after midnight took me away. Somehow I had managed to break the blue and white china urn. I left the fragments in the compartment when I got out at Paddington.

I was at Christian's house where they had taken Priscilla. Later I was with Rachel in a garden. This was no dream. And somebody was flying a kite.

I found a note from Rachel waiting, and Rachel herself came early, very early, soon after I had arrived, to tell me what had happened: how Priscilla had become upset, how Christian had telephoned, how Arnold had come, how Francis had come. When I failed to appear Priscilla had become as fretful as a little child awaiting its tardy mother, tears, fears. Late in the evening Christian had carried Priscilla off in a taxi. Arnold and Christian had laughed a great deal. Rachel thought I would be angry with her. I was not. 'Of course you could do nothing if *they* decided otherwise.'

Priscilla was wearing Christian's black *négligée* and sitting upright against a pile of snowy pillows. Her deadened dyed hair was unkempt and scanty, her face without make-up looked soft, like clay or dough, the wrinkles lightly imprinted upon its puffy surface. Her mouth drooped extremely. She could have been seventy, eighty. Christian was in dark green with real pearls and the radiant look of one who has organized and controls a successful gathering. Her eyes were glistening and moist as with washed tears of laughter or the tears people shed when they are pleased and touched. She kept combing her undulating red-brown hair with thin pretty fingers. Arnold was boyish and excited, apologetic to me but constantly exchanging looks with Christian and laughing. He wore his 'interested writer's air': I am merely a spectator, a watcher, but one who *understands*. His face was sallow and sweaty and he kept pulling his floppy colourless hair down over his pale clever eyes in a deliberately childish way. Francis was sitting apart and rubbing his hands, once he silently clapped them, his little close-set bear's peepers roving over the company. He kept nodding towards me as if he were bowing, and murmuring, 'It's all right, it's all right, it's going to be all right, it's going to be all right.' Then he thrust his hand down inside his trousers and started scratching with a preoccupied air. Rachel was standing still with the stillness of one who apes repose but is really embarrassed. She smiled vaguely, her sugary-pink lipsticked lips parted a little, her smile broadening, fading then broadening again, as if under the impulse of private thoughts, but not very convincingly.

'It's not a plot, Bradley, don't look like that.'

'He's furious with us.'

'He thinks you're holding Priscilla as a hostage!'

'I am holding Priscilla as a hostage!'

'Whatever happened to you? Priscilla was terribly upset.'

'I missed the train. I'm very sorry.'

'Why did you miss the train?'

'Why didn't you telephone?'

'How guilty he looks! Look, Priscilla, how guilty he looks!'

'Poor Priscilla thought you'd been run over or something.'

'You see, Priscilla, we told you he'd turn up like an old bad penny.'

'Be quiet everybody, Priscilla's trying to say something.'

'Bradley, don't be cross.'

'Silence for Priscilla!'

'Did you get my things?'

'Sit down, Brad, you look awful.'

'I'm sorry I missed the train.'

'It's going to be all right.'

'I did telephone.'

'Did you get my things?'

'Dear Priscilla, don't throw yourself around so.'

'I'm afraid I didn't get your things.'

'Oh I knew it would go wrong, I knew it would, I knew it would, I told you so!'

'What happened, Bradley?'

'Roger was there. We had a chat.'

'A chat!'

'You're on his side now.'

'Men always stick together, dear.'

'I'm not on his side. Did you want me to fight him?'

'Battling Brad the Bruiser!'

'You talked to him about me.'

'Of course I did!'

'They agreed that women were hell.'

'Well, women *are* hell!'

'Is he unhappy?'

'Yes.'

'Was the house all dirty and awful?'

'Yes.'

'But what about my things?'

'He said he'd send them on.'

'But didn't you bring anything, not anything?'

'He said he'd pack them up.'

'Did you ask him specially about the jewels and the mink?'

'He'll send everything on.'

'But did you ask him specially?'

'It's all right, it's going to be all right.'

'Yes, I did!'

'He won't send them, I know he won't –'

'Priscilla, will you please get dressed?'

'He won't send my things ever, he won't, he won't, I know he won't, I've lost them forever and ever!'

'I'll wait for you downstairs. Then we can both go home.'

'Those jewels are all I've got.'

'Oh but Priscilla's going to stay here with me.'

'Did you look for them, did you see them?'

'Priscilla, get up, get dressed.'

'Aren't you, darling, going to stay here with me?'

'Bradley, you mustn't talk to her like that.'

'Brad, be reasonable. She needs medical attention, she needs psychiatric help, I'm going to engage a nurse –'

'She doesn't need a nurse, for Christ's sake.'

'You know you're not a looker-after, Bradley.'

'Priscilla –'

112

'After all, look what happened yesterday.'

'I think I must go,' said Rachel who had so far said nothing, still smiling vaguely as at secret thoughts.

'Oh please don't go.'

'Is it too early for a drink?'

'You are not going to take over my sister. I will not have her pitied and patronized.'

'No one's pitying her!'

'I pity her,' said Francis.

'You can just shut up, you're leaving here in three minutes, the real doctor is coming and I don't want you arsing around –'

'Come on, Priscilla.'

'Steady on, Bradley, maybe Chris is right.'

'And don't call her Chris.'

'You can't have it both ways, Brad, disown me *and* –'

'Priscilla is perfectly well, she just needs to pull herself together.'

'Bradley doesn't believe in mental illness.'

'Well, neither do I as it happens, but –'

'You are all persuading her she's ill, while what she needs –'

'Bradley, she needs rest and quiet.'

'Is *this* rest and quiet?'

'Brad, she's a sick woman.'

'Priscilla, *get up*.'

'Brad, do stop shouting.'

'I think I really must go.'

'You do want to stay here with me, don't you, darling, you said so, you want to stay with Christian?'

'He won't send my things, I know he won't, I'll never see them again, never.'

'It's going to be all right.'

In the end Rachel and Arnold and Francis and I left the house together. At least, I just turned and walked out, and the others followed somehow.

The scene had been taking place in one of the new rooms which belonged to the upstairs flat in the old days. It was a pretentious, but now shabby, room with an oval 'film star' bed and the walls covered with pseudo-bamboo. I felt trapped there as if some trick of false perspective were bringing the ceiling down at such a sharp angle that a step would bring it into contact with my head. There are days when a tall man feels taller. I towered above the others as above puppets and my feet were many inches above the floor. Perhaps this was still the effect of drink.

Out in the street some blackness boiled in my eyes. Sun, filtered through hazy cloud, dazzled me. People loomed in front of me in bulky shadowy shapes and passed me by like ghosts, like trees walking. I could hear the others hurrying after. I had heard them clattering down the stairs, but I did not look round. I felt sick.

'Bradley, you look as if you've gone blind, here, don't walk out into the roadway like that, you ass.'

Arnold had hold of my sleeve. He held on to me. The other two crowded up, staring.

Rachel said, 'Leave her there for a day or two. Then she'll have recovered and you can take her away.'

'You don't understand,' I said. My head ached and my eyes were intolerant of the light.

'I understand perfectly, as a matter of fact,' said Arnold. 'You've just lost this round and you'd better relax. I'd go to bed if I were you.'

'I'll come and look after you,' said Francis.

'No, you won't.'

'Why do you keep shading your eyes and screwing them up like that?' said Rachel.

'What made you miss the train?' said Arnold.

'I think I'll go to bed, yes.'

'Bradley,' said Arnold, 'don't be cross with me.'

'I'm not cross with you.'

'It was all an accident, my being there I mean, I called in because I thought you'd be back, then Christian rang and then she turned up, and Rachel had had about enough of Priscilla and there was no sign of you. I know it seems hurtful, I do understand, but really it was just common sense, and it amused Christian so much, and you know how I love a scandal and a little bit of turmoil. You've got to forgive us. We're not all conspiring against you.'

'I know you're not.'

'I only went along today because –'

'Oh never mind. I'm going home.'

'Let me come with you,' said Francis.

'You'd better come with me,' said Rachel. 'I'll give you lunch.'

'That's a good idea. You go along with Rachel. I must go to the library and get on with my novel. I've wasted quite enough time on this little drama. I'm such an incorrigible Peeping Tom. You're sure you're not cross with me, Bradley?'

Rachel and I got into a taxi. Francis ran along beside it trying to say something, but I pulled the window up.

Now at last there was peace. Rachel's big calm woman's face beamed upon me, the beneficent full moon, not the black moon dagger-armed and brimming with darkness. The bruise seemed to have faded, or perhaps she had covered it with make-up. Or perhaps it had only ever been a shadow after all.

Feeding my hangover, I had consumed a lunch which consisted of three aspirins, followed by a glass of creamy milk, followed by milk chocolate, followed by shepherd's pie, followed by Turkish delight, followed by milky coffee. I felt physically better and clearer in the head.

We were sitting on the veranda. The Baffins' garden was not big, but in the flush of early summer it seemed endless. A dotting of fruit trees and ferny bushes amid longish red-tufted grass obscured the nearby houses, obscured even the creosoted fence. Only a hint of pink rambler roses between the trunks suggested an enclosure. The garden was a curved space, a warm green shell smelling of earth and leaves. At the foot of the veranda steps there was a pavement covered with the mauve flowers of creeping thyme, beyond this a clipped grassy path starred with white daisies. It stirred some memory of a childhood holiday. Once in an endless meadow, just able to peer through the tawny haze of the grass tops, the child who was myself had watched a young fox catching mice, an elegant newly minted fox, straight from the hand of God, brilliantly ruddy, with black stockings and a white-tipped brush. The fox heard and turned. I saw its intense vivid mask, its liquid amber eyes. Then it was gone. An image of such beauty and such mysterious sense. The child wept and knew himself an artist.

'So Roger's blissfully happy?' said Rachel, to whom I had told all.

'I can't tell Priscilla, can I?'

'Not yet.'

'Roger and that young girl. God, it sickens me!'

'I know. But Priscilla is the problem.'

'What am I to do, Rachel, what am I to do?'

Rachel, relaxed, barefoot, did not reply. She was gently stroking her face where I had imagined the bruise. We were reposing now in deck chairs. She was relaxed yet animated, in a characteristic way: what Arnold called her 'exalted look'. A bright expectancy blazed in her pale freckled face and in her light brown eyes. She looked alert and handsome. Her reddish golden hair was deliberately frizzed out and untidy.

'How mechanical they look,' I said.

'Who? What?'

'The blackbirds.'

Several blackbirds were walking jerkily about like little wound-up toys upon the clipped grass path.

'Just like us.'

'What are you talking about, Bradley?'

'Mechanical. Just like us.'

'Have some more milk chocolate.'

'Francis likes milk chocolate.'

'I feel sorry for Francis, but I do see Christian's point.'

'All this intimate friendly talk about "Christian" makes me feel ill.'

'You mustn't mind so much. It's all in your head.'

'Well, I live in my head. I wish she was dead. I wish she'd died in America. I bet she killed her husband.'

'Bradley. You know I didn't mean any of those violent things I said about Arnold the other day.'

'Yes, I know.'

'In marriage one says things which are, yes, mechanical, but it doesn't affect the heart.'

116

'The what?'

'Bradley, don't be so –'

'How heavy mine is, like a great stone in my breast. Sometimes one feels suddenly doomed by fate.'

'Oh brace up, for God's sake!'

'You don't hate me for having seen – you know, you and Arnold, the other day –'

'No. It just makes you seem closer.'

'I wish, I wish she hadn't met Arnold.'

'You're very attached to Arnold, aren't you?'

'Yes.'

'It's not just that you care what he thinks?'

'No.'

'It's odd. He's awkward with you. I know he often hurts you. But he cares very much for you, very much.'

'Do you mind if we change the subject a bit?'

'You're such a funny fellow, Bradley. You're so unphysical. And you're as shy as a schoolboy.'

'That woman coming back bang into the middle of everything has been such a bloody shock. And she's got her claws into Arnold already. And Priscilla.'

'She's beautiful, you know.'

'And you.'

'No. But I appreciate her. You never described her properly.'

'She's changed.'

'Arnold thinks you're still in love with her.'

'If he thinks that it must be because he's in love with her himself.'

'Are you in love with her?'

'Rachel, do you want me to scream and scream and scream?'

'You *are* a schoolboy!'

'Only because of her I understand hatred.'

'Are you a masochist, Bradley?'

'Don't be daft.'

'I sometimes thought you enjoyed it when Arnold went for you.'

'Is Arnold in love with her?'

'Where do you suppose he went to when he left us today?'

'To the – Oh, you mean he went back to her?'

'Of course.'

'Hell. He's only met her twice, three times –'

'Don't you believe in love at first sight?'

'So you think he is – ?'

'He had a pretty long session with her in that pub. And again last night when –'

'Don't tell me. Is he?'

'He keeps his head. He's physical but cold. You're unphysical but warm. He loves any sort of tumult, as he told you, he loves a drama. He's terribly curious, he wants to pry into everything, to appropriate it by knowing about it. He'd like to be everybody's father confessor. He wouldn't be a bad one either, he can help people when he tries. He got Christian to tell him about your marriage.'

'Oh Jesus Christ.'

'That was in the pub. Last night I gather they – All right, all right! I just wanted to say I'm on your side. We'll bring Priscilla here if you like.'

'It's too late. Oh Christ. Rachel, I don't feel terribly well.'

'Oh confound you, Bradley. Here. Take my hand. Take it.'

Under the opaque glass of the veranda it had become very hot and sultry. The earth smells and the grass smells were exotic now, like incense, not rainy and fresh. Rachel had edged her deck chair close up against mine. I could feel the nearby weight of her sagging body like a gravitational pull upon my own. She had wound her arm in underneath my arm and rather awkwardly taken hold of my hand. So two corpses might ineptly greet each other on resurrection day. Then she began to turn over towards me, her head pressing on to my shoulder. I could smell her perspiration and the fresh clean scent of her hair.

One is very vulnerable in a deck chair. I had been wondering what kind of hand-holding this was. I did not know what sort of pressure to give her hand or how long to retain it. When her head came thrusting on to my shoulder with that gauche aggressive nuzzling gesture I felt a sudden not unpleasant helplessness. At the same time I said, 'Rachel, get up, please, let's go inside.'

She shot up out of the chair. I got up more slowly. The slack canvas gave little leverage, and her speed was remarkable. I followed her into the dark drawing-room.

'I beg your pardon, Bradley.' She had already thrown open the door into the hall. Her staccato voice and manner made clear what she thought. I realized that if I did not take her in my arms at once, some quite irreparable 'incident' would have occurred. I closed the door into the hall and took her in my arms. I was not reluctant to do so. I felt the hot plumpness of her shoulders and again the heavy nuzzling head.

'Come and sit down, Rachel.'

We sat down on the sofa and immediately her lips were pressed against mine.

Of course this was not the first time I had touched Rachel. But casual social pecking and patting can be, in some cases, almost an inoculation against strong feeling. It is a strange fact that the barriers which guard the degrees of intimacy are immensely strong, and yet can be overthrown by a light touch. Only take someone's hand in a certain way, even look into their eyes in a certain way, and the world is changed forever.

At the same time, like the excellent Arnold, I was keeping my head, or trying to. I kept my lips upon Rachel's and we remained immobile for a time which began to seem absurdly long. I held her meanwhile rather stiffly, but firmly, one arm still round her shoulder and the other holding her hand. I felt as if I were, in two senses, arresting her. Then we drew apart and studied each other's eyes: possibly to find out what had happened.

The first glimpse of someone's face after they have made an irrevocable gesture of affection is always instructive and moving. Rachel's face was radiant, tender, rueful, questioning. I felt bucked. I wanted to convey pleasure, gratitude. 'Oh, dear Rachel, thank you.'

'I'm not just trying to cheer you up.'

'I know.'

'There's a real something here.'

'I know. I'm so glad.'

'I've wanted to – draw you closer – before. I felt shy. I feel shy now.'

'So do I. But – Oh, thank you.'

We were silent for a moment, tense, almost embarrassed.

Then I said, 'Rachel, I think I must go.'

'Oh you are ridiculous,' she said. 'All right, all right. Schoolboy. Running away. Off you go then. Thank you for kissing me.'

'It's not that. It's just so perfect. I'm afraid of spoiling something or something.'

'Yes, off you go. I've done enough – damage or whatever.'

'No damage. Oh silly Rachel! It's beautiful. We are closer, aren't we?'

We got up and stood holding hands. I suddenly felt extremely happy and laughed.

'Am I absurd?'

'No, Rachel. You've given me a piece of happiness.'

'Well, hold on to it then. It's mine too.'

I pushed the sturdy wiry gingery hair back from the pale freckled puzzled tender face, straining it back with both hands, and I kissed her on the brow. We went out into the hall. We were awkward, moved, pleased, anxious now to carry off a good parting without spoiling the mood. Anxious to be alone to think.

A copy of Arnold's latest novel, *The Woeful Forest*, was lying on the table near the front door. I saw it with a shock, and my hand shot to my pocket. My review of the novel was still there, folded up. I took it out and handed it to Rachel. I said, 'Do something for me. Read that and tell me whether or not I should publish it. I'll do whatever you tell me.'

'What is it?'

'My review of Arnold's book.'

'But of course you must publish it.'

'Read it. Not now. I'll do whatever you say.'

'All right. I'll see you to the gate.'

Coming out into the garden everything was different. It had become evening. There was a lurid indistinct light which made things blurry and hard to locate. Near things were illuminated by a rich hazed sunlight, while the sky farther off was dark with cloud and the promise of night, although in fact it was not yet very late. I felt upset, confused, elated, and very much wanting now to be by myself.

The garden in front of the house was rather long, a lawn planted with small bushes, shrubby roses and the like, with a 'crazy paving' path down the centre. The paths glimmered white, with dark patches where tufty rock plants were growing between the stones. Rachel touched my hand. I squeezed her fingers but did not hold on. She went first down the path. About half-way to the gate a sense of something behind me made me turn round.

A figure was sitting in an upstairs window, sitting up half reclined upon a window seat, or even it seemed upon the window sill itself. Without seeing the face except as a blur I recognized Julian, and felt an immediate pang of guilt at having kissed the mother when the child was actually in the house. However what more strongly attracted my attention was something else. The window, which was of the hinged casement variety, had been pushed wide open to leave a rectangular space within which the girl, dressed in some kind of white robe, perhaps a dressing gown, half lay, her knees up, her back against the wooden frame. Her left hand was extended. And I saw that she was flying a kite.

Only it was not an ordinary kite, but a sort of magical kite. The string was invisible. Up above the house there hovered motionless, some thirty feet up, a huge pale globe with a long trailing ten-foot tail. The curious light made the globe seem to glow with a sort of milky alabaster radiance. The tail, evidently hanging free from the suspending string, since a slight movement of air had towed the balloon out of the vertical, consisted of a number of white bows, or as they looked, blobs, which hung invisibly supported in a motionless row beneath their parent form. Behind the balloon, whose size was hard to estimate – its diameter, if one may use this term of a globe, could have been as great as four feet – the sky, towards the sunnier quarter, was a purplish colour which might have indicated light cloud or simply open sky verging to twilight.

Rachel had turned round now, and we both stood in silence looking up. The figure above was so odd and separate, like an image upon a tomb, it did not occur to me that I could speak to it. Then as I gazed up at the featureless face, the girl slowly brought her other hand round towards the taut invisible string. There was a faint flash and a faint click. The pale globe up above curtsied for a moment, and then with an air of suddenly collected dignity and purpose rose and began to move slowly away. Julian had cut the string.

The deliberation of the action, and the evident and histrionic way in which it was addressed to its impromptu audience, produced physical shock, like that of some sort of assault. I felt a thrill of pain and dismay. Rachel gave a brief exclamation, a sort of 'ach!' and moved quickly on towards the gate. I followed her. She did not pause at the gate but went on into the road and began to walk briskly along the pavement. I hurried and joined her where she had stopped, out of sight of the house, under a big copper beech tree at the corner of the road. It was getting dark.

'Whatever was that?'

'The balloon? Oh some boy gave it to her.'

'But how does it stay up?'

'It's filled with hydrogen or something.'

'Why did she cut the string?'

'I can't imagine. Just some sort of act of aggression. She's full of strange fancies just now.'

'Is she unhappy?'

'Girls of that age are always unhappy.'

'Love, I suppose.'

'I don't think she's had love yet. She feels she's somebody very special and she's just beginning to realize that she's not very talented.'

'That sounds like the human condition.'

'She's spoilt as they all are, she's had everything done for her, not like my generation. They fear ordinariness so. She'd like to go off with the raggle taggle gipsies or something. As it is her life is dull. Arnold is disappointed in her and she feels it.'

'Poor child.'

'Oh she's all right, she's lucky. And as you say, it's the human condition. Well, good night, Bradley. I know you want to get away from me.'

'No, no –'

'I don't mean it in a nasty way! You're so shy. I love it. Kiss me.'

I kissed her quickly but very fully in the darkness underneath the tree.

'I may write to you,' she said.

'Do that.'

'Don't worry. Nothing for worry.'

122

'I know. Good night. And thanks.'

Rachel gave a weird little laugh and vanished into the obscurity. I began to walk quickly along the next road in the direction of the tube station.

I found that my heart was beating rather violently. I could not make out whether something very important had happened or not. I thought, I shall know tomorrow. Now there was nothing to be done except to rest upon an immediate sense of the experience. Rachel still hovered round me like a perfume. But in my mind with great clarity I saw Arnold, as if he were looking at me from the far end of an illuminated corridor. Whatever had happened had happened to Arnold too.

Just then I saw the balloon again. It was moving slowly along, a little ahead of me, over the tops of the houses. It was lower than it had been before and seemed to be very gradually descending. The street lamps had been turned on, giving a local ineffectual light beneath a sky which was glowing but nearly dark, and in which the pale object was barely visible. A few people were walking along the road, but no one except myself seemed to have noticed the strange wanderer. I began to hurry, trying to gauge its direction. In the suburban villas rectangles of light were appearing in the lower rooms. Sometimes undrawn curtains showed insipid pastel-shaded interiors and sometimes the blue flicker of television. Up above, the neat silhouettes of roofs and the bunchy silhouettes of trees were outlined against a dark bluish sky through which the faint globe, its tail now entirely invisible, floated onward. I began to run.

I turned down a little-frequented side road of more modest houses. I was now ahead of the balloon which was, though still moving very slowly, descending more rapidly. I watched it coming towards me like an errant moon, mysterious, invisible to all except myself, the bearer of some potent as yet unfathomed destiny. I wanted it. The question of what I would do with it when I captured it was quite unformulated. The question was rather what would it do with me. I moved along the road, feeling in my body its direction and rate of descent.

For a moment it was invisible behind a tree. Then suddenly, wafted faster by a momentary breeze, it swept down over the street, moving into the arc of the lamplight. For a second or two it appeared in front of me, huge and yellow, its tail of pendant bows swaying crazily. I could even see the string. I raced towards it. Something lightly brushed my face. The street lamps dazzled me as I clutched above my head, and clutched again. And then it was all gone. The balloon had vanished, descending into some dark and further maze of suburban gardens. I continued for some while to hurry to and fro among the little intersecting streets, but I did not set eyes again upon the travelling portent.

At the tube station I saw Arnold coming through the ticket barrier, smiling secretively to himself. I moved to the other side and he did not see me. When I reached my flat Francis Marloe was waiting outside the door. I amazed him by asking him in. Of what passed between us then I shall speak later.

One of the many respects, dear friend, in which life is unlike art is this: characters in art can have unassailable dignity, whereas characters in life have none. Yet of course life, in this respect as in others, pathetically and continually aspires to the condition of art. A sheer concern for one's dignity, a sense of form, a sense of style, inspires more of our baser actions than any conventional analysis of possible sins is likely to bring to light. A good man often appears *gauche* simply because he does not take advantage of the myriad mean little chances of making himself look stylish. Preferring truth to form, he is not constantly at work upon the façade of his appearance.

A decent proper man (such as I am not) would have run awkwardly away from Rachel before anything had 'happened'. Of course I did not want to 'offend' her. But I was far more concerned about cutting a masterly figure. I was quite interested in kissing her before: very much more so after. So things begin and work. A serious kiss can alter the world and should not be allowed to take place simply because the scene will be disfigured without it. These considerations will no doubt seem to the young unutterably prudish and fussy. But precisely because they are young they cannot see how all things have their consequences.

(This thing had its consequences, including some very unexpected ones.) There are no spare unrecorded encapsulated moments in which we can behave 'anyhow' and then expect to resume life where we left off. The wicked regard time as discontinuous, the wicked dull their sense of natural causality. The good feel being as a total dense mesh of tiny interconnections. My lightest whim can affect the whole future. Because I smoke a cigarette and smile over an unworthy thought another man may die in torment. I kissed Rachel and hid from Arnold and got drunk with Francis. I also put myself into a totally different 'life-mood' which had extensive and surprising results. Of course, my dear, I cannot, how could I, altogether regret what has happened. But the past must be justly judged, whatever marvels may have sprung out of one's faults through the incomprehensible operation of grace. *O felix culpa!* does not excuse anything.

For an artist, everything connects with his work, and can feed it. I should perhaps explain more fully what my frame of mind was at that time. The context of this could be: on the day after the evening of the balloon I awoke with a crippling sense of anxiety. I asked myself, should I not go at once to Patara and take Priscilla with me? To do this would solve several problems. I would be tending my sister. A simple hard obligation to do this remained with me, a palpable thorn in the flesh of my versatile egoism. I would also be getting her away from Christian, and I would be getting away from Christian myself. Sheer physical distance can help, perhaps always helps, in the case of these cruder enchantments. I saw Christian as a witch in my life, and a low demon, though I did not in doing so excuse myself. There are people who occasion in one, as it seems automatically, obsessive egoistic anxiety and preoccupying resentment. When confronted with such people one should if possible run: or else deaden the mind to them. (Or behave in some 'saintly' manner not here relevant.) I knew that if I stayed in London I should certainly see Christian again. I would have to do so because of Arnold, to find out what was going on. And I would have to do so because I would have to do so. Those who have such obsessions will understand my state.

When I say that I *also* thought I ought to leave London because of what had just happened between me and Rachel I would not be understood as suggesting that I was entirely moved by delicate conscientious scruples, though I did in fact feel such scruples. I felt rather more, about Rachel, a kind of curious detached satisfaction which had many ingredients. One ingredient of a less than worthy sort was a crude and simple sense of scoring off Arnold. Or perhaps that indeed puts it too crudely. I felt that I was now, in a new way, defended against Arnold. There was something important to him which I knew and he did not. (Only later did it occur to me that Rachel might decide to tell Arnold of our kisses.) Such knowledges are always deeply reassuring. Though, to do myself justice, there was in this no intent of going any further with the matter. What was remarkable was how far we had, in our little exchange, actually gone. And that we had gone so far suggested, as Rachel herself later said, that in both our minds the ground had long been prepared. Such dialectical leaps from quantity into quality are common in human relations. This was another reason for going away. I now had more than enough to brood upon and I wanted to brood without the intrusive interference of any real developments. As it was, we had carried the thing off well, with dignity and intelligence. It had a certain completeness. Rachel's gesture had enormously comforted me. I felt no guilt. And I wanted to bask at peace in the rays of that comfort.

However it appeared, when I attempted to be realistic about it, that I could not thus solve my problems all together. Priscilla and myself at Patara was simply not a viable idea. I knew I could not possibly work with my sister in the house. Not only would her sheer nervous presence make work impossible. I knew that she would soon irritate me into all sorts of beastliness. Besides, how ill was she really? Ought she to have medical attention, psychiatric treatment, electric shocks? What ought I to do now about Roger and Marigold and the crystal and lapis necklace and the mink stole? Until these things were clarified Priscilla would have to remain in London and so would I.

The burden of all these unpredictable arrangements annoyed me, when I reflected upon them, to the point of screaming. My desire to get away and write had been coming to a climax. I felt, as artists so felicitously sometimes do, 'under orders'. I was not at this time my own master. That which I had long served with

126

such exemplary humility and with so little return was preparing to reward me. I had within me at last a great book. There was a fearful urgency about it. I needed darkness, purity, solitude. This was not a time for wasting with the trivia of superficial planning and *ad hoc* rescue operations and annoying interviews. To begin with there was the problem of extracting Priscilla from Christian, who had even *said* that she regarded her in the light of a hostage. Could this be done without a confrontation? Would I have to invoke Rachel's help and muddy those waters after all?

I let Francis into my house because Rachel had kissed me. At that stage, a fluid all-conquering confidence was still making me feel benevolent and full of power. So I surprised Francis by letting him in. Also I wanted a drinking companion, I wanted for once to *chatter*: not about what had happened of course, but about quite other things. When one has a secret source of satisfaction it is pleasing to talk of everything in the world *but* that. It was also important that I felt myself so immeasurably superior to Francis. Some clever writer (probably a Frenchman) has said: it is not enough to succeed; others must fail. So I felt gracious that evening towards Francis because he was what he was and I was what I was. We both took in a lot of drink and I let him play the fool for my benefit, encouraging him to speculate about methods of getting money out of his sister, a subject on which he was droll. He said, 'Of course Arnold wants to bring you and Christian together again.' I laughed like a maniac. He also said, 'Why shouldn't I stay here and nurse Priscilla?' I laughed again. I threw him out just after midnight.

The next morning I had a headache and that illusion of not having slept at all, which insomniacs know so well. I decided I must telephone my doctor for more pills. The awful anxiety about Priscilla was combined with a frenetic desire to get away and write my book. I also felt, together with this, a tender gratitude in the direction of Rachel and a self-indulgent desire to write her an ambiguous letter. In this respect however it turned out that she had forestalled me. As I emerged again into my little hallway after finishing my breakfast, or rather after drinking my tea, since I never eat at breakfast time, I found on the mat a long letter from her which had evidently just been delivered by hand. This letter ran as follows.

My dearest Bradley, please forgive my writing to you at once like this. (Arnold is asleep. I am alone in the lounge. It is one in the morning. An owl is hooting.) You ran away so quickly, I was not able to say properly half the things which I wanted to say. What a schoolboy you are. Do you know that you *blushed* so beautifully? It is years since I have seen a man blush like that. It is also years since I have kissed anybody properly. And it was a very important kiss, wasn't it? (Two very important kisses!) My dear, I have wanted to kiss you like that for a long time. Bradley, I want and need your love. I don't mean an affair. I mean your *love*. I said to you yesterday that I did not mean what I said about Arnold when you saw me on that awful day up in the bedroom. That was not entirely true. I half meant it. Of course I love Arnold, but I can hate him too, and it can go along with love that one never forgives certain things. I thought for a short while that I should never forgive *you* for having seen me in that unspeakable moment of defeat – a wife crying upstairs while her husband shrugs his shoulders and talks about 'women' to a man friend. (That's what hell is about.) But it has worked otherwise. In fact, it made me kiss you. I have *got* to have you as an ally now. Not in any 'battle' against my husband. I cannot fight him. But just because I am a lonely ageing woman and you are an old friend and I want to put my arms round your neck. It is also important that you love and admire Arnold so much. Bradley, you asked me if I thought Arnold was in love with Christian and I gave you no answer. After seeing him tonight I begin to think that he is. He *laughed* and *laughed*, he seemed so *happy*. (I suspect he spent the day with her.) He kept talking about you, but he was thinking about her. I cannot express to you what pain this gives me. This is, my dear, another reason why I *need* you. Bradley, we must have an alliance which is forever. Nothing else will do, and only *you* will do. I must live with my husband as best I can, with his infidelities and his tempers, which no outsider, not even you, really knows of or will believe in, and also with my own indelible hate, which is part of my love. I cannot cannot forgive. When I lay that day with the sheet over my bruised face I made a pact with hell. Yet I love him. Isn't that odd, and can one keep sane so? *You must help me.* You are the only person who does and can know the truth, some of it anyway, and I love you with a special love which you *must* reciprocate. There is a bond between us now which cannot be broken and also a vow of silence. I will never speak of our 'alliance' to Arnold, and I know that you will not. Bradley, I must see you *soon* now, and see you *often*. You *must* get Priscilla away from Christian and bring her here, and you can visit her here, and I will look after her. Will you *please* telephone me this morning? I will drop this in on you early and then go home again. If Arnold is in the house when you ring I'll talk in a conventional way, you'll understand at once, and then you can ring again later. Oh Bradley, I need your love so much, I'm relying on you now and forever. Much much love

R.

PS I've read the review and enclose it with this letter. I think you shouldn't publish it. It would hurt Arnold so much. You and he must love each other. That is so important. Oh help me to remain sane.

I was upset, touched, annoyed, pleased and thoroughly frightened by this emotional and jumbled missive. What large new thing was happening now and what consequences would it have? Why did women have to make things so definite? Why could she not have let our strange experience drift in a pleasant vagueness? I had dimly thought of her as an 'ally' against (against?) Arnold. She had made this horrible idea explicit. And if I was to be made mad by a relationship between Arnold and Christian would it help me at all that Rachel was made mad too? How I feared these 'needs'. I now wanted very much to see Arnold and have a frank talk, even a shouting match. But a frank talk with Arnold was something which seemed to be becoming more and more impossible. In utter dismay I sat down where I was upon a chair in the hall to think it all over. Then the telephone rang.

'Hello, Pearson? Hartbourne here. I'm thinking of giving a little office party.'

'A little what?'

'A little office party. I thought of inviting Bingley and Matheson and Hadley-Smith and Caldicott and Dyson, and the wives of course, and Miss Wellington and Miss Searle and Mrs Bradshaw –'

'How nice.'

'But I want to be sure you can come. You'll be by way of being the guest of honour, you know!'

'How kind.'

'Now you tell me a day that would suit you and I'll issue the invitations. It'll be quite like old times. People so often ask after you, I thought –'

'Any day suits me.'

'Monday?'

'Fine.'

'Good. Then eight o'clock at my place. By the way, shall I invite Grey-Pelham? He won't bring his wife, so it should be all right.'

'Fine. Fine.'

'And I'd like to make a lunch date with you.'

'I'll ring you. I haven't got my diary.'

'Well, don't forget about the party, will you?'

'I'm writing it down now. Thank you so much.'

As I put the telephone down someone began ringing the door bell. I went and opened the door. It was Priscilla. She marched past me into the sitting-room and immediately began to cry.

'Oh God, Priscilla, do stop.'

'You only want me to stop crying.'

'All right, I only want you to stop crying. *Stop crying.*'

She lay back in the big 'Hartbourne' armchair and in fact stopped. Her hair was in ugly disorder, the darkened parting zigzagging across her head. She lay back limply, gracelessly, with her legs spread and her mouth open. There was a hole in her stocking at the knee through which pink spotty flesh bulged in a little mound.

'Oh Priscilla, I am so sorry.'

'Yes. Be sorry. Bradley, I think you're right. I'd better go back to Roger.'

'Priscilla, you *can't* –'

'Why not? Have you changed your mind? You were saying so much I should go back. You said he was so unhappy and the house was so awful. He needs me, I suppose. And it is my home. Nowhere else is. Perhaps he'll be nicer to me now. Bradley, I think I'm going mad, I'm going out of my mind. What's it like when people go mad, does one know one's going mad?'

'Of course you aren't going mad.'

'I think I'll go to bed if you don't mind.'

'I'm sorry, I still haven't made up the spare bed.'

'Bradley, your cabinet looks different, something's gone. Where have you put the water buffalo lady?'

'The water buffalo lady?' I looked at the gaping empty space. 'Oh yes. I gave her away. I gave her to Julian Baffin.'

'Oh Bradley, how *could* you, she was *mine*, she was *mine*.'

Priscilla gave a little moan and the tears began to flow again. She started to fumble vainly in her bag looking for a handkerchief.

I remembered that technically speaking she was quite right. I had given the water buffalo lady to Priscilla years and years ago for her birthday, but finding the pretty thing once put away in a drawer had reappropriated it. 'Oh dear!' I felt the blush upon which Rachel had remarked.

'You couldn't even keep that for me.'

'I'll get it back.'

'I only let you take her because I knew I could visit her here. I liked visiting her here. She had her place here.'

'I'm terribly sorry –'

'I'll never get my jewels and now even she's gone, my last little thing gone.'

'Please, Priscilla, I really will –'

'You gave her to that wretched girl.'

'She asked for it. I *will* get it back, please don't worry. Now please go to bed and rest.'

'She was mine, you gave her to me.'

'I know, I know, I'll get it back, now come on, you can have my bed.'

Priscilla trailed into the bedroom. She got straight into the bed.

'Don't you want to undress?'

'What's the point. What's the point of anything. I'd be better dead.'

'Oh buck up, Priscilla. I'm glad you've come back though. Why did you leave the other place?'

'Arnold made a pass at me.'

'Oh!'

'I pushed him away and he turned nasty. He must have told Christian about it. They were downstairs laughing and laughing and laughing. They must have been laughing at me.'

'I don't suppose they were. They were just happy.'

'Well, I hated it, I hated it.'

'Was Arnold there in the afternoon?'

'Oh yes, he came straight back after you'd left, he was there nearly all day, they made a huge lunch downstairs, I could smell it, I didn't want any, and I heard them laughing all the time. They didn't want me, they left me alone nearly all day.'

'Poor Priscilla.'

'I can't stand that man. And I can't stand her either. They didn't really want me there at all, they didn't care about me really to help me, it was just part of a game, it was like a joke.'

'You're right there.'

'They were just playing with me and triumphing and showing off. I hate them. I feel half dead. I feel as if I'm sort of bleeding inwardly. Do you think I'm going mad?'

'No.'

'She said a doctor was coming but he didn't come. I feel terrible, I think I've got cancer. Everyone despises me, everyone knows what's happened to me. Bradley, could you ring up Roger?'

'Oh no, please –'

'I'll have to go back to Roger. I could see Dr Macey at home. Or else I'll kill myself. I think I'll kill myself. No one will care.'

'Priscilla, do get properly undressed. Or else get up and comb your hair. I can't bear to see you lying dressed in bed.'

'Oh what does it matter, what does it matter.'

The front door bell rang again. I ran to open it. Francis Marloe was outside, his little eyes screwed up with ingratiating humility. 'Oh Brad, you must forgive me for coming –'

'Come in,' I said. 'You offered to nurse my sister. Well, she's here and you're engaged.'

'Really? Oh goodie, goodie!'

'You can go in and nurse her now, she's in there. Can you give her a sedative?'

'I always carry –'

'All right, go on.' I picked up the telephone and dialled Rachel's number. 'Hello, Rachel.'

'Oh – Bradley –'

I knew at once from her voice that she was alone. A woman can put so much into the way she says your name.

'Rachel. Thanks for your sweet letter.'

'Bradley – can I see you – soon – at once – ?'

'Rachel, listen. Priscilla's come back and Francis Marloe is here. Listen. I gave Julian a water buffalo with a lady on it.'

'A what?'

'A little bronze thing.'

'Oh. Did you?'

'Yes. She asked for it, here, you remember.'

'Oh yes.'

'Well, it's really Priscilla's only I forgot and she wants it back. Could you get it off Julian, and bring it round, or send her? Tell her I'm very sorry –'

'She's out, but I'll find it. I'll bring it at once.'

'The place is full of people. We won't be –'

'Yes, yes. I'll come.'

'He cut down my magnolia tree,' Priscilla was saying. 'He said it shaded the flower bed. The garden was always *his* garden. The house was *his* house. Even the kitchen was *his* kitchen. I've given my whole *life* to that man. I haven't *got* anything else.'

'The human lot is sad and awful,' murmured Francis. 'We are demons to each other. Yes, demons.' He was looking pleased, pursing up his red lips and casting delighted coy glances at me with his little eyes.

'Priscilla, let me comb your hair.'

'No, I can't bear to be touched, I feel as if I were a leper, I feel my flesh is rotting, I'm sure I smell –'

'Priscilla, do take your skirt off, it must be getting so crumpled.'

'What does it matter, what does anything matter, oh I am so unhappy.'

'At least take your *shoes* off.'

'Sad and awful, sad and awful. Demons. Demons. Yes.'

'Priscilla, do try to relax, you're as rigid as a corpse.'

'I wish I was a corpse.'

'Do at least make an effort to be comfortable!'

'I gave him my life. I haven't got another one. A woman has nothing else.'

'Fruitless and bootless. Fruitless and bootless.'

'Oh I'm so *frightened* –'

'Priscilla, there's nothing to be frightened of. Oh God, you are getting me down!'

'Frightened.'

'Do please take your shoes off.'

The front door bell rang. I opened the door to Rachel and was making her a rueful face when I saw that Julian was standing just behind her.

Rachel was wearing a light green rather military-looking macintosh. She had her hands in her pockets and her face, directed at me, communicating privately, blazed with a sort of euphoric purpose. The immediate eye to eye communication showed me how far we had moved even since our last meeting. One does not usually look deep into people's eyes. There was a pleasant shock. Julian was wearing a tawny corduroy jacket and trousers and a brown and gold Indian scarf. She looked raffish, but had put on a self-consciously humble young person's expression, the kind of expression which says: I know I'm the youngest person and very inexperienced and unimportant but I shall do my best to be helpful and it is very kind of you to pay any attention to me at all. This attitude is of course a special kind of vanity. The young are self-satisfied really and utterly ruthless. I saw that she was carrying the water buffalo and a large bouquet of irises.

Rachel said meaningfully, 'Julian arrived back and insisted on bringing the thing along herself.'

Julian said, 'Of course I'm *very* glad to bring it back to Priscilla, of course it's hers and she must have it. I do so hope it will make her feel happier and better.'

I let them in and ushered them into the bedroom where Priscilla was still talking to Francis. 'He had no idea of equality between us, I suppose no man has, they all despise women –'

'Men are terrible, terrible –'

'Visitors, Priscilla!'

Priscilla, her shoes humping the edge of the quilt, was propped up on several pillows. Her eyes were red and swollen with crying, and her mouth was rectangular with complaint, like the mouth of a letter box.

Julian went directly and sat on the bed. She laid the irises down reverently beside Priscilla and then pushed the water buffalo lady along the coverlet, as if she was amusing a child, and thrust it up against Priscilla's blouse, in the hollow between her breasts. Priscilla, now knowing what the thing was, and looking terrified, gave a little cry of aversion. Julian then took it into her head to kiss her and made a dive at her cheek. Their two chins collided with a click.

I said soothingly, 'There you are, Priscilla. There's your water buffalo lady. She came back home to you after all.'

Julian had retreated to the bottom of the bed. She stared at Priscilla with a look of agonized and still rather self-conscious pity. She opened her lips and put her hands together as if praying. It looked as if she were begging Priscilla's pardon for being young and good-looking and innocent and unspoilt and having a future, while Priscilla was old and ugly and sinful and wrecked and had none. The contrast between them went through the room like a spasm of pain.

I felt the pain, I felt my sister's anguish, I said, '*And* lovely flowers for you, Priscilla. *Aren't* you a lucky girl.'

Priscilla murmured, 'I'm not a child. You needn't all be so – sorry for me. You needn't all stare at me – and treat me as if I were a –'

She fumbled for the water buffalo and for a moment it looked as if she were going to fondle it. Then she threw it from her across the room where it crashed against the wainscot. Her tears began again and she buried her face in the pillow. The irises fell to the floor. Francis, who had picked up the bronze, hid it within his hands and smiled. I motioned Rachel and Julian out of the room.

In the sitting-room Julian said, 'I'm terribly sorry.'

'It wasn't your fault,' I told her.

'It must be so awful to be like that.'

'You can't imagine,' I said, 'what it is to be like that. So don't bother to try.'

'I'm so awfully sorry for her.'

Rachel said, 'You run along now.'

Julian said, 'Oh I do wish – Ah well –' She went to the door. Then she said to me, 'Bradley, could I have just a word with you? Could you just walk with me to the corner. I won't keep you more than a moment.'

I gave a complicit wave to Rachel and followed the child out of the house. She walked confidently down the court and into Charlotte Street without looking round. The cold sun was shining brightly and I felt a great sense of relief at being suddenly out in the open among busy indifferent anonymous people under a blue clean sky.

We walked a few steps along the street and stopped beside a red telephone box. Julian now wore a rather jaunty boyish air. She was clearly feeling relieved too. Above her, behind her, I saw the Post Office Tower, and it was as if I myself were as high as the tower, so closely and so clearly could I see all its glittering silver details. I was tall and erect: so good was it for that moment to be outside the house, away from Priscilla's red eyes and duller hair, to be for a moment with someone who was young and good-looking and innocent and unspoilt and who had a future.

Julian said with a responsible air, 'Bradley, I'm very sorry I got that all wrong.'

'Nobody could have got it right. Real misery cuts off all paths to itself.'

'How well you put it! But a saintly person could have comforted her.'

'There aren't any, Julian. Anyway, you're too young to be a saint.'

'I know I'm stupidly young. Oh dear, old age is so awful, poor Priscilla. Look, Bradley, what I wanted to say was just thank you so much for that letter. I think it's the most wonderful letter that anybody ever wrote to me.'

'What letter?'

'That letter about art, about art and truth.'

'Oh that. Yes.'

'I regard you as my teacher.'

'Kind of you, but –'

'I want you to give me a reading list, a larger one.'

'Thank you for bringing the water buffalo back. I'll give you something else instead.'

'Oh will you, please? Anything will do, any little thing. I'd so like to have something from you, I think it would inspire me, something that's been with you a long time, something that you've handled a lot.'

I was rather touched by this. 'I'll look out something. And now I'd better –'

'Bradley, don't go. We hardly ever talk. Well, I know we can't now, but do let's meet again soon, I want to talk to you about *Hamlet*.'

'*Hamlet!* Oh all right, but –'

'I have to do it in my exam. And Bradley, I say, I did agree with that review you wrote about my father's work.'

'How did you see that review?'

'I saw my mother putting it away, and she looked so secretive –'

'That was very sly of you.'

'I know. I'll never become a saint, not even if I live to be as old as your sister. I do think my father should be told the truth for once, everyone has got into a sort of mindless habit of flattering him, he's an accepted writer and a literary figure and all that, and no one really looks at the stuff critically as they would if he were unknown, it's like a conspiracy –'

'I know. All the same I'm not going to publish it.'

'Why not? He ought to know the truth about himself. Everyone should.'

'So young people think.'

'And another thing, about Christian, my father says he's working Christian on your behalf –'

'What?'

'I don't know what he thinks he's at, but I'm sure you should go and see him and ask him. And if I were you I'd get away like you told them you were going to. Perhaps I could come and see you in Italy, I'd love that. Francis Marloe can look after Priscilla, I rather like him. I say, do you think Priscilla will go back to her husband? I'd rather die than do that if I was her.'

So much hard clarity all at once was a bit hard to react to. The young are so direct. I said, 'To answer your last question, I don't know. Thank you for the observations which preceded it.'

'I do love the way you talk, you're so precise, not like my father. He lives in a sort of rosy haze with Jesus and Mary and Buddha and Shiva and the Fisher King all chasing round and round dressed up as people in Chelsea.'

This was such a good description of Arnold's work that I laughed. 'I'm grateful for your advice, Julian.'

'I regard you as my *philosopher*.'

'Thank you for treating me as an equal.'

She looked up at me, not sure if this was a joke. 'Bradley, we will be friends, won't we, real friends?'

'What was the meaning of the air balloon?' I said.

'Oh, that was just a bit of exhibitionism.'

'I pursued it.'

'How lovely!'

'It escaped me.'

'I'm glad it got lost. I was very attached to it.'

'It was a sacrifice to the gods?'

'Yes. How did you know?'

'Mr Belling gave it to you.'

'Yes, how did –'

'I'm your philosopher.'

'I really loved that balloon. I did sometimes think of letting it go, it was a sort of nervous urge. But I didn't know I'd cut the string –'

'Until you saw your mother in the garden.'

'Until I saw you in the garden.'

'Well, Julian, now I must let you go, cut the string, your mother is waiting –'

'When can we talk about *Hamlet*?'

'I'll ring up –'

'Don't forget you're my guru.'

I turned back into the court. When I got to the sitting-room Rachel moved towards me and enveloped me with a spontaneous yet planned movement. We swayed together, nearly falling over her piled macintosh upon the floor, and then slumped down on to Hartbourne's armchair. She tried to nudge me back into the depths of the chair, her knee climbing over mine, but I kept her upright, holding her as if she were a large doll. 'Oh Rachel, let us not get into a muddle.'

'You cheated me out of those minutes. Whatever it is, we're in it. Christian just rang up.'

'About Priscilla?'

'Yes. I said Priscilla was staying here. She said –'

'I don't want to know.'

'Bradley, I want to tell you something and I want you to think about it. It's something I've discovered since I wrote you that letter. I don't really mind all that much about Christian and Arnold. I suddenly feel that it's sort of set me free. Do you understand, Bradley? Do you know what that means?'

'Rachel, I don't want a muddle. I've got to work and I've got to be alone, I'm just going to write a book I've been waiting all my life to write –'

'You look so Bradleian at this moment I could cry over you. We're not young and we're not fools. There'll be no muddle except for the one that Arnold makes. But a new world has come into being which is yours and mine. There will always be a place where we can be together. I need love, I need more people to love, I need you to love. Of course I want you to love me back, but even that's less important, and what we *do* isn't important at all. Just holding your hand is marvellous and makes my blood move again. Things are happening at last, I'm developing, I'm changing, think of all that's happened since yesterday. I've been dead for years and unhappy and terribly secretive. I thought I'd be loyal to *him* till the end of time, and of course I will be and of course I love him, that's not in question. But loving him seemed like being in a box, and now I'm out of the box. Do you know, I think quite accidentally we may have happened upon the key to perfect happiness. I suspect one can't be happy anyway until one's over forty. You'll see how little drama there'll be. Nothing will change except the deep things. I'm Arnold's wife forever. And you can go and write your book and be alone and whatever you want. But we'll each have a resource, we'll have each other, it will be an eternal bond, like a religious vow, it will save us, if only you will let me love you.'

'But Rachel – this will be a secret –?'

'No. Oh, everything's changed so since even a little while ago. We can live in the open, there's nothing to be secretive about. I feel free, I've been set free, like Julian's balloon, I'm sailing up above the world and looking down at it at last, it's like a mystical experience. We don't have to keep secrets. Arnold has somehow forged a new situation. I shall have friends at last, real friends, I shall go about the world, I shall have you. And Arnold will accept it, he'll have to, he might even learn humility, Bradley, he's our slave. I've got my will back at last. We've become gods. Don't you see?'

139

'Not quite,' I said.

'You do love me a bit, don't you?'

'Of course I do, I always have, but I can't exactly define –'

'Don't define! That's the point!'

'Rachel, I don't want to feel guilty. It would interfere with my work.'

'Oh Bradley, Bradley –' She began to laugh helplessly. Then she drew her knees up again and threw the weight of her torso forward against me. We toppled over backwards into the chair with her mainly on top. I felt her weight and saw her face close to mine, leering and anarchic with emotion, unfamiliar and undefended and touching, and I relaxed and felt her body relax too, falling like heavy liquid into the interstices of my own, falling like honey. Her wet mouth travelled across my cheek and settled upon my mouth, like the celestial snail closing the great gate. As blackness fell for a moment I saw the Post Office Tower, haloed with blue sky, aslant and looking in at the window. (This was impossible, actually, since the next house blocks any possible view of the tower.)

Francis Marloe came into the room, said 'Oh, sorry', and went out again. I slowly unwound from Rachel, not because of Francis (I minded him no more than if he had been a dog) but because I was feeling sexually excited and correspondingly alarmed. Guilt and fear, endemic in my blood, prickled, indistinguishable at that moment from desire, but prophetically announcing themselves. At the same time, I was deeply moved by Rachel's confidence in me. Perhaps the new world of which she had spoken really existed. Could I enter it without disloyalty? And at that moment it was not disloyalty to Arnold which concerned me most. I would have to think. I said, 'I shall have to think.'

'Of course you will. You are a chap who thinks.'

'Rachel –'

'I know. You're going to tell me to go.'

'Yes.'

'I'm going. See how docile I am. Don't be frightened by anything I said. *You* haven't got to do anything at all.'

'The unmoved mover.'

'I'll run. Can I see you tomorrow?'

'Rachel, I'm so terrified of being tied by anything just now. You'll think me so mean and spiritless – I do care and I'm very grateful – but I've got to write this book, I've got to, and I've got to be *worthy* to –'

'I do respect and admire you, Bradley. That's part of it. You're so much more serious about writing than Arnold is. Don't worry about tomorrow or about anything. I'll ring you. Don't get up. I want to leave you sitting there looking so thin and tall and solemn. Like a – like a – Inspector of Taxes. Just remember, freedom, a new world. Perhaps that's just what your book needs, what it's been waiting for. Oh you're such a schoolboy, such a puritan. It's time for you to grow up and be free. Good-bye, Bradley. May your own god bless you.'

She ran out. I stayed where I was, as she had told me to. I was greatly struck by what she had just said. I reflected upon it. Perhaps after all Rachel was the destined angel. How very *peculiar* it all was, and how brimful I was of sexual desire and how *unusual* this was.

I found that I was staring at the face of Francis Marloe. He had, I realized, been in the room for some time. He was making curious grimaces, closing up his eyes in a way that involved wrinkling his nose and dilating his nostrils. He looked, while doing this, as unselfconscious as an animal in the zoo. Perhaps he was shortsighted and was trying to focus on my face.

'Are you all right, Brad?'

'Yes, of course.'

'You've got a funny look.'

'What do you want?'

'Do you mind if I go out and have some lunch?'

'Lunch? I thought it was the evening.'

'It's after twelve. There's only baked beans in the kitchen. Do you mind –'

'Yes, yes, go.'

'I'll bring some light stuff in for Priscilla.'

'How is she?'

'She's asleep. Brad –'

'Yes?'

'Could you give me a pound?'

'Here.'

'Thanks. And, Brad –'

'What?'

'I'm afraid that bronze thing got broken. It won't stand up properly.'

He thrust the warm bronze into my hand and I put it down on the table. One of the water buffalo's legs was crumpled. It fell over lopsidedly. I stared at it. The lady smiled. She resembled Rachel. When I looked up Francis was gone.

I went softly into the bedroom. Priscilla was sleeping high up on her pillows, her mouth open and the neck of her blouse pulling at her throat. Relaxed in sleep, a softer less peevish dejection made her face look a little younger. Her breath made a soft regular sound like 'eschew . . . eschew . . .' She still had her shoes on. Very gently I undid the top button of her blouse. The neck fell open, revealing the badly soiled interior of the collar. I eased off her shoes, holding them by the long pointed heels, and pulled the blankets over her plump sweat-darkened feet. The breathing-murmur ceased, but she did not waken. I left the room.

I went into the spare room and lay down on the bed. I thought about my two recent encounters with Rachel and how calm and pleased I had felt after the first one, and how disturbed and excited I now felt after the second one. Was I going to 'fall in love' with Rachel? Should I even play with the idea, utter the words to myself? Was I upon the brink of some balls-up of catastrophic dimensions, some real disaster? Or was this perhaps in an unexpected form the opening itself of my long-awaited 'break-through', my passage into another world, into the presence of the god? Or was it just nothing, the ephemeral emotions of an unhappily married middle-aged woman, the transient embarrassment of an elderly puritan who had for a very long time had no adventures at all? Indeed it is true, I said to myself, it *is* a long time since I had an adventure of any sort. I tried to think soberly about Arnold. But quite soon I was conscious of nothing except a flaming sea of vague undirected physical desire.

It is customary in this age to attribute a comprehensive and quite unanalysed causality to the 'sexual urges'. These obscure forces, sometimes thought of as particular historical springs, sometimes as more general and universal destinies, are credited with the power to make of us, delinquents, neurotics, lunatics, fanatics, martyrs, heroes, saints, or more exceptionally, integrated fathers, fulfilled mothers, placid human animals, and the like. Vary the mixture, and there's nothing 'sex' cannot be said to explain, by cynics and pseudo-scientists such as Francis Marloe, whose views on these matters we are shortly to hear in detail. I am myself however no sort of Freudian and I feel it important at this stage of my 'explanation' or 'apologia', or whatever this malformed treatise may be said to be, to make this clear beyond the possibility of misunderstanding. I abominate such half-baked tosh. My own sense of the 'beyond', which heaven forbid anyone should confuse with anything 'scientific', is quite other.

I say this the more passionately because I think it just conceivable that an obtuse person might mistake some of my attitudes for something of that sort. Have I not just been speculating whether Rachel's sweet unexpected affections might not set free the talent which I had so long known of, believed in, and nursed in vain? What sort of picture of me has my reader received? I fear it must lack definition, since as I have never had any strong sense of my own identity, how can I characterize sharply that which I can scarcely apprehend? However my own delicacy cannot necessarily cozen judgement and may even provoke it. 'A frustrated fellow, no longer young, lacking confidence in himself as a man: of course, naturally, he feels that a good fuck would set him up, release his talents, in which incidentally he has given us no good reason to believe. He pretends he is thinking about his book, while really he is thinking about a woman's breasts. He pretends he is apprehensive about his moral uprightness, but really it is quite another sort of rectitude that is causing him anxiety.'

I would like to make it clear that any explanation along these lines is not only over-simplified and 'coarse', it is also entirely wide of the mark. In so far as I thought about the possibility of making love to Rachel (which by this time I did, but with a deliberately controlled vagueness) I did not, I was not such a shallow fool as to, imagine that a trivial sexual release would bring me the great freedom for which I had sought, nor had I in any way confused animal instinct with godhead. And yet, so complex are minds and so deeply intermingled are their faculties that one kind of change often images or prefigures another of, as it seems, a quite different sort. One perceives a subterranean current, one feels the grip of destiny, striking coincidences occur and the world is full of signs: such things are not necessarily senseless or symptoms of incipient paranoia. They can indeed be the shadows of a real and not yet apprehended metamorphosis. Coming events do cast shadows. Writers know that their books are often prophetic. One gratuitously imagines what is really going to happen. Though since these fates are as teasing as oracles, the happening may be curiously different from its prefiguration. As it was in this case.

It was not frivolous to connect my sense of an impending revelation with my anxiety about my work. If some great change was pending in my life this could not but be part of my development as an artist, since my development as an artist was my development as a man. Rachel might indeed be the messenger of the god. She was certainly confronting me with a challenge to which I would have to respond boldly or otherwise. It had often, when I thought most profoundly about it, occurred to me that *I was a bad artist because I was a coward.* Would now courage in life prefigure and even perhaps induce courage in art?

However, and this is just another way of putting my whole dilemma, the grandiose thinker of the above thoughts had to coexist in me with a timid conscientious person full of sensitive moral scruples and conventional fears. Arnold was someone to be reckoned with. If it should come to it, had I the nerve to provoke and to face Arnold's just anger? Christian was also

144

someone to be reckoned with. I had not even begun to *settle* the matter of Christian in my mind. She prowled in my consciousness. *I wanted to see her again.* I even felt about her bright new friendship with Arnold an emotion which strongly resembled jealousy. Her vital prying faintly wrinkled face appeared in my dreams. Was Rachel *strong* enough to protect me from such a menace? Perhaps this was what it was all about, my search for a protector.

I was much struck in retrospect by Rachel's cry about her husband: he is our slave. What an extraordinary thing to say and how much I had felt at the time that I understood it. Yet what did it mean? And could it be true without other awful things being true as well? Ought I not to *decide* that everything here was trivial? Was this very brooding not itself a sin? A 'feeling of destiny' can lead too into the most idiotic of servitudes. A dramatic sense of oneself is probably something which one ought never to have and which saints are entirely without. However not being a saint I could not effectively follow up that line of thought very far. The best I could do by way of penance was to try to think more carefully about Arnold: and even that induced a certain histrionic pleasure. I decided I must see Arnold soon and (but how?) talk frankly with him. Was he not the key figure? What did I really feel about him? The question was interesting. I decided, and the decision brought some peace, that I must talk at length with Arnold before seeing Rachel again.

So I reflected, attempting to achieve calm. But by about five o'clock of that same day I was in a frenzy again, an *obscure* frenzy. What was this, love, sex, art? I felt that strong urge to do something, to act, which often afflicts people in unanalysable dilemmas. If one can only act, depart, return, send a letter, one can ease the anxiety which is really fear of the future in the form of fear of the darkness of one's present desires: 'dread', such as philosophers speak of, which is not so much really an experience of void as the appalling sense that one is in the grip of some very strong but as yet undeclared motive. Under the influence of this feeling I put my review of Arnold's book into an envelope and posted it off to him. But first of all I read it carefully through.

Arnold Baffin's new book will delight his many admirers. It is, what readers often and innocently want, 'the mixture as before'. It tells of a stockbroker who, at the age of fifty, decides to become a monk. His course is thwarted by the sister of his abbot-to-be, an intense lady returned from the east, who attempts to convert the hero to Buddhism. These two indulge in very long discussions of religion. The climax comes when the abbot (a Christ figure he) is killed by an immense bronze crucifix which accidentally (or is it accidentally?) falls upon him while he is celebrating mass.

Such a novel is typical of Arnold Baffin's work. The blurb says: 'Baffin's new book succeeds in being both serious and funny. It is a profound study of comparative religion which is also as gripping as a thriller.' Is it ungenerous to carp? What the blurb claims is at least partly true. The book is quite serious and quite funny. (Most novels are.) It contains a vague and casual and I thought rather boring study of comparative religion. One misses the bite and savour of real thought, and there is not even the pretence of scholarship. (The author confuses Mahayana and Theravada and seems to imagine that Sufism is a form of Buddhism!) The story, when one can get at it, is certainly melo-dramatic, though I would be inclined to describe it as being 'a thriller' rather than as being 'like a thriller'. The sequence where the heroine, who has put herself into a trance to overcome the pain of a broken ankle, is nearly drowned by an overflowing reservoir is pure 'Cowboys and Indians'. Naturally the film rights have already been sold. However one must ask not just, is it amusing, is it exciting, but *is it a work of art*? And the answer to this question in this case, and I fear in the case of the rest of Mr Baffin's *œuvre*, is alas no.

Mr Baffin is a fluent writer. He is a prolific writer. It may indeed be this facility which is his worst enemy. It is a quality which can be mis-taken for imagination. And if the artist himself so mistakes it he is doomed. The writer who is facile needs, to become a writer of any merit, one quality above all; and that is courage: the courage to destroy, the courage to wait. Mr Baffin, judging by his output, is incapable of either destroying or waiting. Only genius can afford 'never to blot a line', and Mr Baffin is no genius. The power of imagination only condescends to lesser men if they are prepared to work, and work consists very often of simply refusing all formulations which have not achieved the density, the special state of *fusion*, which is the unmistakable mark of art . . .

And so on for another two thousand words. When I had folded this up and posted it I felt a solid, but still rather mysterious, sense of satisfaction. My action would at least precipitate a new phase in our relationship, too long stagnant. I even thought it possible that this careful assessment of his work might actually *do Arnold good*.

That evening Priscilla seemed to be a little bit better. She slept all the afternoon and woke up saying she was hungry. However she took only a little of the clear soup and chicken which Francis had prepared. Francis, my view of whom was undergoing modification, had taken over the kitchen. He came back with no change from my pound, but with a fairly plausible account of how he had spent it. He had also fetched a sleeping bag from his digs and said he would sleep in the sitting-room. He seemed humble and grateful. I was busy stifling my misgiving about the risk of so 'engaging' him. For I had decided, though I had not yet told Priscilla, that I would shortly depart for Patara leaving Francis in charge. That much of the future I had settled. How Rachel would fit in was yet unclear. I imagined myself writing her long emotional letters. I had also had a long and reassuring conversation with my doctor on the telephone. (About myself.)

For the moment, however, behold me sitting with Priscilla and Francis. A domestic interior. It is about ten o'clock in the evening and the curtains are drawn.

Priscilla was again wearing my pyjamas, the cuffs liberally turned back. She was drinking some hot chocolate which Francis had made for her. Francis and I were drinking sherry.

Francis was saying, 'Of course one's memories of childhood are so odd. Mine look all *dark*.'

'How funny,' said Priscilla, 'so do mine. It's as if it's always a rainy afternoon, that sort of light.'

I said, 'I suppose we think of the past as a tunnel. The present is lighted. Farther back it gets more shadowy.'

'Yet,' said Francis, 'we often recall the remote past with greater clarity. I can remember going to the synagogue with Christian –'

'To the *synagogue*?' I said.

Francis was sitting cross-legged in a small armchair, filling it completely, looking like an image in a niche. His floppy wide-legged trousers were stiff with dirt and grease near to the turn-ups. The strained knees thereof were threadbare and shiny and hinted at pink flesh beyond the veil. His hands, podgy and also very dirty, were folded in his lap in a complacent position which looked faintly oriental. He was smiling his red-lipped apologetic smile.

'Why, yes. We're Jewish. At least we're partly Jewish.'

'I don't mind your being Jewish. Only oddly enough no one ever told me!'

'Christian is sort of, well, not exactly ashamed of it – or she was. Our maternal grandparents were Jewish. The other grand-parents were goy.'

'Rather funny about Christian's name, isn't it?'

'Yes. Our mother was a Christian convert. At least, she was the slave of our father, an awful bully. You never met our parents, did you? He wouldn't have anything to do with our Jewish background. He made our mother break off relations. Calling Christian "Christian" was part of the campaign.'

'Yet you went to the synagogue?'

'Only once, we were quite small. Dad was ill and we stayed with the grandpops. They were very keen for us to go. At least for me to go. They didn't care what Christian did, she was a girl. And her name disgusted them, though they did call her by her other one.'

'Zoé. Yes. I remember her getting her initials C.Z.P. put on a rather expensive suitcase – God.'

'He killed my mother, I think.'

'Who did?'

'My father. She was supposed to have died after falling down-stairs. He was a very violent man. He beat me horribly.'

'Why did I never know – Ah well – The things that happen in marriage – murdering your wife, not knowing she's Jewish –'

'Christian got to know a lot of Jews in America , I think that made a difference –'

I stared at Francis. When you find out that somebody is Jewish they look different. I had only after many years of knowing him discovered that Hartbourne was a Jew. He im-mediately began to look much cleverer.

Priscilla was restive at being left out of the conversation. Her hands moved ceaselessly, creasing the sheet up into little fan-like shapes. Her face was thickly patchily powdered. She had combed her hair. Every now and then she sighed, making a woo-woo-woo sound with a palpitating lower lip.

'Do you remember hiding in the shop?' she said to me. 'We used to lie on the shelves under the counter and we'd think the counter was a boat and we were in our bunks and the boat was sailing? And when Mummy called us we'd just lie there ever so quietly – it was – oh it was exciting –'

'And the door with the curtain on it and we'd stand behind the curtain and when someone opened the door we'd move quietly back underneath the curtain.'

'And the things on the upper shelves that had been there for years. Big old dried-up inkpots and bits of china that had got chipped.'

'I often dream about the shop.'

'So do I. About once a week.'

'Isn't that odd. I always feel frightened, it's always a nightmare.'

'When I dream about it,' said Priscilla, 'it's always empty, huge and empty, a wooden shell, counter and shelves and boxes, all empty.'

'You know what the shop means, of course,' said Francis. 'The womb.'

'The empty womb,' said Priscilla. She made her woo-woo-woo sound and began to cry, hiding her eyes behind the large pendant sleeve of my pyjama jacket.

'Oh bosh,' I said.

'No, not empty. You're in it. You're remembering your life in the womb.'

'Rubbish! How could you remember that! And how could anyone ever prove it anyway? Now, Priscilla, do stop, it's time you went to sleep.'

'I've slept all day – I can't sleep now –'

'You will,' said Francis. 'There was a sleeping pill in your chocolate.'

'You're drugging me. Roger tried to poison me –'

149

I motioned Francis away and he left the room murmuring, 'Sorry, sorry, sorry.'

'Oh, whatever shall I do –'

'Go to sleep.'

'Bradley, you won't let them certify me, will you? Roger said once I was mad and he'd have me certified and shut up.'

'He ought to be certified and shut up.'

'Bradley, whatever will happen to me? I'll have to kill myself, there's nothing else to do. I can't go back to Roger, he was killing my mind, he was making me mad. He'd break things and say I'd done it and couldn't remember.'

'He's a very bad man.'

'No, I'm bad, so bad, I said such cruel things to him. I'm sure he went with girls. I found a handkerchief once. And I only use Kleenex.'

'Settle down, Priscilla. I'll do your pillows.'

'Hold my hand, Bradley.'

'I'm holding it!'

'Is wanting to kill yourself a sign of going mad?'

'No. Anyway, you don't want to kill yourself. You're just a bit depressed.'

'"Depressed"! Oh if you knew what it's like to be me. I feel as if I were made of old rags, a corpse made of old rags. Oh Bradley, don't leave me, I shall go mad in the night.'

'Do you remember when we were very small we used to tell Mummy to stay awake all night and look after us? And she'd say she would, and we'd be asleep the next moment and she'd creep away.'

'And the night-light. Bradley, do you think I could have a night-light?'

'I haven't got one and it's too late. I'll get one tomorrow. The lamp is just beside you, you can turn it on.'

'At Christian's there was a fanlight over the door and the light shone in from the corridor.'

'I'll leave the door ajar, you'll see the landing light.'

'I think I'd die of terror in the dark, my thoughts would kill me.'

'Look, Priscilla, I'm going into the country the day after

150

tomorrow for a while to work. You'll be all right here with Francis –'

'No, no, no, Bradley, you mustn't leave me, Roger might come –'

'He won't come, I *know* he won't –'

'I'd die of shame and fear if Roger came – Oh my life is so awful, it's just so awful to be me, you don't know what it's like waking every morning and finding the whole horror of being yourself still there. Bradley, you won't go away, will you, I haven't anybody but you.'

'All right, all right –'

'You promise you won't go, you promise – ?'

'I won't go – not yet –'

'Say "promise", say it, say the word –'

' "Promise".'

'My mind's all hazy.'

'That's sleep. Good night, there's a good girl. I'll leave the door ajar a little. Francis and I will be quite near.'

She protested still, but I left her and returned to the sitting-room. Only one lamp was lit and the room was ruddy and dusky. There were murmurs from the bedroom, then silence. I felt exhausted. It had been a long day.

'What's that vile smell?'

'It's the gas, Brad. I couldn't find the matches.'

Francis was sitting on the floor beside the glowing gas fire with the bottle of sherry. The level in the bottle had dropped considerably.

'Of course you can't remember being in the womb,' I told him. 'It's impossible.'

'It isn't impossible. You can.'

'Nonsense.'

'We can remember what it was like when we were in the womb and our parents had sex.'

'If you can believe that you can believe anything.'

'I'm sorry I upset Priscilla.'

'She keeps talking about suicide. They say if people talk about suicide they don't do it.'

'That's not so. I think she could.'

151

'Would you stay with her if I went away?'

'Of course, I'd only want board and lodging and a bit –.'

'I can't go though. Oh God.' I leaned back against one of the armchairs and closed my eyes. The calm image of Rachel rose before me like a tropical moon. I wanted to talk to Francis about myself, but I could only talk in riddles. I said, 'Priscilla's husband is in love with a young girl. They've been lovers for ages. He's so happy now he's got rid of Priscilla. He's going to marry the girl. I haven't told Priscilla, of course. Isn't falling in love odd? It can happen to anyone at any time.'

'So,' said Francis. 'Priscilla is in hell. Well, we all are. Life is torture, consciousness is torture. All our little devices are just morphia to stop us from screaming.'

'No, no,' I said, 'good things can happen. Like, well, like falling in love.'

'We're each of us screaming away in our own private padded cell.'

'Not at all. When one really loves somebody –'

'So you're in love,' said Francis.

'Certainly not!'

'With who? Well, I know actually and can tell you.'

'What you saw this morning –'

'Oh, I don't mean *her*.'

'Who then?'

'Arnold Baffin.'

'You mean I'm in love with – ? What perfectly obscene nonsense!'

'And he's in love with you. Why has he taken up with Christian, why have you taken up with Rachel?'

'I haven't –'

'Just to make the other one jealous. You're both unconsciously trying to bring about a new phase in your relationship. Why do you have nightmares about empty shops, why are you obsessed with the Post Office Tower, why do you keep worrying about smells –'

'It's Priscilla who dreams about empty shops, my shops are crammed –'

'Well, there you are!'

152

'And every man in London is obsessed with the Post Office Tower, and –'

'Have you never realized that you're a repressed homosexual?'

'Look,' I said, 'I'm grateful to you for your help with Priscilla. And don't misunderstand me, I am a completely tolerant man. I have no objection to homosexuality. Let others do as they please. But I just happen to be a completely normal heterosexual –'

'One must accept one's body, one must learn to relax. Your thing about smells is a guilt complex because of your repressed tendencies, you won't accept your body, it's a well-known neurosis –'

'I am not a neurotic!'

'You're trembling with nerves and sensibility –'

'Of course I am, I'm an artist!'

'You have to pretend to be an artist because of Arnold, you identify with him –'

'I discovered him!' I shouted. 'I was writing long before him, I was well known when he was in the cradle!'

'Sssh, you'll wake Priscilla. The emotion rubs off on the women, but the source of the emotion is you and Arnold, you're crazy about each other –'

'I am *not* homosexual, I am *not* neurotic, I *know* myself –'

'Oh all right,' said Francis, suddenly changing his posture and turning away from the fire. 'All right. Have it your own way.'

'You're just inventing this out of spite –'

'Yes, I'm just inventing it. I *am* neurotic and I *am* homosexual and I'm bloody unhappy about it. Of course you don't know yourself, lucky old you. I just know myself too bloody well.' He began to cry.

I have rarely seen a man crying and the sight inspires disgust and fear. Francis was whimpering loudly, producing suddenly a great many tears. I could see his fat reddened hands wet with them in the light of the gas fire.

'Oh, cut it out!'

'Sorry, Brad. I'm such a bloody sod – I've been so unhappy in my life – when they struck me off the register – I thought I'd

153

die of unhappiness – and I've never had a happy relationship, never – I crave for love, everybody does, it's as natural as pissing – and I've never had a bloody crumb of it – and I've given so much love to people – I really can love people, I can, I let them walk over me – but nobody's ever loved me, even my bloody parents didn't love me – and I haven't a home, I'll never have a home, everyone throws me out sooner or later, usually sooner. I'm a wanderer on the face of the earth – I thought Christian might be nice to me, Christ I'd sleep in the hallway – I just want to serve and help people and be good to everybody, only it always goes wrong somehow – I think about suicide all the time, every bloody day I want to die and stop this torture, but I go crawling on, shitting with misery and fear – I'm so Christ awful bloody lonely I could scream with it for hours on end –'

'Stop talking this foul rubbish!'

'All right, all right. Sorry, Brad. Forgive me. Please forgive me. I expect I just want to suffer. I'm a masochist. I must like pain or I wouldn't go on living, I'd have taken my bottle of sleeping pills years ago, I've thought of it often enough. Oh Christ, now you'll think I'm bad for Priscilla and boot me out –'

'Stop making that horrible noise, I can't bear it.'

'Forgive me, Brad. I'm just a –'

'Try to be a man, try to –'

'I can't – Oh God – it's just the bloody pain – I'm not like other people, my life just doesn't work, it never has – and now you'll throw me out, and, oh God, if you only knew –'

'I'm going to bed,' I said. 'Have you got your sleeping bag here –'

'Yes, it's –'

'Well, get into it and shut up.'

'I want to have a pee.'

'Good night!'

I left the room abruptly and went across the passage and listened outside Priscilla's door. At first I thought she was crying too. No, she was snoring. After a while it began to sound like Chaine-Stokes respiration. I went on into the spare room, where I had still not remembered to make up the bed, and lay down clothed with the light on. The house was gently creaking with the

154

footsteps of my upstairs neighbour, a shadowy youth called
Rigby who sold ties in Jermyn Street. The heavy stealthy steps
of another man followed him up. Whatever they did above they
fortunately did it quietly. There was another sound, a kind of
muffled knocking. It was my heart. I resolved to go and see
Rachel early on the following morning.

'Where's Arnold?'
'Gone to the library. So he says. And Julian's gone to a pop
festival.'
'I sent Arnold that review. Did he say anything?'
'I never see him reading his letters. He said nothing. Oh
Bradley, thank God you've come!'
I hugged Rachel in the hall, behind the stained glass of the
front door, beside the hall stand, next to the coloured print of
Mrs Siddons which I could see through the red haze of her hair.
Still imprinted on my eyes was the vision of her broad pale face
as she opened the door, crumpled into an ecstasy of relief. It is a
privilege to be received in this way. There are human beings who
have never been so welcomed. Something of Rachel's age, of her
being weary, no longer young, was visible too and touching.
'Look, come upstairs.'
'Rachel, I want to talk –'
'You can talk upstairs, I'm not going to eat you.'
She led me by the hand, and in a moment we were in the
bedroom where I had seen Rachel lying like a dead woman with
the sheet over her face. As we came in Rachel pulled the curtains
and then dragged the green silk counterpane off the bed.
'Now, Bradley, sit down beside me.'
We sat down rather awkwardly side by side and stared at each
other. I felt the roughness of the blankets under my limp hand.
The welcoming image had faded and I was rigid with confusion
and anxiety.
'I just want to touch you,' she said. And she did touch me

155

with her finger tips, lightly touching my face and neck and hair, as if I were a holy image.

'Rachel, we must know what we're doing, I don't want to behave badly.'

'Guilt would interfere with your work.' She lightly closed my eyes with her finger tips.

I jerked away from her. 'Rachel, you aren't just doing this to spite Arnold?'

'No. I think I started thinking about it, somehow out of self-defence, and then that awful time, you know, in this room, you were here, you were inside the barrier as it were, and I've known you so long, it's as if you had a special role, like a knight with a charge laid upon him, my knight, so necessary and precious, and I've always seen you a little as a wise man, a sort of hermit or ascetic –'

'And it always gives ladies particular pleasure to seduce ascetics.'

'Perhaps. Am I seducing you? Anyway, I've got to perform an act of will. Otherwise I shall die of humiliation or something. I feel it's a holy time.'

'This could be a pretty unholy idea.'

'It's your idea too, Bradley. Look where you are!'

'We are both conventional middle-aged people.'

'I'm not conventional.'

'Well, I am. I'm pre-permissive. And you are my best friend's wife. And one doesn't with one's best friend's wife –'

'What?'

'Start anything.'

'But it's started, it's here, the only question is what we do with it. Bradley, I'm afraid I do rather enjoy arguing with you.'

'You know where arguments like this end.'

'Between the sheets.'

'God, we might as well be eighteen.'

'Look, is all this because Arnold is having an affair with Christian? *Is* he having an affair with Christian?'

'I don't know and it no longer matters.'

'You still love Arnold, don't you?'

'Oh yes, yes, yes, but that doesn't matter either. He's just

156

played the tyrant for too long. I must have new love, I must have love outside the Arnold-cage –'

'I suppose women of your age –'

'Oh don't start that, Bradley.'

'I just mean, naturally one might want a change, but let's not do anything –'

'Bradley, with all your philosophy, surely you know that it doesn't really matter what we do.'

'It does. You were saying we wouldn't deceive Arnold. It matters if we do, it matters if we don't.'

'Are you afraid of Arnold?'

I reflected. 'Yes.'

'Well, you must stop being. Oh my dear, don't you see that this is somehow the point? I must see you unafraid. This is what being my knight is. That will really let me out. And it will do something great for you too. Why can't you write? Because you're all timid and repressed and tied up. I mean in a spiritual way.'

This was close to what I had thought myself. 'Then are we to love each other in a spiritual way?'

'Oh Bradley, look, enough of this argument, let's undress.'

All this time we had been sitting sideways facing each other, not touching, except when the tips of her fingers lightly tapped my face, then the lapels of my jacket, my shoulders and arms, as if she were putting a spell upon me.

Rachel turned away, and in a single quick contorted movement peeled off her blouse and brassière. Naked to the waist she now regarded me. This was a very different matter.

She was blushing and her face had become suddenly more tentative. She had very full round breasts with huge brown mandalas. The unclothed body wears a very different head from the clothed body. The blush extended down her neck and faded into the deep V of mottled sunburn which stained the flesh between her breasts. Her body had an air of unexhibited chasteness. I knew that this was a most unwonted gesture. And indeed it was a long time since I had seen a woman's breasts. I looked but did not move.

'Rachel,' I said. 'I am very touched and moved, but I really think this is most unwise.'

'Oh stop it.' She suddenly clasped my neck and rolled me

157

back on the bed. There was a pushing and a scrambling and in a moment she was entirely naked beside me. Her body was hot. She was panting and her lips were against my cheek. She said, 'Oh God.'

To lie fully clothed, with one's shoes on, beside a panting naked woman is not perhaps very gentlemanly. I raised myself on one elbow so that I could see her face. I did not want to be submerged by this warm gale. I looked intently down at her face. There was a grimace upon it which reminded me of certain Japanese pictures, a mingling of pain and joy, the eyes narrowed, the mouth squared. I touched her breasts, moving my hand over them very lightly, scrutinizing them with my touch. I looked down and regarded her body, which was plump, fleshy. I drew my hand down over her stomach which contracted under my fingers. I felt excited, stunned, but this was not quite desire. I seemed to be outside, seeing myself as in a picture, a fully dressed elderly man in a dark suit and a blue tie lying beside a pink naked pear-shaped lady.

'Bradley, undress.'

'Rachel,' I said, 'I am, as I say, moved. I am very grateful But I cannot make love to you. I don't mean I don't want to, I cannot. The machinery will not work.'

'Do you always – have – difficulties?'

' "Always" has no force here. I haven't been with a woman for many years. This privilege is unwonted and unexpected. And I cannot rise to it.'

'Undress. I just want to hold you.'

I felt appallingly cool, still seeing myself. I took off my shoes and socks, my trousers, pants and tie. Some sort of self-protective instinct made me retain my shirt, but I let Rachel with hot trembling fingers undo the buttons. As I lay in her arms quite still and physically chilled, and her hands moved timidly about me, I saw above the haze of her hair through a gap in the curtains the leaves of a tree moving about in the breeze, and I felt that I was in hell.

'You're icy cold, Bradley. You look as if you're going to cry. Don't worry, my darling, it doesn't matter.'

'It does matter.'

'It'll be better next time.'

There won't be a next time, I thought. And then I felt so overpoweringly sorry for Rachel that I really put my arms round her and drew her up against me. She gave an excited little sigh.

Then. 'Rachel! Hey, where are you?' Arnold's voice below.

Like spirits of the damned pricked by the devil's fork we bounded up. I began scrabbling for my clothes which had got into a tangle on the floor. They appeared to be plaited into each other. Rachel had pulled on her blouse and skirt with no underclothes. She leaned on me as my hands still plucked vainly at inside-out trousers and her breath tickled my ear. 'I'll take him down the garden.' Then she was gone, closing the door behind her. I heard voices below.

Of course it took me many minutes to get dressed. My trousers seemed to be knotted up at the ends and something tore as I eventually drove my foot through. I put on my shoes without socks, began to take them off again, then changed my mind. My braces were a tangled ball. I stuffed my tie and socks and pants into my pockets. When at last I tiptoed to the window and peered through the slit in the curtain I saw Arnold and Rachel down at the bottom of the garden. Rachel had got her hand on Arnold's shoulder and she was pointing to a plant. They looked pastoral.

I glided out and down the stairs and opened the front door. I pulled it to very softly after me but it would not close. I pulled it harder and it banged. I ran down the path and slipped upon some moss and came down with a crash. I staggered up and began to run away down the road.

At the end of the next road I was slowing down to a quick walk when, just as I rounded the corner, I cannoned straight into somebody. It was a girl dressed in a very short striped garment, she had bare legs and bare feet, she was Julian.

'So sorry. Oh Bradley, how super. You've been visiting the parents. What a shame I missed you. Are you going to the station? May I walk along with you?' She turned and we walked on together.

'I thought you were at a pop festival,' I said, breathless, frantic with emotion, but concealing it.

'I couldn't get on the train. At least I could have done if I didn't mind being squashed, but I do, I'm a bit of a claustrophobe.'

'So am I. Pop festivals are no places for us claustrophobes.' I was speaking calmly, but now I was thinking: she will tell Arnold that she met me.

'I suppose not. I've never been to one. Now you're going to lecture me about drugs, aren't you?'

'No. Do you want a lecture?'

'I wouldn't mind one from you. But I'd rather it was on *Hamlet*. Bradley, do you think Gertrude was in league with Claudius to kill the king?'

'No.'

'Do you think she was having an affair with Claudius before her husband died?'

'No.'

'Why not?'

'Too conventional,' I said. 'Not enough courage. It would have needed tremendous courage.'

'Claudius could have persuaded her, he was very powerful.'

'So was her husband.'

'We only see him through Hamlet's eyes.'

'No. The ghost was a real ghost.'

'How do you know?'

'I just know.'

'Then the king must have been an awful bore.'

'That's another point.'

'I think some women have a nervous urge to commit adultery, especially when they reach a certain age.'

'Possibly.'

'Do you think the king and Claudius ever liked each other?'

'There's a theory that they were in love. Gertrude killed her husband because he was having a love affair with Claudius. Hamlet knew of course. No wonder he was neurotic. There are lots of veiled references to buggery. "A mildewed ear blasting his wholesome brother." Ear is phallic and wholesome is a pun –'

'I say! Where can I read about it?'

'I'm teasing you. They haven't thought of that yet, even in Oxford.'

I was walking fast and Julian had to give a little run every now and then to keep up. She kept turning towards me as she did so, performing a sort of dance beside me. I looked down at her bare brown very dirty feet executing these hops, skips and jumps.

We had nearly reached the place where I had seen her in the twilight tearing up the love letters, when I had at first taken her for a boy. I said, 'How is Mr Belling?'

'Please, Bradley –'

'Sorry.'

'No, you know you can say anything you like to me. All that's over and done, thank God.'

'Your balloon didn't come sailing back to you? You didn't wake up one morning and find it tied to your window?'

'No!'

Her face, turning to mine, with the sun and shade dappling over it, looked very young, almost that of a child, with the anxious focused seriousness of the young. How very whole and unspoilt she seemed to me at that moment with her silly bare feet and her naïve preoccupations about her 'set book'. And I felt a regret which was really a sort of shame before her. What had I just been doing and why? A man's life should be simple and lived in the open. It is very much more rarely worth lying, even for hedonistic purposes, than is generally supposed in sophisticated circles. I felt entangled and ashamed, and frightened about it. At the same time, I felt a loving pity for Rachel, mingled with a memory of the smell of her warm plump body. Of course I would not abandon her in her need. Some formula must be available. But oh what infernally bad luck it was to have run into Julian. Could I conceivably ask her not to tell her father that she had met me? Could I think of some ingenious reason for this request which would not make me look unutterably shabby? I could not simply ask her and let her guess. The mean words would dirty me forever in her eyes. Yet was I not already soiled enough and did it really matter at all what Julian thought? It mattered very much more what Arnold knew.

At that moment Julian stopped outside the same shoe shop where I had parted from her on the previous occasion. 'Oh I adore those boots, the purple ones, I do wish they weren't so expensive!'

On impulse I said, 'I'll buy them for you.' I wanted to gain a little time to think of a suitably plausible way of asking her to keep quiet.

'Oh Bradley, you *can't*, they're *far* too much, how awfully kind of you but you *can't* –'

'Why not? It's ages since I gave you a present. I used to when you were little. Come on, be brave.'

'Oh Bradley, I'd love it, and you're so kind, which is even better than the boots, but I can't –'

'Why not?'

'I haven't any stockings. I can't try them on with my feet like this.'

'I see. I think incidentally that this barefoot cult is perfectly idiotic. Suppose you step on some glass?'

'I know. I think it's idiotic too, I won't do it again, it was just for the festival, it's terribly uncomfortable, my feet are hurting like anything already. Oh dear, what a shame though.'

'Can't you buy some stockings!'

'There isn't a shop near –'

I had been fumbling in my pocket looking for my wallet. Suddenly as my hand emerged a pile of stuff fell out on to the pavement: my tie, underpants and socks. My face blazing with guilt, I swooped on them.

'Oh look, what luck, I could wear your socks. It's so warm, I don't wonder you took them off. May I, would you mind?'

'Of course you can – they were clean this morning – but they're not exactly –'

'Oh nonsense, that really *is* conventional, not like not liking bare feet. Oh Bradley, I *do* want those boots, but it's such a lot of money. Suppose I were to pay you back when I –'

'No. Stop arguing. Here are the socks.'

She put them on immediately, balancing on each foot and holding on to my sleeve. We went into the shop.

It was cool and dim inside. Not at all like the nightmare shop that haunted my sister and myself; and not at all like the remembered interior of the womb either. More like the temple of some old unpassionate rather ascetic cult. The tiers of white containers (perhaps containing relics or votive gifts), the quiet darkly clad acolytes, the lowered voices, the rows of seats for meditation, the oddly shaped stools. The shoe horns.

We sat down side by side and Julian asked for her size. The black-clad girl began to ease the purple boot on over Julian's foot and my grey nylon sock. The high boot enveloped her leg and the zip fastener moved smoothly upward.

'It fits beautifully. May I try the other?' The other boot slid on.

Julian stood in front of the mirror and I looked at her reflection. The boots looked stunning on her. Above the knee there was a piece of bare thigh, only faintly brown, and then the blue and green and white striped hem of her brief dress.

Julian's delight was literally indescribable. Her face dissolved and glowed, she quite unconsciously clapped her hands, she rushed back to me and shook me by the shoulders and then rushed back to the mirror. Her innocent pleasure would have moved me very much upon a better occasion. Why had I thought of her as an image of vanity? This delight of the young animal in itself was something pure. I could not help smiling.

'Bradley, you do like them, they don't look absurd?'

'They look smashing.'

'I'm so pleased, oh you are so sweet – Thank you so much!'

'Thank you. Present-giving is a form of self-indulgence.' I asked for the bill.

Julian, exclaiming, began to pull off the boots. Then, still wearing my socks which she had rolled down to the ankles, and gloating over her prize, she crossed one leg over the other. As I looked at the purple boots lying on the floor, and then at Julian's feet and her legs, slightly browner below the knee and lightly furred with auburn hair, something very unexpected and extraordinary happened. The experience which I had sought in vain when I was holding Rachel naked in my arms came to me suddenly with a pang and a flurry: physical desire with its absurd, alarming, unmistakable symptoms, the anti-gravitational as-

piration of the male organ, one of the oddest and most unnerving things in nature. I felt an embarrassment so intense that it
transcended the concept altogether. I also felt a ridiculous un-
classifiable sort of glee. At the same time, the simple pleasure
which I might have had in buying the child a present was somehow released and for a moment I felt happy. I lifted my eyes.
Julian was beaming her gratitude at me. I laughed, because of
the physical sensation which her legs had inspired, and because
she knew nothing about it. To conceal our transports may be
painful sometimes, but it is also a privilege and may have its
funny side. I laughed, and Julian in childish delight over her
boots, laughed back.

'No, I won't wear them, it's too hot,' Julian was explaining
to the sales girl. 'Bradley, you are an angel. May I come and see
you soon and we'll talk about Shakespeare? I'm free any time –
Monday, Tuesday – how about Tuesday morning at your place
at eleven? Or whenever you like?'

'All right, all right.'

'And we'll talk seriously and look at the text in detail?' .

'Yes, yes.'

'Oh I am so pleased with the boots.'

When we parted company at the station and I looked into those
purely coloured blue eyes I could not bring myself to dim her
joy by asking her to lie, even though I had by then thought of a
fairly ingenious cock and bull story.

It was not until later that I remembered that she had gone away
still wearing my socks.

Somehow or other it was twelve noon. Returning eastward to
my flat I felt a good deal more sober, and I soon regretted my
'high-minded' failure to silence Julian. Out of some ridiculous
sense of dignity I had failed to take an absolutely essential precaution. When Julian blurted out about meeting me, what would
Arnold guess, what would Rachel devise, what would she confess?
Trying, and failing, to get the problem into focus I felt a guilty
excited painful feeling not unlike sexual desire. Julian must be
home by now. What was happening? Perhaps nothing. I felt an

intense need to telephone Rachel at once, but knew that this would be profitless. 'Knowing the worst' would have to wait a while.

I had left Charlotte Street about nine-thirty. Now, with a sudden distressed anxiety about Priscilla, I let myself into the flat, and knew at once that something odd had happened. The door of Priscilla's room was wide open. I rushed in. Priscilla was gone. Christian was lying on the bed reading a detective story.

'Where's Priscilla?'

'Don't take on, Brad. She's back at my place.'

Christian had taken off her shoes, which were lying on the bed. Her trim pearly-silk legs were neatly crossed. Legs are ageless.

'How dare you interfere!'

'I didn't, I just came to visit her, and she was so tearful and low and saying you were going to go away and leave her, so I said "Why not come back to me", and she said she wanted to, so I sent her and Francis off in a taxi.'

'My sister is not a sort of ping pong ball.'

'Don't be so cross, Brad. Now you can go away with a clear conscience.'

'I don't want to go away.'

'Well, Priscilla thought you did.'

'I'm going right away now to fetch her back.'

'Brad, don't be silly. It's far better for her to be at Notting Hill. I've asked a doctor to see her this afternoon. Do leave her in peace for a bit.'

'Did Arnold come to you this morning?'

'He came to see me. Why do you say "come to you" in that meaningful way? He was very upset by your spiteful review. Why ever did you send it to him? Why cause pain just like that? You wouldn't like it if someone did it to you.'

'Did he come to cry on your shoulder?'

'No. He came to discuss a business project.'

'Business?'

'Yes. We're going into business together. I have a lot of spare money, so has he. I didn't spend all my time in Illinois at the

165

Ladies' Guild. I helped Evans run his business. At the end I ran his business. I'm not going to idle around over here. I'm going into lingerie. And Arnold is going with me.'

'Why did you never tell me you were Jewish?'

'You were never interested enough to find out.'

'So you and Arnold are going to make money together. Has it occurred to you to wonder how Rachel might feel?'

'I'm not after Arnold. And I should have thought you were in rather a weak position to criticize people for being after people.'

'What do you mean?'

'Aren't you after Rachel?'

'What makes you imagine that?'

'Rachel told Arnold you were.'

'Rachel told Arnold I was after her?'

'Yes. They had a good laugh together.'

'You're lying,' I said. I left the room. Christian called after me, 'Brad, let's be friends, please.'

I had reached the front door with some general intention of going to fetch Priscilla and with a more immediate need to get away from Christian when the bell rang. I opened the door at once and there was Arnold.

He gave a well-prepared smile, apologetic, ironical, rueful.

I said, 'Your business partner is here.'

'So she told you?'

'Yes. You're going into lingerie. Come in.'

'Hello, honey,' said Christian behind me, welcoming Arnold. They trooped into the sitting-room, and after a moment's hesitation I followed them. Christian, who was still putting her shoes on, was wearing a handsome cotton dress of an exceptionally vivid shade of green. Of course I could see now that she was Jewish: that curvy clever mouth, that wily rounded off nose, those veiled snaky eyes. She was as handsome as her dress, a queen in Israel.

I said to Arnold, 'Did you know that she was Jewish?'

'Who? Christian? Of course. I found it out on our first meeting.'

'How?'

'I asked.'

166

'Brad thinks we're having some sort of romance,' said Christian.

'Look,' said Arnold, 'there's nothing between Chris and me except friendship. You've heard of that, haven't you?'

'It can't exist between a man and a woman,' I said. I had only just, with sudden clairvoyance, realized this for certain.

'It can if they're intelligent enough,' said Christian.

'Married people can't have friendships,' I said. 'If they do, they're faithless.'

'Don't worry about Rachel,' said Arnold.

'But I do, oddly enough. I felt very worried about her when I saw her the other day with a black eye you'd given her.'

'I didn't give her the black eye. It was accidental. I explained to you.'

'Before we continue,' I said, 'could you ask your business partner, who has just kidnapped my sister for the second time, to go away, please?'

'I'll go,' said Christian, 'but let me just make a little speech before I do. Gee, I'm sorry about all this. But honestly, Brad, you're living in a dream world. I was very emotionally disturbed when I got back here and I came straight to you. Some men would have been flattered. I may be over fifty but I'm not a has-been. I got three proposals of marriage on the boat, and all from people who didn't know I was rich. Anyway, what's wrong with being rich? It's a quality, it's attractive. Rich people are nicer, they're less nervy. I'm quite a proposition. And I came to you. As it happened I met Arnold and we talked and he asked a lot of questions, he was interested. That makes people friends and we are friends. But we haven't started up a love affair. Why should we? We're too intelligent. I'm not a little girl in a mini-skirt looking for kicks. I'm a damned clever woman who wants to have fun for the rest of her life, real fun, and happiness, not just emotional messes. I guess I can see into my motivation by now. I was years in deep analysis back in Illinois. I want friendships with men. I want to help people. Do you know that helping people is the way to be happy? And I'm curious. I want to know lots of people and see what makes them tick. I'm not going to get stuck in any hole and corner dramas. I'm going to live in the open. And right out in the open is where Arnold and I have been. You just haven't understood. I want to be friends with you, Brad. I want us to redeem the past by our friendship, like sort of redemptive love –'

I groaned.

'Don't mock me, I'm trying, I know I may seem ridiculous –'

'Not in the least,' I said.

'Women my age can easily look damn silly when they're being really serious, but in a way, because we've less to lose, we can be wiser too. And because we're women it's our part to sort of help people and spread a bit of warmth and caring around the place. I'm not trying to capture you or corner you or anything, I just want us to get to know each other again and maybe like each other. I had a damn lot of misery out there in Illinois, growing apart from poor old Evans and remembering how much you got to resent me and thought I was always getting at you, and maybe I was, I'm not defending myself. Only I'm a little wiser now and hopefully I'm a better person maybe. Why don't you and me get together and talk about the old days, talk about our marriage –'

'Which, I gather, you've already discussed with Arnold.'

'Well why not, naturally he was interested, and I was truthful. It's not a sacred subject, why shouldn't I talk about it. I guess you and I ought to try to be honest with each other and talk it all out of our systems. I know it would do me a power of good. Say, have you ever been analysed?'

'*Analysed!!* Certainly not!!'

'Well, don't be too sure it would be a waste of time. You seem pretty snarled up to me.'

'Ask your friend to go, would you?' I said to Arnold. He smiled.

'I'm going, I'm going, Brad. Look, don't answer me now, but think about this. I do beg you most humbly, and I *mean* humbly, to talk to me sometime soon, to talk properly, talk about the past, talk about what went wrong, and do it not because it will help you but because it will help me. That's all. Think it over. See you.'

She made for the door. I said, 'Wait a minute. To someone

who has spent years in deep analysis this may seem crude, but
I simply do not like you and I do not want to see you.'

'I know you're sort of scared –'

'I am not scared. I just happen to detest you. You are the sort
of insinuating power-mongering woman that I detest. I cannot
forgive you and I do not want to see you.'

'I guess this sort of classical love-hate –'

'Not love. Just hate. Be honest enough to see that, since you're
so intelligent. And another thing. When I have had my little
talk with Arnold I am coming over to fetch my sister, and after
that any connection between you and me ceases.'

'Look, Brad, there's something more I want to say after all. I
guess I see into your motivation –'

'Get out. Or do you want me to resort to violence?'

She laughed a red-tongued white-toothed laugh, merrily.
'Oh-ho, what would *that* mean, I wonder? You'd better watch
it, I learnt Karate at the Ladies' Guild. Well, I'm off. But think
over what I said. Why *choose* hatred? Why not choose happiness
and doing a little good to each other for a change? All right, all
right, I'm off, cheery-bye.'

She clacked out and I could hear her laughing as she pulled
the front door to behind her.

I turned on Arnold, 'I don't know what you think that
Rachel –'

'Bradley, I didn't hit Rachel purposely, I know it was my fault,
but it was accidental. Do you believe me?'

'No.' The feeling of sheer loving pity for Rachel came back to
me, no nonsense about legs, just pity, pity.

'Wait a bit, wait a bit. Rachel's all right. It's *you* who's getting
all steamed up about me and Christian. Of course you naturally
feel possessive about Christian –'

'I do not!'

'But there's really and truly nothing there except friendship.
Rachel understands that now. You're the one who has invented
this myth about me and your ex-wife. And you seem to be using
it as an excuse for pestering Rachel in a way I might resent if I
were more old-fashioned. Fortunately Rachel has a sense of
humour about it. She told me how you came round this morning,

accusing me and all ready to comfort her! Of course I know, we all know, that you're keen on Rachel. Your being so has been an aspect of our friendship. You were keen on both of us. And don't misunderstand me, Rachel hasn't just regarded this as a joke, she's been very touched. Any woman likes a suitor. But when you start pestering her with attentions and suggesting I'm unfaithful at the same time it becomes something that she rightly won't put up with. I don't know whether you really think that Chris and I are lovers, or whether you pretend to Rachel that you think it. But *she* certainly doesn't believe anything of the sort.'

Arnold was sitting with his legs straight out in front of him, balancing on the heels. A characteristic pose. His face wore the affectionate quizzical ironical expression which I had once liked so much.

I said, 'Let's have a drink.' I went to the walnut hanging cupboard.

It had not occured to me that Rachel might defend herself by sacrificing me. I had imagined, in the event of a revelation, a flaming row, mutual accusations, Rachel in tears. Or rather, to be more honest, I had not imagined anything in detail. When we do ill we anaesthetize our imagination. Doubtless this is, for most people, a prerequisite of doing ill, and indeed a part of it. I thought there would be trouble and I appeared on the evidence to have been so resigned to it that I had not even bothered to tell Julian a tale, or simplest of all, deny that I had been to the house. ('I was going to call, but suddenly I felt sick': anything would have been better than nothing.) But what the trouble would amount to my vision had shied from. So they always act, who prowl upon the confines of marriages, unconcerned with the real quality of the dramas enacted behind that mysterious and sacred barrier.

I should of course have been, and in a way I was, relieved that the thing had been done so quietly. But I was also upset and annoyed and felt an impulse to shatter Arnold's complacency by showing him Rachel's letter. The letter was in fact lying on the Pembroke table, where I could even see the corner of the envelope protruding from under some papers. Naturally such treachery was not to be seriously envisaged. It is the woman's privilege to save herself at the man's expense. And though, as it seemed at that moment, whatever had happened had been Rachel's idea and not mine, I had to take full responsibility and suffer the consequences. I decided at once that I must not discuss or dispute the proffered view, but just pass the matter off as coolly as possible. It then came to me: but is Arnold lying? He could well be lying about Christian. Was he also lying about Rachel? What had passed between Arnold and his wife and would I ever know it for certain?

I looked at Arnold and found him looking at me. He seemed hugely amused. He looked well and strong and young, his lean greasy brown face had the look of a keen undergraduate. He looked like a clever undergraduate teasing his tutor.

'Bradley, it's true what I said about me and Chris. I care far too much about my work to indulge in muddles. And Christian is rational too. In fact she's the most rational woman I've ever met. What a grip on life that woman has!'

'Having a grip on life would be quite compatible with having a fling with you, I daresay. Anyway, as you have politely indicated, it's not my business. I'm sorry if I offended Rachel. I certainly wasn't intending to pester her with attentions. I was depressed and she was sympathetic. I'll try to be less disorderly. Can we leave it at that?'

'I read your so-called review with some interest.'

'Why call it a so-called review? It's a review. I'm not going to publish it.'

'You oughtn't to have sent it to me.'

'True. And if it's any satisfaction to you I regret having done so. Could you just tear it up and forget it?'

'I've already torn it up. I thought I might be tempted to read it again. I can't forget it. Bradley, you know how vain and touchy we artists are.'

'I know from my own case.'

'I wasn't excluding you, for Christ's sake. We, you too. When one's attacked through one's work it goes straight into the heart. I don't mean that one bothers about journalists, I mean people one knows. They sometimes imagine that you can despise a man's

171

book and remain his friend. You can't. The offence is unforgivable.'

'So our friendship is at an end.'

'No. Because in rare cases one can overcome the offence by moving much closer to the other person. I think this is possible here. But there are one or two things I must say.'

'Go on.'

'You, and you aren't the only one, every critic tends to do this, speak as if you were addressing a person of invincible complacency, you speak as if the artist had never realized his faults at all. In fact most artists understand their own weaknesses far better than the critics do. Only naturally there is no place for the public parade of this knowledge. If one is prepared to publish a work one must let it speak for itself. It would be unthinkable to run along beside it whimpering "I know it's no good". One keeps one's mouth shut.'

'Quite.'

'I know I'm a second-rater.'

'Uh-hu.'

'I believe that the stuff has some merits or I wouldn't publish it. But I live, I *live*, with an absolutely continuous sense of failure. I am always defeated, always. Every book is the wreck of a perfect idea. The years pass and one has only one life. If one has a thing at all one must do it and keep on and on and on trying to do it better. And an aspect of this is that any artist has to *decide* how fast to work. I do not believe that I would improve if I wrote less. The only result of that would be that there would be less of whatever there is. And less of me. I could be wrong, but I judge this and stand by the judgement. Do you understand?'

'Yes.'

'Also I enjoy it. For me writing is a natural product of *joie de vivre*. Why not? Why shouldn't I be happy if I can?'

'Why indeed.'

'An alternative would be to do what you do. Finish nothing, publish nothing, nourish a continual grudge against the world, and live with an unrealized idea of perfection which makes you feel superior to those who try and fail.'

'How clearly you put it.'

'You're not angry with me?'

'Nope.'

'Bradley, don't be cross, our friendship has suffered because I'm successful and you aren't, I mean in a worldly way. I'm afraid that's true, isn't it?'

'Yep.'

'Believe me, I'm not trying to make you angry, I'm in a quite instinctive way defending myself against you. Unless I do this reasonably effectively I shall feel deep resentment and I don't want to feel deep resentment. Isn't that sound psychology?'

'No doubt.'

'Bradley, we simply mustn't be enemies. I don't only mean it would be nice not to be, I also mean it would be fatal to be. We could destroy each other. Bradley, do say something for God's sake.'

'You do like melodrama,' I said. 'I couldn't destroy anybody. I feel old and stupid. All I care about is getting my book written. There is a book, I care about that absolutely. The rest is rubble. I'm sorry I upset Rachel. I think I'd better leave London for a while. I need a change.'

'Oh stop being so self-absorbed and quiet. Shout and wave your arms about! Curse me, question me. We must come closer to each other, otherwise we're lost. Most friendships are a sort of frozen and undeveloping semi-hostility. We've got to fight if we're going to love. Don't be cold with me.'

I said, 'I don't believe you about you and Christian.'

'You're jealous.'

'You're wanting to make me shout and wave my arms, but I won't. Even if you aren't making love to Christian, your "friendship", as you call it, must hurt Rachel.'

'My marriage is a very strong organism. Any wife has moments of jealousy. But Rachel knows she's the only one. When you have slept beside a woman for years and years and years she becomes part of you, separation isn't possible. Wishful thinking outsiders often tend to under-estimate the strength of a marriage.'

'I daresay.'

'Bradley, let's meet again soon and talk properly, not about these nervy things, but about literature, like we used to. I'm going to write a critical reassessment of Meredith. I'd love to know what you think.'

'Meredith! Yes.'

'And I do wish you'd see Christian and talk to her properly. She needs that talk, it wasn't nonsense about redemption. It would be a *good* thing to. I *want* you to see her.'

'What Christian would call your motivation is dark to me.'

'Don't take refuge in irony. God, I seem to be wooing you all the time now! Wake up, you're going along in a trance. We've got to wrestle into some sort of decent directness with each other. It's worth it, isn't it?'

'Yes. Arnold, would you go now? Do you mind? Perhaps I'm getting old, but I can't stand emotional conversations the way I used to.'

'Write to me. We used to write to each other. Let's not rapidly mislay each other.'

'OK. I'm sorry.'

'I'm sorry too.'

'Oh fuck off, for Christ's sake.'

'Dear old Bradley, that's better! Good-bye then. Till soon.'

I waited till I heard Arnold's footsteps well out of the court, then I rang the Baffins' number. Julian answered. I put the phone down at once.

I thought: what did they say to Julian?

'He knows you're with me?'

'He sent me to you.'

It was the next morning and Rachel and I were sitting on a bench in Soho Square. The sun was shining and there was a dusty defeated smell of midsummer London: oily, grimy, spicy, melancholy and old. A number of tousled and rather elderly-looking pigeons stood around us, staring at us with their hard insentient eyes. Despairing people sat on other benches. The sky above Oxford Street was a sizzling unforgiving blue. Though it was still quite early in the morning I was sweating.

Rachel, who kept rubbing her eyes and drooping her head, seemed today like an ill person. Her listlessness and her puffy tired face reminded me of Priscilla. Her eyes were vague and she would not look at me. She was wearing a sleeveless cream-coloured dress. The back was unhooked, the zip not fully up, revealing lumpy vertebrae covered with reddish down. A satiny shoulder strap, not clean, had flopped down over the vaccination mark on her plump pallid upper arm. The armholes of the dress cut into the bulging flesh of the shoulder. Her gingery-red hair was in a tangle and her fingers constantly twisted and twisted it, pulling it down over her face with an instinctive gesture of concealment. I found her slightly sluttish unkempt shabbiness physically attractive. There was a kind of intimacy in it, and I felt much closer to her than when we had lain on the bed together. *That* now seemed like a bad dream. I felt too that confused pity for her which I had experienced and recognized earlier. It is not really true that pity is an inferior substitute for love, though many of its recipients feel this. Often it is love itself.

I said thoughtlessly, 'Poor Rachel, oh poor Rachel.'

She laughed with a kind of snarl, tugging at her hair. 'Yes. Poor old Rachel!'

'Sorry, I – Oh hell – You mean he actually said to you, "Go and see Bradley"?'

'Yes.'

'But what words *exactly* did he use? People who aren't writers never describe things *exactly*.'

'Oh I don't know. I can't remember.'

'Rachel, you must remember. It can't be more than two hours since –'

'Oh Bradley, don't *torture* me. I just feel I'm being cut and scratched and ridden over by everything, I feel I'm under the plough.'

'I know that feeling.'

'I don't think you do. Your life is perfectly OK. You're free. You've the money. You fuss about your work, but you can go away to the country or go abroad and meditate in some hotel. God, how I'd like to be alone in a hotel! It would be paradise!'

' "Fussing about one's work" can describe a kind of hell.'

'All that's superficial, what's the word I want, frivolous. It's all – what's the word –'

'Gratuitous.'

'It's not part of real life, of what's compulsory. My life is all compulsory. My child, my husband, compulsory. I'm caged.'

'I could do with a few more compulsory things in my life.'

'You don't know what you're saying, Bradley. You've got dignity. Solitary people can have dignity. A married woman has no dignity, no thoughts which really stand up separately. She's a subdivision of her husband's mind, and he can release misery into her consciousness whenever he pleases, like ink spreading into water.'

'Rachel, I think you're raving. A striking simile, but really I never heard such tosh.'

'Well, perhaps I'm just describing how it is with me and Arnold. I'm just a growth on him. I have no being of my own. I can't get at him. I couldn't do so even by killing myself. It would interest him, he'd have a theory about it. He'd soon find another woman he could get on with better, and they'd discuss my case.'

'Rachel, these are very base thoughts.'

'Bradley, how I adore your simplicity. As if I understood that language any more! You're talking to a toad, to an earthworm cut in two and wiggling.'

'Rachel, do stop, you're upsetting me.'

'You are a sensitive plant, aren't you? And to think that I saw you as a sort of knight errant!'

'Such a bedraggled one –'

'You were a *separate place*. Do you understand?'

'A wide plain where you could set up your tent? Or are these similes getting out of hand?'

'You mock everything.'

'I don't, it's just a habit of speech. Surely you know me by now.'

'Yes, yes, I do actually. Oh I've messed everything up. I've even spoilt *you*. Now Arnold has taken you over too. He cares for you far more than he cares for me. He takes everything.'

'Rachel. Listen. My relation to you is not part of my relation to Arnold.'

'Brave words. But it is now.'

'Please try to remember what he said this morning, you know, when he asked you –'

'Oh how you do hurt and annoy me! He said **something like,**

"Don't feel you can't go and see Bradley now. In fact you'd better go and see him straightaway. He'll be in a frenzy to see you and discuss our conversation. Why not go and see him and have a frank chat, have it all out. He'll talk more to you than to me. He's a bit sore and it'll do him good. Off you go." '

'God. Does he think you'll report your conversation with me to him?'

'Maybe.'

'And will you?'

'Maybe.'

'I don't understand this situation.'

'Ha ha.'

'Is Arnold having an affair with Christian?'

'You're in love with Christian.'

'Don't be silly. Is Arnold –'

'I don't know. I'm getting bored with that question. Possibly not in the strict sense. But I don't care. He acts as a free man, he always has. If he wants to see Christian he sees her. They're going into business together. I couldn't care less whether they get into bed together too.'

'Rachel, now do try to be more *precise*. Does Arnold really believe that I'm just pestering you against your will? Or did he invent that to smooth things over?'

'I don't know what he believes and I don't care.'

'Please try. Truth does matter. What exactly happened yesterday after Arnold arrived back and we were – Please describe the events in detail. I want a description beginning, "I ran down the stairs." '

'I ran down the stairs. Arnold had gone out on to the veranda. So I dodged through the kitchen and into the side passage and then came into the garden as if I'd just seen him, and I took him down to the end of the garden to show him something and I kept him there and that seemed all right. Then about half an hour later Julian turned up and said she'd met you and you'd said you'd been at our place.'

'I didn't say it. She assumed it and I didn't deny it.'

'Well, that comes to the same thing. Then Julian started to talk about the boots you'd bought her. I must say I was rather surprised. You are a cool customer. Anyway, Arnold raised his eyebrows, you know the way he does. But he said nothing while Julian was with us.'

'Wait a moment. Did Arnold notice that Julian was wearing my socks?'

'Ha! That's another thing. No, I don't think so. Julian went straight on upstairs to try the boots on. I didn't see her again till after Arnold had gone to see you. Then she explained about the socks. She thought it was a great joke.'

'You see, I just shoved them in my pocket and –'

'All right, I imagined it all. Here they are, by the way. I washed them. They're still a bit damp. I told Julian not to mention you to Arnold for a while. I said he was so cross about that review. So I trust the sock incident is closed.'

I thrust the limp grey objects away out of sight, a sordid reminder. 'Go on, what did Arnold say after Julian had gone?'

'He asked me why I hadn't said you'd been.'

'What did you say?'

'What could I say? I was completely taken by surprise. I laughed and said you'd annoyed me. I said you'd been rather emotional and I'd turned you out, and felt it would be kinder to you not to tell Arnold.'

'Couldn't you think of anything better than that?'

'No, I couldn't. While Julian was there I couldn't think, and then I just had to say something. My head was full of nothing but the truth. The best I could do was to tell half of it in a garbled form.'

'You could have invented a complete falsehood.'

'So could you. There was no need to let Julian assume you'd been visiting us.'

'I know, I know. Did Arnold believe you?'

'I'm not sure. He knows I'm a liar, he's often enough caught me in lies. He lies too. We accept each other as liars, most married couples do.'

'Oh Rachel, Rachel –'

'You grieve over such an imperfect world, do you? Anyway, he doesn't really mind. If I have some sort of thing on it eases his conscience and leaves him more free. And as long as he's in control and can bait you a bit it may even amuse him. He doesn't take you seriously as a threat to his marriage.'

178

'I see.'

'And of course he's quite right. There is no threat.'

'Isn't there?'

'No. You've just played along out of vague affection and pity.
Oh don't protest, I know. As for Arnold not taking you seriously
as a libertine, that can hardly surprise you. The funny thing is,
Arnold does care for you a lot.'

'Yes,' I said. 'And the funny thing is that though I think in
some ways he's a real four-letter man, I care for him a lot.'

'So you see, the real drama is between you and him. I'm just a
side issue as usual.'

'No, no.'

'When men talk together they naturally betray women, they
can't help it. There was a sort of contempt in Arnold pretending
to you that he believed what I said. Contempt for me and contempt for you. But he'd give you a wink all the same.'

'He never winked.'

'I don't mean a literal wink, you fool. Ah well, my little bid for
freedom didn't last long, did it. It ended in a sordid undignified
scrabbling little muddle and Arnold taking over once again. Oh
God, marriage is such an odd mixture of love and hate. I detest
and fear Arnold and there are moments when I could kill him.
Yet I love him too. If I didn't love him he wouldn't have this
awful power over me. And I admire him, I admire his work, I
think his books are marvellous.'

'Rachel, you can't!'

'And I think that review of yours was spiteful and stupid.'

'Well, well.'

'You're just eaten up with envy.'

'Let's not argue about that, Rachel, please.'

'I'm sorry. I feel so sort of broken. I feel resentment against
you for not having had the grace or luck to – rescue me or
defend me or something. I don't even know what I mean. It
isn't that I want to leave Arnold, I couldn't, I'd die. I just want a
little privacy, a little secrecy, a few things of my own which
aren't absolutely dyed and saturated with Arnold. But it seems
to be impossible. You and he are going to start up again –'

'What a phrase!'

'You'll be talking your intellectual talk together and I'll be outside washing up and hearing your voices going on and on and on. It'll be just like the old days.'

'Listen, dear Rachel,' I said. 'Why shouldn't you have a private place? I don't mean a love affair, neither of us has the temperament for that. I dare say I'm terribly repressed, not that I mind. And an affair would involve us in lies and would be wrong –'

'How simply you put it!'

'I don't want to encourage you to deceive your husband –'

'I'm not asking you to!'

'We've known each other for years without ever coming really close. Now we suddenly blunder up against each other and it goes all wrong. We might now recede again to the previous distance or even further. I suggest we don't. We can be *friends*. Arnold was holding forth about how he and Christian were friends –'

'Was he?'

'I suggest that you and I settle down to construct a friendship, nothing clandestine, all cheerful and above board –'

'*Cheerful?*'

'Why not? Why should life be sad?'

'I often wonder.'

'Why shouldn't we love each other a bit and make each other happier?'

'I like your "a bit". You're such a weights and measures man.'

'Let's try. I need you.'

'That's the best thing you've said yet.'

'Arnold could hardly object –'

'He'd love it. That's the trouble. Sometimes, Bradley, I wonder whether you have it in you at all to be a writer. You have such naïve views about human nature.'

'When you *will* something a simple formulation is often the best. Besides, morals is simple.'

'And we must be moral, mustn't we?'

'In the end, yes.'

'In the end. That's rich. Are you going to leave Priscilla with Christian?'

This took me aback. I said, 'For the present.' I could not decide what to do about Priscilla.

'Priscilla is a complete wreck. You've got her on your hands for life. I've had second thoughts about minding her, by the way. She'd drive me mad. Anyway, you'll leave her with Christian. And you'll go there to see her. And you'll start to talk with Christian and you'll start discussing how your marriage went wrong, just like Arnold said you ought to do. You don't realize how confident Arnold is that he's the centre of every complex. It's little people like you and me who are mean and envious and jealous. Arnold is so self-satisfied that he's really generous, it's real virtue. Yes, you'll come to Christian in the end. That's where the end is. Not morality but power. She's a very powerful woman. She's a great magnet. She's your fate. And the funny thing is that Arnold will regard it all as his doing. We are all his people. But you'll see. Christian is your fate.'

'Never!'

'You say "never", but you smile secretively all the same. You're fascinated by her too. So you see, our friendship can never be, Bradley. I'm just an appendage, you can't *separate* me, you'd have to focus your attention on me very hard to do that, and you won't. You'll be thinking about Christian and what's going to happen there. Even in our thing you were really just jealous about her and Arnold –'

'Rachel, you know this is all very unworthy and unkind and also completely dotty. I'm not a cold schemer. I'm just a muddler hoping to be forgiven, same as you.'

'A muddler hoping to be forgiven. That sounds humble and touching. It would possibly be very effective in one of your books. But I've got a kind of misery that makes me blind and deaf. You wouldn't understand. You live in the open with all of you spread out around you. I'm mangled in a machine. Even to say it's my own fault doesn't mean anything. However don't worry too much about me. I expect all married people are like this. It doesn't prevent me from enjoying cups of tea.'

'Rachel, we will be friends, you won't run away into remoteness? There's no need to be dignified with me.'

'You're so self-righteous, Bradley. You can't help it. You're a deeply censorious and self-righteous person. Still, you mean well, you're a nice chap. Maybe later I shall be glad you said these things.'

'Then it's a pact.'

'All right.' Then she said, 'You know there's a lot of fire in me. I'm not a wreck like poor old Priscilla. A lot of fire and power yet. Yes.'

'Of course –'

'You don't understand. I don't mean anything to do with simplicity and love. I don't even mean a will to survive. I mean *fire, fire*. What tortures. What kills. Ah well –'

'Rachel, look up. The sun's shining.'

'Don't be soppy.'

She threw her head back and suddenly got up and started off across the square like a machine which had just been quietly set in motion. I hurried after her and took her hand. Her arm remained stiff, but she turned to me with a grimacing smile such as women sometimes use, smiling through weariness and a self-indulgent desire to weep. As we neared Oxford Street the Post Office Tower came into view, very hard and clear, glittering, dangerous, martial and urbane.

'Oh look, Rachel.'

'What?'

'The tower.'

'Oh that. Bradley, don't come any farther. I'm going to the station.'

'When shall I see you?'

'Never, I expect. No, no. Ring up. Not tomorrow.'

'Rachel, you're sure Julian doesn't know anything about – anything?'

'Quite sure. And no one's likely to tell her! Whatever possessed you to buy her those expensive boots?'

'I wanted time to think of a plausible way of asking her to say she hadn't met me.'

'You don't seem to have employed the time very profitably.'

'No I – didn't.'

'Good-bye, Bradley. Thanks ever.'

Rachel left me. I saw her disappear into the crowd, her battered blue handbag swinging, the plump pale flesh on her upper arm oscillating a little, her hair tangled, her face dazed and tired. With an automatic hand she had scooped up the hanging shoulder strap. Then I saw her again, and again and again. Oxford Street was full of tired ageing women with dazed faces, pushing blindly against each other like a herd of animals. I ran across the road and northwards towards my flat.

I thought, I must get away, I must get away, I must get away. I thought, I'm glad Julian doesn't know about all *that*. I thought, maybe Priscilla really is better off at Notting Hill. I thought, perhaps I will go and see Christian after all.

As I now approach the first climax of my book let me pause, dear friend, and refresh myself once again with some direct converse with you.

Seen from the peace and seclusion of our present haven the events of these few days between the first appearance of Francis Marloe and my Soho Square conversation with Rachel must seem a tissue of absurdities. Obviously life is full of accidents. But to the intensity of this impression we contribute too by our anxiety and fear. Anxiety most of all characterizes the human animal. This is perhaps the most general name for all the vices at a certain mean level of their operation. It is a kind of cupidity, a kind of fear, a kind of envy, a kind of hate. Now, a favoured recluse, I can, as anxiety diminishes, measure both my freedom and my previous servitude. Fortunate are they who are even sufficiently aware of this problem to make the smallest efforts to check this dimming preoccupation. Perhaps without the circumstances of a dedicated life it is impossible to make more than the smallest efforts.

The natural tendency of the human soul is towards the protection of the ego. The Niagara-force of this tendency can be readily recognized by introspection, and its results are everywhere on public show. We desire to be richer, handsomer, cleverer, stronger, more adored and more apparently good than anyone else. I say 'apparently' because the average man while he covets real wealth, normally covets only apparent good. The burden of genuine goodness is instinctively appreciated as intolerable, and a desire for it would put out of focus the other and ordinary wishes by which one lives. Of course very occasionally and for an instant even the worst of men may wish for goodness. Anyone who is an artist can feel its magnetism. I use the word 'good' here as a veil. What it veils can be known, but not further named. Most of us are saved from finding self-destruction in a chaos of brutal childish egoism, not by the magnetism of that mystery, but by what is called grandly 'duty' and more accurately 'habit'. Happy is the civilization which can breed men accustomed from infancy to regard certain at least of the ego's natural activities as unthinkable. This training, which in happy circumstances can be of life-long efficacy, is however seen to be superficial when horror breaks in: in war, in concentration camps, in the awful privacy of family and marriage.

With these observations I introduce an analysis of my recent (as it were) conduct which I now wish, my dear, to deploy before you. As far as Rachel was concerned, I acted out a mixture of rather graceless motives. I think the turning point was her emotional letter. What dangerous machines letters are. Perhaps it is as well that they are going out of fashion. A letter can be endlessly reread and reinterpreted, it stirs imagination and fantasy, it persists, it is red-hot evidence. It was a long time since I had received anything resembling a love letter. And the very fact that it was a letter and not a *viva voce* statement gave it a sort of abstract power over me. We often make important moves in our life in a de-individualized condition. We feel suddenly that we are typifying something. This can be a source of inspiration and also a way of excusing ourselves. The intensity of Rachel's letter communicated self-importance, energy, the sense of a role.

I was also moved, as I have said, by the idea of scoring off Arnold, especially by excluding him from a secret. This instinct too can often lead us into ill-doing. To see someone as not 'in the know' is to see them as diminished. My resentment against Arnold was not entirely concerned with our general and time-honoured relationship. It derived also from the *shock* which I had received when I saw Rachel lying on her bed in the curtained room and covering over her face with the sheet. It was then that I conceived

184

the strong pity for her which, though it was contaminated as perhaps all pity is by feelings of superiority, represented the tiny fragment of moderately clean emotion in the amalgam. Did I believe Arnold when he said it was 'an accident'? Perhaps I did. Perhaps in the darkness of my egoistic pity, I was nevertheless beginning to see Rachel through Arnold's eyes, as a faintly hysterical and not always truthful middle-aged woman. When dealing with a married couple one can never be neutral. The hot magnetic power of each one's view of the other makes the spectator sway. Also of course I felt resentment against Rachel because she had made me behave in a ridiculous way. Those who occasion loss of dignity are hard to forgive.

Vanity and anxiety had involved me with Rachel, and envy (of Arnold) and pity and a sort of love and certainly an intermittent play of physical desire. As I have explained I was even then (and of course without any particular merit) generally indifferent to bodies. I experienced them involuntarily and without positively shuddering in crowded tube trains. But on the whole I did not now concern myself much with these integuments of the soul. Faces, of course, my friends had, but as far as I was concerned the rest could have been ectoplasm. I was not by nature a toucher or a starer. So it was that I was interested to find that I wanted to kiss Rachel, that I wanted, after a considerable interval, to kiss a particular woman. This was part of my excitement in the idea of playing a new role. In kissing her I had however no thought of proceeding further. What happened afterwards was just an unintentional muddle. Of course I did not disown it and I thought it might have serious consequences. And it did.

I suspect that I have not yet succeeded in purveying the peculiar quality of my relationship with Arnold. Perhaps I should attempt once more to describe this friendship. I was, as I said, his 'discoverer': at first his patron. He was my grateful protégé! I can even remember at that time thinking of him as a pet dog. (Arnold resembles a terrier.) There was even a 'dog' joke between us, now lost in history. Only gradually did the poison get in, deriving mainly from the fact of his (worldly) success and my (worldly) failure. (How hard it is for the best of us to be genuinely indifferent to the world!) Even then we were, to a remarkable extent, gentlemen about this. That is, I feigned a magnanimity and he a humility which in part we genuinely felt. Such feigning is essential in the lives of us imperfect beings. Our relationship in fact was never idle. It was obvious that we constantly thought about each other. He was (but of course not in Marloe's sense) the most important man in my life. And this was noteworthy, since I had many male acquaintances, persons in the office such as Hartbourne and Grey-Pelham, also literary and journalistic persons, lawyers and scholars, whom I do not mention simply because they were not actors in this particular drama. It would not be too strong to say that Arnold fascinated me. There was a sort of gritty not quite 'engaging' feel about our friendship which gave me a sense of reality. A conversation with him always stimulated a fresh flow of thought. Also, and paradoxically, he sometimes seemed like an emanation of myself, a strayed and alien *alter ego*. He made me laugh *deeply*. I liked his doggy greasy humorous face and pale ironical eyes. He was abrasive, always slightly teasing, always slightly aggressive, always slightly (I cannot avoid the word) flirting with me. He was well aware of being the disappointing and even slightly menacing son-figure. He played the role wittily and usually with kindness. Only in later years, and after several open quarrels, did I begin to feel him the cause of such pain that I had to withdraw a little. His remarks now all seemed 'needles'. And as my life passed on without the great visitation in which I believed, I became more and more irritated by Arnold's facile success.

Am I unjust to him as a writer? It is possible. Someone said that 'all contemporary writers are either our friends or our foes'; and it is certainly hard to be objective about the contemporary crew. The scandalized annoyance which I could not prevent myself from feeling when I saw one of Arnold's books favourably reviewed had of course its base sources. But I had also, at various times, tried quite hard to reflect rationally upon the value of Arnold's work. I think I objected to him most because he was such a *gabbler*. He wrote very carelessly of course. But the gabble was not just casual and slipshod, it was an aspect of what one might call his 'metaphysic'. Arnold was always trying, as it were, to take over the world by emptying himself over it like scented bath water. This wide catholic imperialism was quite alien to my own much more exacting idea of art as the condensing and refining of a conception almost to nothing. I have always felt that art is an aspect of the good life, and so correspondingly difficult, whereas Arnold, I regret to say, regarded art as 'fun'. This was certainly the case in spite of the sort of 'mythological' pomposity which has made some critics take him seriously as a 'thinker'. Arnold never really *worked* on his 'symbolism'. He saw significance everywhere, everything was vaguely part of his myth. He liked and accepted everything. And although he was 'in life' a clever man and an intellectual and a tough arguer, 'in art' he went soft and failed to make distinctions. (The making of distinctions is the centre of art, as it is the centre of philosophy.) The cause of his failure was, in part at least, a kind of enthusiastic garrulous religiosity. He was in a somewhat shadowy way a disciple of Jung. (I mean no special disrespect to that theorist, whose work I just happen to find unreadable.) For Arnold, the artist, life was simply one big gorgeous metaphor. I think perhaps I will forbear to characterize him further here, as I can already hear the venom creeping into my tone. My friend P. has taught me much about the absolute spiritual necessity of silence. As an artist I knew of this in humbler ways and instinctively at an earlier time and my knowledge informed a kind of contempt which I always felt for Arnold.

My relations with my sister were much simpler and also much more complex. Sibling relationships are usually complicated and yet also so taken for granted that unsophisticated participants are often unconscious of being caught in such a spider's web of love and hate, rivalry and solidarity. As I explained earlier, I identified myself with Priscilla. My horrified distress at Roger's happiness was a reaction of self-defence. I was affronted by the impunity with which this husband had exchanged his elderly wife for a young girl. That is every husband's dream, no doubt: only in this context I was the elderly wife. Indeed in an odd way my sympathy for Rachel derived from my sympathy for Priscilla, despite the fact that Rachel was such a different case, so much tougher, more intelligent, more interesting and more attractive. On the other hand, Priscilla irritated me to the point of ruthlessness. In general I cannot stand weepers and whimperers. (I was moved when Rachel spoke of 'fire'. Affliction should strike sparks, not induce self-pity.) The silence which I have always valued has included a determination to keep the mouth shut under blows. Nor do I encourage tearful confidences. The readers will have seen how promptly I shut Francis Marloe up. This was another point on which I differed from Arnold. Arnold, even affirming that this was part of his 'job' as a writer, constantly encouraged people quite indiscriminately to tell him their troubles. (He exercised this talent on Christian the first time they met.) This had of course more to do with malicious curiosity than with compassion and often led to misunderstandings and subsequent bitterness. Arnold was a great 'leader up the garden' of persons of both sexes. I despised this. To return however to Priscilla, I felt very troubled by her afflictions and yet very unwilling to be involved. I have always felt that a realistic sense of one's limitations as a helper is an essential part of being a good neighbour. (Arnold entirely lacked this sense.) I was not going to let Priscilla interfere with my work. And I was determined not to view her, as Rachel did, as 'done for'. People are not so easily destroyed.

Christian's take-over of Priscilla, though utterly 'obscene', was already becoming more of a problem than an outrage. I was more inclined to let the situation ride. Christian would get no profit from her hostage. But I did not think that she would therefore abandon or 'drop' Priscilla. Perhaps here again I had been influenced by Arnold. In some people sheer *will* is a substitute for morality. What Arnold called 'grip'. When she was my wife Christian had employed this will in an attempt to invade and conquer me. A lesser man would have surrendered in exchange for a marriage which might even have been a happy one. One can see many men who live happily, possessed and run (indeed *manned*, the way a ship is manned) by women of tremendous will. What saved me from Christian was art. My artist's soul rejected this massive invasion. (It was like an invasion of viruses.) The hatred for Christian which I had nursed all these years was a natural product of my struggle for survival and its original spearhead. To overthrow a tyrant, whether in public or in private, one must learn to hate. Now however, no longer really threatened and with an incentive to be more objective, I could see how well, how *intelligently*, Christian had organized herself. Perhaps learning that she was Jewish had altered my vision. I felt almost ready for a new kind of contest in which I would defeat her casually. The final exorcism would be a display of cool amused indifference. But these were shadowy thoughts. The main point was that now I felt ready to trust Christian to be business-like and reliable about Priscilla, since I felt like being neither.

In the light of later events I was disposed to regard almost everything I did during the period so far narrated as blame-worthy. I daresay human wickedness is sometimes the product of a sort of conscious leeringly evil intent. (I used to think of Christian as evil in this way, though later this seemed at least exaggerated.) But more usually it is the product of a semi-deliberate inattention, a sort of swooning relationship to time. As I said at the beginning, any artist knows that the space between the stage where the work is too unformed to have committed itself and the stage where it is too late to improve it can be as thin as a needle. Genius perhaps consists in opening out this needle-like area until it covers almost the whole of the working time. Most artists, through sheer idleness, weariness, inability to attend, drift again and again and again from the one stage straight into the other, in spite of good resolutions and the hope with which each new work begins. This is of course a moral problem, since all art is the struggle to be, in a particular sort of way, virtuous. There is an analogous transition in the everyday proceedings of the moral agent. We ignore what we are doing until it is too late to alter it. We never allow ourselves quite to focus upon moments of decision; and these are often in fact hard to find even if we are searching for them. We allow the vague pleasure-seeking annoyance-avoiding tide of our being to hurry us onward until the moment when we announce that we can no other. There is thus an eternal discrepancy between the self-knowledge which we gain by observing ourselves objectively and the self-awareness which we have of ourselves subjectively: a discrepancy which probably makes it impossible for us ever to arrive at the truth. Our self-knowledge is too abstract, our self-

189

awareness is too intimate and swoony and dazed. Perhaps some kind of integrity of the imagination, a sort of moral genius, could verify the scene, producing minute sensibility and control of the moment as a function of some much larger consciousness. Can there be a *natural*, as it were Shakespearean felicity in the moral life? Or are Eastern sages right to set as a task to their disciples the gradual total destruction of the dreaming ego?

In fact the problem remains unclarified because no philosopher and hardly any novelist has ever managed to explain what that weird stuff, human consciousness, is really made of. Body, external objects, darty memories, warm fantasies, other minds, guilt, fear, hesitation, lies, glees, doles, breathtaking pains, a thousand things which words can only fumble at, coexist, many fused together in a single unit of consciousness. How human responsibility is possible at all could well puzzle an extra-galactic student of this weird method of proceeding through time. How can such a thing be tinkered with and improved, how can one change the quality of consciousness? Around 'will' it flows like water round a stone. Could constant prayer avail? Such prayer would have to be the continuous insertion into each of these multifarious units of one recurring pellet of anti-egoistic concern. (This has, of course, nothing to do with 'God'.) There is so much grit in the bottom of the container, almost all our natural preoccupations are low ones, and in most cases the rag-bag of consciousness is only unified by the experience of great art or of intense love. Neither of these was relevant to my messy and absent-minded goings-on.

I have perhaps not even now sufficiently emphasized how much I was dominated during this time by an increasingly powerful sense of the imminence in my life of a great work of art. *This* pellet irradiated each of the 'frames' of my awareness in such a way that even when I was, for example, listening to Rachel's voice or looking at Priscilla's face, I was also thinking: the time has come. At least I was not thinking these words, I was not thinking anything in words: I was simply aware of a great dark wonderful *something* nearby in the future, magnetically connected with me: connected with my mind, connected with my body, which sometimes literally shook or swayed under that tremendous and authoritative *pull*. What did I imagine that the book would be like? I did not know. But I intuitively grasped both its being and its excellence. An artist in a state of power has a serene relationship to time. Fruition is simply a matter of waiting. The work announces itself, emerges often quite whole, when the moment comes, if the apprenticeship has been correct. (As the sage looks for years at the bamboo branch, then draws it quickly and without effort.) I felt that all I needed was solitude.

What the fruits of solitude are, my dearest friend, I know now very much better and more profoundly than I did then: because of my experiences and because of your wisdom. The person that I was then seems captive and blind. My instincts were true and my sense of direction was sound. Only the way turned out to be very much longer than I expected.

The following morning, that is the day after my dispiriting conversation with Rachel, I started to pack my suitcase again. I had had a disturbed night, the bed seeming to burn under me. I had decided to depart for the country. I had also decided to go to Notting Hill and see Priscilla and have a cool business-like talk with Christian. I would not attempt to see Rachel or Arnold again before I went. I would write them both long letters from my retreat. I rather looked forward to writing these letters: affectionate and steadying to Rachel, rueful and ironical to Arnold. I felt that if I could only reflect for a while I could sort out that situation, defend myself and satisfy them. For Rachel, an *amitié amoureuse*, for Arnold a fight.

The mind, so constantly busy with its own welfare, is always sensitively filing and sorting the ways in which self-respect (vanity) has been damaged. In doing so it is at the same time industriously discovering methods of making good the damage. I had felt chagrined and ashamed because Rachel regarded me as a failed muddler, and Arnold was posing as having, in some unspecified sense, 'found me out'. (And, what was worse, 'forgiven me'!) Reflection on what had happened was already re-painting this picture. I was quite strong enough to 'hold' them both, to comfort Rachel and to 'play' Arnold. The sense of challenge involved already made my bruised vanity cease a little to droop.

I would console Rachel with *innocent* love. This resolution and the ring of the good word made me feel, on that momentous morning, a better man. But what rather preoccupied my thoughts was the image of Christian: her image rather than any definite proposition about her. These images which float in the mind's cave (and whatever the philosophers may say the mind *is* a dark cave full of drifting beings) are of course not neutral apparitions but already saturated with judgement, lurid with it. I still felt in waves my old poisonous hatred of this bully. I also felt the not very edifying desire before-mentioned to erase, by a show of indifference, the undignified impression which I had made. I had displayed too much emotion. Now instead I must stare with cold curiosity. As I practised staring at her charged and glowing image it seemed to be dissolving and changing before my eyes. Was I beginning to *remember* at last that I had once loved her?

I shook myself and closed the suitcase and snapped the catch to. If I could only *get started* on the book. A day of solitude, and I could write down something, a precious pregnant something like a growing seed. With that for company I could make terms with the past. And I was not now thinking of reconciliations or even of exorcisms, but just of the shedding of the load of sheer biting *remorse* which I had carried with me through my life.

The telephone rang.

'Hartbourne here.'

'Oh hello.'

'Why didn't you come to the party?'

'What party?'

'The office party. We specially put it on a day that suited you.'

'Oh God. Sorry.'

'Everyone was very disappointed.'

'I'm terribly sorry.'

'So were we.'

'I – er – hope it was a good party all the same –'

'In spite of your absence it was an excellent party.'

192

'Who was there?'

'All the old gang. Bingley and Grey-Pelham and Dyson and Randolph and Matheson and Hadley-Smith and –'

'Did Mrs Grey-Pelham come?'

'No.'

'Oh good. Hartbourne, I am sorry.'

'Never mind, Pearson. Can we make a lunch date?'

'I'm leaving town.'

'Ah well. Wish I could get away. Send me a postcard.'

'I say, I am sorry –'

'Not at all.'

I put the telephone down. I felt the hand of destiny heavy upon me. Even the air was thickening as if it were full of incense or rich pollen. I looked at my watch. It was time to go to Notting Hill. I stood there in my little sitting-room and looked at the buffalo lady who was lying on her side in the lacquered display cabinet. I had not dared to try to straighten out the buffalo's crumpled leg for fear of snapping the delicate bronze. I looked where a line of sloping sun had made a flying buttress against the wall outside, making the grime stand out in lacy relief, outlining the bricks. The room, the wall, trembled with precision, as if the inanimate world were about to utter a word.

Just then the door bell rang. I went to the door. It was Julian Baffin. I looked at her blankly.

'Bradley, you've forgotten! I've come for my *Hamlet* tutorial.'

'I hadn't forgotten,' I said with a silent curse. 'Come in.'

She marched before me into the sitting-room and pulled the two lyre-back chairs up to the marquetry table. She sat down and opened her book before her. She was wearing the purple boots, pink tights, and a short mauve shirt-like dress. She had combed or tossed the mass of browny gold hair back into a great coxcomb behind her head. Her face looked shiny, summery, healthy.

'You're wearing the boots,' I said.

'Yes. It's a bit hot for them, but I wanted to show them off to you. I'm so cheered up and grateful. Are you sure you don't mind discussing Shakespeare? You look as if you were going somewhere. Did you really remember I was coming?'

'Yes, of course.'

'Oh Bradley, you are so good for my nerves. Everybody irritates me like mad except you. I didn't bring two texts. I suppose you've got one?'

'Yes. Here.'

I sat down opposite to her. She sat side saddle on her chair, the boots side by side, very much on display. I sat astride on mine, gripping it with my knees. I opened my copy of Shakespeare in front of me on the table. Julian laughed.

'Why are you laughing?'

'You're so matter-of-fact. I'm sure you weren't expecting me. You'd forgotten I existed. Now you're just like a school teacher.'

'Perhaps you are good for my nerves too.'

'Bradley, this is fun.'

'Nothing's happened yet. It may not be fun. What do you want to do?'

'I'll ask questions and you answer them.'

'Go on then.'

'I've got a whole list of questions, look.'

'I've answered that one already.'

'About Gertrude and – Yes, but I'm not convinced.'

'You're going to waste my time with these questions and then not believe my answers?'

'Well, it can be a starting point for a discussion.'

'Oh, we're to have a discussion too, are we?'

'If you have time. I know I'm lucky to get *any* of your time, you're so busy.'

'I'm not busy at all. I have absolutely nothing to do.'

'I thought you were writing a book.'

'Lies.'

'I know you're teasing again.'

'Well, come on, I haven't got all day.'

'Why did Hamlet delay killing Claudius?'

'Because he was a dreamy conscientious young intellectual who wasn't likely to commit a murder out of hand because he had the impression that he had seen a ghost. Next question.'

'But, Bradley, you yourself said the ghost was real.'

'I know the ghost is real, but Hamlet didn't.'

'Oh. But there must have been another deeper reason why he delayed, isn't that the point of the play?'

'I didn't say there wasn't another reason.'

'What is it?'

'He identifies Claudius with his father.'

'Oh really? So that makes him hesitate because he loves his father and so can't touch Claudius?'

'No. He hates his father.'

'Well, wouldn't that make him murder Claudius at once?'

'No. After all he didn't murder his father.'

'Well, I don't see how identifying Claudius with his father makes him not kill Claudius.'

'He doesn't enjoy hating his father. It makes him feel guilty.'

'So he's paralysed with guilt? But he never says so. He's fearfully priggish and censorious. Think how nasty he is to Ophelia.'

'That's part of the same thing.'

'How do you mean?'

'He identifies Ophelia with his mother.'

'But I thought he loved his mother.'

'That's the point.'

'How do you mean that's the point?'

'He condemns his mother for committing adultery with his father.'

'Wait a minute, Bradley, I'm getting mixed.'

'Claudius is just a continuation of his brother on the unconscious level.'

'But you can't commit adultery with your husband, it isn't logical.'

'The unconscious mind knows nothing of logic.'

'You mean Hamlet is jealous, you mean he's in love with his mother?'

'That is the general idea. A tediously familiar one I should have thought.'

'Oh *that*.'

'That.'

'I see. But I still don't see why he should think Ophelia is Gertrude, they're not a bit alike.'

'The unconscious mind delights in identifying people with each other. It has only a few characters to play with.'

'So lots of actors have to play the same part?'

'Yes.'

'I don't think I believe in the unconscious mind.'

'Excellent girl.'

'Bradley, you're teasing again.'

'Not at all.'

'Why couldn't Ophelia save Hamlet? That's another of my questions actually.'

'Because, my dear Julian, pure ignorant young girls cannot save complicated neurotic over-educated older men from disaster, however much they kid themselves that they can.'

'I know that I'm ignorant, and I can't deny that I'm young, but I do *not* identify myself with Ophelia!'

'Of course not. You identify yourself with Hamlet. Everyone does.'

'I suppose one always identifies with the hero.'

'Not in great works of literature. Do you identify with Macbeth or Lear?'

'No, well, not like that –'

'Or with Achilles or Agamemnon or Aeneas or Raskolnikov or Madame Bovary or Marcel or Fanny Price or –'

'Wait a moment. I haven't heard of some of these people. And I think I do identify with Achilles.'

'Tell me about him.'

'Oh Bradley – I can't think – Didn't he kill Hector?'

'Never mind. Have I made my point?'

'I'm not sure what it is.'

'*Hamlet* is unusual because it is a great work of literature in which everyone identifies with the hero.'

'I see. Does that make it less good than Shakespeare's other plays, I mean the good ones?'

'No. It is the greatest of Shakespeare's plays.'

'Then something funny has happened.'

'Correct.'

'Well, what is it, Bradley? Look, do you mind if I write down some notes on what we were talking about earlier about Hamlet thinking his mother was committing adultery with his father, and all that. Gosh, how hot it is in here. Please may we open the window? And do you mind if I take off my boots? They're simply baking me alive.'

196

'I forbid you to take notes. You may not open the window. You may take off your boots.'

'For this relief much thanks.' She unzipped the boots and revealed, in pink tights, the legs. She admired the legs, waggled the toes, undid another button at her neck, then giggled.

I said, 'Do you mind if I take off my jacket?'

'Of course not.'

'You'll see my braces.'

'How exciting. You must be the last man in London who wears any. They're getting as rare and thrilling as suspenders.'

I took off my jacket, revealing grey army surplus braces over a grey shirt with a black stripe. 'Not exciting, I'm afraid. I would have put on my red ones if I'd known.'

'So you weren't expecting me?'

'Don't be silly. Do you mind if I take off my tie?'

'Don't be silly.'

I took off my tie and undid the top two buttons of my shirt. Then I did one of them up again. The hair on my chest is copious but grizzled. (Or if you prefer, a sable silvered.) I could feel the perspiration trickling down my temples, down the back of my neck, and winding its way through the forest on my diaphragm.

'You aren't sweating,' I said to Julian. 'How do you manage it?'

'I am. Look.' She thrust her fingers in under her hair and then stretched her hands towards me across the table. The fingers were long but not unduly slim. They were faintly dewy. 'Now, Bradley, where were we. You were saying *Hamlet* was the only –'

'Let's fold up this conversation shall we?'

'Oh Bradley, I knew I'd just bore you! And now I won't see you again for months, I know you!'

'Shut up. That dreary stuff about Hamlet and his ma and pa you can get out of a book. I'll tell you which one.'

'So it's not true?'

'It is true, but it doesn't matter. A sophisticated reader takes such things in his stride. You are a sophisticated reader *in ovo*.'

'In what?'

'Of course Hamlet is Shakespeare.'

'Whereas Lear and Macbeth and Othello are –'

'Aren't.'

'Bradley, was Shakespeare homosexual?'

'Of course.'

'Oh I see. So Hamlet's really in love with Horatio –'

'Be quiet, girl. In mediocre works the hero is the author.'

'My father is the hero of all his novels.'

'It is this that induces the reader to identify. Now if the greatest of all geniuses permits himself to be the hero of one of his plays, has this happened by accident?'

'No.'

'Is he unconscious of it?'

'No.'

'Correct. So this must be what the play is about.'

'Oh. What?'

'About Shakespeare's own identity. About this urge to externalize himself as the most romantic of all romantic heroes. When is Shakespeare at his most cryptic?'

'How do you mean?'

'What is the most mysterious and endlessly debated part of his *œuvre*?'

'The sonnets?'

'Correct.'

'Bradley, I read such an extraordinary theory about the sonnets –'

'Be silent. So Shakespeare is at his most cryptic when he is talking about himself. How is it that *Hamlet* is the most famous and accessible of his plays?'

'But people argue about that too.'

'Yes, but nevertheless it is the best known work of literature in the world. Indian peasants, Australian lumberjacks, Argentine ranchers, Norwegian sailors, members of the Red Army, Americans, all the most remote and brutish specimens of mankind have heard of *Hamlet*.'

'Don't you mean Canadian lumberjacks? I thought Australia –'

'How can this be?'

'I don't know, Bradley, you tell me.'

'Because Shakespeare, by the sheer intensity of his own meditation upon the problem of his identity has produced a new language, a special rhetoric of consciousness –'

'I'm not with you.'

'Words are Hamlet's being as they were Shakespeare's.'

'Words, words, words.'

'What work of literature has more quotable lines?'

'Oh what a noble mind is here o'erthrown.'

'How all occasions do inform against me.'

'Since my dear soul was mistress of her choice.'

'Oh what a rogue and peasant slave am I.'

'Absent thee from felicity awhile.'

'Something too much of this. As I was saying. The thing is a monument of words, it is Shakespeare's most rhetorical play, it is his longest play, it is his most inventive and involuted literary exercise. See how casually, with what a lucid easy grace he lays down the origins of modern English prose –'

'What a piece of work is a man –'

'*Hamlet* is nearer to the wind than Shakespeare ever sailed, even in the sonnets. Did Shakespeare hate his father? Of course. Was he in love with his mother? Of course. But that is only the beginning of what he is telling us about himself. How does he dare to do it? How can it not bring down on his head a punishment which is as much more exquisite than that of ordinary writers as the god whom he worships is above the god whom they worship? He has performed a supreme creative feat, a work endlessly reflecting upon itself, not discursively but in its very substance, a Chinese box of words as high as the tower of Babel, a meditation upon the bottomless trickery of consciousness and the redemptive role of words in the lives of those without identity, that is human beings. *Hamlet* is words, and so is Hamlet. He is as witty as Jesus Christ, but whereas Christ speaks Hamlet is speech. He is the tormented empty sinful consciousness of man seared by the bright light of art, the god's flayed victim dancing the dance of creation. The cry of anguish is obscure because it is overheard. It is the eloquence of direct speech, it is *oratio recta* not *oratio obliqua*. But it is not addressed to us. Shakespeare is passionately exposing himself to the ground and author of his being. He is speaking as few artists can speak, in the first person and yet at the pinnacle of artifice. How veiled that deity, how dangerous to approach, how almost impossible with impunity to

199

address, Shakespeare knew better than any man. *Hamlet* is a wild act of audacity, a self-purging, a complete self-castigation in the presence of the god. Is Shakespeare a masochist? Of course. He is the king of masochists, his writing thrills with that secret. But because his god is a real god and not an *eidolon* of private fantasy, and because love has here invented language as if for the first time, he can change pain into poetry and orgasms into pure thought –'

'Bradley, wait, please, do stop, I'm not understanding you –'

'Shakespeare here makes the crisis of his own identity into the very central stuff of his art. He transmutes his private obsessions into a rhetoric so public that it can be mumbled by any child. He enacts the purification of speech, and yet also this is something comic, a sort of trick, like a huge pun, like a long almost pointless joke. Shakespeare cries out in agony, he writhes, he dances, he laughs, he shrieks, and he makes us laugh and shriek ourselves out of hell. Being is acting. We are tissues and tissues of different *personae* and yet we are nothing at all. What redeems us is that speech is ultimately divine. What part does every actor want to play? Hamlet.'

'I played Hamlet once,' said Julian.

'What?'

'I played Hamlet once, at school, I was sixteen.'

I had closed the book and had my two hands flat on the table. I stared at the girl. She smiled, and then when I did not, giggled and blushed, thrusting back her hair with a crooked finger. 'I wasn't very good. I say, Bradley, do my feet smell?'

'Yes, but it's charming.'

'I'll put the boots on again.' She began to point one pink foot, thrusting it into its purple sheath. 'I'm sorry, I interrupted you, please go on.'

'No. The show's over.'

'Please. What you were saying was marvellous, though I can't really understand much of it. I do wish you'd let me take notes. Can't I now?' She was zipping up the boots.

'No. What I was saying is no good for your exam. That's esoteric lore. You'd plough if you tried to utter that stuff. In fact you don't understand any of it. It doesn't matter. You'd better just learn a few simple things. I'll send you some notes and one or two books to read. I know what questions they'll ask you and I know what answers will get you top marks.'

'But I don't want to do the easy stuff, I want to do the difficult stuff, besides, if what you say is *true* –'

'You can't conjure with that word at your age.'

'But I do want to understand. I thought Shakespeare was a sort of business man, I thought he was really interested in making money –'

'He was.'

'But then how could he –'

'Let's have a drink.'

I got up. I felt suddenly exhausted, almost dazed, damp with sweat from head to foot as if I were outlined with warm quicksilver. I opened the window and a breath of slightly cooler air entered the room, polluted and dusty, yet also somehow bearing the half-obliterated ghosts of flowers from distant parks. A massed-up buzz of various noise filled the room, cars, voices, the endless hum of London's being. I opened the front of my shirt all the way down to the waist and scratched in my curly mat of grey hair. I turned to face Julian. Then I went to the walnut hanging cupboard and brought out glasses and the sherry decanter. I poured out sherry.

'So you played Hamlet. Describe your costume.'

'Oh the usual. All Hamlets dress the same, don't they. Unless they're in modern dress, and we weren't.'

'Do what I ask please.'

'What?'

'Describe your costume.'

'Well, I wore black tights and black velvet shoes with silvery buckles and a sort of black slinky jerkin with a low opening and a white silk shirt underneath that and a big gold chain round my neck and – What's the matter, Bradley?'

'Nothing.'

'I thought I looked a lot like a picture I saw of John Gielgud.'

'Who is he?'

'Bradley, he's an actor –'

'You misunderstand me, child. Go on.'

'That's all. I enjoyed it ever so much. Especially the fight at the end.'

'I think I'll close the window again,' I said, 'if you don't object.' I closed it and the London buzz became indistinct, something internal, something in the mind, and we were alone in a warm small thingy solitude. I stared at the girl. She was dreamy, combing her layers of greeny-golden hair with long fingers, seeing herself as Hamlet, sword in hand.

' "Here thou incestuous murderous damned Dane –" '

'Bradley, you must be a mind-reader. Look, do tell me something more about what you were saying, couldn't you sort of put it in a nutshell?'

'*Hamlet* is a piece *à clef*. It is about someone Shakespeare was in love with.'

'But Bradley, you didn't say that, you –'

'Enough, enough. How are your parents.'

'Oh you are a tease. They're much as usual. Dad's out at the library all day, scribble, scribble, scribble. Mum stays at home and moves the furniture about and broods. It's such a pity she never had any education. She's so intelligent.'

'Don't be so bloody sorry for them,' I said. 'They're marvellous people, both of them, marvellous people with real private lives of their own.'

'Sorry. I must have sounded awful. I suppose I am awful. Perhaps all young people are awful.'

'Lay not that flattering unction to your soul. Only some.'

'Sorry, Bradley. I say, I do wish you'd come and see the parents oftener, I think you do them good.'

I felt some shame in asking her about Arnold and Rachel, but I wanted to be, and now was, sure that they had said nothing damaging about me.

'So you want to be a writer?' I said. I was still leaning back against the window. She was pointing her alert secretive little face at me. With her mane of hair she looked more like a nice dog than like Royal Denmark. She had crossed her legs now, one lying horizontal upon the other, showing off the purple boots and a maximum amount of pink tights. Her hand played at her neck, opening another button, questing within. I could smell her sweat, her feet, her breasts.

'I feel I can. I'm ready to wait. I won't rush into it. I want to

202

write hard dense impersonal sort of books, not a bit like me.'

'Good girl.'

'I certainly won't call myself Julian Baffin –'

'Julian,' I said. 'I think you'd better go.'

'I'm so sorry – Oh Bradley, I have enjoyed this. Do you think we could meet again before long? I know you hate to be tied down. Aren't you going away?'

'No.'

'Then please let me know sometime if we can meet.'

'Yes.'

'Well, I suppose I must be off –'

'I owe you a thing.'

'What?'

'A thing. In return for the buffalo lady. Remember?'

'Yes. I didn't like to remind you –'

'Here.'

I took two strides to the chimney piece and picked up a little oval gilt snuff box, one of my most treasured pieces. I gave it into her hand.

'Oh Bradley, how frightfully kind of you, it looks so sort of elegant and valuable, and something's written on it, *A Friend's Gift*, oh my dear, how nice! We are friends, aren't we?'

'Yes.'

'Bradley, I *am* grateful –'

'Off you go. Out, out.'

'You won't forget all about me – ?'

'Out.'

I saw her to the front door and closed it immediately after her as soon as she had stepped outside it. I went back into the flat, into the sitting-room, and closed the door. The room was sweet with heavy dusty sunlight. Her chair was where it had been. She had left her copy of *Hamlet* behind on the table.

I fell on my knees and then lay full length face downward on the rug in front of the fireplace. Something very extraordinary indeed had just happened to me.

Part Two

What it was that had happened the percipient reader will not need to be told. (Doubtless he saw it coming a mile off. I did not. This is art, but I was out there in life.) I had fallen in love with Julian. At what point during our conversation I realized this fact is hard to determine. The consciousness darts back and forth in time like a weaver and can occupy, when busy with its mysterious self-formings and self-gatherings, a very large specious present. Perhaps I realized it when she said, in that beautiful resonant tone of hers, 'Since my dear soul was mistress of her choice.' Perhaps it was when she said 'Black tights and black velvet shoes with silvery buckles'. Or perhaps it was when she took her boots off. No, not as early as that. And when I had had that mystical experience, looking at her legs in the shoe shop, had that been a veiled realization of being in love? It had not seemed so. Yet that too was part of it. Everything was part of it. After all, I had known this child since her birth. I had seen her in her cradle. I had held her in my arms when she was twenty inches long. Oh Christ.

'I had fallen in love with Julian.' The words are easily written down. But how to describe the thing itself? It is odd that falling in love, though frequently mentioned in literature, is rarely adequately described. It is after all an astounding phenomenon and for most people it is the most astonishing event that ever happens to them: more astonishing, because more counter-natural, than life's horrors. (I do not of course refer to mere 'sex'.) It is sad that, like the experience of bereavement, the experience of love is usually, like a dream, *forgotten*. Furthermore, those who have never fallen desperately in love with someone whom they have known for a long time may doubt whether this can occur. Let me assure them that it can. It happened to me. Was it always there cooking, incubating, in the warm inwards of time, as the girl grew and filled out into bloom? Of course I had always liked her, especially when she was a little child. But nothing really had prepared me for this blow. And it was a *blow*, I was felled by it physically. I felt as if my stomach had been shot away, leaving a gaping hole. My knees dissolved, I could not stand up, I shuddered and trembled all over, my teeth chattered. My face felt as if it had become waxen and some huge strange weirdly smiling mask had been imprinted upon it, I had become some sort of god. I lay there with my nose stuck into the black wool of the rug and the toes of my shoes making little ellipses on the carpet as I shook with possession. Of course I was sexually excited, but what I felt transcended mere lust to such a degree that although I could vividly sense my afflicted body I also felt totally alienated and changed and practically discarnate.

Of course the mind of the lover abhors accident. 'I wonder by my troth what thou and I did till we loved' is a question intimate to his amazement. My love for Julian must have been figured before the world began. Surely it was lovers who discovered astrology. Nothing less than the great chamber of the stars could be large and steady enough to be context, origin, and guarantee of something so eternal. I realized now that my whole life had been determinedly travelling towards this moment. *Her* whole life had been travelling towards it, as she played and read her school books and grew and looked in the mirror at her breasts. This was a predestined collision. But it had not only just happened, it had happened aeons ago, it was of the stuff of the original formation of earth and sky. When God said 'Let there be light' this love was made. It had no history. Yet too my awakening consciousness of it had a history of bottomless fascination. When, how, did I begin to realize the charm of this girl? Love generates, or rather reveals something which may be called *absolute charm*. In the beloved nothing is gauche. Every move of the head, every tone of the voice, every laugh or grunt or cough or twitch of the nose is as valuable and revealing as a glimpse of paradise. And in fact lying there absolutely limp and yet absolutely taut with my brow on the ground and my eyes closed I was actually not just glimpsing but in paradise. The act of falling in love, of really falling in love (I do not mean what sometimes passes by this name), floods the being with immediate ecstasy.

I am not sure how long I lay upon the floor. Perhaps an hour, perhaps two or three hours. When at last I pulled myself up into a sitting posture it appeared to be afternoon. It was certainly another world and another time. Of course there was no question of eating anything, I should instantly have been sick. Sitting on the floor I reached out and drew towards me the chair upon which she had sat and leaned against it. I could see my own sherry untouched upon the table, hers half drunk. A fly was drowned in it. I would have drunk it fly and all, only I knew I could keep nothing down. I clasped the chair (it was the tiger lily one) and stared at her copy of *Hamlet*. The pleasure of picking that up and fingering it, perhaps seeing her name written in the front, was hundreds of years ahead in a delightful future of perfectly satis- fying preoccupations. There was no hurry. Time had already become eternity. There was a huge warm globe of conscious being within which I moved with extreme slowness, or which perhaps I was. I had only to gaze, to stretch my hands out slowly like a chameleon. It no longer mattered where I looked or what I did. Everything in the world was Julian.

Some readers may feel that what I am describing is a condition of insanity, and in a way this is true. Were it not reasonably common, men could surely be locked up for such a change of consciousness. However it is one of the peculiarities, perhaps one of the blessings, of this planet that anyone can experience this transformation of the world. Also, anyone can be its object. What a commonplace girl, the reader may say: naïve, ignorant, thought- less, not even particularly beautiful. Or else you have misdescribed her. I can only say that until that moment I could not *see* her. And I have tried, as an honest narrator, to reveal her so far only dimly, through the casual blinded consciousness of the person that I *was*. Now I could see. Can any lover doubt that *now* he sees truly? And is the possessor of this enlivened vision not really more like God than like a madman?

The conventional notion of the Christian God pictures Him as *having* created and being *about* to judge. A more intimate theology, and one more consonant with the nature of what we know of love, pictures a demonic force engaged in continuous creation and participation. I felt that I was, at every instant, creating Julian and supporting her being with my own. At the same time I saw her too in every way as I had seen her before. I saw her simplicity, her ignorance, her childish unkindness, her unpretty anxious little face. She was not beautiful or brilliantly clever. How false it is to say that love is blind. I could even judge her, I could even condemn her, I could even, in some possible galactic loop of thought, make her suffer. But this was still the stuff of paradise because I was a god and I was involved with her in some eternal activity of making to be which was of sole and absolute value. And with her the world was made, nothing was lost, not a grain of sand nor a speck of dust, since she was the world and I touched her everywhere.

The rather flowery ideas which I have set out above were not of course as such at all clear in my mind while I was sitting on the floor hugging the chair which she had sat in. (I did this too for some considerable time: perhaps until the evening.) I was, for that period, largely dazed with happiness: joy in my marvellous *achievement* of absolute love. In this blaze of light of course a few more mundane thoughts flitted to and fro like little birds, scarcely descried by one who was dazzled by emergence from the cave. I will mention here two of these thoughts since they are germane to events which happened later. They were, I should say, not posterior to my discovery of being in love: they were innate in it and born with it.

I spoke earlier in this rigmarole of my whole life as travelling towards what had now occurred. Perhaps my friend the percipient reader may be excused for having interpreted this conception in the following terms: that all this dream of being a great artist was simply a search for a great human love. Such things have been known, indeed such discoveries are common, especially among women. Love can soon dim the dream of art and make it seem secondary, even a delusion. I should say at once that this was not my case. Of course since everything was now connected with Julian, my ambitions as a writer were connected with Julian. But they were not cancelled thereby. Rather something more like the opposite seemed to be happening. She had filled me with a previously unimaginable power which I knew that I would and could use in my art. The deep causes of the universe, the stars, the distant galaxies, the ultimate particles of matter, had fashioned these two things, my love and my art, as aspects of what was ultimately one and the same. They were, I *knew*, from the same source. It was under the same orders and recognizing the same authority that I now stood, a man renewed. Of this conviction I will speak more and explain more later.

The second thing which was from the start perfectly clear to me, not something which I realized even as much later as one second, was this. I could never never never tell my love. That this knowledge did not immediately produce a pain of which I died is a proof of the immense power, that is *ipso facto* the purity, of the love which I felt for this girl. It was enough happiness to love her. The extra piece which would be telling her about it was like a pinpoint compared with the heavenly joy of simply apprehending her. (Any further joys my beatified imagination not only did not covet but did not even conceive.) I did not even mind when I saw her again. I had no plans to see her again. Who was I to have plans? If I had been told that I would never see her again I would have felt some sort of distress but it would instantly have been carried up and lost in the great creative upsurge of my adoration. This was no delirium. Those who have loved so will understand me. There was an overwhelming sense of reality, of being at last real and seeing the real. The tables, the chairs, the sherry glasses, the curls on the rug, the dust: real.

Nor did I envisage suffering. 'I will run the gauntlet of a thousand blows but I will keep my mouth shut.' No. To the pure lover in his moments of purity the idea of suffering is vulgar, it portends the return of self. What I rather felt was a dazzled gratitude. Yet I understood at once in a clear *intellectual* way that I could not ever tell Julian that I loved her. The details of this certainty (what it involved) became clearer to me later, but it stood flaming in my way at the very start. I was fifty-eight, she was twenty. I could not puzzle, burden, and bedevil her young life with the faintest hint or glimpse of this huge terrible love. How fearful that dark shadow is when we catch sight of it in the life of another. No wonder those at whom that black arrow is aimed so often turn and flee. How unendurable it can be, the love another bears us. I would never persecute my darling with that dread knowledge. From now onward until the world ended everything must remain, although utterly changed, exactly as it was before.

The reader, especially if he has not had the experience I have been describing, may feel impatient with the foregoing lyricism. 'Pshaw!' he will say, 'the fellow protests too much and intoxicates himself with words. He admits to being a thoroughly repressed man, no longer young. All he means is that he suddenly felt intense sexual desire for a girl of twenty. We all know about that.' I will not pause to answer this reader back, but will go on as faithfully as I can to recount what happened next.

I slept exceptionally well that night and awoke into the glow of an immediate knowledge of what had occurred. I lay in bed, floating in my secret bliss. For my first consciousness also brought that with it: that I was a man dedicated to a secret task. And forever. There was no doubt about that either. If I love thee not, chaos is come again. The foreverness of real love is one of the reasons why even unrequited love is a source of joy. The human soul craves for the eternal of which, apart from certain rare mysteries of religion, only love and art can give a glimpse. (I will not pause to answer the cynic, possibly the same one whom we heard from just now, who will say: 'And how long does your romantic foreverness last, pray?' or rather, I will simply reply: 'True love is eternal. It is also rare; and no doubt *you*, Sir, were never lucky enough to experience it!') Love brings with it also a vision of selflessness. How right Plato was to think that, embracing a lovely boy, he was on the road to the Good. I say a *vision* of selflessness, because our mixed nature readily degrades the purity of any aspiration. But such insight, even intermittent, even momentary, is a privilege and can be of permanent value because of the intensity with which it visits us. Ah, even once, to *will* another rather than oneself! Why could we not make of this revelation a lever by which to lift the world? Why cannot this release from self provide a foothold in a new place which we can then colonize and enlarge until at last we will *all* that is not ourselves? That was Plato's dream. It is not impossible.

210

I cannot say that I thought all these sage thoughts as I lay in bed on that first morning of the first full day of the new world. Perhaps I thought some of them. I certainly felt made anew, I felt corporeally glorified, as one might feel oneself to be with humble amaze upon the day of the bodily resurrection. My limbs were made of butter or lilies or pale wax or manna or something. Of course the flame of physical desire warmed and informed this scene of unsullied pallor, yet without seeming separate from it, or indeed feeling separate from anything. When sexual desire is also love it connects us with the whole world and becomes a new mode of experience. Sex then reveals itself as the great connective principle whereby we overcome duality, the force which made separateness as an aspect of oneness at some moment of bliss in the mind of God. I yearned absolutely, yet I had never felt more relaxed in my life. I lay in bed and thought about Julian's legs, now bare and egg-shell brown, now encased in tights, pink, mauve, black. I thought about her mane of dry shining greeny-golden hair and the way it grew down the back of her neck. I thought about the intense concentration of her strokable nose and pouting mouth, pointing like an animal's muzzle. I thought about the sky-cleanness of her English water-colour eyes. I thought about her breasts. I felt completely happy and I felt good. (I mean virtuous.)

I got up and shaved. What physical pleasure there is in shaving when a man is happy! I examined my face in the mirror. It looked fresh and young. The waxen imprint was still upon it. I really did look a different person. A radiant force from within had puffed out my cheeks and smoothed the wrinkles round my eyes. I dressed with care and took some time to select a tie. Eating was still, of course, out of the question. I felt as if I should never need to eat again, but could live indefinitely simply by breathing. I drank a little water. I squeezed an orange, more out of a theoretical idea that I should nourish myself, than because of any return of appetite, but the juice was too rich and heavy, I could not even sip it. Then I went into the sitting-room and dusted it a little. At least I dusted a few visible surfaces. As a lifelong Londoner, I am easily tolerant of dust. The sun had not yet come round to the position whence it could illuminate the brick wall opposite, but there was so much sunny brightness in the sky that the room was glowing in a subdued way. I sat down and wondered what I was going to do with my new life.

All this may sound ridiculous. But being in love is a life-occupation. I suppose this concept resembles, or rather is a special case of, the idea of doing everything for God and making the whole of life into a sacrament, 'sweeping the room as for Thy laws', as in Herbert's poem. I had just been dusting the room for Julian, without of course even conceiving that she might ever visit it again. I now allowed myself to pick up her copy of *Hamlet*, which was still lying in its place on the marquetry table. It was a school edition. In the front the name of a previous owner, *Hazel Bingley*, had been crossed out, and *Julian Baffin* written in a childish hand, obviously some time ago. What did Julian's handwriting look like now? I had only received a child's postcards. Would I ever receive a letter from her? I felt quite faint at the idea. I examined the book. The text was scrawled over with extremely silly observations by Hazel. There were also a few observations by Julian (equally silly, I have to admit), dating from her school studies rather than from her 'second innings' with the play. 'Feeble!' she had written beside Ophelia's 'Oh what a noble mind' speech, which I thought was a bit unfair. And 'Hypocrite!' beside Claudius's attempted prayer of repentance. (Of course no young person can understand Claudius.)

I spent some time examining the book and culling these flowers. Then hugging it against my shirt, I began to meditate. It had not ceased to be clear that my new 'occupation' was not in any sense an alternative to my life's work. The same agency had sent me both these things, not to compete but to complete. I would soon be writing and I would write well. I do not mean that I thought of anything so vulgar as writing 'about' Julian. Life and art must be kept strictly separate if one is aiming at excellence. But I felt those dark globules in the head, those tinglings in the fingers which token the advent of inspiration. The children of my fancy were already hosting. Meanwhile however there were simpler tasks to be performed. I must set my life in order and I now had the strength to do so. I must see Priscilla, I must see Roger, I must see Christian, I must see Rachel, I must

212

see Arnold. (How easy it all suddenly looked!) I did not say to myself 'I must see Julian', and over that divine lacuna I gazed out with wide peaceful eyes at a world devoid of evil. There seemed to be no question, at the moment, of leaving London. I would perform my tasks and I would not lift a finger to see my darling again. And I felt, as I meditated upon her, glad to think that I had so immediately given her one of my best treasures, the gilt snuffbox, *A Friend's Gift*. I could not have given it to her now. This innocent thing had gone away with her, a pledge, did she but know it, of a love dedicated in silence to her quite separate and private happiness. Out of this *silence* I would forge my power. Yes, this was a yet clearer revelation and I held on to it. I would be able to create because I would be able to keep silent.

After I had been brooding upon this truly awe-inspiring insight for some time my heart suddenly nearly fell out of me because the telephone rang and I thought it might be her.

'Yes?'

'Hartbourne here.'

'Oh hello, my dear fellow!' I felt a sort of cordial relief though I could hardly still breathe with excitement. 'I'm so glad you rang. Look, let's meet soon, how about lunch – could you manage lunch today?'

'Today? Well, yes, I think I could actually. Shall we say one o'clock at the usual place?'

'Yes, that's fine! I'm afraid I'm on a diet by the way, and won't be able to eat much, but I'd love to see you, I do look forward to it.' I put the phone down smiling. Then the front-door bell rang. My heart performed the same swoop into emptiness. I scrabbled at the door, almost moaning.

Rachel stood outside.

When I saw her I came straight out of the flat and closed the door behind me and said, 'Oh Rachel, how marvellous to see you! I'm just going to do some urgent shopping, would you like to walk along with me?' I did not want to let her in. She might have gone into the sitting-room and sat down on Julian's tiger lily chair. Also I felt I must talk to her unintimately, out in the open air. I was glad to see her.

'Can't I come in and sit down for a minute?' she said.

213

'I must have a breath of air, do you mind? It's such a lovely day. Come along then.'

I set off along the court and then along Charlotte Street, walking rather fast.

Rachel was dressed more smartly than usual in a silky dress with red and white blotches on it and a low square neckline. Her collar bones, sun-browned and mottled, were prominent above the dress. Her neck was dry and wrinkled, faintly reptilian, her face was smoother, more made-up than usual, and wearing the expression the French call *maussade*. She seemed to have lately washed her hair which made a smooth frizzy ball around her head. She looked, in spite of the above description, a handsome woman, tired, but not defeated, by her life.

'Bradley, don't walk so fast.'

'Sorry.'

'Before I forget, Julian said would I pick up her copy of *Hamlet* which she left with you.'

I had no intention of parting with this book. I said, 'I'd like to keep it for a while. It's rather a good edition, and I wanted to note one or two things.'

'But it's a school book.'

'Excellent edition all the same. Not available any more.' Later I would feign to have lost it.

'It was so kind of you to see Julian yesterday.'

'I enjoyed it.'

'I hope she hasn't been pestering you.'

'Not at all. Here we are.'

I turned into a stationer's shop in Rathbone Place. I can browse indefinitely in a stationer's shop, indeed there is hardly anything in a good stationer's which I do not like and want. What a scene of refreshment and innocence! Loose leaf paper, writing paper, notebooks, envelopes, postcards, pens, pencils, paper-clips, blotting paper, ink, files, old-fashioned things like sealing wax, new-fangled things like sellotape.

I dashed among the shelves followed by Rachel. 'I must buy some more of my special notebooks. I'm going to be doing a lot of writing soon. Rachel, let me buy you something, I must, I'm in a present-giving mood.'

214

'Bradley, whatever is the matter with you, you seem quite delirious.'

'Here, let me give you these nice things!' I had to load some-body with presents. I collected for Rachel a ball of red string, a blue felt-tipped pen, a pad of special calligrapher's paper, a magnifying glass, a fancy carrier bag, a large wooden clothes peg with URGENT written on it in gold, and six postcards of the Post Office Tower. I paid for the purchases and loaded the bag with all Rachel's spoil into her arms.

'You seem in a good mood!' she said, pleased, but still a bit *maussade*. 'Now can we go back to your place?'

'I'm awfully sorry. I've got a rather early lunch engagement, I'm not going back.' I was still worrying about the chair and whether she wouldn't try again to remove the book. It was not that I was unwilling to talk to Rachel, I was greatly enjoying it.

'Well, let's sit somewhere.'

'There's a seat in Tottenham Court Road, just opposite Heals.'

'Bradley, I am not going to sit in Tottenham Court Road and contemplate Heals. Aren't the pubs open yet?'

They were. I must have spent longer than I realized in medita-tion. We went into one.

It was a featureless modern place, ruined by the brewers, all made of light plastic (pubs should be dark holes), but with the sun shining in and the street door open it had a sort of southern charm. We visited the bar and then sat at a plastic table which was already wet with beer. Rachel had a double whisky which she proposed to drink neat. I had a lemonade shandy for the sake of appearances. We looked at each other.

It occurred to me that this was the first time since I had been *smitten* that I had looked another human being in the eyes. It was a good experience. I beamed. I almost felt that my face had the power to bless.

'Bradley, you *are* looking odd.'

'Peculiar?'

'Very nice. You look awfully well today. You look younger.'

'Dear Rachel! I'm so glad to see you. Tell me all. Let's talk about Julian. Such an intelligent girl.'

'I'm glad you think so. I'm not sure that I do. I'm grateful to you for taking an interest in her at last.'

'At last?'

'She says she's been trying to attract your attention for years. I warned her you probably won't keep it up.'

'I'll do what I can for her. I like her, you know.' I laughed crazily.

'She's like all of them now, so vague and inconsiderate and doing everything on the spur of the moment, and so full of contempt for everything. She adores her father but she can't help needling him all the time. She told him this morning that you thought his work was "sentimental".'

'Rachel, I've been thinking,' I said. (I had not in fact, it had just come into my head.) 'I may be being completely unjust to Arnold. It's years since I read the whole of his work. I must read it all through again, I may see it quite differently now. You like Arnold's novels, don't you?'

'I'm his wife. And I'm a totally uneducated woman, as my dear daughter never tires of telling me. But look, I don't want to talk about these things. I want to say – well, first of all forgive me for bothering you again. You'll begin to think I'm a neurotic woman with a fixation.'

'Never, my dear Rachel! I'm so glad to see you. And what a pretty dress! How charming you look!'

'Thanks. Oh I feel so unhappy about everything that's happened lately. I know life is always a muddle but the muddle's got suddenly worse and I can't bear it. You know when things get inside you and you can't stop going round and round the same piece of misery. That's why I just have to come and see you. And Arnold always puts me in the wrong and I dare say I am in the wrong –'

'I've been in the wrong too,' I said, 'but I feel now that everything can be put right. There's no need to have warfare when one can have peace. I'll go and see Arnold and we'll have a long talk –'

'Wait a moment, Bradley. Are you getting drunk on that shandy? You haven't even had any yet. I don't see any point in your talking all solemnly to Arnold. Men are so pompous about having things out and talking things through. I'm not sure that I want you to see Arnold at all at present. I just wanted to say this. Are you listening to me, Bradley?'

'Yes, my dearest creature.'

'You said some very kind and probably very wise things last time we met about friendship. I feel I was rather churlish –'

'Not at all.'

'I want to say now that I accept and need your friendship. I also want to say – it's hard to find the words – I'd be wretched if I felt you just saw me as a desperate middle-aged harpy trying to pull someone into bed to spite her husband –'

'I assure you –'

'It's not like that, Bradley. There's something I feel I didn't make absolutely clear. I wasn't just looking for a man to console me after a married row –'

'You did make it clear –'

'It could only have been you. We've known each other for centuries. But it's only lately come to me – how much I really care about you. You're a very special person in my life. I esteem you and admire you and rely on you and – well, I love you. That's what I wanted to say.'

'Rachel, what a delightful thing, it's made my day!'

'Be serious for a moment, Bradley.'

'I am serious, my dear. People should love each other more in simple ways, I've always felt this. Why can't we just comfort each other more? One tends to live at a sort of level of anxiety and resentment where one's protecting oneself all the time. Climb above it, climb above it, and feel free to love! That's the message. I know in my relations with Arnold –'

'Never mind your relations with Arnold. This is about me. I want – I must be a bit drunk – let me put it crudely – I want a special relationship with you.'

'You've got it!'

'Be quiet. I don't want an affair, not because I don't want an affair, maybe I do, it's not worth finding out, but because it would be a mess and belong with all that anxiety and resentment you were talking about, anyway you haven't got the guts or temperament or whatever for an affair, but, Bradley, I want *you*.'

217

'You've got me!'

'Oh don't be so gay and flippant, you look so horribly pleased with yourself, what's the matter?'

'Rachel, don't worry. I can be everything that you want me to be. It's all perfectly simple. As Julian's namesake remarked, obscurely but with *élan*, all shall be well and all shall be well and all manner of thing shall be well.'

'I wish I could hold you to some sort of seriousness, you're so terribly sort of slippery today. Bradley, this matters so much – you will love me, you will be faithful?'

'Yes!'

'A real true friend to me forever?'

'Yes, yes!'

'I don't know – thank you – all right – You're looking at your watch, you must go to your lunch date. I'll stay here and – think – and – drink. Thank you, thank you.'

The last I saw of her, through the window as I went off, she was staring at the table and very slowly making patterns in the beer drips with her finger. Her face had a heavy sullen dreamy remembering look which was very touching.

Hartbourne asked after Christian. He had known her slightly. The news of her return must have somehow got around. I talked about her frankly and at ease. Yes, I had seen her. She was much improved, not only in looks. We were on quite good terms, very civilized. And Priscilla? She had left her husband and was staying with Christian, I was just going to visit them. 'Priscilla staying with Christian? How remarkable,' said Hartbourne. Yes, I supposed it was, but it just showed what good friends we all were. In turn I asked Hartbourne about the office. Was that ridiculous committee still sitting? Had Matheson got his promotion yet? Had the new lavatories materialized? Was that comic tea lady still around? Hartbourne remarked that I seemed 'very fit and relaxed'.

I had indeed decided to go to Notting Hill that afternoon, but I decided to return to my flat first. I had to refresh myself with some silence and solitude and thinking about Julian. So holy men return to temples and crusading knights feed upon the blessed sacrament. I felt a bit inclined to go home and stay home in case she rang up, but I knew this to be a temptation and I resisted it. If all was indeed to be well I must not alter the pattern of my life in any way: apart, that is, from the tidyings and reconcilings which I now felt so sure that I could effect. At a bookshop on the way home I stopped and ordered Arnold's complete works. There were, of course, far too many to carry, and anyway they were not all in stock. The shopman promised to send them to me soon. Looking at a list, I realized that I had not even read all his books, and some of them I had read so long ago that I could remember nothing about them. How could I judge the man on that basis? I realized that I had been completely unjust. I smiled upon the shopman. 'Yes, all of them please, every one.' 'And the poems, sir?' 'Yes.' I had not even realized that Arnold had published any poems. What a skunk I was! I also purchased the London edition of Shakespeare complete in six volumes, to give to Julian in exchange for her *Hamlet* when the time came, and I went away still smiling.

As I was just turning into the court I saw Rigby, my upstairs neighbour. I stopped him and had begun some cordial conversation about the fine weather when he said, 'There's someone waiting outside your door.' I gasped and excused myself and quickly ran. A man, however, was awaiting me. A well-dressed distinguished-looking figure with a soldierly air.

When he saw me Roger started to say, 'Look here, before you tell me –'

'My dear Roger, come in and have some tea. Where's Marigold?'

'I left her in a sort of café down there.'

'Well, go and get her at once, go on, I'd love to see her again! I'll be putting the kettle on and putting the tea things out.'

Roger stared and shook his head as if he thought I must be mad, but he went off all the same to fetch Marigold.

Marigold was looking very dressed-up for town with a little blue linen cap and a white linen pinafore dress and a dark blue silk blouse and a rather expensive-looking red, white and blue scarf. She looked a bit like a musical comedy sailor girl. She was rounder however and had the self-conscious self-satisfied pouting stance of the pregnant woman. Her tanned cheeks were deeply ruddy with health and happiness. She smiled all the time with her eyes and one simply could not help smiling back. She must have left a trail of happiness behind her down the street.

'Marigold, how lovely you look!' I said.

'What's your game?' said Roger.

'Sit down, sit down, please forgive me, it's just that you both look so happy, I can't help myself. Marigold, will you be mother?'

'I suppose this is some sort of sick joke?'

'No, no'! I was serving tea on the mahogany night-table. I had put Julian's chair well back out of the way.

'You'll be turning nasty in a minute.'

'Roger, please relax, please just talk to me quietly, let's be gentle and reasonable with each other. I'm very sorry I was so unpleasant to you both down in Bristol. I was upset for Priscilla, I still am, but I don't regard you as wicked, I know how these things happen.'

Roger grimaced at Marigold. She beamed back. 'I wanted to put you in the picture,' he said. 'And I want you to do something for us, if you will. First of all, here's this.' He put a large gaping carrier bag on to the floor beside my feet.

I peered down and then began to dig into it. Necklaces and things. The enamel picture. The little marble, or whatever it was, statuette. Two silver cups, other oddments. 'That's good of you, Priscilla will be so pleased. What about the mink?'

'I was coming to that,' said Roger. 'I'm afraid I sold the mink. I'd already sold it when I saw you last. I agreed with Priscilla it was a sort of investment. I'll let her have half the proceeds. In due course.'

'She mustn't worry,' said Marigold. She had advanced her smartly shod blue patent leather foot up against Roger's shoe. She kept moving her arm so that her sleeve lightly and rhythmically brushed his.

'All the jewels are there,' said Roger, 'and the little things from her dressing table, and Marigold has packed all the clothes and so on into three trunks. Where shall we send them?'

I wrote down the Notting Hill address.

'I didn't pack all the old cosmetics,' said Marigold, 'and there were a lot of old suspender belts and things –'

'And could you tell Priscilla we want the divorce to get going at once? Naturally I will make her an allowance.'

'We won't be poorly off,' said Marigold, sweeping her sleeve across Roger's. 'I shall go on working after the little one is born.'

'What do you do?' I asked.

'I'm a dentist.'

'Good for you!' I laughed out of sheer *joie de vivre*. Fancy, this charming girl a dentist!

'You've told Priscilla about us, of course?' said Roger, sedate.

'Yes, yes. All shall be well and all shall be well, as Julian remarked.'

'Julian?'

'Julian Baffin, the daughter of a friend of mine.'

'Is she the daughter of Arnold Baffin?' said Marigold. 'I do so admire his books, he's my favourite writer.'

'You must go, my children,' I said, rising. I could not bear any longer not being alone with my thoughts. 'I will arrange everything for the best with Priscilla. It remains to wish you both every happiness.'

'I confess you've surprised me,' said Roger.

'Being beastly to you two won't help Priscilla.'

'You've been *sweet*,' said Marigold. I think she would have kissed me, only Roger piloted her off.

'Cheery-bye to my favourite dentist!' I shouted after them.

'He must be drunk,' I heard Roger say as I shut the door.

I went back to lying face downwards on the black woolly rug.

'Guess what I've got in this bag!' I said to Priscilla.

It was the same evening. Francis had let me in. There was no sign of Christian.

Priscilla was still occupying the upstairs 'new' bedroom with the rather tattered-looking walls of synthetic bamboo. The oval bed, which had black sheets, was tousled, doubtless just vacated. Priscilla, in a rather clinical white bath robe, was sitting on a stool in front of a low very glittering dressing-table. She had been staring at herself in the mirror when I came in, and returned to doing so after greeting me without a smile. She had powdered her face rather whitely and reddened her lips. She looked grotesque, like an elderly geisha.

She did not reply. Then she suddenly reached out to a big jar of greasy cold cream and started plastering it upon her face. The red lipstick melted into the grease, tingeing it with red. Priscilla spread the pinkish mess all over her face, still gazing devouringly into her own eyes.

'Look,' I said, 'look who's here!' I put the white statuette on to the glass top of the dressing-table. I laid the enamel picture and the malachite box beside it. I drew out a mass of entangled necklaces.

Priscilla stared. Then without touching the stuff she reached out and took a paper tissue and began wiping the red mess off her face.

'Roger brought them for you. And look, I've brought you the buffalo lady again. I'm afraid she's a bit lame, but –'

'And the mink stole? Did you see him?'

'Yes, I saw him. Now, Priscilla, I want to tell you –'

Priscilla's face, cleaned of the grease, looked raw and mottled. She dropped the soggy reddish screw of tissue on to the floor. She said, 'Bradley, I've decided to go back to Roger –'

'Oh, Priscilla –'

'It's no good. I should never have left him. It isn't fair to him. And I think away from him I'm literally going mad. All chances of happiness are gone from me. Just being with myself is hell all the time anyway. And here in this meaningless place I'm with myself more. Even hating Roger was something, it meant something, being made unhappy by him did, after all he belongs to me. And I was used to things there, there was something to do, shopping and cooking and cleaning the house, even though he didn't come home for his supper, I'd cook it and put it ready for him and he wouldn't come home and I'd sit and cry watching the television programme. Still it was all part of something, and

222

waiting for him at night in the dark when I went to bed, listening for his key in the door, at least there was something to wait for. I wasn't alone with my mind. I don't really care if he went with girls, secretaries in the office, I suppose they all do. I don't feel now that it matters much. I'm connected with him forever, it's for better and worse, worse in this case, but any tie is something when one's drifting away to hell. You can't look after me, obviously, why should you. Christian's been very kind, but she's just curious, she's just playing a game, she'll soon get tired of me. I know I'm awful, awful, I can't think how anyone can bear to look at me. I don't want to be looked after anyway. I can feel my mind decaying already. I feel I must smell of decay. I've been in bed all day. I didn't even make up my face until just before you came, and then it looked so terrible. I hate Roger and the last year or two I've been afraid of him. But if I don't go back to him I'll just dissolve, all my inwards will come pouring out, like people who are just going to be hanged. I can't tell you what the misery's like that I'm in.'

'Oh, Priscilla, do stop. Here, look, pretty things. You're pleased to see them again, so there's something that gives you pleasure.' I plucked up a long necklace with blue and glassy alternate beads out of the pile and shook it free and opened it out into a big O to put round her neck, but she gestured it violently away.

'Did he send the mink?'

'Well –'

'I'm going back anyway so it doesn't matter. It was kind of him to bring – What did he say, did he want to see me, did he say I was awful? Oh my life has been such hell, but when I go back it won't be worse than now, it couldn't be. I'll try to be resigned and quiet. I'll try to do little things, I'll go to the cinema more. I won't shout and cry. If I'm quiet he won't hurt me, will he? Bradley, would you come with me to Bristol? I'd like you to *explain* to Roger –'

'Priscilla,' I said, 'listen, dear. There's no question or possibility of your going back now, not ever again. Roger wants a divorce. He's got a mistress, a young girl called Marigold whom he's been living with for ages, for years, and he wants to marry her now. I saw them this morning. They're very happy and they love each other and they want to marry each other and Marigold's pregnant –'

Priscilla got up and walked stiffly towards the bed. She got into it. It was like a corpse climbing into its coffin. She pulled up the bedclothes.

'He wants to get married –' Her mouth had become flabby and her speech blurred.

'Yes, Priscilla –'

'He's had this girl for a long time –'

'Yes.'

'She's pregnant –'

'Yes.'

'So he wants a divorce –'

'Yes. Dear Priscilla, you've understood it all and you must face it all –'

'Death,' she murmured, 'death, death, death –'

'Don't give way, my dear –'

'Death.'

'You'll soon feel better. You're well rid of that heel. Honestly. We'll make a new world for you, we'll spoil you, we'll all help, you'll see. You said yourself you'd go to the cinema more. Roger will give you an allowance, and Marigold is a dentist –'

'And perhaps I could pass my time knitting little things for the baby!'

'That's better, show a bit of spirit!'

'Bradley, if you knew how much I hated even you, you'd know how far beyond any human hope I am now. As for Roger – I'd like to stick – a red-hot knitting needle – into his liver –'

'Priscilla!'

'I read about it in a detective story. You die slowly and in terrible agony.'

'Please –'

'You understand nothing of – the horror – no wonder you can't write real books – you don't see – the horror –'

'I know of horrors,' I said. 'I know of joys too. Life has good surprises, prizes, glories. We'll protect you and give you treats –'

'Who's "we"? Ach – I have nobody in the world. I'll kill myself. That's best. Everyone will say, it's for the best that she killed herself, she's better off dead. I hate you, I hate Christian, I hate myself so much I could spend hours and hours just screaming with hatred and with the pain of it, oh the pain of it, oh Roger, Roger, Roger, the pain of it –'

She had turned on her side and was sobbing quietly, rather breathlessly, her mouth shuddering, her eyes awash with tears. I had never seen anyone so inaccessibly miserable. I felt an urge to *put her to sleep*, not for good of course, but if only one could have given her a shot of something just to stop this awful weeping, to give some intermission to the tormented consciousness.

The door opened and Christian came in. Gazing at Priscilla she greeted me inattentively with a sort of 'holding' gesture which, it occurred to me, was the height of intimacy. 'What is it *now*?' she said to Priscilla sternly.

'I've just told her about Roger and Marigold,' I said.

'Oh God, did you have to?'

Priscilla suddenly started to scream quietly. 'Scream quietly' may sound like an oxymoron, but I mean to indicate the curiously controlled rhythmic screaming which goes with a certain kind of hysterics. Hysterics is terrifying because of its willed and yet not willed quality. It has the frightfulness of a deliberate assault on the spectators, yet it is also, with its apparently unstoppable rhythm, like the setting going of a machine. It is no use asking someone in hysterics to 'control themselves'. By 'choosing' to become hysterical they have put themselves beyond ordinary communication. Priscilla, now sitting upright in bed, gave a gasping 'Uuuh!' then a screamed 'aah!' ending in a sort of bubbling sob, then the gasp again and the scream and so on. It was an appalling sound, both tortured and cruel. I have four times heard a woman in hysterics, once my mother when my father hit her, once Priscilla when she was pregnant, once another woman (would that I could forget that occasion) and now Priscilla again. I turned to Christian raising my hands distractedly.

Francis Marloe came in grinning.

Christian said, 'Out you go, Brad, wait downstairs.'

I ran down the first flight, then went more slowly down the second flight. By the time I reached the door of the dark brown

225

and indigo drawing-room the house had become entirely silent. I went in and stood with my feet well apart, breathing.

Christian entered.

'She's stopped,' I said. 'What did you do?'

'I slapped her.'

I said, 'I *think* I'm going to faint.' I sat down on the sofa and covered my face with my hand.

'Brad! Quick, here, some brandy –'

'Could I have some biscuits or something? I haven't eaten all day. Or yesterday.'

I really did feel, for that moment, faint: that odd absolutely unique sensation of a black *baldacchino* being lowered like an extinguisher over one's head. And now, as brandy, bread, bis-cuits, cheese, plumcake became available, I also knew that I was going to cry. It was many many years since I had wept. What a very strange phenomenon it is, little perhaps they realize who use it much. I recalled the dismay of the wolves when Mowgli sheds tears, in the *Jungle Book*. Or rather, it is Mowgli who is dismayed, and thinks he is dying. The wolves are better informed, dignified, faintly disgusted. I held the glass of brandy in both hands and stared at Christian and felt the warm water quietly rising into my eyes. The quiet inevitability of the sensation gave satisfaction. It was an achievement. Perhaps all tears are an achievement. Oh precious gift.

'Brad, dear, don't –'

'I hate violence,' I said.

'It's no good letting her go on and on, she tires herself so, she did it for half an hour yesterday –'

'All right, yes, all right –'

'Why, you poor pet! I'm doing my best, honest. It's no fun having a near-crazy in the house. I'm doing it for you, Brad.'

I had managed to swallow a piece of cheese, but it felt like eating soap. The brandy did good though. I was terribly upset by this glimpse of Priscilla, it was such a vista of hopelessness. But the precious tears, what were they? They were, they could not but be, tears of pure joy, a miraculous portent of my changed state. All of me, material and spiritual, all my substance, all my humours, was composed of the ecstasy of love. I stared ahead of me through the warm silvery veil of my tears and saw Julian's face, eager and intent, like a bird-mask, hanging there in space, like a vision of the Saviour come to console some starving and crazed ascetic in a desert cave.

'Brad, what is it, you look extraordinary, something's happened to you, you're beautiful, you look like a saint or something, you look like some goddam picture, you look all young again –'

'You won't abandon Priscilla, will you, Chris?' I said, and I mopped the tears away with my hand.

'Did you just notice something, Brad?'

'What?'

'You called me "Chris".'

'Did I? Like old days. Well, but you won't? I'll pay you –'

'Oh never mind the dough. I'll look after her. I got on to a new doc. There's a treatment with injections she can have.'

'Good. Julian.'

'What was that?'

I had just uttered Julian's name aloud. I got up, 'Chris, do you mind, I must go. I've got something very important to do.' Think about Julian.

'Brad, please – Oh, all right, I won't keep you. But I want you to say something to me.'

'What?'

'Oh that you forgive me or something. That there's peace between us or something. You know I just loved you, Brad. You saw my love as a sort of crushing force or a will to power or something but I just wanted to hold you. And I did really truly come back here to you and for you. I thought about you out there and what a fool I'd been. Of course I'm not a romantic crazy. I know our thing couldn't work then, we were so young and God we were stupid with each other. But there was something I saw in you which didn't leave me alone. I used to dream we were reconciled, you know in dreams at night, real dreams.'

'Me too,' I said.

'Oh God! And it was such a dream of happiness. And then I'd wake up and remember the way we parted in such hatred and there'd be Evans's silly old face beside me, we shared a bed almost right up to the end. I say, I said some mean things about poor Evans to you, I wished I hadn't afterwards, I must have made a pretty poor impression – I didn't really despise Evans or hate him or want him to die, it wasn't like that at all, I was just so bored with him and with the whole place. The only thing that kept me going out there was making money. Not painting or breathing exercises or deep analysis. I even took up pottery, Christ, I tried everything. In the end only money was real. But I always felt that there was another world, a sort of spiritual world, I guess, waiting for me somewhere. And I just hoped when I came back here that I was coming to a sort of home, a sort of home right in your heart –'

'What tosh, my dearest dearest Chris.'

'Oh sure, but all the same – you know something, suddenly I feel you're open to me, right open to me – I can walk straight in and there's *welcome* written on the mat – Brad, say those good words, will you, say you forgive me, say we're really reconciled and friends again at last.'

'Of course I forgive you, Chris, of course we're reconciled. You must forgive me too, I wasn't a patient man –'

'Sure I do . Now thank God we can talk at last, talk all about how things were and about the bloody fools we used to be, make it all good again, buy it back, that's what "redeem" means, doesn't it, what happens in the pawn shop. When I saw you crying for Priscilla I knew it was possible. You're a good man, Bradley Pearson, we can make it together if only we open our hearts –'

'Chris, dear. Please!'

'Brad, you know in a way you *are* my husband, I've never really stopped thinking of you that way, after all we were married in church, with my body I thee worship and the whole sacred caboodle, we were pure in heart once, we meant well by each other, we really cared, didn't we, didn't we care?'

'Possibly, but –'

'When it went wrong I thought I'd become a cynic forever – I married Evans for his money. Well, that was a real action anyway, I never left him, he died holding my hand, the poor old bugger. But now I feel as if the past has all fallen away. I came back to you to say this, Brad, to *find* this, and now we're

228

older and wiser and sorry for what we did, why don't we try again?'

'Chris darling, you're dotty,' I said. 'But I'm very touched.'

'Gee, Brad, you look so young. You look all dewy and spiritual like a cat with kittens.'

'I'm going. Good-bye.'

'You can't go just when we've established a new deal. I wanted to say all this to you before only I couldn't because you were sort of different, sort of closed, I couldn't sort of see you properly, but now you're all here, every bit of you, and so am I, it's the real thing, we must have another go, Brad, we must. Of course you don't have to decide at once, think it over peacefully at your leisure – we could live anywhere you like and you could get on with your work quietly, we could get a house in France or Italy, anywhere you like –'

'Chris –'

'Switzerland.'

'Not Switzerland. I hate mountains.'

'Well, then –'

'Look, I must –'

'Kiss me, Bradley.'

A woman's face changes in tenderness. It may become scarcely recognizable. Christian *en tendresse* looked older, more animal-like and absurd, her features all squashed up and rubbery. She was wearing an open-necked cotton dress of rich Chinese red and a gold chain round her neck. The flesh of her neck was stained and dry behind the fresh gold of the chain. Her dyed hair was glossy and animal-sleek. She was looking at me in the cool north indigo duskiness of the room with such a humble pleading diffident rueful tender look upon her face, and her drooping hands were opened to me in a sort of Oriental gesture of abandonment and homage. I stepped forward and took her in my arms.

At the same time I laughed, and holding her, not kissing her, continued to laugh. I saw over her shoulder a quite other face of happiness. But I held her very consciously and laughed, and then she began to laugh too, her forehead moving to and fro against my shoulder.

Arnold came in.

I released Christian slowly and she looked at Arnold and went on laughing in a weary almost contented sort of way, 'Oh dear, oh dear –'

'I'm just off,' I said to Arnold.

He had sat down quietly immediately on entering, like a man in a waiting-room. He had his wet look (his drenched albino aspect) as if he had been in the rain, his colourless hair darkened with grease, his face shiny, his nose pointing like a greased pin. His very pale blue eyes, washed almost to whiteness, were cool as water. I had seen, before he had time to smooth it, the expression of chagrin with which he had greeted our little scene.

'You will think it over, Brad, won't you, dear?'

'Think what over?'

'Oh, he's priceless, he's forgotten it already! I just proposed to Brad and he's forgotten it!'

'Christian has taken leave of her senses,' I said in a kindly tone to Arnold. 'I've just ordered all your books.'

'Why?' said Arnold, now affecting a friendly gloomy detachment and still sitting sedately on his chair, while Christian, chuckling to herself, was reeling or dancing in little steps about the room.

'I'd like to make a reappraisal. I feel I may have been unjust to you, completely wrong in fact.'

'Decent of you.'

'Not at all. I want to be – at peace with everybody – at this time –'

'Is it Christmas?' said Arnold.

'No, just – I'll read your books, Arnold – I'll do it – humbly and without prejudice – please believe that – and please forgive me for – all my – shortcomings and –'

'Brad's become a saint.'

'Are you feeling all right, Bradley?'

'Just look at him. I guess it's the transfiguration!'

'I must go – good-bye, good-bye – and – be well – be well –' waving rather awkwardly to them both and eluding the hand which Christian stretched out to me I got to the door and swung myself through the tiny hall and out into the street. It appeared to be evening. What had happened to the day?

230

As I neared the corner of the street I heard running steps behind me. It was Francis.

'Brad, I just wanted to say – Wait, please, wait – I wanted to say I'll stick by her whatever happens, I'll –'

'Who?'

'Priscilla.'

'Oh yes. How is she?'

'Asleep.'

'Thank you for helping poor Priscilla.'

'Brad, I wanted to make sure you weren't angry with me.'

'Why should I be?'

'Not sick with me after all the things I said and crying on you and all, some people it just sickens them if you throw up all your woes like that, and I'm afraid I –'

'Forget it.'

'And Brad. I wanted to say, just one more thing – I just wanted to say – whatever happens – I'm on your side.'

I stopped and looked at him and he smirked and bit his fat lower lip and the little eyes came questing slyly up. 'In the coming – great – battle,' I said, 'whatever it – may turn out – to be – thank you, Francis Marloe.'

He looked a little surprised. I gave a sort of military salute and walked on. He ran after me again.

'I'm very fond of you, Brad, you know that.'

'Bugger off!'

'Brad, please could I have some more cash – I'm sorry to bother you but Christian keeps me so short –'

I gave him five pounds.

The division of one day from the next must be one of the most profound peculiarities of life on this planet. It is, on the whole, a merciful arrangement. We are not condemned to sustained flights of being, but are constantly refreshed by little holidays from ourselves. We are intermittent creatures, always falling to little ends and rising to little new beginnings. Our soon-tired consciousness is meted out in chapters, and that the world will look quite different tomorrow is, both for our comfort and our discomfort, usually true. How marvellously too night matches sleep, sweet image of it, so neatly apportioned to our need. Angels must wonder at these beings who fall so regularly out of awareness into a fantasm-infested dark. How our frail identities survive these chasms no philosopher has ever been able to explain.

The next morning – it was another sunny day – I woke early to an exact perception of my state; yet knowing too that something had changed. I was not quite as I had been the day before. I lay, testing myself, as someone after an accident might test himself for broken limbs. I certainly still felt very happy, with that curious sense of the face as waxen, dissolving into bliss, the eyes swimming with it. Desire, still cosmic, was perhaps more like physical pain, like something one could die of quite privately in a corner. But I was not dismayed. I got up and shaved and dressed with care and looked at my new face in the mirror. I looked so young it was almost uncanny. Then I drank a little tea and went to sit in the sitting-room, with my hands folded, looking through the window at the wall. I sat as still as a Buddhist and experienced myself.

After the initial revelation, love does demand a strategy: that this is often the beginning of the end makes it no less imperative. I knew that today, and presumably every other day forever, I would have to busy myself concerning Julian. Yesterday this had not seemed so precisely necessary. Yesterday what had happened was simply that, through no merit of my own, I had become virtuous. And yesterday that had been enough. I loved, and the joy of love made a void in me where my self had been. I was purged of resentment and of hate, purged of all the mean anxious fears that compose the vile ego. It was enough that she existed and that she could never be mine. I had to live and love alone, and the sense that I could do so had almost made me a god. Today I was no less virtuous, no more illusioned, but my will was just a trifle busier and fussier. Of course I could never tell her, of course silence and work would felicitously absorb the great power with which I was endowed. But all the same I felt a new need for some rather more localized Julian-directed activity.

I sat motionless for I am not sure how long. Perhaps I really went into some sort of trance. Then the telephone rang and my heart went off in a black explosion as I was instantly certain that it was Julian. I ran to the instrument and fumbled and dropped it twice before I got it to my ear. It was Grey-Pelham, ringing up to say that since his wife was indisposed he had an extra ticket for Glyndebourne and would I like it? I would not! Glyndebourne forsooth! When I had politely got rid of him I rang Notting Hill. Francis answered and told me that Priscilla was calmer this morning and had agreed to see a psychiatrist. After that I sat and wondered if I would ring Ealing. Not to talk to Julian of course. Perhaps I *ought* to ring Rachel? But supposing Julian were to answer?

As I was scorching and freezing my mind with this possibility the phone rang again and again my heart exploded, and this time it was Rachel. Our conversation was as follows:

'Hello, Bradley. It's dreary old me.'

'Rachel – dear – nice – happy – you – so glad –'

'You can't be drunk at this hour of the morning.'

'What time is it?'

'Eleven-thirty.'

'I thought it was about nine.'

'You'll be glad to hear that I'm not coming round to see you.'

'But I'd love you to.'

'No, I've got to get hold of myself. It's so – below me – to persecute my old friends.'

'We are friends, aren't we?'

'Yes, yes, yes. Oh Bradley, I mustn't start – I'm glad you're there, I won't bother you more than I can help. Bradley, was Arnold at Christian's place yesterday?'

'No.'

'He was, I know. Never mind. Oh God, I mustn't *start* –'

'Rachel –'

'Yes?'

'How's – how's – Julian – today?'

'Oh much as usual.'

'She's not – by any chance – going to come round here – to get her *Hamlet* – is she?'

'No. She seems to be off *Hamlet* today. She's down the road with a young couple who are digging a conversation pit in their garden playroom.'

'A what?'

'A conversation pit.'

'Oh. Ah well. I see. Tell her – No. Well – '

'Bradley, you do – never mind what it means – love me, don't you?'

'Yes, of course.'

'Sorry to be so sort of – limp and wet – Thanks for listening – I'll ring again – 'Bye –'

I forgot Rachel. I decided I would go out and buy Julian a present. I still felt ill and rather faint and given to fits of trembling. At the idea of buying the present a lot of trembling came on. Present-buying is a fairly universal symptom of love. It is certainly a *sine qua non*. (If you don't want to give her a present you don't love her.) It is I suppose a method of touching the beloved.

When I felt that I could walk all right I left the house and went as far as Oxford Street. Love transforms the world. It had transformed the big Oxford Street shops into diplays of possible presents for Julian. I bought a leather purse, a box of handkerchiefs, an enamel bracelet, a fancy sponge bag, a pair of lace gloves, a set of ballpoint pens, a key ring, and three scarves. Then I ate a sandwich and went home and laid all the presents out together with the six-volume London edition of Shakespeare upon the marquetry table and the mahogany night table, and contemplated them. Of course I could not give her all these things at once, it would look odd. But I could give her one now, another later: and meanwhile here they were and they were *hers*. I tied one of the scarves round my neck and felt giddy with physical desire. I was on a high building and wanted to hurl myself down, I was being burnt and nearly losing consciousness, I was in pain, pain.

The telephone rang. I staggered to it and gasped into it.

'Oh Brad. It's Chris.'

'Oh – Chris – hello, dear.'

'I'm glad I'm still Chris today.'

'Today – yes –'

'Have you thought over my proposition?'

'What proposition?'

'Gee, Brad, you are a tease. Look, can I come over and see you right now?'

'No.'

'Why not?'

'I've got a bridge party.'

'But you can't play bridge.'

'I learnt in the thirty or so years of your absence. I had to pass the time somehow.'

'Brad, when can I see you, it's kind of urgent?'

'I'll come round to see Priscilla – this evening – probably –'

'OK, I'll wait. Mind you come.'

'And God bless you, Chris, God bless you, dear, God bless you.'

I sat in the hall beside the telephone and fingered Julian's scarf. Since I retained it with me, although it was hers, it was as if she had given me a present. I sat and looked through the open door of the sitting-room at Julian's things arranged upon the tables. I listened to the silence of the flat in the midst of the murmur of London. Time passed. I waited. Being your slave what should I do but tend upon the hours and times of your desire. I have no precious time at all to spend, nor services to do till you require.

It now seemed to me incredible that I could have had the nerve to leave the house that morning. Suppose she had telephoned, suppose she had come, when I was away? She could not spend the whole day digging a conversation pit, whatever that was. She would surely come round soon to get her *Hamlet*. How good it was that I had that hostage. After a while I moved back into the sitting-room and picked up the shabby little book and sat caressing it in Hartbourne's armchair. My eyelids drooped and the material world grew dim and I waited.

I had not forgotten that I was soon going to start writing the greatest book of my life. I knew that the black Eros which had felled me was consubstantial with another and more secret god. If I could keep my silence and my nerve I would be rewarded with power. But for the moment writing was out of the question. I could only have committed to paper the scrawlings of the unconscious.

The telephone rang and I ran to it, jolting the table and knocking the six volumes of Shakespeare off on to the floor.

'Bradley. Arnold here.'

'Oh God. It's you.'

'What's the matter?'

'Nothing.'

'Bradley, I hear –'

'What time is it?'

'Four o'clock. I hear you're coming round this evening to see Priscilla.'

'Yes.'

'Well, could I see you after that? There's something important I want to tell you.'

'Yes. Fine. What's a conversation pit?'

'What?'

'What's a conversation pit?'

'A sunken area in a room where you put cushions and people sit and converse.'

'What's the point of it?'

'It has no point.'

'Oh Arnold, Arnold –'

'What?'

'Nothing. I'll read your books. I'll start to like them. Everything will be different.'

'Have you got softening of the brain?'

'Good-bye, good-bye –'

I returned to the sitting-room and I picked up the Shakespeares from the floor and I sat down in the armchair and I said to her in my heart, I will suffer, you will not. We will do each other no harm. You will cause me pain, it cannot be otherwise. But I shall cause you none. And I will feed upon my pain like one who feeds on kisses. (Oh God.) I am simply happy that you exist, happy in the absolute that is you, proud to live with you in the same city, in the same era, to see you occasionally, seldom . . .

But how occasionally, how seldom? When would she communicate with me again? How soon could I communicate with her? I had already worked it out that if she wrote or telephoned I would make an appointment with her for several days later. Everything must be as usual, the world for all that it was utterly changed must remain utterly the same, just as it was, as it would have been, in every detail. I would make not the tiniest haste nor hint at the faintest urgency nor by any slightest gesture depart from what I once was, what I would have been. Yes, I would even put off seeing her, and devote, like a holy man, the precious deprived time to meditation; and so the world would be the same yet different, as it is for the sage who has returned from the mountain and lives an ordinary life in the village though seeing all with the eyes of vision, a god-head that resembles a peasant, that resembles an inspector of taxes: and so we would be saved.

The telephone rang. I reached it. This time it was Julian.

'Oh Bradley, hello, it's me.'

I made some sort of sound.

'Bradley – sorry – it's me – you know, Julian Baffin.'

I said, 'Hold on a minute, would you?' I covered the mouth-piece and closed my eyes tightly, groped for a chair, panting, trying to control my breath. In a few moments I said, coughing a little to disguise the tremor, 'Sorry. The kettle was just boiling.'

'I'm so sorry to bother you, Bradley. I promise I won't become a pest, always ringing up and coming round.'

'Not at all.'

'I just wondered if I could pick up my *Hamlet* whenever you've finished with it.'

'Certainly.'

'But there's no hurry at all – any time in the next fortnight would do. I'm not working on that at the moment. And there's one or two more questions I've thought of. If you like I could send them by post, and you could post me the book. I don't want to interrupt your work.'

'In the next – fortnight –'

'Or month. I may be going to the country actually. My school has still got the measles.'

'Perhaps you could drop in some time next week,' I said.

'Fine. How about Thursday morning about ten?'

'Yes. That's – fine.'

'Thank you so much. I won't keep you. I know you're so busy. Good-bye, Bradley, and thanks.'

'Wait a minute,' I said.

There was silence.

'Julian,' I said, 'are you free this evening?'

The restaurant at the top of the Post Office Tower revolves very slowly. Slow as a dial hand. Majestic trope of lion-blunting time.

How swiftly did it move that night while London crept behind the beloved head? Was it quite immobile, made still by thought, a mere fantasy of motion in a world beyond duration? Or was it spinning like a top, whirling away into invisibility, and pinning me against the outer wall, kitten-limbed and crucified by centrifugal force?

Concerning absence love has always been eloquent. The subject admits of an explicit melancholy, though doubtless there are certain pains which cannot be fully rendered. But has it ever sufficiently hymned presence? Can it do so? The presence of the loved one is perhaps always accompanied by anxiety. Mortals must tremble, where angels might enjoy. But this one grain of darkness cannot be accounted a blemish. It graces the present moment with a kind of violence which makes an ecstasy of time.

To speak more crudely, what I experienced that evening on the Post Office Tower was a kind of blinding joy. It was as if stars were exploding in front of my eyes so that I literally could not see. Breathing was fast and difficult, not unpleasant. I was conscious of a certain satisfaction in being able to go on pumping myself full of oxygen. A quiet and perhaps outwardly imperceptible shuddering possessed my whole frame. My hands vibrated, my legs ached and throbbed, my knees were in the condition described by the Greek poetess. This *dérèglement* was completed by a sense of giddiness produced by the sheer conception of being so high above the ground and yet still connected to it. Giddiness of this kind in any case locates itself in the genitals.

These are the merest physical symptoms. *They* can readily be sketched in words. But how to convey the rapture of the mind, as it mingles with the body, draws apart into itself, and mingles again, in a wild and yet graceful dance? The sense of being absolutely in the right and longed-for place is fixed and guaranteed by every ray in the universe. The beatific vision would be a similar experience if one also *was* what one *saw*. (Perhaps that is indeed the meaning of the beatific vision?) Consciousness half swoons with its sense of humble delighted privilege while keen sight, in between the explosions of the stars, devours every detail of the real presence. I am here now, you are here now, we are here now. To see her among others, straying like a divine form among mortals, is to become faint with secret knowledge. There is also a gleeful calm as one realizes that these passing seconds are the fullest and most perfect, not even excluding sexual union, which can be allotted to human beings.

All this, and further hues and saturations of bliss which I cannot describe at all, I felt on that evening as I sat with Julian in the Post Office Tower restaurant. We talked, and our communion was so perfect that it might have been telepathic for all I could make out afterwards about how it actually occurred. The evening had darkened to an intense blue, but it was not yet night. The forms of London, some already chequered with yellow light, glided onward through a dim shimmering corpuscular haze. The Albert Hall, the Science Museums, Centre Point, the Tower of London, St Paul's Cathedral, the Festival Hall, the Houses of Parliament, the Albert Memorial. The precious and beloved skyline of my own Jerusalem processed incessantly behind that dear mysterious head. Only the royal parks were already places of darkness, growing inkily purple with night-time and its silence.

Mysterious head. Oh the tormenting strangeness of our ignorance of other minds, the privileged comfort of the secrecy of our own! In fact on that night what I felt most in her was her lucidity, her transparency almost. That purity and unmuddied simplicity of the young, after the anxious self-guarding deviousness of later ages. Her clear eyes looked at me and she was *with* me and spoke to me with a directness which I had never received before. To say that there was no element of flirting is to speak with a totally inappropriate grossness. We conversed as angels might converse, not through a glass darkly but face to face. And yet: I was – again to say that I was playing a part is a barbarism. I was blazing with secrecy. As my eyes and my thoughts caressed and possessed her and as I smiled into her open attentive gaze with a passion and even with a tenderness which she could not see, I felt ready to fall to the ground fainting, perhaps dying, with the enormity of what I knew and she did not.

'Bradley, I think it's *swaying*.'

'It can't be. I believe it does sway a little in the wind. But there's no wind tonight.'

'There might be a wind up here.'

'Well, there might be. Yes, I think it *is* swaying.' How could I tell? Everything was swaying.

Of course I had merely pretended to eat. I had drunk very little wine. Alcohol still seemed a complete irrelevancy. I was drunk with love. Julian had both eaten and drunk a good deal, indiscriminately praising everything that passed her lips. We had talked about the view, about her college, about her school with the measles, about how soon one could tell whether one was a poet, about whether the novel, about why the theatre. I had never talked so easily to anyone. Oh blessed weightlessness, oh blessed space.

'Bradley, I wish I'd understood that stuff you spouted about *Hamlet*.'

'Forget it. No high theory about Shakespeare is any good, not because he's so divine but because he's so human. Even great art is jumble in the end.'

'So the critics are just stupid?'

'It needs no theory to tell us this! One should simply try to like as much as one can.'

'Like you now trying to like what my father writes?'

'That's more special. I feel I've been unjust. He has huge vitality and he tells a good story. Stories are art too, you know.'

'His stuff is awfully ingenious, but it's as dead as a door nail.'

'So young and so untender.'

'So young, my lord, but true.'

I was nearly on the floor at that moment. I also thought, in so far as thinking occurred, that she was probably right. Only I was not going to utter any harsh things that evening. I was mainly now, since I had realized that I could not keep her with me for much longer, wondering about whether and if so how I could kiss her on parting. Kissing had never been customary between us, even when she was a child. Briefly, I had never kissed her. Never. And now tonight perhaps I would.

'Bradley, you aren't listening.'

She constantly used my name. I could not use hers. She had no name.

'Sorry, my dear, what were you saying?' I was slipping little endearments in slyly. This was no breach of security. Would she notice anything? Certainly not. But the pleasure was mine.

'Ought I to read Wittgenstein?'

What I wanted to do was to kiss her in the lift going down should we chance to have that momentary love nest to ourselves. But of course that was out of the question. There must be no, absolutely no, show of marked interest. She had, as young people with their charming egoism and their impromptu modes so felicitously do, taken it quite calmly for granted that I should suddenly have felt like dining on the Post Office Tower and should, since she had happened to ring up, have happened to ask her to come too.

'No. I shouldn't bother.'

'You think I wouldn't understand him?'

'Yes.'

'Yes, I wouldn't?'

'Yes. He never thought of you.'

'What?'

'I'm quoting again. Never mind.'

'We are full of quotations tonight, aren't we. When I'm with you I feel as if the whole of English literature were inside me like a warm stew and coming out of my ears. I say, what an inelegant metaphor! Oh Bradley, what fun that we're here. Bradley, I do feel so happy!'

241

'Good.' I asked for the bill. I did not want to ruin what was perfect by any hint of anxious hanging-on. An over-stayed welcome would have been torture afterwards. I did not want to see her looking at her watch.

She looked at her watch. 'Oh dear, I must go soon.'

'I'll see you to the tube.'

We had the lift to ourselves going down. I did not kiss her. I did not suggest that she should come back to my flat. As we walked along Goodge Street I did not touch her, even 'accidentally'. I was beginning to wonder how in the world it would be possible to part from her.

Outside Goodge Street station I stopped and casually cornered her against a wall. I did not put my two hands on the wall on either side of her shoulders as I wanted to do. She looked up at me smiling and tossing back her lion mane, so utterly confident, so utterly trusting. She was dressed tonight in a black cotton dress with sort of yellow mandalas on it, Indian I suppose. She looked like a court page. The lamplight shone down on to her tender true face and the V of her throat which I had so intensely wanted during dinner to reach across and touch. I was still in a state of total and now utterly agonizing indecision about the kiss.

'Well, then – Well, then –'

'Bradley, you've been sweet, thank you, I've so much enjoyed it.'

'Oh, I quite forgot to bring your *Hamlet*.' I had of course done no such thing.

'Never mind, I'll get it another time. Good night, Bradley, and thanks.'

'Yes, I – let me see –'

'I must run.'

'Won't you – Shall we fix a time for you to come – You said you had some – I'm so often out – Or shall I – Will you –'

'I'll ring you. Good night, and thank you so much.'

It was now or never. With a sense of moving very slowly, of executing some sort of precise figure in a minuet, I stepped a little in front of Julian, who was turning away, took her left wrist lightly in my right hand, thereby halting her, and then leaned down and pressed my judiciously parted lips against her cheek. The effect could not be casual. I straightened up and we stood for a moment looking at each other.

Julian said, 'Bradley, if I asked you, would you come to Covent Garden with me?'

'Yes, of course.' I would go to hell with her, and even to Covent Garden.

'It's *Rosenkavalier*. Next Wednesday. Meet in the foyer about half past six. I've got quite good tickets. Septimus Leech got us two, only now he can't come.'

'Who is Septimus Leech?'

'Oh he's my new boy-friend. Good night, Bradley.'

She was gone. I stood there dazed in the lamplight among the hurrying ghosts. And I felt as a man might feel who, with a whole skin on him and a square meal inside him, sits in a cell having just been captured by the secret police.

The next morning, of course, I awoke in torment. The reader may think it was unconscionably stupid of me not to have foreseen that I could not continue simply to derive happiness from this situation. But the reader, unless he is at this moment of reading himself madly in love, has probably mercifully forgotten, if indeed he ever knew, what this state of mind is like. It is, as I have re-marked, a form of insanity. Is it not insane to concentrate one's attention exclusively on one person, to drain the rest of the world of meaning, to have no thoughts, no feelings, no being except in relation to the beloved? What the beloved 'is like' or 'is really like' matters not a fig. Of course some people go crazy about people whom other people think worthless. 'Why did she fall for the leader of the band?' is an eternal question. We are stunned when we see those whom we esteem enslaved by the vulgar, the frivolous, or the base. But even if a man or a woman were so fine and so wise that their claim to be such could be denied by no one, it would still be a form of madness to direct upon him or upon her the kind of exclusive worshipping attention in which being in love consists.

A common though not invariable early phase of this madness, the one in fact through which I had just been passing, is a false loss of self, which can be so extreme that all fear of pain, all sense of time (time is anxiety, is fear) is utterly blotted out. The sensation itself of loving, the contemplation of the existence of the beloved, is an end in itself. A mystic's heaven on earth must be just such an endless contemplation of God. Only God has (or would have if He existed) characteristics at least not totally inimical to the continuance of the pleasures of adoration. As the so-called 'ground of being' He may be considered to have come a good deal farther than half-way. Also He is changeless. To remain thus poised in the worship of a human being is, from both sides of the relationship, a much more precarious matter, even when the beloved is not nearly forty years younger and, to say the least of it, detached.

I had in fact lived through almost the whole history of 'being in love' in just over two days. (I say 'almost the whole history' because there is yet more to come.) The condensed phenomenology of the business had been enacted within me. On the first day I was simply a saint. I was so warmed and vitalized by sheer gratitude that I overflowed with charity. I felt so privileged and glorified that resentment, even memory of any wrong done to me, seemed inconceivable. I wanted to go around touching people, blessing them, communicating my great happiness, the good news, the *secret* of how the whole universe was a place of joy and freedom filled and running over with selfless rapture. I did not even want to see Julian on that day. I did not even need her. It was enough to know that she existed. I could *almost* have forgotten her, as perhaps the mystic forgets God, when he becomes God.

On the second day I began to need her, though even 'anxiety' would be too gross a word for that delicate silken magnetic tug, as it manifested itself at any rate initially. Self was reviving. On the first day Julian had been everywhere. On the second day she was, yes, somewhere, located vaguely, not yet dreadfully required, but needed. She was, on the second day, absent. This inspired the small craving for strategy, a little questing desire to make plans. The future, formerly blotted out by an excess of light, reappeared. There were once more vistas, hypotheses, possibilities. But joy and gratitutde still lightened the world and made possible a gentle concern with other people, other things. I wonder how long a man could remain in that first phase of love? Much longer than I did, no doubt, but surely not indefinitely. The second phase, I am sure, given favourable conditions, could continue much longer. (But again, not indefinitely. Love is history, is dialectic, it *must* move.) As it is, I lived in hours what another man might have lived in years.

The transformation of my beatitude could, as that second day wore on, be measured by a literally physical sense of strain, as if magnetic rays or even ropes or chains were delicately plucking, then tugging, then dragging. Physical desire had of course been with me from the first, but earlier it had been, though perceptually localized, metaphysically diffused into a general glory. Sex is our great connection with the world, and at its most felicitous and spiritual it is no servitude since it informs everything and enables us to inhabit and enjoy all that we touch and look upon. At other times it settles in the body like a toad. It becomes a drag, a weight: not necessarily for this reason unwelcome. We may love our chains and our stripes too. By the time Julian telephoned I was in deep anxiety and yearning but not in hell. I could not then willingly have put off seeing her, the craving was too acute. But I was able, when I was with her, to be perfectly happy. I did not expect the inferno.

Even then, when I got back to my flat after leaving her, I was confused and frightened and wounded, but not writhing, not screaming. My spiritual liberation from alcohol appeared to be over. I got out the secret bottle of whisky which I keep for emergencies and drank a lot of it neat. After that I drank some sherry. I also ate, spooning it out of the tin, some chicken curry which Francis had evidently introduced into the house. I felt then, as I remember having felt in childhood, very unhappy, somehow humiliated, but determined not to think, determined to seek refuge in sleep. I knew that I would sleep well and I did. I rushed towards unconsciousness as a ship that flies towards a black storm cloud which covers the whole of the horizon.

I woke with a clear head, a slight headache, and the knowledge that I was completely done for. Reason which had been – where had it been, during the last days? – somehow absent or dazed or altered or in abeyance, was once more at its post. (At least it was audible.) But in a rather specialized role and certainly not in that of a consoling friend. Reason was not, needless to say, uttering any coarse observations, such as that Julian was after all a very ordinary young woman and not worth all this fuss. Nor was it even pointing out that I had put myself in a situation where the torments of jealousy were simply endemic. I had not yet got as far as jealousy. That too was still to come. What the cold light showed me was that my situation was simply unlivable. I wanted, with a desire greater than any desire which I had ever conceived could exist without instantly killing its owner by spontaneous combustion, something which I simply could not have.

There were no tears now. I lay in bed in an electric storm of physical desire. I tossed and panted and groaned as if I were wrestling with a palpable demon. The fact that I had actually touched her, kissed her, grew (I am sorry about these metaphors) into a sort of mountain which kept falling on top of me. I felt her flesh upon my lips. Phantoms were bred from this touch. I felt like a grotesque condemned excluded monster. How could it be that I had actually kissed her cheek without enveloping her, without becoming her? How could I at that moment have refrained from kneeling at her feet and howling?

I got up but was suffering such extreme local discomfort that I could hardly get dressed. I started making tea, but its smell sickened me. I drank a little whisky in a glass of water and began to feel very ill. I could not stand still but wandered distractedly and rapidly about the flat rubbing against the furniture as a tiger in a cage endlessly brushes its bars. I had ceased groaning and was now *hissing*. I tried to compose a few thoughts about the future. Should I kill myself? Should I go at once to Patara and barricade myself in and blow my mind with alcohol? Run, run, run. But I could not compose thoughts. All that concerned me was finding some way of getting through these present *minutes* of pain.

I have said that I did not yet feel jealousy. Jealousy after all is a sort of exercise or play of the reason. And my state of love was still too monumentally complete in itself to let reason get inside. Reason stood, as it were, beside it, playing its torch over the monument. It was not yet worming about within. It was not really until the following day, day four that is (but I will describe it now), that I began to *think* that Julian was twenty and as free as a bird. Did I dare question with my jealous thought where she might be, and her affairs suppose? Yes, I did, it was ultimately unavoidable. At that very moment she could be anywhere in anybody's arms. Of course I must have 'known' that at the start, since it was so obvious. But it had not then seemed to concern *me* or to touch the saint that I was. She had dwelt with me then in a kind of unlocalized communion of consciousness. Now it began suddenly to concern me so much that it felt like a red-hot knitting needle thrust into the liver. (Where had I picked up that appalling simile?)

Jealousy is the most dreadfully involuntary of all sins. It is at once one of the ugliest and one of the most pardonable. In fact, in relation to its badness it is probably the most pardonable. Zeus, who smiles at lovers' oaths, must also condone their pangs and the venom which these pangs engender. Some Frenchman said that jealousy was born with love, but did not always die with love. I am not sure whether this is true. I would think that where there is jealousy there *is* love, and its appearance when love has apparently ceased is always a proof that the cessation *is* apparent. (I believe this is not just a verbal point.) Jealousy is certainly a measure of love in some, though as my own case illustrates not in all, of its phases. It also (and this may have prompted the Frenchman's idea) seems like an alien growth – and *growth* is indeed the word. Jealousy is a cancer, it can kill that which it feeds on, though it is usually a horribly slow killer. (And thereby dies itself.) Also of course, to change the metaphor, jealousy *is* love, it is loving consciousness, loving vision, darkened by pain and in its most awful forms distorted by hate.

What is so terrible about it is the sense that a part of oneself has been irrecoverably alienated and stolen. I realized this now, first vaguely and then with increasing precision, in the case of Julian. It was not simply that I frenziedly desired what I could

247

not have. That was but a blunt and unrefined kind of suffering. I was condemned to be *with* her even in her very rejection of me. And how long and how slow and how long-drawn-out that rejection would be. Still temptation would follow where she was. Endlessly she would give herself to others taking me with her. Like an obscene puny familiar I would sit in the corners of bedrooms where she kissed and loved. She would make consort with my foes, she would adore those that mocked me, she would drink contempt for me from alien lips. And all the time my very soul would travel with her, invisible and crying soundlessly with pain. I had acquired a dimension of suffering which would poison and devour my whole being, as far as I could see, for ever.

The idea that one recovers from being in love is, of course, by definition (by my definition anyway) excluded from the state of love. Besides, one does not always recover. And certainly no such banal would-be comfort could have existed for a second in the scorching atmosphere of my mind at that time. As I said earlier, I knew that I was completely done for. There was no ray of light, no comfort *at all*. Though I will now also mention something which dawned upon me later. There was of course no question now of writing, of 'sublimating' it all (ridiculous expression). But the sense remained that this *was* my destiny, that this was ... the work of ... the same power. And to be pinned down by *that* power, even though one was writhing upon a spear which passed through the liver, was to be in some terrible sense in one's own place.

To speak of matters which are less obscure, I soon of course decided that I could not 'run'. I could not go away to the country. I had to see Julian again, I had to wait through those awful days until the appointment at Covent Garden. Of course I wanted to ring her up at once and ask her to see me. But I somehow kept blindly thrusting this temptation away. I would not let my life degenerate into madness. Better to be alone with *him* and to suffer than to pull it all down into some sort of yelling chaos. Silence, though now with a different and utterly unconsoling sense, was my only task.

Somewhere in the middle of that morning, which I will not

248

attempt to describe further (except to say that Hartbourne rang up: I replaced the receiver at once), Francis Marloe came.

I went back into the sitting-room and he followed me, already staring at me with surprise. I sat down and started rubbing my eyes and my brow, breathing heavily.

'What's the matter, Brad?'

'Nothing.'

'I say, there's some whisky. I didn't know you had any. You must have hidden it jolly well. May I have some?'

'Yes.'

'Would you like some?'

'Yes.'

Francis was putting a glass into my hand. 'Are you ill?'

'Yes.'

'What's the matter?'

I drank some whisky and choked a bit. I felt extremely sick and also unable to distinguish physical from mental pain.

'Brad, we waited all evening for you.'

'Why? Where?'

'You said you'd come to see Priscilla.'

'Oh. Priscilla. Yes.' I had totally and absolutely forgotten Priscilla's existence.

'We rang up here.'

'I was out to dinner.'

'Had you just forgotten?'

'Yes.'

'Arnold was there till after eleven. He wanted to see you about something. He was in a bit of a state.'

'How is Priscilla?'

'Much the same. Chris wants to know if you'd mind if she had electric shock treatment.'

'Yes. Fine.'

'You mean you don't mind? You know it destroys cells in the brain?'

'Then she'd better not have it.'

'On the other hand –'

'I ought to see Priscilla,' I said, I think, aloud. But I knew that I just *couldn't*. I had not got a grain of spirit to offer to any other

249

person. I could not expose myself in my present condition to that poor rapacious craving consciousness.

'Priscilla said she'd do anything *you* wanted.'

Electric shocks. They batter the brain cage. Like hitting the wireless, they say, to make it go. I must pull myself together. Priscilla.

'We must go – into it –' I said.

'Brad, what's the matter?'

'Nothing. Destruction of cells in the brain.'

'Are you ill?'

'Yes.'

'What is it?'

'I'm in love.'

'Oh,' said Francis. 'Who with?'

'Julian Baffin.'

I had not intended to tell him. It was something to do with Priscilla that I did. The pity of it. And then a sense of being battered beyond caring.

Francis took it coolly. I suppose that was the way to take it. 'Oh. Is it very bad, I mean your sickness?'

'Yes.'

'Have you told her?'

'Don't be a fool,' I said. 'I'm fifty-eight. She's twenty.'

'I don't see that that decides anything much,' said Francis. 'Love is no respecter of ages, everyone knows that. Can I have some more whisky?'

'You don't understand,' I said. 'I can't – before that – young girl – make a display of feelings such as I – feel. It would appal her. And as I can envisage – no possible relationship with her of *that* kind –'

'I don't see why not,' said Francis, 'though whether it would be a good idea is another matter.'

'Don't talk such utter – It's a question of morals and of – everything. She cannot possibly feel – for me – almost an old man – It would just disgust her – she simply wouldn't want to see me again.'

'There's a lot of assumptions there. As for morals well maybe, though I don't know. Everything is another matter, especially

250

these days. But will you enjoy going on and on meeting her and keeping your mouth shut?'

'No, of course not.'

'Well, then. Sorry to be so simple-minded. Hadn't you better start pulling out?'

'You've obviously never been in love.'

'I have actually. And *awfully*. And – always – without hope – I've never had my love reciprocated ever. You can't tell *me* –'

'I can't pull out. I'm only just in. I don't know what to do. I feel I'm going mad, I'm trapped.'

'Cut and run. Go to Spain or something.'

'I can't. I'm seeing her on Wednesday. We're going to the opera. Oh Christ.'

'If you want to suffer I suppose it's your affair,' said Francis, helping himself again to the whisky, 'but if you want to get *out*, I think I should tell her if I were you. Reduce the tension and let the thing get more ordinary. That'll help the cure. Secret brooding always makes it worse. Tell her in a letter. You're a writer chap, you'd enjoy writing it all down.'

'It would sicken her.'

'You could do it with a sort of light touch –'

'There's a dignity and a power in silence.'

'Silence?' said Francis. 'You've broken that already.'

O my prophetic soul. It was true.

'Of course I won't tell anybody,' said Francis. 'But why after all did you tell me? You didn't intend to and you'll regret it. You'll probably hate me for it. But please, please don't if you can. You told me because you were frantic, because you felt an irresistible nervous urge. You'll tell her, sooner or later, for the same reason.'

'Never.'

'There's no need to make such heavy weather of it. As for her being sickened, it's far more likely that she'll laugh.'

'*Laugh?*'

'Young people can't take too seriously the feelings of oldies like us. She'll be rather touched, but she'll regard it as an absurd infatuation. She'll be amused, fascinated. It'll make her day.'

'Oh get out,' I said, 'get out.'

'Brad, you are cross with me, don't be, it wasn't my fault you told me.'

'Get out.'

'Brad, what about Priscilla?'

'Do anything you think fit. I leave it to you.'

'Aren't you coming over to see her?'

'Yes, yes. Later. Give her my love.'

Francis got as far as the door. I was still sitting and rubbing my eyes. Francis's funny bear face was all creased up with anxiety and concern and he suddenly resembled his sister, when she had become so absurd, looking at me tenderly in the indigo dark of our old drawing-room.

'Brad, why don't you make a thing of Priscilla?'

'What do you mean?'

'Make her your life-line. Go all out to help her. Really make a job of it. Take your mind off this.'

'You don't know what this is like.'

'Then do the other. Try and make her. Why not?'

'What?'

'Why shouldn't you have an affair with Julian Baffin? It wouldn't do her any harm.'

'You vile – thing – Oh why did I tell you, why did I tell *you*, I must have been insane –'

'Well, I'll keep mum. All right, all right, I'm going.'

When he was gone I simply ran berserk round the house. Why oh why oh why had I broken my silence. I had given away my only treasure and I had given it to a fool. Not that I was concerned about whether Francis would betray me. Some much more frightening things had been added to my pain. In my chess game with the dark lord I had made perhaps a fatally wrong move.

Later on I sat down and began to think over what Francis had said to me. At least I thought over some of it. About Priscilla I did not think at all.

My dear Bradley,

I have lately got myself into the most terrible mess and I feel that I must lay the whole matter before you. Perhaps it won't surprise you all that much. I have fallen desperately in love with Christian. I can imagine your dry irony at this announcement. 'Falling in love? At your age? Really!' I know how much you despise what is 'romantic'. This has been, hasn't it, one of our old disagreements. Let me assure you that what I feel now has nothing to do with rosy dreaming or 'the soppy'. I have never been in a *grimmer* mood in my life, nor I think in a more horribly *realistic* one. Bradley, this is the real thing, I'm afraid. I am completely floored by a force in which, I suspect, you simply do not believe! How can I convince you that I am *in extremis*? I hoped to see you on several occasions lately to try to explain, to *show* you, but perhaps a letter is better. Anyway, that's point one. I am *really* in love and it's a terrible experience. I don't think I've ever felt quite like this before. I'm turned inside out, I'm living in a sort of myth, I've been depersonalized and made into somebody else. I feel sure, by the way, that I've been *completely transformed* as a writer. These things connect, they must do. I shall write much better *harder* stuff in future, as a result of this, whatever happens. God, I feel hard, hard, hard. I don't know if you can understand.

This brings me to point two. There are two women, one of whom I love, the other of whom I do not propose at all to abandon. Of course I care for Rachel. But there is alas such a thing as getting tired of somebody. Our marriage is there, but it is thoroughly tired, exhausted, the spirit has left it I fear for ever. I see this so clearly *now*. There is no deep enlivening connection any more. I have for some time had to look elsewhere for real love, and my affection for Rachel has become something so habitual as to be almost feigned. However I shall hold on to her, I shall hold on to them both because I've *got* to, to abandon either now would be some sort of death, so what must be will be, and that much is clear. And if it means running two establishments it means running two establishments. Other men have done this. Thank God I can afford it. Rachel guesses a bit (nothing like the shattering truth) but I have not spoken to her yet. I know that I can, in terms of my affections, *hold* them both. (Why should one feel there's only a limited amount of love to be distributed?) It is only the first phase which will be difficult, I mean setting up. Habit will smooth ruffled feathers. I will hold them and give them both love. I know this is the sort of talk that disgusts you. (You are rather easily disgusted actually.) But believe me this is something I see with great clarity and *purity*, it is not anything romantic or 'messy'. And I don't think it's easy, I just think it's necessary.

The third point is about you. How do you come in? Well, you just *are* absolutely in. I wish you weren't, but you can in fact be useful. Excuse this cold directness. Perhaps now you can see what I mean by 'hard', 'pure' and the rest. Briefly, I have *got* to have your help. I know in the past we have feuded, we have loved. We are old friends and old enemies, but much more friends, or rather the friend includes the enemy and not vice versa. You understand. You are connected with both of these women. If I say that I want you to release the one and console the other I am saying very roughly and boorishly what I want from you. Rachel cares for you very much, I know that. What there may have been, lately or at some stage, 'between you', I do not ask. I am not a jealous man and I know that Rachel has had, at various times and of course especially now, a good deal to put up with. I think that, in this unavoidable tribulation, you can be a great support to her. It will do her good to have a *friend* to whom she can complain about me! I want you, and this is the immediate specific thing, to see her and to tell her about me and Chris. I think it is psychologically right that you should tell her and that will sort of set the scene for what follows. Tell her this really is 'something big', not just momentary like things in the past. Tell her about 'two establishments' and so on. Break it to her and make her both see the worst and see how it can all work and be not too bad. This sounds awful on paper. But I have, I suppose, become through the power of love, awful, relentless. I am sure that if you will speak to Rachel frankly about this (and I mean soon, today, tomorrow) she will become at once resigned to it. It will also of course create a very special bond between you and her. As to whether this will please you I do not inquire.

About Christian, there is a problem too which concerns you. I have not yet said, though of course I have implied, how she feels. Well, she loves me. A lot has happened in the last few days. They have been probably the most eventful days of my whole life. What Christian was saying to you the last time you saw her was of course a sort of joke, a mere result of high spirits, as I imagine you realized. She is such a gay affectionate person. However she is not indifferent to you and she wants something from you now which is rather hard to name: a sort of *ratification* of the arrangement I have been describing, a sort of final

254

reconciliation and settling of old scores and also the assurance, which
I'm sure you can give, that you will still be her friend when she is living
with me. I might add that Christian, who is a very scrupulous person, is
extremely concerned about Rachel's rights and whether Rachel will be
able to 'manage'. I hope that here too you can give some reassurance.
Rachel is strong too. They are really two marvellous women. Bradley,
do you follow all this? I feel such a mixture of joy and fear and sheer
hard *will*, I'm not sure if I'm expressing myself clearly.

I shall deliver this by hand and will not try to see you at once. But
soon, I mean later today or tomorrow I would like to talk to you. You
will be coming to see Priscilla of course, and we could meet then. There
is no need to delay your talk with Rachel till you've seen me. The sooner
that happens the better. But I'd like to see you before you see Chris
alone. God, does this make sense? It is an *appeal*, and that should
tickle your vanity. You are in a strong position for once. Please help
me. I ask in the name of our friendship.

Arnold.

PS If you hate all this for God's sake be at least kind and don't give me
any sort of hell about it. I may sound rational but I'm feeling terribly
crazy and upset. I so much don't want to hurt Rachel. And please don't
rush round to Chris and upset her, just when some things have become
clear. And don't see Rachel either unless you can do it quietly and like
I asked. Sorry, sorry.

I received this curious missive on the following morning. A
little while ago it would have caused me a mixture of strong
emotions. As it was, love can so deaden one to external matters
that I might as well have been perusing the laundry bill. I read
it through once and then put it away and forgot it. The only
difference it made was that it established the impossibility now
of my going to see Priscilla. I went to a flower shop and gave them
a cheque to send her flowers every day.

I will not attempt to describe how I got through the next few
days. There are desolations of the spirit which can only be hinted
at. I sat there huge-eyed in the wreck of myself. At the same time
there was an awful crescendo of excitement as Wednesday
approached, and the idea of simply *being with her* began to shed
a lurid joy, a demonic version of the joy which I had felt upon
the Post Office Tower. Then I had been in innocence. Now I felt
both guilty and doomed. And, in a way that concerned myself

255

alone, savage, extreme, rude, cruel . . . Yet: to be with her again. Wednesday.

Of course I had to answer the telephone in case it was her. Every time it sounded was like a severe electric shock. Christian rang, Arnold rang. I put the receiver down at once. Let them make what they liked of it. Arnold and Francis both came and rang the bell, but I could see them through the frosted glass of the door and did not let them in. I did not know if they could see me, I was indifferent to that. Francis dropped a note in to say that Priscilla was having shock treatment and seemed better. Rachel called, but I hid. Later she telephoned in some state of emotion. I spoke briefly and said I would ring her later. Thus I beguiled the time. I also started several letters to Julian. My dear Julian, I have lately got myself into the most terrible mess and I feel that I must lay the whole matter before you. Dear Julian, I am sorry that I must leave London and cannot join you on Wednesday. Dearest Julian, I love you, I am in anguish, oh my darling. Of course I tore up all these letters, they were just for private self-expression. At last, after centuries of sick emotion, Wednesday came.

Julian was holding my arm. I had made no attempt to take hers. She had taken mine and was squeezing it convulsively, probably unconsciously, out of excitement. We were jostling our way through a lot of noisy people in the foyer of the Royal Opera House, having just come in out of the evening sunshine into this brilliantly lit crowd scene. Julian was wearing a red silk dress, rather long, covered with an *art nouveau* design of blue tulips. Her hair, which she had been combing carefully and surreptitiously when I first caught sight of her, was unusually casque-like, glowing softly like long slightly dulled strips of flattened metal. Her face was unfocused, joyfully *distrait*, laughing with pleasure. I was feeling a sick delighted anguish of desire, as if I had been ripped by a dagger from the groin to the throat. I also felt frightened. I fear crowds. We got into the auditorium, Julian now pulling me, and found our seats, half-way back in the stalls. People stood up to let us in. I hate this. I hate theatres. There was an intense subdued din of human chatter, the self-satisfied yap of a civilized audience awaiting its 'show': the frivolous speech of vanity speaking to vanity. And now there began to be heard in the background that awful and inimitably menacing sound of an orchestra tuning up.

How I feel about music is another thing. I am not actually tone deaf, though it might be better if I were. Music can touch me, it can get at me, it can torment. It just, as it were, reaches me, like a sinister gabbling in a language one can almost understand, a gabbling which is horribly, one suspects, *about oneself.* When I was younger I had even listened to music deliberately, stunning myself with disorderly emotion and imagining that I was having a great experience. True pleasure in art is a cold fire. I do not wish to deny that there are some people – though fewer than one might think from the talk of our self-styled experts – who derive a pure and mathematically clarified pleasure from these medleys of sound. All I can say is that 'music' for me was simply an occasion for personal fantasy, the outrush of hot muddled emotions, the muck of my mind made audible.

Julian had let go of my arm but was sitting now leaning towards me, so that the whole length of her right arm from the shoulder to the elbow was lightly touching my left arm. I sat stiffly in possession of this contact. At the same time I very cautiously advanced my left shoe up against her right shoe in such a way that the shoes were contiguous without any pressure being exerted on the foot. As if one had secretly sent one's servant to suborn the servant of the beloved. I was breathing very short in I hoped not audible pants or gasps. The orchestra was continuing its jumbled keening of crazed birds. I felt a void the size of an opera house where my stomach might have been and through the middle of it travelled the great scar of desire. I felt a cringing fear of which I could not determine whether it was physical or mental, and a sense that soon I might somehow lose control of myself, shout, vomit, faint. I felt the heavenly continued steady light pressure of Julian's arm upon mine. I smelt the clean rapier smell of the silk of her dress. I felt, delicately, delicately, as if I were touching an egg shell, her shoe.

The softly cacophonous red and gold scene swung in my vision, beginning to swirl gently like something out of Blake: it was a huge coloured ball, a sort of immense Christmas decoration, a glittering shining twittering globe of dim rosy light in the midst of which Julian and I were suspended, rotating, held together by a swooning intensity of precarious feather-touch. Somewhere above us a bright blue heaven blazed with stars and round about us half-naked women lifted ruddy torches up. My arm was on fire, my foot was on fire, my knee was trembling with the effort of keeping still. I was in a golden scarlet jungle full of the chattering of apes and the whistling of birds. A scimitar of sweet sounds sliced the air and entered into the red scar and became pain. I was that sword of agony, I was that pain. I was in an arena, surrounded by thousands of grimacing nodding faces, where I had been condemned to death by pure sound. I was to be killed by the whistling of birds and buried in a pit of velvet. I was to be gilded and then flayed.

'Bradley, what's the matter?'

'Nothing.'

'You weren't listening.'

'Were you talking?'

'I was asking you if you knew the story.'

'What story?'

'Of *Rosenkavalier*.'

'Of course I don't know the story of *Rosenkavalier*.'

'Well, quick, you'd better read your programme –'

'No, you tell me.'

'Oh well, it's quite simple really, it's about this young man, Octavian, and the Marschallin loves him, and they're lovers, only she's much older than he is and she's afraid she'll lose him because he's bound to fall in love with somebody his own age –'

'How old is he and how old is she?'

'Oh I suppose he's about twenty and she's about thirty.'

'*Thirty?*'

'Yes, I think, anyway quite old, and she realizes that he just

258

regards her as a sort of mother-figure and there can't be any real lasting relations between them, and it begins with them in bed together and of course she's very happy because she's with him but she's also very unhappy because she knows she's sure to lose him and –'

'Enough.'

'Don't you want to know what happens next?'

'No.'

At that moment there was a pattering noise of clapping, rising to a rattling crescendo, the deadly sound of a dry sea, the light banging of many bones in a tempest.

The stars faded and the red torches began to dim and a terrifying packed silence slowly fell as the conductor lifted up his rod. Silence. Darkness. Then a rush of wind and a flurry of sweet pulsating anguish has been set free to stream through the dark. I closed my eyes and bowed my head before it. Could I transform all this extraneous sweetness into a river of pure love? Or would I be somehow undone by it, choked, dismembered, disgraced? I felt now almost at once a pang of relief as, after the first few moments, tears began to flow freely out of my eyes. The gift of tears which had been given and then withdrawn again had come back to bless me. I wept with a marvellous facility, quietly relaxing my arm and my leg. Perhaps if I wept copiously throughout I could bear it after all. I was not listening to the music, I was undergoing it, and the full yearning of my heart was flowing automatically out of my eyes and soaking my waistcoat, as I hung, so easily now, together with Julian, fluttering, hovering like a double hawk, like a double angel, in the dark void pierced by sorties of fire. I only wondered if it would soon prove impossible to cry quietly, and whether I should then begin to sob.

The curtain suddenly fled away to reveal an enormous double bed surrounded by a cavern of looped-up blood-red hangings. This consoled me for a moment because it reminded me of Carpaccio's Dream of Saint Ursula. I even murmured 'Carpaccio' to myself as a protective charm. But these cooling comparisons were soon put to flight and even Carpaccio could not rescue me from what happened next. Not on the bed but upon some cushions near the front of the stage two girls were lying in a close embrace. (At least I suppose one of them was enacting a young man.) Then they began to sing.

The sound of women's voices singing is one of the bittersweetest noises in the world, the most humanly piercing, the most terribly significant and yet contentless of all sounds: and a duet is more than twice as bad as a single voice. (Perhaps boys' voices are worst of all: I am not sure.) The two women were conversing in pure sound, their voices circling, replying, blending, creating a trembling silver cage of an almost obscene sweetness. I did not know what language they were singing in, and the words were inaudible anyway, there was no need of words, these were not words but the highest coinage of human speech melted down, become pure song, something vilely almost murderously gorgeous. No doubt she is crying for the inevitable loss of her young lover. The lovely boy protests but his heart is free. Only it has all been changed into a sort of plump luscious heart-piercing cascade of sugary agony. Oh God, not much more of this can be endured.

I became aware that I had uttered a sort of moan, because the man on my other side, whom I noticed now for the first time, turned and stared at me. At the same moment my stomach seemed to come sliding down from somewhere else and then quickly arched itself up again and I felt a quick bitter taste in my mouth. I murmured 'Sorry!' quickly in Julian's direction and got up. There was a soft awkward scraping at the end of the row as six people rose hastily to let me out. I blundered by, slipped on some steps, the terrible relentless sweet sound still gripping my shoulders with its talons. Then I was pushing my way underneath the illuminated sign marked *Exit* and out into the brightly lit and completely empty and suddenly silent foyer. I walked fast. I was definitely going to be sick.

Selection of a place to be sick in is always a matter of personal importance and can add an extra tormenting dimension to the graceless horror of vomiting. Not on the carpet, not on the table, not over your hostess's dress. I did not want to be sick within the precincts of the Royal Opera House, nor was I. I emerged into a deserted shabby street and a pungent spicy smell of early dusk. The pillars of the Opera House, blazing a pale gold behind me, seemed in that squalid place like the portico of a ruined or perhaps imagined or perhaps magically fabricated palace, the green and white arcades of the foreign fruit market, looking like something out of the Italian Renaissance, actually clinging to its side. I turned a corner and confronted an array of about a thousand peaches in tiers of boxes behind a lattice grille. I carefully took hold of the grille with one hand and leaned well forward and was sick.

Vomiting is a curious experience, entirely *sui generis*. It is involuntary in a peculiarly shocking way, the body suddenly doing something very unusual with great promptness and decision. One cannot argue. One is *seized*. And the fact that one's vomit moves with such a remarkable drive contrary to the force of gravity adds to the sense of being taken and shaken by some alien power. I am told that there are people who enjoy vomiting, and although I do not share their taste I can, I think, faintly imagine it. There is a certain sense of achievement. And if one does not fight against the stomach's decree there is perhaps some satisfaction in being its helpless vehicle. The relief of having vomited is of course another thing.

I leaned there for a moment, looking down at what I had done, and aware too of the tear-wetness of my face upon which a faint breeze was coolly blowing. I remembered that casket of agony, steel coated in sugar. The inevitable loss of the beloved. And I *experienced* Julian. I cannot explain this. I simply felt in a sort of exhausted defeated cornered utmost way that she *was*. There was no particular joy or relief in this, but a sort of absolute categorical quality of *grasp* of her being.

I became aware that someone was standing beside me. Julian said, 'How are you feeling now, Bradley?'

I began to walk away from her, fumbling for my handkerchief. I wiped my mouth carefully, trying to cleanse it within with saliva.

I was walking along a corridor composed entirely of cages. I was in a prison, I was in a concentration camp. There was a wall composed of transparent sacks full of fiery carrots. They looked at me like derisive faces, like monkeys' bottoms. I breathed carefully and regularly and interrogated my stomach, stroking it gently with my hands. I turned into a lighted arcade and tested my stomach against a smell of decaying lettuce. I walked onward occupied in breathing. Only now I felt so empty and so faint. I felt that I had reached the end of the world, I felt like a stag when it can run no further and turns and bows its head to the hounds, I felt like Actaeon condemned and cornered and devoured.

Julian was following me. I could hear the soft tap-tap of her shoes on the sticky pavement and my whole body apprehended her presence behind me.

'Bradley, would you like some coffee? There's a stall there.'

'No.'

'Let's sit down somewhere.'

'Nowhere to sit.'

We passed between two lorries loaded with milky white boxes of dark cherries and came out into the open. It was becoming dark, lights had come on revealing the sturdy elegant military outline of the vegetable market, resembling a magazine, a seedy eighteenth-century barracks, though quiet at this time and sombre as a cloister. Opposite to us the big derelict eastern portico of Inigo Jones's church was now in view, cluttered up with barrows and housing at the far end the coffee stall referred to by Julian. Some mean and casual lamp-light, itself seeming dirty, revealed the thick pillars, a few lounging market men, a large pile of vegetable refuse and disintegrating cardboard boxes. It was like a scene in some small battered Italian city, rendered by Hogarth.

Julian seated herself on the plinth of one of the pillars at the dark end of the portico, and I sat down next to her, or as near next to her as the bulge of the column would allow. I could feel the thick filth and muck of London under my feet, under my bottom, behind my back. I saw, in a diagonal of dim light, Julian's silk dress hitched up, her tights, smoky blue, coloured by the flesh within, her shoes, also blue, against which I had so cautiously placed my own.

'Poor Bradley,' said Julian.

'I'm sorry.'

'Was it the music?'

'No, it was you. Sorry.'

We were silent then for what seemed ages. I sighed and leaned back against the pillar and felt a few more tears, latecomers to the scene, quiet and gentle, come slowly brimming up and overflowing. I contemplated Julian's blue shoes.

Then Julian said, 'How me?'

'I'm terribly in love with you. But please don't worry about it.'

Julian whistled. No, this does not quite convey the sound she made. She let her breath out thoughtfully, judiciously.

After a while she said, 'I thought perhaps you were.'

'How on earth did you know?' I said, and I rubbed my face and dabbed my lips with my wet hand.

'The way you kissed me last week.'

'Oh really. Well, I'm sorry. Now I think I'd better go home. I'll be leaving London tomorrow. I'm very sorry to have spoilt your evening. I hope you'll excuse my animal behaviour. J hope you haven't dirtied your pretty dress. Good night.' I actually got up. I felt quite empty and light, able to walk. First the flesh, then the spirit. I started to walk away in the direction of Henrietta Street.

Julian was in front of me. I saw her face, the bird-mask fox-mask very intense and clear. 'Bradley, don't go. Come and sit down again, just for a moment.' She put her hand on my arm.

I jerked myself away. 'This is not something for little girls to play with,' I said to her. We faced each other.

'Come back. Please.'

I came back. I sat down again and covered my face. Then I felt Julian's hand trying to come through the crook of my arm. I shook her off again. I felt determined and violent, as if at that moment I hated her and could kill her.

'Bradley, don't – be like that – Please talk to me.'

'Don't try to touch me,' I said.

'All right, I won't. But please talk.'

'There's nothing to talk about. I have done what I swore to myself I would never do, told you about my condition. I don't have to emphasize, I think you must already have gathered, that this is all rather extreme. I shall tomorrow do what I should have done earlier, go away. What I do not propose to do is to gratify your girlish vanity by a display of my feelings.'

'Bradley, listen, listen. I'm not good at explaining or arguing

263

but – You see, you can't just unload all this on to me and then run off. It isn't fair. You must see that.'

'I'm beyond fairness,' I said. 'I just want to survive. I'm sure you feel a curiosity which it is natural to try to gratify. Even perhaps politeness suggests that one should be a little less abrupt. But I honestly don't care a hang about considering your feelings and all that. It's possibly the worst thing I've ever done. But now it's done there's little point in lingering over a post-mortem, however much satisfaction you might derive from it.'

'Don't you want to talk to me about your love?'

The question had a striking simplicity. I was clear about the answer. 'No. It's all spoilt. I endlessly *imagined* talking to you about it, but that just belonged to the fantasy world. I can't talk love to you in the real world. The real world rejects it. It's not that it would be a crime so much as – absurd. I feel quite cold and – dry. What do you want? To hear me praise your eyes?'

'Has telling your love – made your love – end?'

'No. But it's – it's not – it has no speech any more – it's just something I've got to carry away and live with. When I hadn't told you I could endlessly imagine myself telling you. Now – the tongue has been cut out.'

'I – Bradley, don't go – I must – oh help me – find the right words – This is important – And it concerns me – You talk as if there was nobody here but you.'

'There is nobody here but me,' I said. 'You're just something in my dream.'

'That's not true. I'm real. I hear your words. I can suffer.'

'Suffer? You?' I got up with a sort of laugh and set off again. This time before I could take more than a step or two Julian, still sitting down, had managed to capture one of my hands in two of hers. I looked down into her face. I willed to pull my hand from her, but somewhere between the brain and the hand the message got lost. I stood looking down into her urgent face which seemed to have hardened and aged. She gazed at me, not tenderly but frowning with intent, the eyes narrowed into thin questioning rectangles, the lips parted, the nose wrinkled with some sort of delicate fastidious doubt. She said, 'Sit down, please.' I sat down, and she released my hand.

264

We looked at each other. 'Bradley, you can't go.'

'It looks like it. Do you know, you are a very cruel young lady.'

'This isn't cruelty. There's something I've got to understand. You say you're just concerned with yourself. All right. I'm just concerned with myself. And you did start it. You can't just stop it now when *you* decide to. I'm an equal partner in this game.'

'I hope you are enjoying the game. It must be pleasant to feel blood on your claws. It'll give you something nice to think about when you lie in bed tonight.'

'Don't be beastly to me, Bradley, it isn't my fault. I didn't invite you to fall in love with me. I never dreamt of it at all. When did it happen? When did you first begin to notice me in that way?'

'Listen, Julian,' I said, 'reminiscences of this sort are very charming to indulge in when two people love each other. But when one person loves and the other doesn't they lose their charm. The fact that I am unfortunately in love with you doesn't mean that I can't see you for what you are, a very young, very undereducated, very inexperienced, and in many ways very silly girl. And I do not propose to pander to your silliness by any coy account of the history of this business. I know it must be very amusing to you. I daresay it'll make your day. But you'll just have to try to be a bit grown-up and be cold and grim about this and just *let it go*. You can't have it for a plaything. Your curiosity will be unsatisfied and your vanity ungratified. And you will, I trust, unlike me, keep your mouth shut. I can't stop you from gossiping and giggling over this, but I ask you not to.'

Julian after a moment said, 'You don't seem to know me at all. Are you sure it's *me* you love?'

'All right, I daresay I can trust your discretion. But I must now ask you to release me from this unkind and unseemly inquisition.'

Julian said, after another short pause, 'So you're going away tomorrow? Where to?'

'Abroad.'

'And what am I supposed to do? Just lock this evening away and forget about it?'

'Yes.'

'You think that's possible?'

'You know perfectly well what I mean.'

'I see. And how long will it take you to get over this, as you put it, unfortunate infatuation?'

'I did not use the word "infatuation".'

'Suppose I say, you just want to go to bed with me?'

'Suppose you say it.'

'You mean you don't care what I think?'

'Not now.'

'Because you've spoilt all the fantasy fun of your love by bringing it out into the real world?'

I got up and got well away from her this time, walking quickly. I saw her as in a vision, her red and blue silk tulip dress spread by her legs, striding like a Spartan maid, her shining blue feet twinkling, her arms held out. And now again she had cut me off and we had stopped beside a lorry loaded with white boxes. A unique but unidentified smell, carrying awful associations, entered my mind like a swarm of bees. I leaned against the tail board of the lorry and groaned.

'Bradley, may I touch you?'

'No. Please go away. If you pity me at all, go away.'

'Bradley, you've upset me and you must let me talk this out, I want to understand myself too, you don't conceive –'

'I know this must nauseate you.'

'You say you aren't thinking about me. Indeed you aren't!'

'What's that bloody smell? What's in those boxes?'

'Strawberries.'

'Strawberries!' The smell of youthful illusion and feverish transient joy.

'You say you love me, but you aren't *interested* in me in the least.'

'Nope. Now good-bye. Please.'

'You evidently don't think at all that I might return your affection.'

'Nope. What?'

'That I might return your affection.'

'Don't be silly,' I said. 'You're being childish.' Pigeons, unsure whether it was day or night, were walking about near our feet. I looked at the pigeons.

'Your love must be very – what's the word – solipsistic if you don't even imagine or speculate about what I might feel.'

'Yes,' I said, 'it is solipsistic. It's got to be. It's a game I play by myself.'

'Then you oughtn't to have told me about it.'

'We agree on that.'

'But don't you *want* to know what I feel?'

'I'm not going to get excited about what you feel,' I said. 'You're a very silly young girl. You're flattered and thrilled because an older man is making a fool of himself about you. Possibly this is the first time this has happened to you, and doubtless it won't be the last. Of course you want to explore the situation a bit, probe your feelings, fake up a few emotions. That's no use to me. And of course I realize that you'd have to be a good deal older and tougher and cooler than you are to be able to drop this thing at once as you ought to do. So you can't do what you ought to do any more than I can. What a pity. Now let's get away from these blasted strawberries. I'm going home.'

I began to walk away, but more slowly this time. Julian was walking by my side. We turned into Henrietta Street. I felt horribly excited but determined not to show it. I also felt that I had just taken, or allowed to be taken, some step that could prove fatal. In protesting that I would not talk love I had talked love and nothing but love. And this had given me an intense bittersweet pleasure. This discussion, this argument, this fight once started could continue and continue and could become for me an addiction. If she wanted to *talk* about it how could I ever be strong enough to refuse? If I could *die* of this talk I would be most happy. And I realized with shock how much, even in this last twenty minutes, this treatment had increased the sum and complexity of my love for her. Before, my love had been huge but lacked detail. Now already there were caverns, there were labyrinths. And soon ... Complexity would make it stronger, deeper, more hopelessly ineradicable. There was so much more now to ponder, so much more to feed upon. Oh God.

'Bradley, how old are you?'

The question took me horribly by surprise, but I replied instantly, 'Forty-six.'

Why I told this lie is hard to explain. Partly it was just a bitter joke. I was so absorbed in prophetic calculation of this evening's damage, of how much more awful the pains of loss and jealousy and despair would now be; to be asked my age was somehow the last straw, the last dash of salt upon the wound. One could only jest. Anyway, surely the girl knew my age. Also however in another part of my mind was the idea: I am not 'really' fifty-eight, how can I be. I feel young, I look young. There was an immediate instinct for concealment. I was in fact about to say forty-eight, and then hopped on to forty-six. That seemed a reasonable age, acceptable, right.

Julian was silent for a moment. She seemed surprised. We turned into Bedford Street. Then she said, 'Oh, then you are a little older than my father. I thought you were younger.'

I began to laugh helplessly, wailing softly to myself, how funny it was, how exquisitely insane. Of course young people do not reckon ages, do not perceive temporal distance. Over thirty it all looks much the same to them. And I had this deceptively youthful mask. Oh funny funny funny.

'Bradley, don't laugh in that horrible way, what is it? *Please* let us stop and talk, I *must* talk to you properly tonight.'

'All right, let us stop and talk.'

'What's this place?'

'Inigo Jones giving us another chance.'

A discreet gateway and two draped urns ushered us towards the west end of the church, accessible only from this side. I turned into the darkened courtyard and went on into the garden. At the end of the path the doorway of the lovely barn, last resting place of Lely, Wycherley, Grinling Gibbons, Arne, and Ellen Terry was dimly lit. Here was its brown and bricky, small and more domestic face of a pretty elegance, a more purely English beauty. I sat down upon one of the seats in the garden, where it was dark. A little way away a lamp shone dimly upon tangerine-coloured roses, making them look like wax. A cat went by, soundless and swift as a bird's shadow. I moved away as Julian sat down beside me. I would not not not touch the girl. Of course it was insanity to continue the argument. But now I was weak with madness, with the insane awful funniness of it all. After the lie about my age all prudence, all efforts at self-preservation, seemed finally pointless.

'No one has ever been sick for me before,' said Julian.

'Don't flatter yourself. It was partly Strauss.'

'Good old Strauss.'

I was sitting Egyptian style, square, with my hands on my knees, looking away into the darkness where the shadow-cat had made himself a play-fellow out of the stuff of the night. A warm hand came questing lightly over my tensed knuckles. 'Don't, Julian. I really am going in a minute. Please try to make it easy.'

She withdrew her hand. 'Bradley, don't be so cold to me.'

'I may behave like a fool, but that's no reason for you to behave like a bloody bitch.'

'To a nunnery go and quickly too. Farewell.'

'I know this amuses you immensely. But please stop, be silent, don't touch.'

'I won't be silent and I will touch.' She put her tormenting hand upon my arm again.

I said, 'You are behaving – so badly – I wouldn't have – believed – you could be so – frivolously – unkind.'

I turned round to face her, taking the offending hand in a strong grip just above the wrist. There was a shock wave, as I apprehended rather than saw her excited half-smiling face. Then I put my arms very evenly and strongly around her shoulders and kissed her with very great care upon the mouth.

There are moments of paradise which are worth millennia of hell, or so one may think, only one is not always fully conscious of this at the moment in question. I was fully conscious. I knew that even if the ruin of the world were to ensue I had made a good bargain. I had imagined kissing Julian, but I had not pre-figured this concentrated intensity of pure joy, this sudden white-hot rapturous pressure of lips upon lips, being upon being.

I was so utterly transported by the quite unexpected experience of holding and kissing her that it was only, I think, in some secondary moment inside this moment that I became aware that she was also holding and kissing me. Both her arms were round my neck and her lips were ardent and her eyes were closed.

I turned my head and began to push her away and she withdrew her arms from my neck. I was aided in releasing her by the innate awkwardness of seated kissing. We drew apart.

I said, 'You shouldn't have done that.'

'Bradley, I love you.'

'Don't talk lying rubbish.'

'What am I to do? You won't listen properly. You think I'm a child, you think I'm playing, it's not so. Of course I'm confused. I've known you such a long time, all my life. I've always loved you. Please don't interrupt. Oh if you only knew how much I always looked forward to your coming, wanted to talk to you, wanted to tell you things. You never noticed, but lots and lots of things weren't real to me at all until I'd told you about them. If you only knew how much I've always admired you. When I was a child I used to say I wanted to marry you. Do you remember? I'm sure you don't. You've been my ideal man for ever and ever. And this isn't just a silly child's thing, it isn't even a sort of crush, it's a deep real love. Of course it's a love I've not questioned or thought about or even named until quite lately – but I have questioned it and thought about it – as soon as I felt and knew that I was grown up. You see, my love has grown up too. I've so much wanted to be with you, I've so much wanted to get to know you properly, since I've been a woman. Why do you think I made all that fuss about discussing the play? I did want to discuss the play. But I much more wanted and needed your affection and your attention. God, I wanted just to *look* at you. You can't think how I've longed to touch you and kiss you sometimes in these last, oh years, only I didn't dare to and thought I never would. And lately, oh ever since that day you saw me tearing up the letters, I've been thinking about you almost all the time – and so especially since last week when I – when I had a sort of premonition about – what you told me tonight – I've thought about nothing else but you.'

'What about Septimus?' I said.

'Who?'

'Septimus. Septimus Leech. Your boy-friend. Haven't you been able to spare a couple of minutes to think about him?'

'Oh that. I just said that. I think I may even have said it out of some sort of instinct to tease you. He isn't my boy-friend, he's just a friend. I haven't got a boy-friend.'

I was staring at her. She was sitting side saddle on the bench, the strained silk outlining one knee. I looked at the little row of blue buttons that led upward in between her breasts. Her hair, disordered, a turban now and not a casque, bushed over the top of her head, where her nervous thoughtless hand was tossing it back from her brow. Her face glowed with a sort of intellectual passion and with emotions which I dared not name. She was certainly no child any more. She had taken full possession of her womanhood and its authority and its power.

I said, 'I see.' I got up lightly and quickly and made for the gateway. I turned along Bedford Street in the direction of Leicester Square station. As I crossed into Garrick Street Julian, walking beside me, thrust her left hand into my right hand. With my left hand I carefully detached hers and dropped it again by her side. We walked on in silence as far as the corner of St Martin's Lane.

Then Julian said, 'I see that you're determined not to believe or attend to anything that I say. You seem to think that I'm still about twelve.'

'No, no,' I said. 'I attended carefully to your statement and found it interesting, even touching. And remarkably well expressed considering you invented it on the spur of the moment. It was not however very detailed or very clear, nor do I yet see what implications it has if any.'

'God, Bradley, I do love you.'

'That's very kind of you.'

'I'm not inventing it, it's true.'

'I am not accusing you of insincerity. Just of not having the faintest idea what you are talking about. You admitted to being confused.'

'Did I?'

'The main source of your confusion is fairly obvious. You have liked me, or as you are gracious enough to say, loved me, when you were a little ignorant innocent child and I was an impressive visitor, a writer, a friend of your father's and so on. Now you are an adult and I am a man, a good deal your senior, but

suddenly seen as inhabiting the same adult world. Even leaving
aside the little shocks which you have had this evening, you are
naturally surprised, possibly a bit elated, to find that we are now
somehow equals. What in this new situation do you do with your
old feeling of affection for the man whom the child used to
admire? Is this question important? In itself probably not. My
inexcusable proceedings have made it so, just for the moment at
any rate. Startled, amused, and thrilled by my idiotic declaration,
you have felt impelled to make a counter-statement which is
totally muddled and unclear and which you will certainly regret
tomorrow. That's all. Here we are at the station, thank God.'

We went down the steps into Leicester Square station. We
stood face to face in the bright light near to the ticket machines,
quite still in the middle of a scattered crowd of moving people.
Our concentration upon each other was so great that we might
have been alone together in the quietest of gardens or upon the
great empty plateaux of Tibet.

'Was that kiss I gave you muddled and unclear?' said Julian.

'You're going home by train,' I said. 'I'll say good night now.'

'Bradley, have you taken in what I said?'

'You don't know what you said. Tomorrow it will seem a bad
dream.'

'We'll see about that! At least you've talked to me, you've
argued.'

'There's nothing to talk about. I've just been irresponsibly
prolonging the pleasure of being with you.'

'Look, I don't have to go now.'

'Yes, you do. It's finished.'

'It isn't. You won't leave London, will you, please?'

'I won't – leave London,' I said.

'You'll see me tomorrow?'

'Maybe.'

'I'll ring up about ten.'

'Good night.'

Without putting my hands on her I leaned down and brushed
her lips very lightly with mine. Then I turned at once and went
back up the steps into Charing Cross Road. I walked along
blindly, grimacing with joy.

I slept, I suppose. I kept being nudged awake by a sort of bliss and then sinking again. My body ached with a painful delightful sensation of desire and gratified desire, somehow merged into a single mode of being. I groaned softly over myself. I was made of something else, something delicious, in which consciousness throbbed in a warm daze. I was made of honey and fudge and marzipan, and at the same time I was made of steel. I was a steel wire vibrating quietly in the midst of blue emptiness. These words do not of course convey my sensations, no words could. I did not think. I was. In so far as any stray thoughts attempted to intrude into this heaven I sent them packing.

I rose early and shaved with majestic slowness and dressed with indulgent care and spent a long time inspecting myself in the mirror. I looked about thirty-five. Well, forty. My recent regime had made me even thinner and this suited me. Faded silky grey-blond hair, straight and quite a lot of it, a large-nostrilled bony nose, not unsightly, granity blue-grey eyes, good cheek bones, a large brow, a thin mouth: an intellectual's face. The face, too, of a puritan. What of him?

I drank some water. Eating was, of course, once more out of the question. I felt sick and shuddery but the night had been heaven and the glory of it had not yet left me. I went into the sitting-room and once again perfunctorily dusted the more obvious surfaces which had once again become dusty. Then I sat down and let a few thoughts set themselves end to end.

I could mainly congratulate myself on having been fairly cool last night. It is true that I had been sick at her feet and had told her that I loved her in accents which, I noted, had conveyed the gravity of the situation to her at once. But after that I had behaved with dignity. (Which of course I had been enabled to do partly by the intense cozening delight of her presence.) I could not accuse myself of having *then* hustled her in any way. But what, oh what, was she feeling about it all by now? Suppose when she telephoned she said coldly that after all she agreed that the matter had best be dropped? I had exhorted her to be adult enough to let go. Perhaps maturer reflection had already made her see the point of this good advice. What had her speech about 'love' meant? Did she know what she was talking about? Was it not just a rigmarole which she had invented because she was touched and flattered and excited by my exhibition? Would she draw back? Or if it were the case that she really loved me, what on earth would happen next? But I did not really wonder about what would happen next. If she really loved me it did not matter what happened next.

I looked at my watch and it said eight o'clock. I dialled TIM on the telephone and he said eight o'clock too. I went outside into the court, though not out of earshot of the telephone, and stood there in a stupor. Rigby and one of his *louche* friends came out and I gave them such a slow strange salute that they kept turning back to stare at me. I wondered if I dared make a dash to the flower shop but decided I dared not. Suppose she simply didn't ring? I went inside and looked at my watch again and then shook it madly. Hours had passed, and it said eight-fifteen. I went into the sitting-room and tried lying on the rug but for some reason this position was no good any more, I had to keep moving and fidgeting. I moved round the flat with my teeth chattering. I tried the hissing noise again, but it didn't serve. I tried deep breathing, but seemed to lose contact with myself between each breath, so that the next one was always an emergency. I began to feel faint.

At about nine o'clock the front-door bell rang. I crept out and peered at the frosted glass panel. It was Julian. With a quick small effort of self-control I opened the door. She flew in. I managed to kick the door to before she pulled me into the sitting-room. She had her arms round my neck and I held her in a sort of vivid darkness and then my chattering teeth had become a laughing and crying act, and she was laughing and shuddering too and we had sat down on the floor.

'Bradley, thank God, I was so afraid you might have changed your mind since yesterday, I couldn't wait till ten.'

'Don't be a fool, girl. Oh – Oh – You're here – you're here –'

274

'Bradley, I do love you, I do, it's the real thing. I realized it for absolute certain last night after I left you. I haven't slept, I've been in a sort of mad trance. This is it. I've never had it before. One can't be in doubt, can one?'

'No,' I said. 'One can't. If there is any doubt it's not it.'

'So you see –'

'What about Mr Belling?'

'Oh Bradley, don't torment me with Mr Belling. That was just a nervous craving. He doesn't exist, nothing exists but this – surely you see – Besides he had no real feelings, no strength, not like you –'

'I've impressed you. You're sure you're not *just* impressed?'

'I love you. I feel shattered but at the same time I feel quite calm. Doesn't that show that something extraordinary has happened, that calm? I feel like an archangel. I can talk to you, I can convince you, you'll see everything. There's plenty of time after all, isn't there, Bradley?'

Her question, which was really an assertion, touched me in the midst of my joy with a coldish finger. Time, plans, the future. 'Yes, my darling, there's plenty of time.'

We were sitting, I with my legs tucked sideways, she kneeling a little above me, her hands caressing my hair and neck. Then she began taking off my tie. I started to laugh.

'All right, Bradley, don't panic, I just want to look at you. I don't want to think about anything except looking at you just now, and touching you so, and feeling what a miracle it is –'

'That A loves B and B loves A. It's rare enough.'

'You've got such a beautiful head.'

'I thrust it through the curtains of your cradle.'

'And I fell in love at first sight.'

'I'd lay it under the wheels of your car.'

'I wish I could remember when I first saw you!'

It occurred to me suddenly as odd that I could probably establish from an old engagement book, for I had kept them all, what I was doing on the day Julian was born. Resolving some tax problem, lunching with Grey-Pelham.

'When did you first start feeling like this about me? We can talk about that now, can't we?'

'We can talk about that now. I think it came on when we were discussing *Hamlet*.'

'Only *then*! Bradley, you terrify me. Honestly, I think you should think twice about this. Aren't you just acting out of some momentary emotional impulse? Aren't you all mixed up? Won't you feel quite different next week? I thought at least –'

'You're not serious, Julian? No, no – you can see that this is something very absolute. The past has folded up. There's no history. It's the last trump.'

'I know –'

'One can't calculate, measure. But – oh my dear – we are in a fix, aren't we. Come here.' I drew her to me and got her liony head up against my chest.

'I don't see any fix about it,' she said into my clean blue pin-striped shirt, of which she was undoing the upper buttons. 'Of course we must move very slowly and test ourselves against time and – not be in a hurry to do – anything –'

'I agree,' I said, 'that we should not be in a hurry to do – anything.' She was not making it easy, however, thrusting her hand inside my shirt, and sighing, and grasping the curly grey hair of my front.

'You don't think that I'm behaving badly, shamelessly?'

'No, Julian, my dear heart.'

'I have to touch you. It's so marvellous, such a sort of privilege –'

'Julian, you're mad, dotty –'

'But I think we must get to know each other slowly and quietly and tell each other the truth and tell everything and look into each other's eyes like this and – I feel I could spend years just – looking into your eyes – it's like – nourishing oneself – just looking – do you feel that?'

'I feel a lot of things,' I said. 'Some of them were expressed by Marvell. But what I mainly feel – no, let me talk – is this. I'm totally unworthy of this love which you are offering to me. I won't go on boringly about my unworthiness, but it's there. I am prepared to carry on slowly as you say and let you convince me and convince yourself that you really feel what you now seem to feel. But meanwhile you mustn't be in any way bound or tied –'

'But I am tied –'

'You must be completely free –'

'Bradley, don't be –'

'I think we even shouldn't use certain words.'

'What words –'

' "Love", "in love".'

'I think that's silly. But while we've got eyes I suppose we can give words a rest. Look. Can't you see what you won't name?'

'Please. I honestly think we shouldn't define this thing at all. We must just be quiet and patient and see what happens.'

'You sound so anxious.'

'I'm terrified.'

'I'm not. I've never felt braver in my life. What are you afraid of? And why did you say we were in a fix? What fix are we in?'

'I'm very much older than you are. *Very* much. That's the fix.'

'Oh that. That's simply a convention. It doesn't touch *us* at all.'

'It does touch us,' I said. I felt its touch.

'Is that all you meant?'

I hesitated. 'Yes.' There was much that I would have some day to lay before her. But not today.

'It's not –'

'Oh Julian, you don't know me, you don't *know* me –'

'It's not Christian?'

'What? Christian? God no!'

'Thank heaven. You know, Bradley, when I heard my father talking about bringing you and Christian together I felt such a pang – and that was before – perhaps that began to make me realize how I really felt about you –'

'Like Emma and Mr Knightley.'

'Yes, exactly. You see, ever since I've known you you've always been alone, just sort of absolutely there, like solitary people are.'

'A pillar in the desert.'

'And I was worrying about Christian last night too –'

'No, no, Chris is a nice person and I don't even hate her any more, but she's nothing to me. You have let me out of so many cages. I'll tell you – later – in the time – that we've got.'

'Well, if it's not that, the age business doesn't matter a pin, lots of girls prefer older men. So everything's quite clear and plain. I didn't say anything to my parents last night or this morning, as I wanted to be sure you hadn't changed. But I'll tell them today –'

'Wait a minute! What'll you say to them?'

'That I love you and want to marry you.'

'Julian! It's impossible! Julian, I'm older than you think –'

'Older than the rocks among which you sit. Yes, yes, we know that!'

'It's impossible.'

'Bradley, you aren't making any sense. Why do you look like that? You do really love me, don't you? You don't just want a love affair and then good-bye?'

'No – I really love you –'

'Isn't that something for ever?'

'Yes. Real love is about for ever – and this is real love – but –'

'But what?'

'You said we'd move slowly and get to know each other slowly – all this has happened so fast – I'm sure you shouldn't– in any way commit yourself –'

'I don't mind committing myself. That won't stop us being slow and patient and all that. Anyway, we already know each other, I've known you all my life, you're my Mr Knightley, and the age gap there –'

'Julian, I think we must keep this thing secret for a while.'

'Why?'

'Because you may change your mind.'

'Or because you may?'

'I won't. But you don't know me, you can't. And I'm more than old enough to be your father.'

'Do you think I care –?'

'No, but society does and you will one day. You'll see me getting older –'

'Bradley, that's *soft*.'

'I'd very much rather you didn't tell your parents at present.'

'All right,' she said, after a pause, drawing apart from me, kneeling there, her face suddenly childish with doubt.

The shadow between us was unbearable to me. If I was embarked upon this thing let me be embarked. I would have to trust myself completely to her sense of truth, even to her naïvety, even to her inexperience, even to her foolishness. I said, 'My perfect darling, you must do whatever you feel is right to do. I leave it entirely to you. I love you absolutely and I trust you absolutely and what will be will be.'

'You think the parents won't like it?'

'They'll hate it.'

After that we talked a bit more about Christian and about my marriage and about Priscilla. We talked about Julian's childhood and the times when we had been together. We talked about when I might have started to love her, and about when she might have started to love me. We did not talk about the future. We continued to sit upon the floor like shy animals, like children, stroking each other's hands and each other's hair. We kissed, not often. I sent her away about midday. I felt we should not exhaust each other. We needed to brood and to recover. Of course there was no question of going to bed.

'You don't quite understand,' I said. 'I am not proposing to go away.'

Rachel and Arnold were occupying the two armchairs in my sitting-room. I was sitting on Julian's chair beside the window. There was a murky cloudy light and I had just turned the lamps on. It was the same day, late afternoon.

'What do you propose to do then?' said Arnold.

He had telephoned. Then he and Rachel had arrived. They had, there is no other word for it, marched in. Their presence was like that of an occupying army. To confront familiar people who are suddenly unsmiling and tense with anger and shock is very frightening. I felt frightened. I knew they would 'hate it'. But I had not expected this big united hostile will. Their sheer incredulity, feigned or otherwise, silenced me, put me to flight. I could

279

explain nothing and felt that I was creating some entirely false impression. Also I knew that I was not only seeming but also feeling appallingly guilty.

'To stay here,' I said, 'see a bit of the girl I suppose –'

'You mean lead her on?' said Rachel.

'To act naturally, get to know her better – After all we – love each other it appears – and –'

'Bradley, get back to reality,' said Arnold. 'Stop blithering. You're in some sort of dream world at the moment. You're nearly sixty. Julian is twenty. She said at the start that you'd told her your age and that she didn't mind, but you can't mean to take advantage of a sentimental schoolgirl who is flattered by your attentions –'

'She's not a schoolgirl,' I said.

'She's very immature,' said Rachel, 'and very easily taken in, and –'

'I am not taking her in! I've told her that the age difference makes this thing practically impossible –'

'It makes it entirely impossible,' said Arnold.

'She said the most extraordinary things this afternoon,' said Rachel. 'I can't think what you can have been saying to her.'

'I didn't want her to tell you.'

'So you suggested that she should deceive her parents?'

'No, no, not like that –'

'I can't make out what has happened,' said Rachel. 'Did you suddenly feel this – urge or whatever it was – and then go and tell her that you found her attractive, and then make a pass at her, or what? What has happened exactly? This must be fairly new?'

'It is new,' I said. 'But it's very serious. I didn't foresee it or will it, it happened. And then when it turned out that she felt the same –'

'Bradley,' said Arnold, 'what you are saying describes nothing which could possibly have happened in the real world. All right, you suddenly felt that she was an attractive girl. London's full of attractive girls. And it's nearly mid-summer and you are, perhaps, reaching the age when men make asses of themselves. I've known several people who started sowing some rather unsavoury wild oats at sixty, it's not unusual. But given that you felt randy about my daughter, why the hell didn't you keep quiet about it instead of annoying and upsetting her and confusing her –'

'She's not annoyed or upset –'

'She was this afternoon,' said Rachel.

'Well, you annoyed and upset her –'

'Why couldn't you act like a gentleman –'

'And she's a good deal less confused than I am. I'm sorry, but *your* words simply don't describe anything here. There are huge cosmic forces at work here. Maybe you just don't know about them. Now I come to think of it, Arnold, you've never in any of your books really described what it's like to be in love –'

Rachel said, 'You talk as if you were fifteen. Of course everyone knows about being in love. That's not the point. The details of what you so suddenly imagine that you feel are your affair. They're just as uninteresting as someone telling their dreams. Julian is certainly not "in love", whatever you suppose that to mean here, with you. She's a very unsophisticated child who thinks it very exciting and amusing that an elderly friend of her father's should pay this sort of attention to her. If you could have seen her this afternoon, telling us all about it and laughing, *laughing*. She was just like a child with a toy.'

'But you said she was upset –'

'We told her it was a bad joke.'

I thought, my darling, I trust you, I trust you, and I *know*. I will keep faith with your faith. But at the same time I felt pain and fright. Could I, after what had happened, now doubt it all? She was so very young. And it was indeed, as they said, something very new in the world. When I thought *how* new I was amazed at the degree of my certainty. But there, above the doubt, *was* the certainty.

'I can see that you are listening to us at last,' said Arnold. 'Bradley, you are a decent rational man and a moral being. You can't seriously propose to settle down and *explore* this emotional mess with Julian? I call it an emotional mess, but thank God it hasn't had time to develop into one. Nor will it do so. I shall stop it.'

'I don't know what we shall do,' I said. 'I agree that the whole thing is fantastic. It's almost too good to be true that Julian should love me. It may even not be true. It has surprised me very much indeed. But I am certainly not going now to let the matter drop. I am not going to go quietly away as you suggested earlier, I am not going to stop seeing Julian, I can't. I must find out whether she really loves me or not. Though what follows if she does I don't know at all, perhaps nothing. All this is extremely unusual and may turn out to be very painful, especially to me. I don't want to cause her pain. I don't think I can do her harm. But at this *particular* point we can't either of us stop. That's all.'

'She can stop and she will,' said Arnold. 'Even if I have to lock her in her bedroom.'

'Of course you can stop,' said Rachel. 'Try to be honest! And do stop saying "we". You can't answer for Julian. You haven't been to bed with her, have you?'

'Oh Christ, *Christ*,' said Arnold, 'of course he hasn't, he's not a criminal.'

'No, I haven't.'

'And you won't.'

'Rachel, I don't know! Please realize that you are talking to a mad person.'

'So you actually *admit* to being irrational and irresponsible and dangerous!'

'Arnold, please don't get so angry. You are both frightening me and confusing me and that does no good. When I said mad I didn't mean irresponsible – I feel as responsible as if – I'd been given something – I don't know – the bloody grail – I swear I won't press her or bother her – I'll leave her quite free – she *is* quite free –'

'You know this is nonsense,' said Arnold, 'and anyway you're contradicting yourself. If you pester her now you'll make her emotional about you, you'll make a *situation* between you. Naturally that's what you want. Of course she doesn't feel anything serious about you, even you seem to realize that it's all in your mind. Just think what a child she is! And please, understand this, I will not have any "situation" coming into being between you and my daughter. There will be no meetings, no interesting discussions, no exploration of feelings, nothing. See this, please. *See* that I regard you in this context as if you were some filthy lustful old man who was following her in the street. I will be ruthless about this, Bradley. And it's the kindest thing to be. You will leave Julian alone. I will protect her from you by imprisoning her, by taking her out of the country, if necessary by lawyers and by police and by physical force. Do not imagine that you can even write to her, she will be completely defended against you. You will never reach her, I am not going to let this thing *start*. My God, just put yourself in my place! Make up your mind to that *now* and do the decent and sensible thing and leave London at once. You were going to go anyway. Please go. Of course it will all blow over. I'm not suggesting that you never see her or us again, of course not. But I recognize that you're in a stupid state of mind at present and I am not going to have my daughter involved in any way, however superficially or histrionically or inconclusively, with an elderly man. The idea sickens me and I will not permit it.'

There was a moment's silence after this speech. I stared at Arnold. He had been sitting very still, speaking quietly but with a spitting staccato emphasis and with that sort of 'edge' to the voice which is intended to terrify. His face under his pale hair was flushed bright pink like a girl's. I tried to check my fear with anger, but could not. I said in a small voice, 'Your eloquence suggests to me that Julian did after all convince you both that she was in love.'

'She doesn't know what she feels –'

'This isn't the eighteenth century –'

'Come!' Arnold got up, and motioned with his head to Rachel who rose too. 'We've said what we came to say. We'll leave you to – digest it – see there's only one course for you to – adopt –'

I opened the sitting-room door. I said, 'Arnold, please don't be so angry with me. I haven't done anything wrong.'

'Yes, you have,' said Rachel. 'You spoke to her about your feelings.'

'All right. I shouldn't have. But to love somebody isn't a sin, there's good in this, we'll find a way to make it – all good – I won't bother her – if you like I won't see her for a week – let her think things over –'

'It won't do,' said Arnold, more gently. 'Any sort of half-measures will only make things worse. You must see that,

Bradley. Christ, you don't want a mess any more than we do. You must go away. If you see her you'll just make more drama. Best thing for all is stop, absolutely, now. Do see it. Sorry.'

Arnold went out of the sitting-room and opened the door of the flat.

Rachel passed me and as she did so she shrank from me and her mouth gave a little wince of disgust. She said tonelessly, 'I want you to know, Bradley, that Arnold and I are entirely united in this matter.'

'Forgive me, Rachel.'

She went on out of the flat, turning her back on me.

Arnold came back. He said, 'There's no need just now to act on the letter I sent you. Could I have it back?'

'I've destroyed it.'

He stood a moment. 'All right. I'm sorry I shouted at you. Will you please give me your word that you won't try to see Julian until I permit it?'

'No.'

'Well. I will not allow any harm to my daughter. Be sure of that. Be – warned.'

He went out, closing the front door softly. I was panting with emotion. I ran to the telephone and dialled the Ealing number. There was a pause and then the high buzz of 'number unobtainable'. I dialled several times, with the same result. I felt as if I had been cut off by an axe at the knees. I held my head in a violent grip, trying to compose myself and *think*. The urgency of the need to see Julian seethed all round me, blotting out my vision. I was being blinded and stung to death by bees. I was suffocating. I ran out into the court and began to walk at random along Charlotte Street, then along Windmill Street, then along Tottenham Court Road. After a while it began to seem probable that if I did not take some violent and decisive action soon I would collapse. I hailed a taxi and told the man to drive to Ealing.

I stood under the copper beech at the corner of the road. I put my hand on the close-grained trunk of the tree and it felt absurdly there, complacent with indifferent reality. It was evening now, twilight time, the evening of that same lengthy fantastic eventful day.

The evening was overcast, the dour thick light turning a little purple, the air warm and motionless. I could smell dust, as if the quiet tedious streets all around me had dissolved into endless dunes of dust. I thought about this morning and how we had seemed to have all the time in the world. And now there seemed to be no more time. I also thought that if only I had had the wit to take that taxi at once I might have arrived here before Arnold and Rachel. What was happening? I crossed the road and began to walk slowly down on the other side.

At the Baffins' house lights were on down below, shining from the curtained dining-room window and through the oval stained glass of the front door. There was one lighted window above, also curtained, that of Arnold's study. Julian's room was at the back, next to the room where I had seen Rachel lying with the sheet over her face, and where, God forgive me, I had lain too, keeping my shirt on. One day I would tell all this to Julian. One day she would be the just judge who understands and forgives. I did not fear her. And even in those seconds, ånd even as I wondered with anguish whether I would ever see her again, I lived with her in some angelic timeless world of quiet communication and absolute understanding.

I stood now upon the opposite pavement and regarded the house and wondered what to do. I considered the idea of hanging around until three o'clock in the morning and then penetrating into the garden and using one of Arnold's ladders to climb up to Julian's window. But I did not want to become a nightmare figure to her, a night intruder, a secret man. The greatness of this morning had been its lucid openness. This morning I had felt like a cave-dweller emerging into the sun. She was the truth of my life. I would not become a sort of burglar or pickpocket in hers. Besides. There were so many unknown things. What was she thinking now?

As I stood there in that thick oppressive urban dusk breathing the breath of fear, smelling the dunes of dust, I became aware of being looked at by a figure standing in the long unlighted landing window of the house I was studying. I could see the figure framed in the window and the pallor of the face regarding me. It was Rachel. We looked at each other in an awful immobility of quietness for about a minute. Then I turned away, like an animal from a human stare, and began to pace the pavement, to and fro, to and fro, waiting. The street lamps came on.

After about five minutes Arnold came out. I recognized his figure though I could not see his face. I began to walk back up the road towards the copper beech and he followed, then walked beside me in silence. A close-by lamp post was illuminating one side of the tree, making the leaves a transparent glowing winey purple, and separating them out with clear shadows, each from each. We stepped into the rich gathered darkness underneath the tree, trying to see each other's faces.

Arnold said, 'I'm sorry I got so excited.'

'OK.'

'Everything's got much clearer now.'

'Good.'

'I'm sorry I said all those ludicrous things – about lawyers and so on.'

'So 'm I.'

'I hadn't realized how little had happened.'

'Oh.'

'I mean, I hadn't got the time scheme. I somehow gathered from what Julian said this afternoon that this whatever it is had been going on for some time. But now I understand it's only been going on since yesterday evening.'

'A lot has happened since yesterday evening,' I said. 'You should understand, you seem to have been fairly busy lately yourself.'

'You must have thought Rachel and I were being ridiculously solemn this afternoon about very little.'

'I see you're playing it differently now,' I said.

'What?'

'Go on.'

'Now Julian has explained everything to us and it's all perfectly clear.'

'And what does it look like?'

'Of course she was upset and touched. She felt pity for you, she said.'

'I don't believe you. But go on.'

'And of course she was flattered –'

'What's she doing now?'

'Now? Lying on her bed and crying her eyes out.'

'Christ.'

'But don't worry about her, Bradley.'

'Oh, I won't.'

'I wanted to explain – She has now told us *everything*, and we can see that this is really nothing at all, just a storm in a teacup, and she agrees.'

'Does she?'

'She asks you to forgive her for being so emotional and silly, and she says will you please not try to see her just now.'

'Arnold, did she really say this?'

'Yes.'

I gripped him by the shoulders and pulled him with me a few steps so that the lamplight fell on to his face. He reacted convulsively for a moment, then stood still in my hold. 'Arnold, did she say that?'

'Yes.'

I let go of him, and we both moved instinctively back into the shadow. His face leered at me, twisted up with will and anxiety and deep intention. It was not the pink angry hostile face of earlier. It was a hard determined face which told me nothing.

'Bradley, try to be decent here. If you just shut up and clear off for a while this will all simply blow away, and later on you can meet each other again in the old style. This nonsense simply rests on two meetings. You can't have got permanently attached to each other in two meetings! It's all a fantasy. Come back into the real world. The fact is Julian's very embarrassed by this stupid business –'

'*Embarrassed?*'

'Yes, and it will be most considerate of you to sheer off. Be kind to the child. Let her recover her dignity. Dignity matters so much to a young girl. She feels she's lost face by taking it all so seriously and she feels she's made a bit of an exhibition of herself.

If you saw her now she'd just giggle and blush and feel sorry for you and ashamed of herself. She sees now it was silly to take it all so seriously and make a drama of it. She admits that she was flattered, it turned her head a bit, and it was an exciting surprise. But when she saw we weren't amused she sobered up. She understands now that it's all an impossible nonsense, well, she *understands*, in practical matters she's an intelligent girl. Do use enough imagination to see how she must feel now! She's not such a fool as to imagine you're suffering from any great passion either. She says she's very sorry and will you please not try to see her for a while yet. It's better to have a bit of an interval. We're going on holiday soon anyway, the day after tomorrow, in fact. I've decided to take her to Venice. She's always wanted to go. We've been to Rome and Florence, but never there, and she's got a thing about it. So we're going to take a flat, probably spend the rest of the summer. Julian's absolutely thrilled. I think a change of scene would help my book too. So there we are. I'm awfully sorry I got so worked up this afternoon. You must have thought me a solemn idiot. I hope you aren't angry with me now?'

'Not at all,' I said.

'I'm just trying to act rightly. Well, we all are. Fathers have duties. Please, please try to understand. It's kindest to Julian to play this quite cool. You will sheer off and keep quiet, please? She won't want any heavy letters or anything. Leave the kid alone and let her begin to enjoy herself again. You don't want to haunt her like a ghost, do you? You will leave her alone now, won't you, Bradley?'

'All right,' I said. 'Yes.'

'I can rely on you?'

'I'm not a complete fool, I do see. I was rather solemn as well this afternoon. The whole sort of flare-up took me by surprise and I was damnably upset. But now I see that – it's probably better for all concerned to play it cool and regard it as a storm in a teacup. All right, all right. Now perhaps I'd better retire and recover my dignity too.'

'Bradley, you do relieve my mind. I knew you'd act decently, for the child's sake. Thank you, thank you. God, I'm relieved. I'll run back to Rachel. She sends her love, by the way.'

'Who does?'

'Rachel.'

'Give her mine. Good night. I hope you have a good time in Venice.'

He called me back. 'By the way, you did really destroy that letter?'

'Yes.'

I made my way home thinking the thoughts which I will describe in the next section. When I got back I found a note from Francis asking me to call on Priscilla.

When we try, especially in times of pain and crisis, to penetrate the mystery of another mind, we are inclined to picture it as being, not a shadowy mass of contradictions like our own, but a casket containing entities which are clear-cut and definite but hidden. So at this time it never occurred to me to think of Julian as being in a state of total confusion. About one per cent of my speculations veered towards the idea of her being roughly in the frame of mind depicted by Arnold: rueful, embarrassed, giggling, feeling she had made a silly bloomer. Ninety-nine per cent of my thought favoured another view. Arnold was lying. He was certainly lying about Rachel 'sending her love'. One sure thing was that I had now earned Rachel's undying hate. Rachel was not a forgiver. He was lying about Julian too. His account was not even consistent. If she was crying her eyes out she was not, at that moment at any rate, in a giggling mood or feeling thrilled about Venice. And why this frantic haste to leave England? No. There had been no illusion. I loved her and she returned my love. I could as soon doubt the ordinary reports and evidences of my senses as doubt that what that girl had affirmed both last night and with such triumphant certainty this morning was indeed the truth.

But then what had happened? Probably they had locked her in her room. I pictured her lying there and crying, a tumbled figure of despair with her shoes off and her hair all tangled. (The vision filled me with pain, but it was rather beautiful too.) There was no doubt that she had thoroughly alarmed her parents by the naïve violence of her declaration. What a mistake that had been. And they had reacted first with unbridled fury and then with devious slyness. Of course they did not think that she had changed her mind. They had changed their tactics. Had Arnold believed in my renunciation of his daughter? Probably not. I am not a good liar.

I had so much loved and trusted Julian's instinct for frankness that I had not even had the sense to advise her to tone it all down a bit. I had not even, fool that I was, really foreseen how awful the thing would look to her parents. I had been far too absorbed in the sacredness of my own feelings to make the cold effort to be objective here. And what an idiot I had been, to go farther back, not to tone it all down myself! I could have broken it to her slowly, moved in on her gradually, wooed her quietly, hinted, insinuated, whispered. There could have been chaste and then less chaste kisses. Why did I have to sick it up all at once like that and put her in a frenzy? But of course this slow motion idea was only tolerable in retrospect in the light of the knowledge that I now had of her love for me. If I had started to tell her anything at all I could not have stopped myself from telling her everything straightaway. The anxiety would have been too terrible. I did not now meditate upon, or even entertain, the thought that I might have been and ought to have been silent. I did not reject this idea. Only it seemed to belong to some very remote period of the past. For better or worse, that was no longer in question, and guilt about it did not form part of my distress.

During the night I was, sleeping and waking, concerned with Venice. If they took her there I would of course follow. It is difficult to hide a girl in Venice. Yet how elusive my lion-darling was that night. I endlessly pursued her along black and white moonlit quays, quiet as etchings beside their glossy waters. Now she had gone into Florian's only I could not open the door. When I got the door open I was in the Accademia and she had gone on into Tintoretto's picture of Saint Mark and was walking across the squared pavement. We were back again in the Piazza San

Marco which had become an enormous chess board. She was a pawn moving steadily forward and I was a knight leaping crookedly after her but always having to turn away to left or to right when I had almost caught her up. Now she had reached the other end and become a queen and turned about to face me. No, she was Saint Ursula's angel, very august and tall, standing at the foot of my bed. I stretched out my arms towards her but she receded down a long path and through the west door of Inigo Jones's church, which had become the Rialto bridge. She was in a gondola, dressed in a red robe, holding a tiger lily, receding, receding, while behind me a terrible drumming of hooves became louder and louder until I turned about and saw that Bartolomeo Colleoni with the face of Arnold Baffin was about to ride me to the ground. The terrible plunging hooves descended on my head and my skull cracked like an egg shell.

I woke to the sound of dustbin lids being clattered by Greeks at the end of the court. I rose quickly into a world which had become, even since last night, much more frightful. Last night there had been horrors, but there had been a sense of drama, a feeling of obstacles to be overcome, and beyond it all the uplifting certainty of her love. Today I felt crazy with doubt and fear. She was only a young girl after all. Could she, against such fierce parental opposition, hold to her faith and keep her vision clear? And if they had lied to me about her was it not likely that they had lied to her about me? They would tell her that I had said I would give her up. And I had said it. Would she understand? Would she be strong enough to go on believing in me? How strong was she? How little in fact I knew her. *Was* it really all in my mind? And supposing they took her away? Supposing I really could not find her? Surely she would write to me. But supposing she did not? Perhaps, although she did love me, she had decided that the whole thing was a mistake? That would, after all, be a thoroughly rational decision.

The telephone rang but it was only Francis asking me to come and see Priscilla. I said I would come later. I asked to talk to her but she would not come to the telephone. About ten Christian rang and I put the receiver back at once. I rang the Ealing number but got 'number unobtainable' again. Arnold must have somehow put the telephone out of action during that period of panic in the afternoon. I prowled about the house wondering how long I could put off the moment when it would be impossible not to go to Ealing. My head was aching terribly. I did try quite hard during this time to put my thoughts in order. I speculated about my intentions and her feelings. I sketched plans for a dozen or so different turns of events. I even tried to feign imagining what it would be like really to despair: that is, to believe that she did not love me, had never loved me, and that all I could decently do was to vanish from her life. Then I realized that I did despair, I was in despair, nothing could be worse than this experience of her absence and her silence. And yesterday she had been in my arms and we had looked forward into a huge quiet abyss of time, and we had kissed each other without frenzy and without terror, with thoughtful temperate quiet joy. And I had even sent her away when she did not want to go. I had been insane. Perhaps that was the only time which we should ever, ever have together. Perhaps it was something which would never, never, never come again.

Waiting in fear is surely one of the most awful of human tribulations. The wife at the pit head. The prisoner awaiting interrogation. The shipwrecked man on the raft in the empty sea. The sheer extension of time is felt then as physical anguish. The minutes, each of which might bring relief, or at least certainty, pass fruitlessly and manufacture an increase of horror. As the minutes of that morning passed away I felt a cold deadly increase of my conviction that all was lost. This was how it would be from now on and for ever. She would never communicate with me again. I endured this until half past eleven and then I decided I must go to Ealing and try to see her by force if necessary. I even thought of arming myself with some weapon. But suppose she was already gone?

It had begun to rain. I had put on my macintosh and was standing in the hall wondering if tears would help. I imagined pushing Arnold violently aside and leaping up the stairs. But what then?

The telephone rang and I lifted it. The voice of an operator said, 'Miss Baffin is calling you from an Ealing call box, will you pay for the call?'

'What? Is that –?'

'Miss Baffin is calling you –'

'Yes, yes, I'll pay, yes –'

'Bradley. It's me.'

'Oh darling – Oh thank God –'

'Bradley, quickly, I must see you, I've run away.'

'Oh good, oh my darling, I've been in such a –'

'Me too. Look, I'm in a telephone box near Ealing Broadway station, I haven't any money.'

'I'll come and fetch you in a taxi.'

'I'll hide in a shop, I'm so terrified of –'

'Oh my darling girl –'

'Tell the taxi to drive slowly past the station, I'll see you.'

'Yes, yes.'

'But, Bradley, we can't be at your place, that's where they'll go.'

'Never mind them. I'm coming to fetch you.'

'What happened?'

'Oh, Bradley, it's been such a nightmare –'

'But what *happened*?'

'I was an absolute idiot, I told them all about it in a sort of triumphant aggressive way, I felt so happy, I couldn't conceal it or muffle it, and they were livid, at least at first they simply couldn't believe it, and then they rushed off to see you, and I should have run away then, only I was feeling sort of combative and I wanted another session and then when they came back they were much worse. I've never seen my father so upset and angry, he was quite violent.'

'God, he didn't beat you?'

'No, no, but he shook me till I was quite giddy and he broke a lot of things in my room –'

'Oh my sweet –'

'Then I started to cry and couldn't stop.'

'Yes, when I came round –'

'You came round?'

'They didn't tell you?'

'Dad said later on that he'd seen you again. He said you'd agreed to give it all up. I didn't believe him of course.'

'Oh my brave dear! He told me you didn't want to see me. Of course I didn't believe him either.'

I was holding her two hands in both of mine. We were conversing in soft voices and sitting in a church. (Saint Cuthbert's Philbeach Gardens, to be exact.) Pale green angelica-coloured light entering through Victorian stained glass failed to dissipate the magnificent and soothing gloom of the place. Framing an elaborate reredos apparently made of milk chocolate, a huge melancholy rood screen which looked as if it had been rescued from a fire at the last moment announced that *Verbum caro factum est et habitavit in nobis*. Behind a sturdy iron railing at the west end a murky dove-pinnacled shrine protected the font, or perhaps the cave of some doom-obsessed sibyl or of one of the more terrible forms of Aphrodite. Powers older than Christ seemed to have casually entered and made the place their own. High above us a black-clad figure paced along a gallery and disappeared. We were alone again.

She said, 'I love my parents. I suppose. Well, of course I do. Especially my father. Anyway, I've never doubted it. But there are things one can't forgive. It's the end of something. And the beginning of something.' She turned to me with gravity, her face very tired, a little puffy and battered and creased with much crying, and grim too. One saw what she would look like when she was fifty. And for an instant her unforgiving face reminded me of Rachel in the terrible room.

'Oh Julian, I've brought irrevocable things to you.'

'Yes.'

'I haven't wrecked your life, have I, you aren't angry with me for having involved you in such trouble?'

'That's your silliest remark yet. Anyway, the row went on for hours, mainly between me and my father, and then when my mother started in he shouted that she was jealous of me, and she shouted that he was in love with me, and then she started to cry and I *screamed*, and, oh Bradley, I didn't know ordinary educated middle-class English people could behave the way we behaved last night.'

'That shows how young you are.'

'At last they went off downstairs and I could hear them going on rowing down there, and my mother crying terribly, and I decided I'd had enough and I'd clear out, and then I found they'd locked me in! I'd never been locked in anywhere, even when I was small, I can't tell you how – it was a sort of moment of – illumination – like when people suddenly know – they've got to have a revolution. I was just eternally not going to stand for being locked in.'

'You shouted and banged?'

'No, nothing like that. I knew I couldn't get out of the window, it's too high. I sat on my bed and I cried a lot of course. You know, it seems silly in the middle of all this real sort of – carnage – but I was so sad about the little things of mine my father broke. He broke two sort of cups and all my china animals –'

'Julian, I can't bear this –'

'And it was so frightening – and sort of humiliating – He didn't find *this*, though, it was under my pillow.' Julian took out of the pocket of her dress the gilt snuff box, *A Friend's Gift*.

'I wish it wasn't open war,' I said. 'Julian, you know, what your parents were saying to you wasn't crazy stuff. In a way they're quite right. It's absurd and improper to have anything to do with me. You're so young and I'm so very much older and you've got your whole life – How *can* you know your mind, it's all happened so quickly, you *ought* to be locked up, it'll end in tears –'

'Bradley, we passed this stage long ago. When I was sitting on my bed and looking at the broken china on the floor and feeling my life so broken, I felt so strong too and calm in the middle of it all and quite certain about you and quite certain about myself. Look at me. Certainty. Calm.' She did look calm too, sitting there beside me with her weary lucid face and her blue dress with white willow leaves on it and her brown shiny young knees and our hands piled together on her lap and the gilt snuff box in the loop of her skirt.

'You must have more time to think, we can't –'

'Anyway, about eleven, and that was another last straw, I had to shout and beg them to let me out to go to the lavatory. Then my father came in again and started off on a new tack, being very kind and understanding. It was then he said that he'd seen you again and that you'd said you'd give me up, which of course I knew wasn't true. And then he said he'd take me to Athens –'

'He told me Venice. I've been in Venice all night.'

'He was afraid you'd follow. I was as cold as ice by this time and I'd already made a plan to pretend to agree with anything he said and then to escape as soon as I could. So I acted a climb down and how a treat like going to Athens made all the difference and – thank God you weren't listening – and –'

'I know. I did the same. I actually did tell him I'd sheer off. I felt like Saint Peter.'

'Bradley, I was so *tired* by then, God yesterday was a long day, and I don't know if I convinced him, but he said he was very sorry he'd been so bad, and I think he was sorry too, only I couldn't bear his becoming emotional and soppy and wanting to kiss me and so on, and I said I must sleep so he went away at last and my God he locked the door again!'

'Did you sleep?'

'The funny thing is I did. I imagined I'd stay awake all night, I'd *seen* myself staying awake and thinking, I was quite looking forward to it, but sleep simply took me, unconsciousness rushed over me, I couldn't even undress, it was as if my mind ran straight into oblivion, it had to. And then this morning they started pretending I was sick, and escorting me to the bathroom, and bringing up trays and so on, it was disgusting and somehow frightening. And my father told me to rest and that we'd be leaving London later on today, and then he left the house. I think he went to the telephone box on the corner to make a call he didn't want my mother to hear, he often does at that time in the morning, and anyway he'd dragged the wire of our telephone out of the wall yesterday when he was in a rage. Well, I'd got dressed by then and I looked for my handbag, only they'd taken it, and when I heard him go I tried my door only of course it was locked and I called to my mother and she wouldn't open it, and then I *kicked* my breakfast tray which was just there on the floor. Have you ever kicked a boiled egg off its cup? When I saw that egg flying through the air I felt somehow that's exactly how things are at the moment, only it wasn't funny at all. And then I told

296

my mother that if she didn't open the door at once I would jump out of the window, and I meant it, and at last she did open the door, and I walked down the stairs with her sort of running backwards in front of me, it was very absurd and odd really, and I went to the front door only it was locked with the mortice lock. And all this time my mother was talking at me and begging and asking me to forgive her, it was pathetic, I'd never heard her talk like that before, as if she was really old. And I said nothing and I marched out into the garden and she followed me and I tried the side gate and that was locked too so I ran down the garden and got up on top of the fence – you know those fences are quite high, I don't know how I did it – and dropped down into the next garden. And I could hear her scrabbling and calling – of course she couldn't get over, she's much too fat – and she stood on a box and we stared at each other and her face was so odd – she looked so sort of *surprised*, like someone might look surprised if their leg was shot off, I felt for a moment so sorry for her. Then I ran off across the next garden and over another fence, that wasn't so high, and among some garages and I ran and ran and then I couldn't find a phone box that worked and then I found one and I called you and here I am.'

'Julian, I feel so terrible, so responsible. I'm glad you felt sorry for your mother. You mustn't hate them, you must pity them. In a way they're right and we're wrong –'

'Ever since they locked that door I began to feel like a monster. But I was a happy monster. Sometimes one has got to become monstrous in order to survive. I'm old enough to know that anyway.'

'You escaped and you came to me –'

'I grazed my leg on the fence. It's all hot. Feel.' She put my hand under her skirt on to her thigh. The skin was reddish and broken, blazing hot.

I touched her, and through my scorched palm felt and desired the whole of this young sweet guileless being so suddenly and so miraculously given to me. I withdrew my hand and moved slightly away from her. It was almost too much.

'Julian, my heroine, my queen – oh where can we go – we can't go back to my flat.'

'I know. They'll be there. Bradley, I must be properly alone with you somewhere.'

'Yes. Even if it's only to think.'

'What do you mean, even if it's only to think?'

'I feel so guilty about all this – what you called carnage. We haven't decided anything, we mustn't, we don't know –'

'Bradley, how brave are you really! Are you going to lead me back to my parents? Are you going to stray me like a cat? You are my home now. Bradley, do you love me?'

'Yes, yes, yes, yes, yes.'

'Then you must be bold and free and show qualities of leadership. Think, Bradley, there must be some sort of secret place we can go, even if it's only a hotel.'

'Oh Julian, we can't go to a hotel. There isn't anywhere secret we can go to – Oh my God, yes there is! There is, there is, there is!'

The door of the flat was open. Had I left it open? Was Arnold inside waiting for me?

I went in quietly and stood in the hall listening. Then I heard a nearby rustling sound which seemed to come from my bedroom. Then a curious noise such as some bird might make, a sort of descending 'woo-oo'. I stood stiffly, prickling with alarm. Then there was the unmistakable sound of someone yawning. I went forward and opened the bedroom door.

Priscilla was sitting on my bed. She was dressed in the familiar navy blue coat and skirt, now looking rather baggy. She had taken her shoes off and was in the process of rubbing her toes through her stockings. She said, 'Oh there you are,' and returned to rubbing and scratching her toes, looking at them closely, her head drooped. She yawned again.

'Priscilla! What are you doing here!'

'I decided to come back to you. They tried to stop me but I came. They turned me over to the doctors. They wanted me to stay in the hospital but I wouldn't. There were mad people there, I'm not mad. I had some of the shock treatment. It makes you feel terrible. You scream and throw yourself across the room.

They ought to hold you. I bruised my arm. Look.' She was speaking very slowly. She began laboriously to pull off the navy blue jacket.

'Priscilla, you can't stay here. I've got somebody waiting for me. We're just going to leave London.' Julian was in Oxford Street buying clothes with my money.

'Look.' Priscilla was rolling up the sleeve of her blouse. There was a large mottled bruise on her upper arm. 'Or do you think they were holding me? Perhaps they were holding me. They have a sort of straitjacket they use but they didn't put it on me. I think. I can't remember. It rattles one's head so. It can't be good. And now they've done something to my brain that won't come right again ever. I didn't understand before what it was. I wanted to ask you about it but you didn't come. And Arnold and Christian were always talking and laughing, I couldn't be quiet in myself for their racket and their cackling. I felt such a stranger there, like a poor lodger. One must be with one's own people. And I want you to help me with the divorce. I felt so ashamed with them because everything in their life was going so well and they were so sort of successful. I couldn't talk about what I wanted with them and they were always in a hurry – and then they got me to start out on these electric shocks. One shouldn't do things in a hurry, one always regrets it. Oh Bradley, I wish I hadn't had those shocks, I can *feel* my brain's half destroyed with them. It stands to reason, people aren't supposed to have electric shocks are they?'

'Where's Arnold?' I said.

'He's just gone away with Francis.'

'He was here?'

'Yes. He came after me. I just walked out after breakfast. Not that I had any breakfast, I can't eat these days at all, I can't bear the smell of food. Bradley, I want you to go with me to the lawyer, and I want you to go with me to the hairdresser, I must get my hair rinsed. I think I can just do that, it won't be too much for me. Then I think I'll rest. What did Roger say about my mink stole? I kept worrying about that. Why didn't you visit me? I kept asking for you. I want you to go with me to the lawyer this morning.'

'Priscilla, I can't go anywhere with you this morning. I've got to get out of London quickly. Oh why did you come here!'

'What did Roger say about my mink stole?'

'He sold it. He'll give you the money.'

'Oh no! It was such a lovely one, such a special one –'

'*Please* don't cry –'

'I'm not crying. I came all the way from Notting Hill by myself, and I shouldn't, I'm ill. I think I'll sit in the sitting-room for a while. Could you make me some tea?' She got up heavily and pushed past me. I smelt a rank animal smell off her mingled with some sort of hospital odour. Formaldehyde perhaps. Her face looked ponderous and sleepy and her lower lip drooped with an effect resembling a sneer. She sat down slowly and carefully in the small armchair and put her feet on a footstool.

'Priscilla, you can't stay here! I've got to leave London!'

She yawned hugely, her nose snubbing up, her eyes squeezed, one hand questing through her blouse to scratch her armpit. She rubbed her eyes and then began to undo the middle buttons of her blouse. 'I keep yawning and yawning and I keep scratching and scratching and my legs ache and I can't keep still. I expect it's the electricity. Bradley, you won't leave me will you, you're all I've got now, you can't go away. What were you saying? Did Roger really sell my mink stole?'

'I'll make you some tea,' I said to get out of the room. I went to the kitchen and actually put the kettle on. I was horribly upset at the sight of Priscilla, but of course there was no question of changing my plans. I just could not think what to do immediately. I had a rendezvous with Julian in half an hour's time. If I failed to turn up she would come straight here. Meanwhile Arnold, unaccountably absent, might turn up at any moment.

Someone came in through the front door. I issued quickly from the kitchen, ready to make a dash for freedom. I charged into Francis with such force that I butted him back out of the doorway. We held on to each other.

'Where's Arnold?'

'I strayed him,' said Francis, 'but you haven't much time.'

I pulled Francis outside into the court. I wanted to be able to see Arnold coming. Francis was such a relief, I held firmly on to both his sleeves in case he should run away, which however he seemed unlikely to do. He smirked at me, looking pleased with himself.

'What did you do?'

'I said I thought I'd seen you and Julian going into a pub in Shaftesbury Avenue, I said I knew it was a haunt of yours, and he rushed off, but he'll be back soon.'

'Has he told you –?'

'He told Christian who told me. Chris is enjoying it all like mad.'

'Francis, listen. I'm going away with Julian today. I want you to stay with Priscilla here, or at Notting Hill, wherever she wants to be. Here's a cheque, a big one, and I'll give you more.'

'I say, thanks! Where are you going?'

'Never mind. I'll telephone you at intervals to see how Priscilla is. Thanks for your help. Now I must pack one or two things and get out.'

'Brad, look. I brought this back. I'm afraid it's properly broken now. I broke off the foot trying to straighten it out.' He thrust something into my hand. It was the little bronze of the buffalo lady.

We went back into the house and I dropped the latch on the street door and shut the door of the flat. There was a sort of screeching noise inside the flat. It was the whistling electric kettle announcing that the water was boiling. 'Make tea, would you, Francis.'

I ran into my bedroom and hurled clothes into a suitcase. Then I returned to the sitting-room.

Priscilla was sitting bolt upright now, looking frightened. 'What was that noise?'

'The kettle.'

'Who is it there?'

'Just Francis. He'll stay with you. I've got to go.'

'When will you be back? You aren't going properly away are you, for days?'

'I'm not sure. I'll ring up.'

'Oh Bradley, please, please don't leave me. It's so frightening, everything frightens me now, I get so frightened at night. You are my brother, I know you'll look after me, you can't leave me with strangers. And I don't know what to do for the best and you're the only person I can talk to. I think I won't go and see the lawyer yet. I don't know what to do about Roger. Oh I wish I'd never left him, I want Roger, I want Roger – Roger would pity me if he saw me now.'

'Here's an old friend anyway!' I said, and I dropped the little bronze on to her lap. She closed her legs instinctively and it fell to the floor.

'It's broken now,' she said.

'Yes. Francis broke it trying to mend it.'

'I don't want it now any more.'

I picked it up. One of the buffalo's front legs was broken off jaggedly near the body. I laid the bronze on its side in the lacquer cabinet.

'It's quite broken now. Oh how sad, how sad –'

'Priscilla, stop it!'

'Oh dear, I do want Roger, Roger was mine, we belonged together, he was mine and I was his.'

'Don't be silly, Priscilla. Roger's a dead loss.'

'I want you to go to Roger and tell him I'm sorry –'

'Certainly not!'

'I want Roger, dear Roger, I want him –'

I tried to kiss her, at least I approached my face to the dark soiled line of the grey hair, but she jerked her head as I stooped and rapped me hard on the jaw. 'Good-bye, Priscilla, I'll ring up.'

'Oh don't go away and leave me, please, please, please –'

I was at the door. She stared up at me now with huge slow tears coming out of her eyes, her gaping mouth all red and wet. I turned from her. Francis was just emerging from the kitchen with the tea tray. I saluted him and ran out of the house and along the court. At the end of the court I paused and peered cautiously out round the corner.

Arnold and Christian were just getting out of a taxi about ten yards away. Arnold was paying the taxi man. Christian saw me. She at once moved, turning her back to me and placing herself between me and Arnold.

I dodged back. There is a tiny slit of an alleyway just before

302

the court debouches and I wedged myself into this, and saw almost instantly Arnold striding past, his face set hard with anxiety and purpose. Christian followed him more slowly, her eyes questing about. She saw me again and she made a gesture of a sort of oriental voluptuousness, a kind of amused sensuous homage, lifting her hands palm upwards and then bringing them sinuously down to her sides like a ballet dancer. She did not pause. I waited some moments and then emerged.

Arnold had gone into the flat. Christian was still standing out-side looking back. I set my suitcase down, put both my fists to my brow and then extended my arms towards her. She waved, a sort of frail fluttering wave, like someone departing on a boat. Then she followed Arnold through the door. I ran into Charlotte Street. I caught Arnold and Christian's taxi and it took me to Julian.

Part Three

She had so much enjoyed our shopping. She conducted it. Boldly she chose food, cleaning stuff, washing stuff, kitchen things. She even bought a pretty blue dustpan and brush with flowers painted on. And an apron. And a sun hat. We loaded up the hired car. Some prophetic wit had made me keep my licence up to date. But, after carless years, I was driving cautiously.

It was five o'clock of the same day and we were far from London. We were in a village, the car was parked outside the village shop. Grass grew between the paving stones and the sloping sun was giving to each blade of grass its own individual brown little shadow. There was still quite a long way to go.

Seeing Julian playing housekeeper so busily and naturally and ordering me about as if we had been married for years made me sick with joy. I dissembled the intensity of my delight so as not to make her self-conscious. I bought some sherry and some wine because that is what couples do, but I felt I should be perpetually drunk on sheer pleasure. At moments I almost wanted to be alone so as to meditate more single-mindedly upon what had happened. When we had driven on a bit and I had stopped to relieve myself in a wood, and as I stood looking down at a criss-crossy linoleum of pine needles, and a little copse of frondy moss in a tree root and a few stars of scarlet pimpernel, I felt like a great poet. These tiny things stood before me, the concrete embodiment of something resonant and huge, of histories and ecstasies and tears.

In the beginnings of dusk we drove on in silence along lanes of plump white-flowering chestnuts and powdery ladies' lace. To drive someone one loves in a car is a special mode of possession: the controlled vibrating vehicle becomes an extension of one's being which now powerfully includes the half-seen person by one's side. Sometimes my left hand sought her right. Sometimes with a shy deliberation she touched my knee. Sometimes she sat sideways, contemplating me, and making me smile like a flower in the sun as I gazed ahead at the moving roadway. The tunnel-like movement of the car contained us and the accomplice murmur of the engine wrapped up our happy silence.

Human happiness is rarely in the best of circumstances without shadows, and an almost pure happiness can be a terror to itself. My happiness at this time, though intense, was far from pure, and in the midst of all this mad joy (watching Julian buy the dust-pan and brush for instance) I soon started rehearsing terrors and miseries. Of course there was vengeful Arnold, resentful Rachel, miserable Priscilla. There was the quaint and curious fact that I had lied about my age. There was a huge question mark over the immediate future. But these matters were, now that I was with Julian, problems rather than nightmares. Soon and in soli-tude I would tell her everything and she would be the just judge. The fact of loving and being loved can make (in a way which is of course sometimes illusory) even the most practical of difficulties seem trivial or even senseless. Nor did I in any vulgar sense fear exposure. We would be secret. No one knew of this place. I had told my plans to nobody.

What troubled me as I drove along in that very blue twilight between fat flowery chestnut trees and saw the full moon like a dish of Jersey cream above a barley field which was still catching the light of the sun, were two things, one vast and cosmic, the other horribly precise. The cosmic trouble was that I was feeling, in some way quite unconnected with ordinary speculations about what might happen, that I should certainly lose Julian. I did not doubt now that she loved me. But I felt a kind of absolute despair, as if we had loved already for a thousand years and were con-demned to become weary of something so perfect. I raced about the planet like lightning, I put a girdle round the galaxy, and was back in the next second gasping with this despair. Those who have loved will understand me. I was giddy with fear. A great loop had been made in the continuum of time and space and across the mouth of it Julian's right hand held my left. All this had happened before, perhaps a million times, and because of

306

this was doomed. There was no ordinary future any more, only this ecstatic tormented terrified present. The future had passed through the present like a sword. We were already, even eye to eye and lip to lip, deep in the horrors to come. My other trouble was wondering, when we reached Patara and I tried to make love to Julian, whether I should succeed.

So we started arguing.

'You're thinking too much, Bradley, I can see you are. We'll solve all these problems. We'll have Priscilla to live with us.'

'We won't be living anywhere.'

'What do you mean?'

'We just won't. There isn't any future. We shall go on and on driving in this car forever. That's all there is.'

'You mustn't speak like that, it's false. Look, I've bought brown bread and toothpaste and a dustpan.'

'Yes. That's a miracle. But it's like the fossils which religious men used to think God put there when He created the world in 4000 BC so that we could develop an illusion of the past.'

'I don't understand.'

'We have an illusion of the future.'

'That's wicked talk and a betrayal of love.'

'Our love is in the nature of a closed system. It is complete within itself. It has no accidents and no extension.'

'Please don't talk that abstract sort of language, it's a way of lying.'

'Maybe. But we have no language in which to tell the truth about ourselves, Julian.'

'Well, I have. I'm going to marry you. You will write a great book. I will try to write a great book.'

'Do you really believe this?'

'Yes. Bradley, you're tormenting me, I think you're doing it on purpose.'

'Perhaps. I feel so connected with you. I am you. I must stir a little, even cause pain, if I'm to apprehend you at all.'

'Cause me pain then, I'll bear it gladly, but it must be inside our security.'

'Oh everything's *inside*. That's the trouble.'

'I don't know what you mean by "inside". But you seem to

be speaking as if it were all an illusion, as if you could leave me.'

'I suppose it could be interpreted like that.'

'But we've only just found each other.'

'We found each other millions of years ago, Julian.'

'Yes, yes, I know. I feel that too, but really, ordinary really, since Covent Garden it's only two days.'

'I'll meditate on that.'

'Well, meditate properly. Bradley, you couldn't leave me, what nonsense are you talking.'

'No, I couldn't leave you, my utter darling, but you could leave me. I don't mean anything about doubting your love. It's just that whatever miracle made us will automatically also break us. We are *for* breaking, our smash is what it's for.'

'I won't let you talk like this. I'll hold you and silence you with love.'

'Mind out. This is tricky light for driving in.'

'Will you stop a minute?'

'No.'

'Do you really think I could leave you?'

'*Sub specie aeternitatis*, yes. You have done so already.'

'You know I don't understand Latin.'

'A pity your education was so neglected.'

'Bradley, I shall get angry with you.'

'So we are quarrelling already. Shall I drive you back to Ealing?'

'You are deliberately hurting and spoiling.'

'I am not a very nice character. You must get to know me sometime.'

'I do know you. I know you inside out and backwards.'

'You do and you don't.'

'Do you doubt my love?'

'I fear the gods.'

'I fear nothing.'

'Perfection is instant despair. Instant despair. Nothing to do with time.'

'If you despair you doubt that I love you.'

'Maybe.'

'Will you *please* stop driving?'

'No.'

'What can I do to prove that I love you absolutely?'

'I don't see that you can do anything.'

'I shall jump out of the car.'

'Don't be silly.'

'I shall.'

And the next moment she had.

There was a sound like a small explosion, a puff of air, and she was gone from my side. The door gaped, cracked open, swung and slammed back. The seat beside me was empty. The car careered on to the grass verge and stopped.

I looked back and saw her in the half light lying in a dark motionless heap by the side of the road.

I had had terrible moments in my life. Many of them came to me after this one. But this was, seen in retrospect, the most beautiful, the purest and the most absolutely punishing.

Gasping with terror and anguish I got myself out of the car and ran back. The road was empty and silent, the air filled with atoms of darkening blue, defeating the sight.

Oh the poor frailty of the human form, its egg-shell vulnerability! How can this precarious crushable machine of flesh and bones and blood survive on this planet of hard surfaces and relentless murderous gravity? I had felt the crash and crunch of her body upon the road.

Her head was in the grass, her legs hunched up on the verge. The moment of stillness when I got to her was the worst. I knelt beside her, moaning aloud, not daring to touch or move that perhaps terribly damaged body. Was she conscious, would she in a moment begin to scream with pain? My hands hovered about her with a condemned tragic helplessness. I had a very different future now as I ineptly questioned that inert and scattered being that I did not dare even to fold in my arms.

Then Julian said, 'Sorry, Bradley.'

'Are you badly hurt?' I said in a grating breathless voice.

'Don't – think – so –' Then she sat up and put her arms round my neck.

'Oh Julian, be careful, are you all right, is anything broken?'

'No – I'm sure – not – Look, I fell on to these humpy cushions of grass or moss or –'

'I thought you fell on the road.'

'No, I just – grazed my leg again – and I banged my face – ouf! I think I'm perfectly all right though, it just hurts – Wait a moment, let me just try moving – Yes, I'm perfectly all right – Oh I am sorry –'

I took her in my arms properly then and we held on to each other, half lying among the little mossy grassy hillocks beside a ditch full of white flowering nettles. The creamy moon had become smaller and paler and more metallic. Darkness began to thicken about us in the dense air as we held each other in silence.

'Bradley, I'm getting cold, I've lost my sandals.'

I let go and swivelled my body round and began kissing her cold wet feet as they lay dinting a cushion of damp spongy moss. Her feet tasted of dew and earth and the little green frond-flowers of the moss, which smelt of celery. I clasped her pale wet feet in my arms and groaned with bliss and longing.

'Bradley, please. I hear a car, someone will come.'

I got up, burning, and helped her up, and then in fact a car did come by and its lights showed her legs, the blue of her dress which matched her eyes, and a flash of her shaggy brown-gold mane. It also showed her sandals lying together upon the road.

'There's blood on your leg.'

'It's just a graze.'

'You're limping.'

'No, just stiff.'

We walked back to the car and I turned on the headlights and made an intricate bower of green leaves in the middle of the dark. We got into the car and held each other's hands.

'It won't be necessary to do that again, Julian.'

'I'm very sorry.'

Then we drove on in silence, her hand on my knee. For the last bit she read the map by torchlight. We crossed a railway line and a canal into a sort of empty flat land. There were no lights of houses to be seen now. The lights of the car showed how the roadway faded into a stony verge of smooth grey pebbles and vivid green wiry grass. We paused and turned at a featureless crossroads where Julian turned her torch on to the finger post. The road turned into a stony track along which we bumped at five miles per hour. And at last the headlights swung round and revealed two white gate posts and the name written in bold Italian lettering: *Patara*. The car moved on to gravel and the lights jerked over red brick walls and we came to a halt outside a narrow latticed porch. Julian already had the key, she had been holding it for miles. I peered at our haven. It was a little square red brick bungalow. The agent had been a trifle romantic. 'It's marvellous,' said Julian. She let me in.

All the lights were on. Julian had run from room to room. She had pulled back the sheets of the double divan bed. 'I don't think this is aired at all, it's quite damp. Oh Bradley, let's go down to the sea straightaway, shall we? Then I'll cook supper.'

I looked at the bed. 'It's late, my darling. Are you sure you're all right after that fall?'

'Of course! I think I'll just change, it's got a bit chilly, and then we'll go down to the sea, it must be just there, I think I can hear it.'

I went out of the front door and listened. The sound of the sea sieving pebbles came in a regular harsh grating sigh from over the top of some little eminence, sand dunes perhaps, just in front of me. The moon was slightly hazed over but giving out a golden, not silvery, illumination by which I could see the white garden fencing, ragged shrubs and the outline of a single tree. A sense of emptiness and level land. Air moving softly, salty. I felt a mixture of bliss and pure fear. After a few moments I went back into the house. Silence.

I went into the bedroom. Julian, in a mauve and white flowered petticoat with a white fringe was lying on the bed deeply asleep. Her glowing brown hair was spread all over the pillow and half over her face in a silky network like part of a beautiful shawl. She lay on her back with her throat exposed as if to the knife. Her shoulders, pale in colour, were as creamy as the moon at dusk. Her knees were a little drawn up, the bare muddied feet sideways and pointed. Her hands, also brown with earth, had found each other and nestled between her breasts like a pair of animals. Her right thigh, below the line of the white fringe, was red and scraped in two places, once where she had climbed over the fence, once where she had thrown herself out of the car. She had indeed had an eventful day.

So had I. I sat and brooded over her and pondered a hundred things. I had no intention of waking her, though I did wonder if I should bathe her thigh. The long scratches looked quite clean. This sudden magical withdrawal into unconsciousness was just what I had been wanting at different times during the day, to be with her and yet not with her. And now as I sat and sighed beside her there was a strange pleasure in not touching her. After a while I lightly lifted the bedclothes over her, laying down the folded sheet just below those clasped and nestling hands, and I wondered what I had done, or more perhaps what she had done, since it was more her will than mine which had so completely transformed our lives. Perhaps tomorrow morning it would all seem to her like a dreadful dream. Perhaps tomorrow I would be driving a weeping girl back to London. For that too I must be faithfully ready, for I had already been given a fortune which I did not deserve in the least. How wonderful and terrible it had been when she leapt out of the car. But what did it mean except that she was young and the young love extremes? She was a child of extremes and I was a puritan and old. Would I ever make love to her? Ought I to? Would I be able to?

'Look, Bradley, an animal's skull, all washed by the sea. What is it, a sheep?'

'A sheep, yes.'

'We'll take it back.'

'There are all those stones and shells to take back too.'

'Well, we can get the car down, can't we?'

'I think so. There's that cry again. What did you say it was?'

'The curlew. It says its name. Oh Bradley, look at this beautiful piece of wood, the way the sea has had it, it looks like Chinese writing.'

312

'Are we to bring that too?'

'Of course.'

I took the square piece of wood, all its wrinkles smoothed and joined by the sea water until it looked like a sort of delicate sketch of an old face, a sketch such as some Italian artist, Leonardo perhaps, might make in a rather abstract way in his notebook. I took the sheep's skull. The skull, bereft of teeth but otherwise fairly complete, had been in the sea for some time. There was nothing sharp upon it. It had been smoothed and caressed and polished until it seemed more like a work of art, some exquisite fabrication in ivory, rather than one of nature's remnants. The bone was densely smooth to the touch, warmed by the sun, the colour of thick cream, the colour of Julian's shoulders.

In fact Julian's shoulders had already changed their hue to a glowing angry-looking reddish-brown. It was the *afternoon* of the next day. My meditations of the previous night had been cut short by an attack of sleep almost as sudden as that which had laid Julian low. Sleep sprang upon me like a jaguar launched from a tree. I had half undressed and was wondering how to array myself as Julian's consort and whether to array myself at all, when the next thing I knew was that it was morning, the sun was shining into the room and I was lying by myself underneath the blankets, dressed in my shirt, underpants and socks. I knew instantly where I was. I felt a shock of fear at Julian's absence, allayed at once by hearing her singing in the kitchen. Then I felt annoyance at having displayed myself to her sleeping in such an undignified garb. Shirt and socks form a most unattractive *deshabillé*. Had I got into bed myself or had she covered me? Then it seemed dreadful, scandalous and *funny* that my beloved and I should have slept side by side all night, stupefied into total unawareness of each other. Oh precious precious night.

'Bradley, are you awake? Tea, coffee, milk, sugar? How little I know about you.'

'Indeed. Tea, milk, sugar. Did you see my socks?'

'I love your socks. We're going straight down to the sea.'

And we did. We had a picnic breakfast with milky tea in a thermos flask and bread and butter and jam, down on the flat stones of the beach, just beside where the sea, much more gently

313

than last night, was touching the clean fringe of the land, which it had itself fashioned to be its pure spouse and counterpart, withdrawing to breathe and returning again to touch. Behind us were wind-combed sand dunes and yellow arches of long reedy grass and blue sky the colour of Julian's eyes. Before us was the calm cold English sea, diamond-sparkling and rather dark even under the sun.

There have been many moments of happiness. But that first breakfast beside the sea had a simplicity and an intensity which it would be hard to match. It was not even plagued by hope. It was just perfect communion and rest and the kind of joy which comes when the beloved and one's own soul become so mingled with the external world that there is a *place* made for once upon the planet where stones and tufts of grass and transparent water and the quiet sound of the wind can really *be*. It was perhaps the other side of the diptych from last night's moment of seeing Julian in the twilight lying motionless beside the road. But it was not really connected, as moments of pure joy are not really connected with anything. And human life which has such moments has surely put a trembling finger upon nature's most transcendent aim.

We walked back, carrying stones and pieces of driftwood – there were already too many to bring in one expedition – over the top of the dunes, and saw inland the graceless but already friendly red brick cube of our home, a ruined farmhouse behind it, and then the flat land, a washed yellowy green in colour, under a huge sky scattered with small cornets of gilded white cloud. Far off, beyond a region of shadow, sun shone upon the long grey back and tall tower of a big church. We left our trophies in a pile at the foot of the dunes, where Julian insisted on covering them with sand in case anyone should steal them, a rather idle precaution since there was no one to be seen except ourselves, and then set off across the sort of huge courtyard of flat seaworn stones which divided us from the house. Here mauve sea cabbage and blue vetch and cushiony pink thrift was growing in profusion and wild yellow tree lupins sprawled their starry leaves and pallid cones of blossom about upon the stripy concentric stones of the natural pavement. Glassy dragon flies whizzed and hovered and

314

butterflies idled in from the sea and blew fluttering away with the breeze, soon becoming invisible in the bright air. The exact whereabouts of the paradise I shall for many reasons conceal, but amateurs of the British coastline may hazard their guess.

As I sat and watched her preparing our lunch (she had told me quite correctly that she could not cook) I marvelled at her sheer grasp of the situation, her absolute hereness, and I tried to put off all anxiety, as it seemed that she had done, and to keep at bay the demons of abstraction in protest against which she had hurled herself from the moving car. In the afternoon we drove across the flowery courtyard to collect our trophies and to look for more and we laid them out on the rough weedy lawn in front of the house. The stones were all elliptical and faintly humped and fairly uniform in size but varied immensely in colour. Some were purple spotted with dark blue, some tawny with creamy blotches, some a mottled lavender grey, many with swirling patterns round a central eye or strikingly decorated with stripes of purest white. As Julian said, it was very difficult to decide to leave any of them behind. It was like being in a huge art gallery and being told to help oneself. The most privileged stones she now took inside together with the sheep's skull and the bits of driftwood. The square piece of wood with the Chinese writing she propped upright like an icon upon the chimney-piece of our little sitting-room, with the sheep's skull on one side of it and the gilt snuff box on the other, and on the window ledges she arranged the stones among pieces of grey worked tree root, like small modern sculptures. I watched her total absorption in these tasks. We had tea.

After tea we drove over to the big church and walked about inside its bony emptiness. A few chairs upon the huge stone floor betokened a tiny congregation. There was no stained glass, only huge perpendicular windows through which the cool sun shone on to the pale rather powdery stone of the floor, casting a little shadow into worn *requiescats* many centuries old. The church in the flat land was like a great ruined ship or ark, or perhaps like the skeleton of an enormous animal, under whose gaunt ribs one moved with awe and pity. We trod in silence with soft feet, padding and prowling, separated from one another and yet connected, pausing and gazing at each other across slanting shafts of powdery air, leaning back against pillars or against the thick wall where the cold damp stone was like the touch of death or truth.

We drove back under a sky of light brown cloud streaked with long mouths full of green or orange light, and I felt exalted and hollow and clean and at the same time burning with desire and wondering, but with no will of my own, what was going to happen next. Julian prattled on and I gave her a short tutorial on English church architecture. Then she announced that she wanted to swim and we drove to the dunes and ran to the sea and it turned out that she had her bathing costume on underneath her dress and she rushed into the water and was soon splashing about and taunting me. (I cannot swim.) I think, however, that the sea was extremely cold for she came out of it fairly quickly.

Meanwhile I sat upon the ridge of patterned stones above the water, holding the hem of her discarded dress and, until I noticed what I was doing and deliberately relaxed, crushing it up spasmodically in my hand. I did not think that Julian was deliberately postponing the moment of love-making or that she was doubting her gift of herself. Nor did I think that she wanted me to force her. I felt entirely given over to her instinct and to the tempo of her being. The moment I longed for and dreaded would come at its natural time, and its natural time would be tonight.'

The absolute yearning of one human body for another particular one and its indifference to substitutes is one of life's major mysteries. There are, I am told, people who just want 'a woman' or 'a man'. I cannot conceive of this state of affairs and it does not concern me. I had rarely wanted another human being absolutely which was the same as to say that I had rarely wanted another human being at all. Holding hands and kissing, that can mean something in friendship, though it had not been my way. But that trembling dedication to the totality of another I had experienced – well, as I sat on the divan bed that evening and waited for Julian I felt, never before: though I knew intellectually that I had been in love with Christian. And there had been another case, of which I do not tell the story here.

It was and was not like the first day of the honeymoon when the newly married pair, in tender deference to each other, feign habits which are not their own. I was not a young husband. I was not young and I was not a husband. I felt none of the youthful spouse's need to take control, his reflective anxiety about the future, his calmingly classified commitment. I feared the future and I was committed but I felt myself that day in a world so entirely weird, in a land of marvels, where all that was required of my courage was that I should walk on and on. I felt no need to take control. It was not that Julian controlled me. We were both of us controlled by something else.

We had had eggs for lunch and sausages for supper. At supper we drank some of the wine. Julian had the healthy young person's indifference to alcohol. I thought I would be too excited to drink, but I downed two glasses with a sort of amazed appreciation. Julian had taken great pleasure in finding a pretty tablecloth and laying the table as elaborately as she could for both meals. Patara was, as advertised, well provided with all household necessities. Julian's dustpan and brush were otiose. (It also, as advertised, had its own electricity from a generator in the abandoned farmyard.) She had brought in flowers from the garden, straggling canterbury bells of a faded cottony blue, yellow loosestrife and wild lupins from beyond the fence, and one white peony streaked with crimson, as gorgeous as a lotus. We sat down formally and laughed with delight. After supper she said suddenly, 'There's nothing to worry about.' 'Uh-hu.' 'You understand me?' 'Yes.' We washed up. She went into the bathroom and I went into the bedroom and looked at myself in the mirror. I inspected my dulled straight hair and my thin discreetly wrinkled face. I looked amazingly young. I got undressed. Then she came and we were together for the first time.

When one has at last got what has been ardently longed for one wishes time to cease. Often indeed at such moments it is miraculously slowed. Looking into each other's eyes we caressed each other without any haste at all, with a sort of tender curious astonishment. I felt none of Marvell's frenzy now. I felt rather that I was privileged to be living out in a brief span some great aeon of the experience of love. Did the Greeks know between 600 and 400 BC what millennia of human experience they were enacting? Perhaps not. But I knew, as I worshipped my darling from head to foot that I was under orders, a sort of incarnate history of human love.

My luxuriant sense of destiny had its nemesis however. I put the essential matter off too long and when I came to it it was over in a second. After that I groaned a good deal and attempted to caress her but she held me very closely pinioning my arms. 'I'm no good.' 'Don't be silly, Bradley.' 'I'm too old.' 'Darling, we'll sleep.' 'I'm going outside for a minute.'

I went out naked into the dark garden where the light from the bedroom showed a dim square of jagged grass and dandelions. A mist was coming in from the sea, drifting slowly past the house, curling and uncurling like cigarette smoke. I listened and could not hear the waves but a train rattled and then cried out like an owl somewhere in the land behind me.

When I came back she had put on a sort of dark blue silk night shirt, unbuttoned to the navel. I pushed it back on to her shoulders. Her breasts were the perfect fruit of youth, rounded and just pendant. Her hair had dried into a soft golden fuzz. Her eyes were huge. I put on a dressing-gown. I knelt in front of her without touching her.

'My darling, don't worry.'

'I'm not worrying,' I said. 'I'm just no bloody good.'

'It will be all right.'

'Julian, I'm old.'

'Nonsense. I can *see* how old you are!'

'No, but – How bruised you are, your poor arm and your leg.'

'I'm sorry –'

'It's beautiful, as if you'd been fingered by a god, stained with purple.'

'Come into bed, Bradley.'

'Your knees smell of the northern sea. Has anyone ever kissed the soles of your feet before?'

318

'No.'

'Good. Sorry to be such a failure.'

'You know there isn't any possible failure here, Bradley. I love you.'

'I'm your slave.'

'We will be married, won't we?'

'It's impossible.'

'Don't frighten me by saying that. You don't mean it, it's just mechanical. There's nothing to stop us. Think of other poor people who want to get married and can't. We are free, we aren't married to anyone else, we've got no responsibilities. Well, there's poor Priscilla, but she can live with us. We'll look after her and make her happy. Bradley, don't just reject happiness stupidly. Well, I know you won't, you can't. If I thought you could I'd be screaming.'

'You needn't scream.'

'Well, why do you say these sort of abstract things that you don't mean?'

'I'm just instinctively protecting myself.'

'You haven't answered properly. You will marry me, won't you?'

'You're quite mad,' I said, 'but as I told you, I'm your slave. Whatever you go on wanting will be the law of my being.'

'That's settled then. Oh dear, I am so tired.'

We both were. After we had turned off the light she said, 'And another thing, Bradley. Today has been the happiest day I have ever had in my whole life.'

I was asleep two seconds later. We woke at dawn and embraced each other again, but with the same result.

The next day the mist was still there, thicker, still moving in from the sea with a sort of relentless marching motion, passing by the house in a steady purposive manner like a shadowy army bound for some distant hosting. We watched it, sitting laced together in the window seat of the little sitting-room in the early morning.

After breakfast we decided to walk inland and look for a shop. The air was chilly and Julian was wearing one of my jackets as an overcoat, since it had not occurred to her to purchase a coat during her shopping spree. We walked along a footpath beside a little stream full of watercress and then came to a signalman's cottage and crossed the railway and then went over a humpy bridge which was reflecting itself in a very quiet canal. The sun was piercing the mist now and rolling it up into great cloudy spheres of gold in the midst of which we walked as between huge balls which never quite touched us or touched each other. I felt very troubled about what had happened, or rather not happened, during the night, but I was also being made insanely happy by Julian's presence. To torment us I said, 'We can't stay here forever, you know.'

'Don't use that tone of voice. That's your "despair". Not again.'

'No, just saying the obvious.'

'I think we must stay here a while to learn happiness.'

'It's not my subject.'

'I know, but I'll teach you. I want to keep you here until you become content in your mind about what is going to happen.'

'You mean about our marriage?'

'Yes. Then later on I'll do my exams, everything will be –'

'Suppose I were much older than –'

'Oh stop worrying, Bradley. You want to sort of justify everything.'

'I am by you eternally justified. Even if your love were to end now I am justified.'

'Is that a quotation?'

'Only from me.'

'Well, it isn't going to end now. And do stop boring me about your age.'

'For all that beauty that doth cover thee is but the seemly raiment of my heart, which in thy breast doth live as thine in me. How can I then be older than thou art?'

'Is *that* a quotation?'

'It's a damn rotten argument.'

'Bradley, have you noticed anything about me?'

'One or two little things, I suppose.'

'Have you noticed that in the last two or three days I've *grown up*?'

I had noticed that. 'Yes.'

'I was a child and perhaps you are still thinking of me as a child. But now I am a woman, a real one.'

'Oh my darling girl, hold on to me, hold on to me, hold on to me, and if I ever try to leave you don't let me.'

We walked across a meadow to a little village and found our shop and as we began to walk back the mist cleared away completely. And now the dunes and our courtyard were huge and glistening with sun, all the stones, dampened a little by the mist, shining in their different colours. We left our basket beside the fence and ran on down towards the sea. Julian suggested that we should collect some wood for a fire, but this proved difficult because every bit of wood we found was far too beautiful to burn. However we did find a few pieces which she consented to immolate, and I was carrying them back through the sandy dunes to our collecting point, leaving her still on the beach, when I saw in the distance something which absolutely froze my blood. A man in uniform on a bicycle was just riding along the bumpy track away from our bungalow.

There could be no doubt that he had been to Patara. There was nowhere else to go to. I immediately dropped the wood and lay down in a hollow of sand and watched through a vault of wet golden grass until the bicyclist had ridden out of sight. A policeman? A postman? I have always dreaded officials. What could he want with us? Was it us he wanted? No one knew we were here. I felt cold with guilt and terror: and I thought, I have been in paradise and I have not been grateful. I have been anxious and destructive and stupid. And now something is going to happen, and I shall learn what it is like to be really afraid. So far I have been playing at fear when there was no need.

I called to Julian that I was going back to the house to get the car to carry the wood, and she should stay and go on collecting. I wanted to see if our bicyclist had left anything. I started off

321

across the courtyard, but in a moment she was calling 'Wait for me!' and racing after me and clasping my hand and laughing. I averted my terrified face from her and she noticed nothing.

When she got to the house she stopped in the garden to inspect some stones which she had placed there in a row. I moved without obvious haste to the porch and went in through the door. A telegram was lying on the mat and I picked it up with a quick swoop. I went on into the lavatory and locked the door.

The telegram was addressed to me. I began to fumble at it with trembling fingers. I tore the whole thing, including the telegram itself, then stood there holding the two halves of the paper together. It read *Please telephone me immediately Francis.*

I stared at these deadly words. They could only mean something catastrophic. And the incomprehensibility of this visitation was terrifying. Francis did not know this address. Someone must have found out, how? Arnold presumably. We had made some slip, how, when, what, some fatal mistake. Even now Arnold was on his way here and Francis was trying to warn me.

Julian called 'Yoo hoo!'

I said, 'Coming,' and emerged. I had to get to the telephone at once and without letting Julian know.

'I think it's lunch-time, don't you?' said Julian. 'Let's fetch the wood after.' She was putting the blue and white check table-cloth on to the table again. She put the jug of flowers in the centre of the table, from which it was always ceremonially removed as we sat down to eat. Already there were these customs.

I said, 'Tell you what, you get lunch and I'll just take the car down to that garage. I want to have the oil done and I could get a bit of petrol. Then we'll be ready if we want to go somewhere this afternoon.'

'But we can go then on the way,' said Julian.

'They may be shut this afternoon. And we may not want to go that way.'

'I'll come with you then.'

'No, you stay here. Why don't you go and pick some of that watercress we saw? I'd love some for my lunch.'

'Oh good, yes, I'll do that! I'll get a basket. Don't be long.' She pranced off.

I went to the car, then failed to start it in my agitation. At last it started and I set off bumping horribly slowly along the track. By road the nearest village was where our big church was. There must be a telephone box there. The church was just outside the village on the side towards the sea, and I could recall nothing of the place from our night arrival. I passed the garage. I had thought of asking the garage man if I could use his telephone, but it might not be private. I drove past the church and turning a corner saw the village street and a public telephone box.

I stopped outside it. Of course the box was occupied. Inside it a girl, gesticulating and smiling, turned her back on me. I waited. At last the door opened. I found I had no change. Then the operator would not answer. Finally I achieved a reverse charge call to my own number and heard Francis, who had picked up the receiver at once, babbling at the other end.

'Francis, hello. How did you know where I was?'

'Oh Bradley – Bradley –'

'What's the matter? Has Arnold found out? What sort of a mess have you made of things?'

'Oh Bradley –'

'What is it, for God's sake? What's happened?'

There was silence, then a high whining sound. At the other end of the line Francis was crying. I felt sick with fear.

'What –?'

'Oh Bradley – it's Priscilla –'

'What?'

'She's dead.'

I became suddenly and strangely conscious of the telephone box, the sunshine, somebody waiting outside, my own staring-eyed face in the mirror.

'How –?'

'She killed herself – she took sleeping tablets – she must have had them hidden – I left her – I shouldn't have done – we took her to hospital – but it was too late – oh Bradley, Bradley –'

'She is really – dead –' I said, and I felt that she simply couldn't be, it was impossible, she was in hospital where people were helped to get better, she simply could not have killed herself, it was another false alarm. 'Really – dead – Are you sure –?'

'Yes, yes – oh I am so – it was all my fault – she's dead, Bradley – she was alive in the ambulance – but then they told me she wasn't alive any more – I – oh Bradley, forgive me –'

Priscilla wasn't alive any more. 'It's not your fault,' I said mechanically. 'It's my fault.'

'Oh I'm so wretched – it's all my fault – I want to kill myself – I can't live after this, how can I –' More whining and crying.

'Francis. Stop that whimpering. Listen. How did you find out where I was?'

'I found a letter in your desk from the agent – I thought you might be there – I had to find you – Oh Bradley, I've been in hell, in hell, not knowing where you were – thinking this had happened and you didn't even know – I sent the telegram late last night but they said it wouldn't arrive till this morning.'

'I've just got it. Hold on. Just keep quiet and hold on.' I stood silent in the slanting ray of the sun, looking at the pitted concrete of the telephone box, and I wanted to cry out, she cannot be dead, has everything been done, everything? I wanted to take Priscilla in my arms and make her live again. I wanted desperately to console her and to make her happy. It would have been so easy.

'Oh God, oh God, oh God –' Francis was saying softly, repeating it again and again.

'Listen, Francis. Does anyone else know I'm here, does Arnold know?'

'No. No one knows. Arnold and Christian came over last night. They rang up and I had to tell them. But I hadn't found the letter then and I told them I didn't know where you were.'

'That's good. Don't tell anybody where I am.'

'But, Brad, you're coming back at once, aren't you? You must come back.'

'I'm coming back,' I said, 'but not at once. It was only chance you found that letter. You must consider that this telephone conversation didn't happen.'

'But, Brad, the funeral and – I haven't done anything – she's in the mortuary –'

'You haven't told her husband, you know, Roger Saxe?'

'No, I –'

'Well, let him know. You'll find his address and phone number in my address book in the –'

'Yes, yes –'

'He'll organize the funeral. If he won't, organize it yourself – Start organizing it anyway – Do whatever you'd do if you really didn't know where I was – I'll come when I can.'

'Oh Brad, I can't do it – you must come, you must – they keep asking – she's your sister –'

'I hired you to look after her. Why did you leave her?'

'Oh God, oh God, oh God –'

'Do as I tell you. There's nothing we can do for – Priscilla – she isn't – there any more.'

'Brad, please come, please – for my sake – Until I see you I'm in hell – I can't tell you what it's been like – I must see you, I must –'

'I can't come now,' I said. 'I can't – come – now. Get on with the arrangements – get hold of Roger Saxe – I leave it all to you. I'll come when I can. Good-bye.'

I put the receiver down quickly and came out of the box into the full sun. The man who had been waiting looked at me curiously and went in. I walked over to the car and stood beside it, touching the bonnet. The dry road had made it dusty. I made trails in the dust with my fingers. I looked along the quiet pretty village street, composed of eighteenth-century houses of different shapes and sizes. Then I got into the car and turned it and began to drive back very slowly past the church and on towards Patara.

There are moments when, if one rejects the simple and obvious promptings of duty, one finds oneself in a labyrinth of complexities of some quite new kind. Sometimes no doubt one acts rightly in resisting these simple promptings, one acts rightly in bringing into being the terrible refinements which lie beyond. I was not in fact then troubled about duty. Perhaps I assumed that I was acting wrongly, but the assumption attracted little of my attention. Of course I was stricken with guilt and horror at my unforgivable failure to keep my dear sister alive. But as I drove along I was also employed in minute calculations about the immediate future. I was perhaps absurdly influenced by the idea that it was a pure accident, a mere contingent by-product of my carelessness, that Francis had known where to find me. And if that terrible telephone call had been so little determined, so casually caused, it made it seem that much less real, that much easier to obliterate from history. In acting as if it had not happened I was scarcely distorting the real course of events at all. It had, because it so absolutely needn't and shouldn't have occurred, but a very shadowy existence. And if that was so I need not torment myself yet further by agonizing over whether I ought not at once to set off for London. Anyway, there was nothing more I could do for Priscilla.

As I drove along the road at about fifteen miles an hour I realized what an ambiguous and suspended state I had been in since our arrival, so long ago, at Patara. I had of course been prepared to *occupy* myself simply with being happy, simply with the miracle of her continued presence. This was right surely. These days of paradise, rescued from the slow anxious mastication of time, should not be marred by pusillanimous fears of the future, or by that despair which Julian called my 'abstraction'. On the other hand, as I now saw, some deep reflection had been at work, must have been at work, within that seemingly thoughtless joy-of-presence. I had, half hidden from myself, terrible purposes. My problem was simply how to keep Julian forever. And although I had said, to myself and to her, it is impossible, I knew at the same time that having once been with her in *this* way I could not now surrender her. The problem of keeping her had once, inconceivably long ago, seemed like the problem of persuading myself that it would, in spite of everything clearly to be said against this, be right to accept her generosity and take every possible advantage of it. But by now the problem had become, within the quiet self-concealed flow of my relentlessly purposive ratiocination, something much more blackly primitive, something which was scarcely problem or scarcely thought any more, but more like a sort of growth in my mind.

It may seem ridiculous or monstrous that after that telephone call I was obsessed not less but even more with the necessity of making love properly to Julian. That failure, of which she made so little, had come to seem to me a symbol of the whole dilemma. It was at any rate *the* next obstacle. After *that* I could think, after

326

that I would see my way. Until *then* I could wait and not be accused. And I had perhaps begun quietly to feel that if I could only get *that* right I should emerge at last into the bright light of certainty; and then it seemed to my dark purposing mind that I was now only an inch away from being able to say to myself with a radiantly clear intent: why should I not marry this girl? Miraculously we love each other. There is nothing, but nothing, except a difference in our ages to prevent us from marrying. And if we simply erase this difficulty then it will no longer exist. How can such loves as ours be wasted? It cannot be. We *can* marry: and as between such loves only marriage will serve. I could, I can, possess Julian forever. But I was not yet at this point and my puritanical conscience was still darkening counsel and I had not even fully realized before the telephone call what the form of my indecision was.

I had of course already decided not to tell Julian about Priscilla's death. If I told her I would have to go back to London at once. And I felt that if we left our refuge now, if we parted now, with our flight unconsummated, the process which would ensure our liberation from doubt and our eternal betrothal might never take place at all. It was something which, for both of us, I had to do, it was my destined ordeal to keep silent in order to bring us both through this darkness. And it must be done now in unbroken continuity with what had happened. The love-making was part of this. I could not and would not chill Julian's young blood now with this tale of suicide. Of course I would have to 'discover' it soon, we would have to go back soon, but not yet, not without my having reached that point of decision which seemed so close and which would enable me and make me worthy to keep her forever. There was nothing more I could do for Priscilla. My duty henceforth was to Julian. The sheer pain of the concealment was itself part of the ordeal. I wanted to tell Julian at once. I needed her consolation and her precious forgiveness. But for both our sakes I had for the moment to do without this.

'What ages you've been. I say, look at me and guess who!'

I came in through the porch and blinked in the comparative

obscurity of the sitting-room. At first I could not see Julian at all, could only hear her voice coming to me out of darkness. Then I saw her face, the rest obscure. Then I saw what she had done.

She was dressed in black tights, black shoes, she wore a black velvet jerkin and a white shirt and a gold chain with a cross about her neck. She had posed herself in the doorway of the kitchen, holding the sheep's skull up in one hand.

'I thought I'd surprise you! I bought them in Oxford Street with your money, the cross is a sort of hippy cross, I got it from one of those men, it cost fifty pence. All I needed was a skull, and then we found this lovely one. Don't you think it suits me? Alas, poor Yorick – What's the matter, darling?'

'Nothing,' I said.

'You're staring so. Don't I look princely? Bradley, you're frightening me. What is it?'

'Nothing.'

'I'll take them off now. We'll have lunch. I got the watercress.'

'We won't have lunch,' I said. 'We're going to bed.'

'You mean now?'

'Yes.'

I strode to her and took her wrist and pulled her into the bedroom and tumbled her on the bed. The sheep's skull fell to the floor. I put one knee on the bed and began to drag at her white shirt. 'Wait, wait, you're tearing it!' She began hastily undoing the buttons and fumbling with the jerkin. I pulled the whole bundle up and over her head, but the chain and cross impeded them. 'Wait, Bradley, please, the chain's got round my throat, please.' I dug in the snowy whiteness of the shirt and the silky tangle of her hair for the chain and found it and snapped it. The clothes came away Julian was desperately undoing her brassière. I began hauling down the black tights, dragging them over her thighs as she arched her body to help me. For a moment, still fully dressed, I surveyed her naked. Then I began to tear my clothes off.

'Oh Bradley, please, don't be so rough, please, Bradley, you're hurting me.'

Later on, she was crying. There had been no doubt about this love-making. I lay exhausted and let her cry. Then I turned her

328

round and let her tears mingle with the sweat which had darkened the thick grey hairs of my chest and made them cling to my hot flesh in flattened curls. I held her in a kind of horrified trance of triumph and felt between my hands the adorable racked sobbing of her body.

'Stop crying.'

'I can't.'

'I'm sorry I broke the chain. I'll mend it.'

'It doesn't matter.'

'I've frightened you.'

'Yes.'

'I love you. We'll be married.'

'Yes.'

'We will, won't we, Julian?'

'Yes.'

'Do you forgive me?'

'Yes.'

'Please stop crying.'

'I can't.'

Later on still we made love again. Then somehow it was the evening.

'What made you like that, Bradley?'

'The Prince of Denmark, I suppose.'

We were exhausted and very hungry and I needed alcohol. We ate our lunch of liver sausage and bread and cheese and watercress without ceremony by lamplight with the windows open to the blue salty night, I drank up all the rest of the wine.

What had made me like that? Had I suddenly felt that Julian had killed Priscilla? No. The fury, the anger, was directed to myself through Julian. Or directed against fate through Julian and through myself. Yet of course this fury was love too, the power itself of the god, mad and alarming. 'It was love,' I said to her.

'Yes, yes.'

I had removed, at any rate, my next obstacle, though the world beyond it looked different again, not what I had expected. I had prefigured the proximity of some simplifying intellectual certainty.

What there was now was my relationship to Julian, stretching away still into the obscurity of the future, urgent and puzzling and historically dynamic, changing it seemed even from second to second. The girl looked different, I looked different. Was that the body which I had worshipped every part of? It was as if the terrible abstraction had been carried by the rush of divine power right into the centre of our passion. I found myself, at moments, trembling, and saw Julian trembling. And the touching thing was that we were comforting each other, like people who had just escaped from a fire.

'I will mend your chain, I will.'

'There's no need to mend it, I can just knot it.'

'And I'll mend the sheep's skull too.'

'It's in too many pieces.'

'I'll mend it.'

'Let's draw the curtains. I feel bad spirits are looking in at us.'

'We are surrounded by spirits. Curtains won't keep them out.' But I pulled the curtains and came round behind her chair, touching her neck very lightly with my finger. Her flesh was cool, almost cold, and she shuddered, arching her neck. She made no other response, but I felt that our bodies were rapt in a communion with each other which passed our understanding. Meanwhile it was a time for quiet communication by words, for speech of a new sort, arcane prophetic speech.

'I know,' she said. 'Swarms of them. I've never felt like this before. Listen to the sea. It sounds so close. Though there's no wind.'

We listened.

'Bradley, would you go and lock the front door?'

I went and locked it and then sat down again facing her. 'Are you cold?'

'No, it's not – coldness.'

'I know.'

She was wearing the blue dress with the white willow-spray pattern which she had been wearing when she fled and a light woollen rug off our bed around her shoulders. She was staring at me with big eyes and every now and then a spasm passed across her face. There had been a lot of tears but none now. She looked so much, and beautifully, older, not the child I had known at all, but some wonderful holy woman, a prophetess, a temple prostitute. She had combed her hair down smoothly and pressed it back and her face had the nakedness, the solitude, the ambiguous staring eloquence of a mask. She had the dazed empty look of a great statue.

'Oh you wonderful, wonderful thing.'

'I feel so odd,' she said, 'quite impersonal, I've never felt like this before at all.'

'It is the power of love.'

'Does love do that? I thought yesterday, the day before yesterday, that I loved you. It wasn't like this.'

'It is the god, the black Eros. Don't be afraid.'

'Oh I'm not – afraid – I just feel shattered and empty. I'm in a place where I've never been before.'

'I'm there too.'

'Yes. It's funny. When we were just tender and quiet together, you know, I felt you were there, more there than anybody ever. Now I feel as if I were alone – and yet I'm not – I'm – I'm you – I'm both of us.'

'Yes. Yes.'

'You even resemble me. I feel I'm looking into a mirror.'

I had the strange feeling that I was speaking these words. I was speaking through her, through the pure echoing emptiness of her being, hollowed by love.

'Then I looked into your eyes and thought: Bradley! Now you have no name.'

'We are possessed.'

'I feel we are joined forever. Sort of – dedicated.'

'Yes.'

'Listen to that train, how clear it sounds.'

We listened to it passing, far off.

'Is it like this in inspiration, I mean when you write?'

'Yes,' I said. I knew it was, though I had never yet experienced it, never yet. But now, empowered, I would be able to create. Though still in the dark, I had come through my ordeal.

'It it the same thing really?'

'Yes,' I said. 'The desire of the human heart for love and for knowledge is infinite. But most people only realize this when they are in love, when the conception of this desire being actually fulfilled is present to them.'

'And art too –'

'Is this desire – purified – in the presence of – it's possibility – in the divine presence.'

'Art and love –'

'Must both envisage eternal arrangements.'

'You will write now, won't you?'

'I will write now.'

'I feel complete,' she said, 'as if why we had to come together had been somehow explained. And yet the explanation doesn't matter. We are together. Oh Bradley, I'm *yawning*!'

'And my name's come back!' I said. 'Come on. To bed and to sleep.'

'I don't think I've ever felt so beautifully tired and *heavy* in my life.'

I led her to bed and she fell asleep in her petticoat as on the first night. I felt wide awake and alert. And as I held her in my arms I knew that I had been right not to go back to London. I had had to stay, for the ordeal. I held her and felt the simple warmth of ordinary domestic tenderness flowing back into my body. I thought about poor Priscilla and how I would share all that pain with Julian on the morrow. On the morrow I would tell her everything, everything, and we would go back to London and face plain tasks and duties and begin the ordinariness of being together.

I was deeply asleep. Some sound was crashing, crashing, crashing into the place where I was. I was a hidden Jew whom the Nazis had found at last. I heard them, like the soldiers in Uccello's picture, beating their halberds on the door and shouting. I stirred, found Julian still in my arms. It was dark.

'What is it?' Her frightened voice woke me into full consciousness and absolute dread.

Someone was banging and banging and banging on the front door.

'Oh who can it be?' She was sitting up. I felt her warm darkness beside me, seemed to see light reflected from her eyes.

'I don't know,' I said, sitting up too and putting my arms round her. We clung together.

'Better keep quiet and not put the light on. Oh Bradley, I'm so frightened.'

'I'll look after you.' I was so frightened myself I could hardly think or speak.

'Sssh. Perhaps they'll go away.'

The banging, which had stopped for a moment, was resumed louder than before. Some metal object was being pounded on the panels of the door. There was a sound of splintering wood.

I turned on a lamp and got up. As I did so I actually saw my bare legs trembling. I pulled on my dressing-gown. 'Stay here. I'll see. Lock yourself in.'

'No, no, I'm coming too –'

'Stay here.'

'Don't open the door, Bradley, don't –'

I put the light on in the little hall. The banging stopped at once. I stood in silence before the door, now knowing who was on the other side of it.

I opened the door very quietly and Arnold came, or rather almost fell, in through it.

I turned on the lights in the sitting-room and he followed me in there and put down on the table the large spanner with which he had been beating on the door. He sat down, not looking at me, breathing hard.

I sat down too, covering my bare knees which were shuddering convulsively.

'Is – Julian – here?' said Arnold, speaking thickly, as if in drunkenness, only he was certainly not drunk.

'Yes.'

'I've come to – take her away –'

'She won't want to go,' I said. 'How did you find us?'

'Francis told me. I asked him and asked him and asked him, and he told me. And about the telephone call.'

'What telephone call?'

333

'Don't pretend,' said Arnold, looking at me now. 'He told me he telephoned you this morning about Priscilla.'

'I see.'

'So you couldn't – drag yourself away – from your love nest – even though your sister – had killed herself.'

'I am going to London tomorrow. Julian is coming with me. We are going to be married.'

'I want to see my daughter. The car is outside. I am going to take her back with me.'

'No.'

'Will you call her, please?'

I got up. As I passed by the table I picked up the spanner. I went to the bedroom. The door was closed, not locked, and I went in and locked the door after me.

Julian was dressed. She was wearing one of my jackets over her dress. It reached down to her thighs. She was very pale.

'Your pa.'

'Yes. What's that?'

I threw the spanner down on the bed. 'A lethal weapon. Not for use. Better come and see him.'

'You will –'

'I'll protect you. There's nothing whatever to worry about. We'll just explain the situation to him and see him off. Come. No, wait a minute. I need some trousers.' I rapidly put on a shirt and trousers. I saw with surprise that it was only just after midnight.

I went back to the sitting-room and Julian followed. Arnold had got up. We faced him across the table, which was still strewn with the remnants of our supper which we had been too worn out to clear away. I put my arm round Julian's shoulder.

Arnold had got a grip on himself and had clearly resolved not to shout. He said, 'My dear girl –'

'Hello.'

'I've come to take you home.'

'This is home,' said Julian. I squeezed her, and then moved to sit down, leaving them facing each other.

Arnold in a light macintosh, with his exhausted denuded emotional face, looked like some sort of fanatical gunman. His pale, pale eyes stared and his lips were moving as if he were soundlessly stammering. 'Oh Julian - come away - You can't stay here with this man - You must have lost your mind - Look, here's a letter from your mother begging you to come home - I'll put it here, please read it - How can you be so pitiless and callous, staying here and - I suppose you've been - after poor Priscilla -'

'What about Priscilla?' said Julian.

'So he hasn't told you?' said Arnold. He did not look at me. His teeth clicked together and there was a spasm in his face, perhaps the attempt to conceal a glare of triumph or pleasure.

'What about Priscilla?'

'Priscilla is dead,' I said. 'She killed herself yesterday with an overdose.'

'He knew this morning,' said Arnold. 'Francis told him by telephone.'

'That's correct,' I said. 'When I told you I was going to the garage I went to telephone Francis and he told me.'

'And you didn't tell me? You hid it - and then we - all the afternoon we were -'

'Ach -' said Arnold.

Julian ignored him, staring at me and drawing my jacket closer about her, its collar turned up enclosing her tousled hair, her hands crossed at the neck. 'Why?'

I rose. 'It's hard to explain,' I said, 'but please try to understand. There was nothing more I could do for Priscilla. And for you - I had to stay - and bear the burden of being silent. It wasn't callousness.'

'Lust might be its name,' said Arnold.

'Oh Bradley - Priscilla is dead -'

'Yes,' I said, 'but there's nothing more I can do about it now, and -'

Tears overflowed Julian's eyes and dropped down on to the lapels of my jacket. 'Oh Bradley - how could you - how could we - oh poor, poor Priscilla - what a terrible thing -'

'He is irresponsible,' said Arnold. 'Or else he's a bit mad. He's totally callous. His sister dies and he won't leave his lovemaking.'

'Oh Bradley – poor Priscilla –'

'Julian, I was going to tell you tomorrow. I was going to tell you everything tomorrow. I had to stay today. You saw how it was. We were both possessed, we were held here, we couldn't have gone, it had to happen as it did.'

'He's mad.'

'Tomorrow we'll go back to ordinary things, tomorrow we'll think about Priscilla and I'll tell you all about it and how much I am to blame –'

'It was my fault,' said Julian, 'it was because of me. Otherwise you would have been with her.'

'One can't stop people from killing themselves if they're determined to. It may even be wrong to do so. Her life had become very sad.'

'A convenient justification,' said Arnold. 'So you think Priscilla is better off dead, do you?'

'No. I'm just saying it – at least could be thought about like that – I don't want Julian to feel that – Oh Julian, I ought to have told you.'

'Yes – It's – I feel a sort of doom on us – Oh Bradley, why didn't you say –?'

'Sometimes one has to be silent even if it hurts awfully. I wanted your consolation, of course I did. But something else was more important.'

'The sexual gratification of an elderly man,' said Arnold. '*Think*, Julian, *think*. He is thirty-eight years older than you are.'

'No, he isn't,' said Julian. 'He's forty-six, and that's –'

Arnold gave a sort of laugh and there was the same spasm in his face. 'He told you that, did he? He's fifty-eight. Ask him.'

'He can't be –'

'Look him up in *Who's Who*.'

'I'm not in *Who's Who*.'

'Bradley, how old are you?'

'Fifty-eight.'

'When you are thirty he will be nearly seventy,' said Arnold. 'Come on. Surely this is enough. We've kept this quiet and there's no need for shouting. I see Bradley even removed the blunt instrument. Let's go, Julian. You can have your cry in the car. Then you'll start feeling what an escape you've had. Come. He won't try to stop you now. Look at him.'

Julian was looking at me. I covered my face.

'Bradley, take your hands away. Please. Are you really *fifty-eight*?'

'Yes.'

'Can't you see he is? Can't you *see* he is?'

She murmured, 'Yes – now –'

'Does it matter?' I said. 'You said you didn't mind what age I was.'

'Oh don't be pathetic,' said Arnold. 'Let's all keep our dignity. Come, Julian, please. Bradley, don't think I'm being unkind. I'm doing what any father would do.'

'Quite,' I said, 'quite.'

Julian said, 'I can't bear it, about Priscilla, I can't bear it, I can't bear it –'

'Steady,' said Arnold. 'Steady. Come now.'

I said, 'Julian, don't go. You can't just *go* like that. I want to explain things to you properly and alone. All right, if you now feel differently about me, that's that. I'll drive you anywhere you want and we'll say good-bye. But I beg you not to leave me now. I ask you in the name of – in the name of –'

'I forbid you to stay,' said Arnold. 'I regard this relationship as a defilement. I'm sorry to use such strong language. I have been very upset and very angry and I am trying hard to be reasonable and to be kind. Do just see this thing objectively. I cannot and I will not go away without you.'

'I want to explain to you,' I said. 'I want to explain about Priscilla.'

'How can you –?' she said. 'Oh dear – oh dear –' She was crying now helplessly, with trembling wet lips.

I felt agony, physical pain, total terror. 'Don't leave me, my darling, I should die.' I went to her and reached out towards her, touching the sleeve of my jacket timidly.

Arnold promptly moved round the table and took her other arm and propelled her out into the hall. I followed. I saw through the open bedroom door the heavy spanner lying on the white sheets of the bed, and with a dart I picked it up. I stood barring the front door.

'Julian, I can't let you go now, I'd go mad, please don't go – you must stay with me long enough to let me defend myself –'

'You are indefensible,' said Arnold. 'Why *argue*? Can't you see it's *over*? You have had a caper with a silly girl and now it's *over*. The spell is broken. And give me that spanner. I don't like to see you holding it.'

I gave him the spanner, but I did not move from the door. I said, 'Julian, decide.'

Julian, making an effort with her tears, pulled herself quickly but firmly away from her father's grip. 'I'm not going with you. I'm going to stay here with Bradley.'

'Oh thank God,' I said, 'thank God.'

'I want to hear what Bradley has to say. I'll come back to London tomorrow. But I'm not going to leave Bradley alone in the middle of the night.'

'Thank God.'

'You're coming with me,' said Arnold.

'No, she isn't. She's said what she wants to do. Now please go away. Arnold, *think*. Do you want us to fight about this? Do you want to crack my head with that spanner? I promise I'll bring Julian to London tomorrow. Nobody shall force her, nobody can force her, she'll do what she wants to do, I'm not trying to kidnap her.'

'Please go,' she said. 'I'm sorry. You've been kind and – quiet, but I must just stay here tonight. I promise I'll come to you and listen to everything you want to say. But please be merciful and leave me now to talk to him. We've got to talk, do understand. You can't really do or undo anything here.'

'She's right,' I said.

Arnold did not look at me. He looked at his daughter with a very concentrated desolate stare. He gave a sort of gasping sigh. 'Do you promise to come home tomorrow?'

'I'll come and see you tomorrow.'

'Do you promise to come home?'

'Yes.'

'And don't – any more tonight – oh hell – you can't think or imagine what you've done to me –'

338

I moved from the door and Arnold marched out into the darkness. I turned on the light in the porch. It was like seeing a guest off. Julian and I stood like husband and wife and watched Arnold get into his car. There was a clang as he threw the spanner into the back. The sudden headlights showed the gravel covered with etiolated flowering weeds, the ragged bright green grass, and a line of white fencing posts. Then the lights swung abruptly round, revealed the open gate, and receded down the track. I pulled Julian back inside, shut the door, and fell on my knees at her feet, embracing her legs and pressing my head against the hem of the blue dress.

She suffered this embrace for a moment, then gently freed herself and went into the bedroom and sat down on the bed. I followed and tried to put my arms around her, but she thrust me away with little gentle half-unconscious gestures.

'Oh Julian, we haven't lost each other, have we? I am so deeply sorry I lied about my age, it was stupid. But it doesn't really matter, does it? I mean, we're beyond where it matters, it can't matter. And I couldn't go back to London this morning. I know it was a crime not to. But it was a crime that I committed because I love you.'

'I feel so *confused*,' she said, 'I feel so awfully *confused* –'

'Let me explain how –'

'Please. I can't hear, I just wouldn't be able to *hear* – Everything's been such a shock – like a – destruction – I'd rather – I think I'll just go to the lavatory and then I'll try to go to sleep.' She went away, returned, and took off her dress and put on her dark blue silk night shirt over her underclothes. She seemed already like a sleep-walker.

'Julian, thank you for staying. I worship you with gratitude for having stayed. Julian, you will be kind to me, won't you. You could break my neck with your little finger.'

She began to get heavily into the bed, moving stiffly, like an old person.

'That's right,' I said. 'We'll talk in the morning, won't we. We'll sleep now. If we can just go to sleep in each other's arms we'll be so much helped, won't we.'

She looked at me sombrely, the tears dry on her face.

'May I stay, Julian?'

'Bradley – darling – I'd rather be by myself just now. I feel as if I'd been invaded or – broken – I've got to become complete again and for that – it's better to be alone – just now.'

'All right. I understand, my dear love and my sweetheart. I won't – we'll talk in the morning. Only say you forgive me.'

'Yes, yes.'

'Good night, my darling.'

I kissed her on the brow and then quickly got up and turned the light out and closed the door. Then I went and locked and bolted the front door. Everything seemed possible tonight, even the return of Arnold with the spanner. I sat in an armchair in the sitting-room and wished I had brought some whisky with me. I resolved to stay awake for the rest of the night.

I felt so hurt and frightened that it was very hard to think at all. I felt like simply doubling up over my pain and groaning. What did it *look* like to her, what would it *do* to her, my being so exposed and humiliated by her father? Arnold did not need to beat me to my knees with a blunt instrument. He had quite sufficiently defeated me. What did that failure about Priscilla *mean*? Oh if only I had been given the time to tell her all myself. Would Julian suddenly see me quite differently? Would I look to her like an old man crazed with lust? I must explain that it was not just because I wanted to go to bed that I concealed Priscilla's suicide, that I abandoned Priscilla, that I left her, alive and dead, to others. It was because these things were greater than themselves, because there was a sort of dedication, a sort of visitation, something else to which I had to be absolutely faithful. Would this seem nonsense to her now? Would, and this I am afraid was the most tormenting thought of all, the difference between forty-six and fifty-eight prove to be fatal?

Later on I started thinking about Priscilla and the sheer sadness of it all and the pitifulness of her end. The shocking fact of her death seemed only now to be reaching my heart, and I felt futile ingenuous love for her. I ought to have *thought* about how to console her. It would not have been impossible. I began to feel sleepy and got up and prowled around. I opened the bedroom door and listened to Julian's steady breathing and prayed. I went into the bathroom and looked at my face in the mirror. The godly radiance had withdrawn from my face. My eyes were hooded by wrinkles, my brow was scored, little blood-red worms crawled in the dull sallow skin, I looked gaunt and old. But Julian was sleeping quietly and all my hope slept with her. I returned to my sitting-room armchair and put my head back and instantly fell asleep. I dreamed that Priscilla and I were young again, hiding under the counter in the shop.

I awoke to a grey awful spotty early morning light which made the unfamiliar room present in a ghastly way. The furniture was humped shapelessly about me like sleeping animals. Everything seemed to be covered with soiled dust sheets. The slits in the clumsily drawn curtains revealed a dawn sky, pale and murky, without colour, the sun not yet risen.

I experienced horror, then memory. I began to get up, felt painfully stiff, and smelt some vile odour, probably the odour of myself. I swung myself to the door, heaving a stiff leg, hanging on to the backs of chairs. I listened at the door of the bedroom. Silence. I very cautiously opened the door and put my head round it.

It was hard to see in the room: the granular dawn light, with the texture of a bad newspaper picture, seemed to obscure rather than promote vision. The bed was in some sort of chaos. I thought I could discern Julian. Then I saw that there were only tossed sheets. The bed, the room, was empty.

I called her name softly, ran into the other rooms. I even looked crazily into cupboards. She was not in the house. I went outside on to the porch and ran all round the house and then out on to the level of the stony courtyard, and down to the dunes, calling her name, shouting now, yelling as loudly as I could. I came back and hooted the horn of the car again and again, making a ghastly tocsin in the empty absolutely quiet twilit scene. But nothing answered. There was no doubt about it. She had gone.

I went back into the house, turning on all the lights, a doom-stricken illumination in the gathering day and searched the place once again. On the dressing-table was a pile of five pound notes, the change from the money I had given her to buy clothes, which I had insisted she should keep in her handbag. The handbag, her new one, which she had bought in the 'shopping spree', had gone. All her new clothes were still hanging in the wardrobe. There was no letter, no communication for me, nothing. She had disappeared into the night with her handbag, in her blue willow pattern dress, without a coat, without a word, creeping out of the house while I slept.

I ran out to the car, searching my trouser pockets for the keys, ran back, scrabbled through my jacket. Was it conceivable that Julian had deliberately taken the keys of the car to evade pursuit? Eventually I found the keys lying on the table in the hall. Outside the still sunless sky had become a clear radiant hazy blue, hung with the huge light of the morning star. Of course I could not start the car. Then at last it started and I jerked it away, scraping the gate post and bumping as fast as I could along the track. Now the sun was rising.

I got to the road and doubled back towards the railway station. At the little toy station the platforms were empty. A railway man walking along the tracks told me that no train had stopped there during the night hours. I drove on to the main road and along it in the direction of London. The sun was shining coldly and brightly and a few cars were already about. But the grassy verges of the road were empty. I turned back and drove the other way, through the village, past the church. I even stopped and went into the church. Of course it was hopeless. I drove back and ran into the cottage with a desperate feigned hope that she might have returned while I was away. The little place with its open door and its ransacked air and all its lights on stood obscenely void in the bright sunshine. Then I drove the car to the dunes, running its bonnet into a dewy wall of wispy wiry grass and sand. I ran about among the dunes and down on to the beach, shouting 'Julian! Julian!' The climbing sun shone on to a quiet sea which without even a ripple drew its level line along the gently shelving wall of many-coloured elliptical stones.

'Wait, Brad, better let Roger go first.'

Christian was holding my arm in a firm grip.

With his face stiff and his false soldier's tread Roger marched self-consciously out of his pew and back towards the door of the chapel. The brocaded curtains had closed upon Priscilla's coffin, now bound for the furnace, and the unspeakable service was over.

'What do we do now, go home?'

'No, we should walk around a bit in the garden, I think it's customary, at least it is in the USA. I'll just say a word to those women.'

'Who are they?'

'I don't know. Friends of Priscilla's. I think one of them's her char. Kind of them to come, wasn't it?'

'Yes, very.'

'You must talk to Roger.'

'I have nothing to say to Roger.'

We walked slowly down the aisle. Francis, fluttering by the doorway, stood aside to let the women pass, sent a ghastly smile in our direction, then followed them out.

'Brad, who was that poetry by that the man read?'

'Browning. Tennyson.'

'It was lovely, wasn't it? So suitable. It made me cry.'

Roger had arranged the cremation and had devised a terrible set of poetry readings. There had been no religious service.

We emerged into the garden. A light rain was falling from a brightish brownish sky. The good weather seemed to be over. I shook Christian's hand off my arm and put up my umbrella.

Roger, looking responsible and manly and bereaved in smart black, was thanking the poetry-reader and another crematorium official. The coffin-bearers had already gone. Christian was talking to the three women and they were affecting to admire the dripping azaleas. Francis, beside me, was trying to get in under my um-

343

brella and was repeating a story which he had already told me, with variations, several times. He was whimpering a little as he spoke. He had wept audibly during the service.

'When I went up I didn't intend to stay. I met him in the court in the afternoon and he said why not come up for tea. And Priscilla seemed OK and I said I'm going up, just to the upstairs flat to have tea and she seemed OK and she said she was going to have a bath. And then when I got upstairs we had a drink and God knows what was in it, I think it must have been drugged or something, honest Brad, I think it was drugged. Christ I'm used to alcohol but that stuff just knocked me for six, and then, oh God, he started making passes at me, I swear it wasn't my idea, Brad, and I was sort of laughing and drunk too I suppose and he said would I stay the night and, oh God, I saw how damn late it was, and I said I'd just go down and see how Priscilla was, and I went down and she was asleep, I looked into her room and she was asleep, she seemed quite ordinary and peaceful and so I went back up again and I spent the night up there with him and we did some drinking and – oh God – and I didn't wake up till quite late in the morning, I must have been drugged, it wasn't ordinary drink at all, and Rigby had already gone off to work, it was sort of horrible, I felt an absolute heel, and I went down and Priscilla was still asleep, and I let her sleep, and then a bit later something funny struck me about her breathing and I tried to wake her and then I rang the hospital and it took ages for an ambulance and I went with her, and she was alive in the ambulance and I waited and then they said she must have taken the tablets ages ago on the afternoon before and it was too late, and oh Christ, Brad, I can't live after this, I can't live, I can't live –'

'Oh shut up,' I said. 'It wasn't your fault. It was my fault.'

'Oh Brad, forgive me.'

'Stop whining like a bloody woman. Go away, will you? It wasn't your fault. It had to happen. It was better like that. You can't save someone who wants death. It was better so.'

'You told me to look after her, and I –'

'Go away.'

'Where can I go to, oh where can I go to at all? Brad, don't drive me away, I'll go mad, I've got to be with you, otherwise

I'll go mad with misery, you've got to forgive me, you've got to help me, Brad, you've got to. I'm going back to the flat now and I'll tidy it up and I'll clean it all, I will, oh please let me stay with you now, I can be useful to you, you needn't give me any money –'

'I don't want you in the flat. Just clear off, will you.'

'I'll kill myself, I will.'

'Get on with it, then.'

'You do forgive me, don't you, Brad?'

'Yes, of course. Just leave me alone. Please.' I jerked the umbrella away, turning my shoulder against Francis, and made for the gate.

Flip-flopping rainy steps caught up with me. Christian. 'Brad, you *must* talk to Roger. He says would you wait for him. He has some business to talk with you. Oh Brad, don't run off in that awful way. I'm coming with you, anyway, don't run off. Do come back and talk to Roger, please.'

'He should be content with having killed my sister without bothering me with his business.'

'Well, wait a moment, wait, *wait*, look here he comes.'

I waited under the arty lych-gate while Roger advanced under his umbrella. He even had a black macintosh.

'Bradley. A sad business. I feel much to blame.'

I looked at him, then turned away.

'As Priscilla's heir.'

I paused.

'Priscilla left a will of course in my favour. But naturally I feel that family things, I daresay there are some, photographs and so on, should come to you. And any little keepsake you might care to have, just let me know, or I'll select something for you, shall I? Some little thing she used to keep on her dressing-table or such.'

His umbrella touched mine and I took a pace back. I could see Christian's live eager face just beyond, watching, with the avid curiosity of the unhurt. She had no umbrella and was wearing a dark green raincoat and a smart black macintosh hat with a wide brim, like a small sombrero. Francis had gone back to the azalea ladies.

I said nothing to Roger, just looked at him.

'The will is very simple, there should be no problem. I'll let you see a copy of course. And perhaps you wouldn't mind returning to me any things of Priscilla's which you have, those jewels for instance, they could be sent by registered post. Or better still, perhaps I could call for them this afternoon at the flat, if you're going to be in? Mrs Evandale has very kindly said I may call for the things Priscilla left at her house –'

I turned my back on him and walked away down the street.

He called after me, 'I'm very upset too, very – but what's the use –'

Christian was walking beside me, having got in underneath the umbrella, taking my arm again. We passed a small yellow Austin which was parked at a meter. Inside at the wheel sat Marigold. She bowed to me as we passed, but I ignored her.

'Who's that?' said Christian.

'Roger's mistress.'

A little later the Austin passed us by. Marigold was driving with one arm thrown round Roger's back. Roger's head lay on her shoulder. No doubt he really was very upset, very.

'Brad, don't walk so fast. Don't you want me to help you? Don't you want me to find out where Julian is?'

'No.'

'But do you know where she is?'

'No. Could you take your hand off my arm, please?'

'All right – but you *must* let me help you, you can't just go off by yourself after all these horrors. Please come and stay at Notting Hill. I'll look after you, I'd love to. Will you come?'

'No, thank you.'

'But, Brad, what are you going to *do* about Julian? You must do something. If I knew where she was I'd tell you, honest I would. Shall I get Francis to look for her? It would do him good to do something for you after this business. Shall I tell him to search?'

'No.'

'But where *is* she, Brad, where can she be, where do you think she is? You don't think she's killed herself, do you?'

'No, of course not,' I said. 'She's with Arnold.'

'Could be. I haven't seen Arnold since –'

346

'He came and took her away in the night against her will. He's got her cooped up somewhere, lecturing her. She'll soon give him the slip and come back to me, like she did before. That's all there is to it.'

'We – ell –' Christian peered up at me, peeking from under her black sombrero. 'How do you feel, Brad, generally in yourself? You know, you need looking after, you need –'

'Just leave me alone, will you. And keep Francis at Notting Hill. I don't want to see him. And now if you'll excuse me I'll take this taxi. Good-bye.'

It was perfectly simple of course, what had happened. I saw it all now. Arnold must have come back while I was asleep and either cajoled or forced Julian to get into the car with him. Perhaps he had asked her to sit in the car to talk to him. Then he had driven off quickly. She must have wanted to hurl herself from that car. But she had promised me not to. Besides, she wanted no doubt to convince her father. Now they were somewhere together, arguing, fighting. Perhaps he had locked her into a room somewhere. But she would soon escape and come back to me. I knew that she could not simply have left me like that without a word.

I had been to Ealing of course. When I had driven back to London I went to my flat first in case there was a message, then on to Ealing. I parked the car opposite the house and went and rang the bell. No one came. I went and sat in the car and watched the house. Then after about an hour I started walking up and down on the opposite pavement. I could now see Rachel who was watching me from the upstairs landing window. After a bit more of this she opened the window and shouted 'She isn't here!' and closed the window again. I drove away and returned the car to the car hire firm and went back to my flat. I decided now to remain on duty at the flat since that was where Julian would come to when she escaped. I had only emerged to attend Priscilla's funeral.

When I got back there now I lay down on my bed. Francis let himself in with a key. He tried to talk to me, said he was making me lunch, but I ignored him. Later Roger called and I told Francis to give him the few things of Priscilla's which were still with me. Roger went away. I did not see him. Towards evening Francis tiptoed in and put the bronze buffalo lady on the chimney piece in my bedroom beside *A Friend's Gift.* I started to cry. I told Francis to leave the house, but an hour afterwards I could still hear him doing something in the kitchen.

The world is perhaps ultimately to be defined as a place of suffering. Man is a suffering animal, subject to ceaseless anxiety and pain and fear, subject to the rule of what the Buddhists call *dukha,* the endless unsatisfied anguish of a being who passionately desires only illusory goods. However within this vale of misery there are many regions. We all suffer, but we suffer so appallingly differently. An enlightened one may, who knows, pity the fretful millionaire with as pure an energy as he pities the starving peasant. Possibly the lot of the millionaire is more genuinely pitiable, since he is deluded by the solace of false and fleeting pleasures, while there may be a compulsory wisdom contained in the destitution of the peasant. Such judgements however are reserved for the enlightened, and ordinary mortals who feigned to utter them would rightly be called frivolous. *We* properly think it a worse fate to starve in poverty than to yawn in the midst of luxury. If the suffering of the world were, as it could be imagined to be, less extreme, if boredom and simple worldly disappointments were our gravest trials, and if, which is harder to conceive, we grieved little at any bereavement and went to death as to sleep, our whole morality might be immensely, perhaps totally different. That this world is a place of *horror* must affect every serious artist and thinker, darkening his reflection, ruining his system, sometimes actually driving him mad. Any seriousness avoids this fact at its peril, and the great ones who have seemed to neglect it have only done so in appearance. (This is a tautology.) This is the planet where cancer reigns, where people regularly and automatically and almost without comment die like flies from floods and famine and disease, where people

348

fight each other with hideous weapons to whose effects even nightmares cannot do justice, where men terrify and torture each other and spend whole lifetimes telling lies out of fear. This is where we live.

Does this background forbid *refinement* in morals? How often, my dear friend, have we not talked of this. And shall the artist have no cakes and ale? Must he who makes happy be a liar, and can the spirit that sees the truth also speak it? What is, what can be, the range of the sufficiently serious heart? Must we be always drying these tears, or at least aware of them, or stand condemned? I have no answer to give here to these questions. Perhaps there is a very lengthy answer or perhaps none at all. The question itself will remain, as long as our planet remains (which may not in fact be long) to bedevil our wise men, indeed quite literally sometimes to make demons of them. Must not the response to such a problem be demonic? How God must laugh. (Himself a demon.)

This preludes, dear friend, my apologia, offered to you not for the first time, concerning this love story. The pains of *love*? Pooh! And yet: the ecstasy of love, the glory of love. Plato lay with a beautiful boy and thought it no shame to see here the beginning of the path to the sun. Happy love undoes the self and makes the world visible. Unhappy love is, or can be, a revelation of pure suffering. Too often of course our reverses are clouded and embittered by jealousy, remorse, hatred, the mean and servile 'if onlys' of a peevish spirit. But there can be intuitions even here of a more sublime agony. And who can say that this is not in some way a fellow feeling with those quite otherwise afflicted? Zeus, they say, mocks lovers' oaths, and we may covertly smile even while we sympathize with the love-lorn, especially if they are young. We believe they will recover. Perhaps they will, whatever recovery may be. But there are times of suffering which remain in our lives like black absolutes and are not blotted out. Fortunate are those for whom these black stars shed some sort of light.

Of course I felt remorse. Love cannot really tolerate death. Experience of death destroys sexual desire. Love must *disguise* death or else perish at its hands. We cannot really love the dead. We love a fantasm that secretly consoles. What love sometimes mistakes for death is a kind of intense suffering, a pain that can be endured and absorbed. But the idea of a real ending, that cannot be envisaged. (The false god punishes, the true god slays.) Indeed, in the language of love the concept of an ending is devoid of sense. (So we must go beyond love or utterly change it.) Of course Priscilla's death was, in relation to my love for Julian, a dreadful and completely fortuitous accident. It was indeed my sense of its utter irrelevance, its almost – not – having – happened-ness, which made me able to commit the sin of concealment and delay which so much shocked my beloved. And this evasion was a *mistake* which resulted in as it were crystallizing the death of my sister into something very much harder for that alien love to assimilate. I saw all this very clearly afterwards. I ought to have trusted the future, I ought to have set everything directly at risk, I ought to have run to Julian and taken her with me back to London straight into the middle of that graceless and irrelevant horror.

I thought this afterwards, lying upon my bed, while Francis padded softly around the house inventing tasks for himself. I lay on my bed with the curtains half pulled and gazed at the chimney piece and at the buffalo lady and at *A Friend's Gift*. I also felt a violent rage against Arnold, which was a kind of jealousy, a vile emotion. At least he was her father and had an indestructible connection with her. I had nothing. Did I really believe, I was asked later, that on that awful night Arnold had really come back and taken Julian away? I cannot answer this clearly. My state of mind, which I shall in a moment attempt to describe, is not easily conveyed. I felt that if I could not build a pattern of at least plausible beliefs to make some just bearable sense out of what had happened I should die. Though I suppose what I was conceiving was not true death, but a torture to which death would be preferable. How could I live with the idea that she had simply left me in the night without a word? It could not be. I knew there was an explanation. Did I desire her during this time? The question is frivolous.

I tried, out of a sort of last-resort self-preserving wisdom, to suffer purely. O you my fellow sufferers, you who mourn in waning hope and in ingenious fantastic yearning the loss of the beloved, let me give you at least this advice: suffer purely. Banish remorse, banish resentment and the screaming contortions of degrading jealousy. Give yourself over to immaculate pain. So, at best you will rejoin your joy with a far purer love. And at worst – you will know the secrets of the god. At best, you will be privileged to forget. At worst, you will be privileged to know. Hope is of course the prime tormentor, and I made a pact with hope. I did hope, but I hid my hope inside a black cloud. Some part of my being *knew* that Julian loved me, was part of me, and could not be taken from me. Another part of my being remembered and waited and moaned. I allowed no commerce between them, no speculation, no discussion, no reduction of one to the other. I passed my time, so far as I could, in a pure burning pain. Can one get beyond that image of pain? Hell is depicted as fire. And men who ran the gauntlet in Imperial Russia could do no better when an inquisitive writer, their fellow prisoner, questioned them about their sufferings.

In waiting time devours itself. Great hollows open up inside each minute, each second. Each moment is one at which the longed-for thing *could* happen. Yet at the same instant the terrified mind has flown ahead through centuries of unlightened despair. I tried to grasp and to arrest these giddy convulsions of the spirit, lying on my back on my bed and watching the window glow from dark to light and fade again from light to dark. Odd that a demonic suffering should lie supine, while a glorified suffering lies prone.

I shall now advance the narrative by quoting several letters.

I know that you will communicate with me as soon as you are able to. I will not leave the flat for a single moment. I am a corpse awaiting its Saviour. Accident and its own force induced the revelation of a passion which duty might have concealed. Once revealed, your miraculous self-

351

giving increased it a thousand fold. I am yours for ever. And I know that you love me and I absolutely trust your love. We cannot be defeated. You will come to me soon, my darling and my queen. Meanwhile, oh my dear, I am in so much pain.

P.

Dear Christian,

Have you now any idea where Julian is? Has Arnold taken her away somewhere? He must be keeping her hidden by force. If you can discover anything at all, however vague, let me know for God's sake.

B.

Please reply *at once* by telephone or letter. I do not want to see you.

Dear Arnold,

I am not surprised that you are afraid to face me again. I do not know how you persuaded or forced Julian to go away with you, but do not believe that any arguments of yours can keep us apart. Julian and I have talked with full knowledge and understand each other. After your first departure all was well between us. Your 'revelations' made and can make no difference. You are dealing with a kind of mutual attachment which, since you make no mention of it in your books, I assume that you know nothing of. Julian and I recognize the same god. We have found each other, we love each other, and there is no impediment to our marriage. Do not imagine that you can constitute one. You have seen that Julian was unwilling even to listen to you. Please now recognize that your daughter is grown up and has made her choice. Accept, as indeed you finally must, her free decision in my favour. Naturally she cares what you think. Naturally too she will not finally obey you. I expect her return hourly. By the time you get this she may even be with me.

Your objection to me as a suitor has of course deep motives. The matter of my age, though important, is certainly not crucial. You have even admitted to me that as a writer you are a disappointed man. And some part of you has always envied me because I have kept my gift pure and you have not. Continual mediocre creation can sour a whole life. The compromise with the second best, which is the lot of almost every man, is by the bad artist externalized into a persisting testimony. How much better the silence and guarded speech of a more strict endeavour. That I should also have gained your daughter's love must seem, I can well understand, like the last straw.

I am sorry that our friendship, or whatever name one may give to the obsessive relationship which has bound us together for so many years,

352

should end in this way. This is not the place to utter its elegy. If I feel vindictive towards you now, it is simply because you are an obstacle in the way of something infinitely more important than any 'friendship'. Doubtless it is wise of you to keep out of my way. And if you visit me again, do not bring a blunt instrument with you. I do not care for threats and hints of violence. I have, I assure you, quite enough violence inside myself ready to be provoked.

Julian and I will settle our future together privately and in our own way. *We* understand each other perfectly. Please accept this fact and cease your cruel and vain attempts to force your daughter to do what she does not want to do.

B.P.

Dearest Old Brad,

Thank you for your letter. I don't know where Julian is (honest!), I believe she is staying with friends. I saw Arnold and he was laughing about the whole matter! I'm afraid I can't quite understand now why you got so excited. (I confess it rather amused me at first!) Of course she is an attractive girl, but doesn't she regard you as some sort of uncle or sugar daddy? I can't make head or tail of it all. Arnold says you took her on a seaside holiday and then when you got a bit too intense she legged it. Anyway, that's his story. I think, all's well that ends well, honi soit qui mal y pense, no smoke therefore no fire, and so on. I expect you will have calmed down somewhat by now. Do please see me. I *know* you were in last time I called, I could see you through the glass of the hall door. (You ought to be told how transparent that glass is, especially if the sitting-room door is open!) I assume you have still got Francis (I don't want him of course) who is crazy about you. No wonder you imagine everyone is! See Below.

Brad (this is the most important part of this letter) I want to say this to you. I wish in a way I hadn't met Arnold so pat on coming back. I like him and I feel sort of curious about him and he amuses me. (And I like to be amused.) But he's a red herring, I guess. I came back for you. (Did you know that?) And I'm still here for you. I go for you in a deep way, I never really gave you up, you know. And in a deep way you're even far more amusing than Arnold. So why not let's get together? If you need consoling, I'll console you. As I told you before, I'm a damned attractive clever rich widow. A lot of people are after me. So what about it Brad? That little old till-death-do-us-part bit did mean something, you know. I'll ring again tomorrow.

Caring for you, Brad old thing, with much love

Chris.

The passage above about 'waiting' may have suggested that weeks had now passed. In fact four days, which seemed like four years, had passed.

Men who live by words and writing can, as I have already observed, attach an almost magical efficacy to a communication in that medium. The letter to Julian I wrote out three times, sending one copy to Ealing, one to her Training College, and one to her school. I could scarcely believe that any would reach her, but it was a relief to pain to write the letters and to drop them in the box.

On the day after the funeral Hartbourne rang up to explain in detail why he had been unable to attend. I forgot to say that he had earlier *dictated* to Francis by telephone a carefully worded message of condolence about Priscilla's death! My doctor also rang to say that my usual brand of sleeping pill was now on the forbidden list.

On the third evening Rachel turned up. Of course whenever the door bell rang I rushed out sick with hope and terror. Twice it was Christian (whom I did not let in), once Rigby asking for Francis. (Francis went out and they talked for some time in the court.) The fourth time it was Rachel. I saw her through the glass and opened the door.

Seeing Rachel there in the flat was like a bad trip in a time machine. There was a memory-odour like a smell of decay. I felt distressed, physically repelled, frightened. Her wide round pale face was terribly familiar, but with the ambiguous veiled familiarity of a dream. It was as if my mother had visited me in her cerements.

She came in tossing her head with a surge of excitement, a perhaps feigned air of confidence, almost of elation. She strode by me, not looking at me, her hands deep in the pockets of her tweed coat which had been cobwebbed-over by the light rain. She was purposeful and handsome and I flinched out of her way. She took off her woollen hat and her coat and shook them lightly and hung them up in the hall. We sat down in the sitting-room in the cold brown early evening light.

"Where's Julian?'

Rachel smoothed her skirt down neatly about her knees. 'Bradley, I wanted to tell you how sorry I was about Priscilla.'

'Where's Julian?'

'Don't you know?'

'I know she'll come back. I don't know where she is.'

'Poor old Bradley,' said Rachel. She gave a nervous ejaculatory laugh like a cough.

'Where is she?'

'She's on holiday. I don't know where she is just now, I really don't. Here's the letter you sent her. I haven't read it.'

I took the letter. The return of a passionate letter unread desolates far regions of the imagination. If somewhere she had read my words the world was changed. Now all blew back upon me like dead leaves.

'Oh Rachel, where is she?'

'Honestly I don't know, I'm not in touch. Bradley, do stop it. Think of your dignity or something. You look terrible, you look a hundred. You might shave at least. This thing is all in your mind.'

'You didn't think so when Julian said she loved me.'

'Julian is a child. This latest business had far more to do with me and Arnold than it had to do with you. You ought to know a bit about human nature, you're supposed to be a writer. Of course it was "serious" in its way, but what people do doesn't mean just one thing. Julian adores us, only she likes to stage little revolts from time to time. I daresay we are rather overwhelming as parents, and she is an only child. So she pushes us with one hand and pulls us with the other. She wants to assure herself that she's free, at the same time she wants our attention, she wants the relationship of being scolded. This isn't the first time she's used somebody else to upset us with. A year ago she thought she was madly in love with one of her teachers, well he wasn't as old as you, but he was married with four children, and she made it into a sort of little "demo" against us. We knew how to take it. It ended happily. You're just the next victim.'

'Rachel,' I said, 'you are talking about someone else. You are not talking about Julian, about my Julian.'

'Your Julian is a fiction. This is what I'm telling you, dear Bradley. I'm not saying she didn't care for you, but a young girl's emotions are chaos.'

'And you are talking *to* another person. You obviously have no conception of what you're dealing with. I live in a different world, I am in love, and –'

'Do you think there is some magic in those words which you utter so solemnly?'

'Yes, I do. All this is happening on a different plane –'

'This is a form of insanity, Bradley. Only the insane think that there are planes which are quite separate from other planes. It's all a muddle, Bradley, it's *all* a muddle. God knows, I'm saying this to you in kindness.'

'Love is a sort of certainty, perhaps the only sort.'

'It's just a state of mind –'

'It's a true state of mind.'

'Oh Bradley, do stop. You've had a terrible time lately, no wonder your head's in a whirl. I am so awfully sorry about Priscilla.'

'Priscilla. Yes.'

'You mustn't blame yourself too much.'

'No –'

'Where did Francis find her? Where was she lying when he found her?'

'I don't know.'

'You mean you didn't ask?'

'No. I suppose she was in bed.'

'I would have wanted to know – all the details – I think – just to picture it – Did you see her dead?'

'No.'

'Didn't you have to identify her?'

'No.'

'Someone must have done.'

'Roger did.'

'Odd about identifying dead people, recognizing them. I hope I don't ever have to –'

'He's keeping her prisoner somewhere, I know he is.'

'Really, Bradley, you seem to be living in some sort of literary dream. Everything is so much duller and more mixed-up than you imagine, even the awful things are.'

'He locked her in her room before.'

'Of course he didn't. The girl was romancing.'

'Do you really not know where she is?'

'Really.'

'Why hasn't she written to me?'

'She's no good at writing letters, never has been. Anyway, give her time. She will write. Perhaps it's just a rather difficult letter to compose!'

'Rachel, you don't know what's inside me, you don't know what it's like to be me, to be where I am. You see it's a matter of absolute certainty, of knowing your own mind and somebody else's with absolute certainty. It's something completely steady and old, as if it's always been, ever since the world began. That's why what you say is simply nonsense, it doesn't make any sense to me, it's a sort of gabbling. She understands, she spoke this language with me at once. We love each other.'

'Bradley dear, do try to come back to reality –'

'This is reality. Oh God, supposing she were dead –'

'Oh don't be silly. You make me sick.'

'Rachel, she isn't dead, is she?'

'No, of course not! And do try to take a look at yourself. You're simply absurd, you're just talking melodrama, and you're talking it to *me*, of all people! A couple of weeks ago you were kissing me passionately and lying beside me in bed. Now you expect me to believe that you've developed a life-long passion for my daughter in the space of four days. You expect *me* to believe that, *and* to sympathize with you, it seems! You are rather out of touch! One would think that some sort of dignity or tact or ordinary human gentleness would check this outpouring. Well, don't look like that. You do *remember* being in bed with me, don't you?'

In a way, the truth was that I did not. I could attach no precise events to the idea of Rachel. Here memory was simply a cold cloud to be shuddered at. She was a familiar person and a familiar presence, but the notion that I had ever *done* anything in relation to her was utterly shadowy, so much had the advent of Julian drained the rest of my life of significant content, separating history from prehistory. I wanted to explain this.

'Yes, I do – of course – remember – but it's as if – since Julian – everything has been – sort of amputated and – the past has quite gone – it didn't mean anything anyway – it was just – I'm sorry this sounds rather unkind, but being in love one simply has to tell the truth all the time – I know you must feel that there was a sort of – betrayal – you must resent it –'

'*Resent* it? Good heavens no. I just feel sorry for you. And it's all a pity and a sort of waste and rather pathetic really. Well, a sad thing, a disappointment perhaps, a disillusionment. It seems odd to me now that I ever felt that you were a sort of strong wise man or that you could help me. I was touched when you talked about eternal friendship. It seemed to mean something at the time. Do you remember talking about eternal friendship?'

'No.'

'Can you really not remember? You are peculiar. I wonder if you're having some sort of breakdown? Can you really not recall our liaison at all?'

'There was no liaison.'

'Oh come come. I agree it was brief and stupid and I suppose rather improbable. No wonder Julian could hardly believe it.'

'*You told Julian?*'

'Yes. Hadn't you thought that I might? Oh but of course you'd forgotten all about it!'

'You told –?'

'And I'm afraid I told Arnold almost straightaway. You're not the only one who has states of mind. With my husband at any rate, I'm not very discreet. It's a risk one runs with married people.'

'When did you tell her – when –?'

'Oh, not till later. When Arnold came down to your love-nest he brought Julian a letter from me. And in that letter I told her.'

'Oh Christ – she must have read that letter – after –'

'Arnold thought it might serve as an argument. He is very thorough. He thought at least she might come running back to cross-examine me.'

'What did you tell her?'

'And when she did get back, I must say –'

'*What did you tell her?*'

'Simply what happened. That you appeared to be in love with me, that you started kissing me passionately, that we went to

358

bed together and it wasn't a great success but you swore eternal devotion and so on, and then Arnold came and you ran out without your socks on and bought Julian that pair of boots –'

'Oh God – you told her – all that –'

'Well, why not? It did happen, didn't it? You don't deny it, do you? It was relevant, wasn't it? It was part of you. It would have been wrong to conceal it.'

'Oh God –'

'No wonder you tried to forget it all. But, Bradley, one is responsible for one's actions, and one's past does belong to one. You can't blot it out by entering a dream world and decreeing that life began yesterday. You can't make yourself into a new person overnight, however much in love you feel you are. That sort of love is an *illusion*, all that "certainty" you were talking about is an *illusion*. It's like being under the influence of drugs.'

'No, no, no.'

'Anyway, it's over now and no harm done. You needn't worry too much or feel remorse or anything, she had already decided it was a mistake. She has some sense. Really, you mustn't take a young girl's feelings so literally. You haven't lost a pearl of great price, my dear Bradley, and you'll appreciate this sooner than you imagine. You'll soon be heaving a sigh of relief too. Julian is a very ordinary little girl. She's immature, not all there yet, like an embryo. Of course there was a lo· of emotion swilling around, but it didn't really signify too much who was at the receiving end of it. It's a very volatile time of life. There's nothing steady or permanent or deep in any of these great crazes. She's been "madly in love" any number of times in the last two or three years. My dear man, did you really imagine you would be the sticking point of a young girl's passion? How could that be? A girl like Julian will have to love a hundred men before she finds the right one. I was just the same. Oh do wake up, Bradley. Look at yourself in a mirror. Come back to earth.'

'And she came straight to you?'

'I suppose so. She arrived pretty soon after Arnold –'

'And what did she say?'

'Do stop looking like King Lear –'

'*What did she say?*'

359

'What could she say? What could anyone say? She was crying like a maniac anyway and –'

'Oh Christ, oh Christ.'

'She got me to repeat it all and give all the details and swear it was true and then she believed me.'

'But what did she *say*? Can't you remember anything she actually *said*?'

'She said, "If only it had been longer ago." I suppose she had a point there.'

'She didn't understand. It wasn't at all like what you said. When you said that, it wasn't true. When you used those words they conveyed something which simply wasn't true. You implied –'

'I'm sorry! I don't know what words you would expect me to have used! Those ones seemed to me to be pretty appropriate and accurate.'

'She can't have understood –'

'I think she did understand, Bradley. I'm sorry, but I think she did.'

'You said she was crying.'

'Oh madly, like a child who was going to be hanged. But she always did enjoy crying.'

'How could you have told her, how could you – But she must have known it wasn't like that, it wasn't like that –'

'Well, I think it *was* like that!'

'How *could* you have told her?'

'It was Arnold's idea. But I didn't honestly feel at that point that I had to be discreet any more. I thought a little shock would bring Julian to her senses –'

'Why have you come here today? Did Arnold send you?'

'No, not particularly. I felt you ought to be told about Julian.'

'But you haven't told me!'

'About it being – well, you must have assumed it anyway – all over.'

'*No!*'

'Don't shout. And I came, you won't care of course, but out of a sort of kindness. I wo dered if I could help you.'

360

'I must see Julian, I must see her, I must find her, I must explain –'

'I wanted to tidy things up. Now that everything has come out right in the end. Ever since that day when Arnold telephoned you and you came over, I feel you've been somehow in the dark, not understanding anything, under all sorts of misapprehensions. I daresay my attempts to help you didn't really help at all. And I did want to help you. I know you have strong emotional needs, I know you're a very lonely person, maybe I shouldn't have meddled. But I felt I *could* meddle simply because my own position was so strong. That I was all right was the assumption I stupidly thought you shared. I mean, I thought you understood how united I am with Arnold and how happy we really are. Perhaps I should have made this clearer. It's not that I misled you, but I must somehow have let you mislead yourself, I'm sorry. When people need you, you have to be careful with them, and I just wasn't careful enough. You see, this is one of the unfair things that married couples sometimes do, I'm afraid. They give sympathy to people, or they seek for sympathy, and then they run straight home and tell each other all about it. I've never deceived Arnold for a moment and he's never deceived me. Perhaps outsiders don't understand, perhaps they can't. A good marriage is very strong and flexible, it's tough. You spoke about betrayal and resentment. I'm afraid it's rather you who have been betrayed and who may have to bear the burden of resentment. I blame myself, I'm sorry, I shouldn't have assumed you'd understand. Married people do sometimes victimize unmarried people in this way, one is just so lucky. Arnold and I are very close, we've even been laughing at it all, at you, at Christian, at Julian. And, thank God, it's all turned out reasonably well in the end. I know you feel rather sore at the moment but you'll soon start feeling better too. It was a voyage into the absurd. It may even do you good. So do cheer up, dear Bradley. It doesn't do to take the world too solemnly.'

I stared at her with amazement, she was handsome, pale and bland, elated and precise, eloquent, vibrating with dignity and purpose. 'Rachel, I don't think we understand each other at all.'

'Well, don't worry. You'll feel relieved later on. Just try not to feel resentment against me or against Julian. You'll only make yourself miserable if you do.'

'We aren't talking the same language. I feel I'm simply listening to gibberish. Sorry, I – Anyway, isn't Arnold in love with Christian? I thought that was the point of –'

'Of course he isn't. That was just something in Christian's mind. She chased Arnold for a bit, you know how much energy she has. He was flattered and amused of course but he never took her seriously. Fortunately she's a sensible woman, she soon saw she was getting nowhere. Bradley, why don't you go and see Christian? Fundamentally she's such a very nice person. You and she could comfort each other a lot. You see, I'm not being unkind, I do still care and want to help.'

I got up and went to the bureau and got out Arnold's letter. I got it out simply with the intention of making sure I had not dreamt it. Perhaps my memory really was disturbed. There was a sort of blank over Arnold's letter and yet I seemed to recall – I said, holding the letter in my hand, 'Julian will come back to me. I know this. I know it just as well as I know –'

'What's that you have there?'

'A letter from Arnold.' I began to look at the letter.

There was a ring at the front-door bell.

I threw the letter on to the table and ran out to the door in heart-agony.

A postman stood outside with a very large cardboard box, which he had placed upon the floor.

'What's that?'

'Parcel for Mr Bradley Pearson.'

'What is it?'

'I don't know, sir. Is that you then? I'll just push it in, shall I? It weighs a ton.' The postman nudged the big square box in through the doorway with his knee and made off. As I returned to the sitting-room I saw Francis sitting on the stairs. He had obviously been listening. He looked like an apparition, one of those ghosts that writers describe which look just like ordinary people and yet not. He smiled obsequiously. I ignored him.

Rachel was standing by the table reading the letter. I sat down. I felt very tired.

'You ought not to have shown me this letter.'

'I didn't show it to you.'

'You don't know what you've done. I shall never never never forgive you.'

'But, Rachel, you said you and Arnold told each other everything, so surely you –'

'God, you are vile, vindictive –'

'It's not my fault! It can't make any difference, can it?'

'You understand nothing. You are a destroyer, a black spiteful destroyer. You are the sort of person who goes around in a dream smashing things. No wonder you can't write. You aren't really here at all. Julian looked at you and made you real for a moment. I made you real for a moment because I was sorry for you. Now that's all over and all that's left of you is a sort of crazy spiteful vampire, a vindictive ghost. God, I pity you. But I shall never forgive you. And I shall never forgive myself for not keeping you where you belong, at a safe distance. You are a dangerous and awful person. You are one of those wretchedly unhappy people who want to destroy happiness wherever they see it. You did this out of foul malice to –'

'Truly, I didn't mean you to read it, it was just a crazy accident, I didn't mean to upset you. Anyway, Arnold has probably changed his mind by now –'

'Of course you meant me to read it. It's your vile revenge. I hate you for this for ever. You can't understand anything here, you can't understand anything at all – And to think of your having that letter and gloating over it and imagining –'

'I didn't gloat –'

'Yes, you did. Why else did you keep it except as a weapon against me, except to show it to me and hurt me because you think I deserted you –'

'Honestly, Rachel, I haven't given you a single thought!'

'*Aaaaah –*'

Rachel's scream flamed out in the darkening room, more visible than the pale round of her face. I saw the disturbed violent agony of her eyes and her mouth. She ran at me, or perhaps she was simply running to the door. I stumbled aside and crashed my elbow against the wall. She passed me like a stampeding animal and I heard the after-sigh of her scream. The front door flew open and through the open street door I saw lamplight reflected in the wet paving stones of the court.

I went out slowly and closed both doors and began turning lights on. The apparition of Francis was still sitting on the stairs. He smiled an isolated irrelevant smile, as if he were a stray minor spirit belonging to some other epoch, and some other story, a sort of lost and masterless Puck, smiling a meditative cringing unprompted affectionate smile.

'You were listening.'

'Brad, I'm sorry –'

'It doesn't matter. What the hell's this?' I kicked the cardboard box.

'I'll open it for you, Brad.'

I watched while Francis tore the cardboard and dragged the top off the box.

It was full of books. *The Precious Labyrinth. The Gauntlets of Power. Tobias and the Fallen Angel. A Banner with a Strange Device. Essays of a Seeker. A Skull on Fire. A Clash of Symbols. Hollows in the Sky. The Glass Sword. Mysticism and Literature. The Maid and the Magus. The Pierced Chalice. Inside a Snow Crystal.*

Arnold's books. Dozens of them.

I looked at the huge compact mountain of smugly printed words. I picked up one of the books and opened it at random. Rage possessed me. With a snarl of disgust I tried to tear the book down the middle, ripping the spine in two, but it was too tough, so I tore the pages out in handfuls. The next book was a paperback and I was able to tug it into two and then into four. I seized another one. Francis watched, his face brightening with sympathy and pleasure. Then he came down the stairs to help me, murmuring 'Hi!' to himself, 'Hi!' as he dragged the books to pieces and then pursued and tore again the white cascading sheaves of print. We worked resolutely through the contents of the box, standing sturdily with our feet apart like men working in a river, as the pile of dismembered debris rose about us. It took us just under ten minutes to destroy the complete works of Arnold Baffin.

'How are you feeling now, Brad?'

'All right.'

I had fainted or something. I had eaten practically nothing since my return to London. Now I was sitting on the black woolly rug on the sitting-room floor with my back against one of the armchairs which was propped against the wall. The gas fire was flaring and popping. One lamp was alight. Francis had made some sandwiches and I had eaten some. I had drunk some whisky. In fact I felt very strange but not faint any more, no more little eruptions in my field of vision, no more heavy black canopies descending and bearing me to the ground. I was now on the ground and feeling very long and leaden. I could see Francis clearly in the flickering light, so clearly that I frowned over it, he was suddenly too close, too present. I looked down and noticed that he was holding one of my hands. I frowned over that too and removed it.

Francis who, as I recalled, had by now drunk a good deal of whisky, was kneeling beside me eagerly and attentively, not in an attitude of repose, as if I were something which he was making. His lips were pushed out coaxingly, the big red underlip curling over and the mucus of the mouth showing in a scarlet line. His little close eyes were sparkling with inward glee. His dispossessed hand joined his other hand, rubbing rhythmically up and down his plump thighs on the shiny shabby material of his blue suit. He made a little sympathetic chortling noise every now and then.

I felt, for the first time since my return to London, that I was in a real place and in the presence of a real person. At the same time I felt as people feel who after much ailing become suddenly far more ill and helpless, relaxed into the awfulness of the situation. I still had wit enough to see how pleased Francis was at my collapse. I did not resent his pleasure.

'Have some more whiskers, Brad, it'll do you good. Don't you worry then. I'll find her for you.'

365

'That's right,' I said. 'I'll stay here, I must. She'll come here, won't she. This is where she'll come to. She could come at any time. I'll leave the front door open again tonight, like I did last night. She can come in then like a little bird coming to its place. She can come in.'

'Tomorrow I'll search for her. I'll go to her college. I'll go to Arnold's publisher. I'll pick up a clue somewhere. I'll go first thing tomorrow morning. Don't you grieve, Brad. She'll be back, you'll see. This time next week you'll be happy.'

'I know she'll come back,' I said. 'It's odd when one knows. Her love for me was an absolute word spoken. It belongs to the eternal. I cannot doubt that word, it is the logos of all being, and if she loves me not chaos is come again. Love is knowledge, you see, like the philosophers always told us. I know her by intuition as if she were here inside my head.'

'I know, Brad. When you really love somebody it's as if the whole world's saying it.'

'Everything guarantees it. Like people used to think everything guaranteed God. Have you ever loved like that, Francis?'

'Yes, Brad. There was a boy once. But he committed suicide. It was years ago.'

'Oh my God, Priscilla. I keep forgetting about her.'

'That was my fault, Brad, will you ever forgive me –'

'It was my fault. I can't help feeling it was inevitable though, as if she were doomed by a cancer. Yet why should I doom her by thinking this? I feel as if she's somehow inside me too, only she isn't. She grew old and lost hope and died. She was crumbled into ashes. Perhaps it is like this with God. He imagines He is holding every little thing safe in His thought, but one day He will look closely and see that everything has died and rotted away and there's only empty thoughts remaining. That's why love is so important. It's the only way of apprehending somebody that really holds them and sustains them in being. Or is this wrong? Your boy killed himself. What was his name?'

'Steve. Don't, Brad.'

'Priscilla died because nobody loved her. She dried up and collapsed inside and died like a poisoned rat. God doesn't love the world, He can't do, look at it. But I hardly seem to care at all. I loved my mother.'

366

'Me too, Brad.'

'A very silly woman, but I loved her. I felt a sense of duty to Priscilla, but that's not enough, is it.'

'I guess not, Brad.'

'Because I love Julian I ought to be able to love everybody. I will be able to one day. Oh Christ, if I could only have some happiness. When she comes back I'll love everybody, I'll love Priscilla.'

'Priscilla's dead, Brad.'

'Love ought to triumph over time, but can it? Not time's fool he said and he knew about love if anybody did, he was bloody crucified if anybody was. Of course one's got to suffer. Perhaps in the end the suffering is all, it's all contained in the suffering. The final atoms of it all are simply pain. How old are you, Francis?'

'Forty-eight, Brad.'

'You're ten years luckier and wiser than I am.'

'I've never had any luck, Brad. I don't even hope for any any more. But I still love people. Not like Steve of course, but I love them. I love you, Brad.'

'She will come back. The world hasn't changed for nothing. It can't change back now. The old world has gone forever. Oh how my life has gone from me, it has ebbed away. I cannot believe I am fifty-eight.'

'Have you loved a lot of women, Brad?'

'I never really loved anybody before Julian came.'

'But there were women, after Chris I mean?'

'Annie. Catharine. Louise. It's odd how names remain, like skeletons with the flesh fallen away. They designate something that happened. They give an illusion of memory. But the people are gone as if they were dead. Perhaps they are dead. Dead as Priscilla, dead as Steve.'

'Don't say his name, Brad, please. I wish I hadn't told you it.'

'Perhaps the reality is in the suffering. But it can't be. Love promises happiness. Art promises happiness. Yet it isn't exactly a promise because you don't need the future. I am happy now I think. I'll write it all down, only not tonight.'

'I envy you being a writer chap, Brad. You can say what you feel. I'm just eaten by feelings and I can't even shout.'

'Yes, I can shout, I can fill the galaxy with bellowings of pain. But you know, Francis, I've never ever really *explained* anything. I feel now as if at last I could explain. It's as if all the matrix of my life which has been as hard and tight and small as a nut has become all luminous and spread out and huge. Everything's magnified. At last I can see it all and visit it all. Francis, I can be a greater writer now, I know I can.'

'Sure, you can, Brad. I always knew you had it in you. You were always like you were a great man.'

'I've never given myself away before, Francis, never gambled myself absolutely. I've been a timid frightened man all my life. Now I know what it's like to be beyond fear. I'm where greatness lives now. I've handed myself over. And yet it's like being under discipline too. I haven't any choice. I love, I worship and I shall be rewarded.'

'Sure, Brad. She will come.'

'Yes. He will come.'

'Brad, I think you'd better go to bed.'

'Yes, yes, to bed, to bed. Tomorrow we'll make a plan.'

'You stay here and I search.'

'Yes. Happiness must exist. It can't all be made of pain. But what is happiness made of? All right, all right, Francis, I'll go to bed. What's the worst image of suffering you can think of?'

'A concentration camp.'

'Yes. I'll meditate on that. Good night. Perhaps she'll come back in the morning.'

'Perhaps you'll be happy this time tomorrow.'

'I think I can be happy now whatever happens. But oh if she would come back in the morning! What was it you said? A concentration camp. I'll meditate on that. Good night. Thank you, thank you. Good night.'

The morning brought the crisis of my life. But it was not anything that I could have conceived of in my wildest imaginings.

'Wake up, wake up, Brad, here's a letter.'

I sat up in bed. Francis was thrusting at me a letter in an unfamiliar hand. It had a French stamp. I knew that it could only be from her. 'Go, go, and close the door.' He went. I opened the letter, shuddering, almost weeping with hope and fear. It read as follows.

Dearest Bradley, I am in France with my father. We are driving to Italy. I am very very sorry that I went away without leaving a note, only I couldn't find anything to write with. *I am so sorry*. I got into a terrible state. My father didn't come back and take me away like he says you think. I just felt I had to be alone and I couldn't talk any more. Suddenly everything became dark and awful inside me and I had to get away by myself. *Forgive me*. Everything seemed suddenly so muddled as if all the pieces were shifting. It was my fault, I ought not to have come with you to the country, I ought to have thought a bit. Then everything happened so fast I felt as if my life was suddenly bursting and I had to get away, *please* understand. I didn't want to leave you, I didn't change my feelings, it wasn't that at all, it was just like having to breathe. I have been very stupid and regret everything I have done lately. When you said you loved me it seemed like a dream come true. If only I had been a little older I would have known what to do for the best for both of us. There was something beautiful which I feel I have spoilt, but I didn't know what to do and everything seemed right at the time. Oh I am so sorry and miserable. (I can't write very clearly here in this hotel, people keep coming into the room. There is no proper table in the bedroom.) I've had long talks about it all with my father and I think I understand myself a little better now. I hope so very much that you are not angry with me and don't hate me and have forgiven me for going away like that. I value you so much and always will. I still feel so confused and almost as if I had forgotten things, like after a car crash. I feel I've had a bad dream, but the badness is all my own stupidity and muddle and not understanding my own emotions. My father says really no one understands these things, everyone says things they don't mean. I don't regret anything though and I hope you don't. You were wonderful to me, you are a wonderful person. You talked so wonderfully about love. My father says I am too young to know about love and perhaps he is right. I can't now feel that I could possibly have been adequate to you or that it was *me* that you needed. You had certain needs and perhaps another person would have done better. I mean, I wasn't the, or the only, person. Sorry, I am not explaining this properly. I am so stupidly young and without any character, I feel I am just a blank page. You deserve someone much better and more mature. Perhaps you feel relieved. Now I think of you intensely, it's terrible not to know what you feel. Oh do please love me though, I need love, I've never felt more in need of it than now. I feel so terribly terribly unhappy. But it was all crazy and I feel I've come out of a dream. Sorry, I think I said that before, I can't concentrate. Father knows I'm writing to you and will give me a stamp. I hope you get this soon. I would have written sooner only my mind was all torn up. I am so unhappy at having been so stupid and I do hope I haven't hurt you and that you don't hate me. Of course you were right to tell me of your feelings, though they were so new. Often one gets rid of feelings by telling them. I feel I was just a second-best though. I felt that night before I went away that it couldn't be me you wanted. And oh I felt such pain, Bradley. There is nothing to me. It was partly the shock of your telling me that made me so much feel I responded. Of course I wasn't lying. I'm sorry, I can't explain clearly, I can't *think*. I feel I've had an enormous experience, but something which can't fit into ordinary time and space at all.

I will try now to write a more ordinary letter, like the letters I used to write to you years ago when I was a child. Father is quite relaxed now about it all and sends you his best wishes by the way. (Everyone at the hotel thinks we are lovers!) He has gone off to take the car to the garage, there is something wrong with the bonnet, it won't shut properly. I think I never made it clear enough to you how much I love my father. (Perhaps he is *the* man in my life!) I wish he hadn't come down to the bungalow though. That banging on the door was a terrible shock, I still feel I'm trembling and I start crying at anything. It didn't really matter though, as between us. I mean, he didn't make me come away. It was something quite general, it wasn't him or anything to do with Priscilla or finding out your age or finding out anything else at all. Nothing anyone told me made any real difference. I suppose continual shocks can alter one's state of mind and make one feel one has to take decisions or something. It was a shock about Priscilla, I am so sorry about that. I feel I ought to have gone to see her more. It's awful when people get old and abandoned, especially a woman. I was crying about that this morning, sometimes I can't stop crying. I am going to stay with a fan of my father's in Italy and he is coming home and leaving me there, and they hardly speak any English so I shall have to speak Italian all the time! I did learn a little last year, I know some words anyway. The Signora will teach me. They live in a quite remote village, a little place in the mountains amid the 'snow and ice', so there won't be any other English speakers around. I think I may start a novel when I'm in Italy too, I've been talking about that with my father, I feel I now really have something to say.

Please, please don't feel badly about me, don't be too sad or cross with me either. Forgive my ignorance of myself, forgive my worthless empty selfish youth. I can't quite now believe that you absolutely loved me, how could you have done. A mature woman would attract you much more deeply. I think that men like 'youthful bloom' and so on but perhaps they don't really distinguish young girls much from one another and quite rightly, one is so unformed. I hope you don't think I behaved like a 'loose woman'. I felt great feelings and at every moment I did what seemed unavoidable. I don't regret anything unless I hurt you and you won't forgive me. I must stop this letter, I keep saying the same things over and over again, you must be quite fed up. I am so very sorry that I went without saying good-bye. (I got a lift back to London quite easily, by the way. I'd never hitch-hiked before.) I felt I had to go, though I didn't think anything else just then, and since then it has seemed more sensible to keep on with that course rather than make more muddle and misery for everybody, though I terribly, terribly want to see you. We will meet again, won't we, later on perhaps, after some time, and try to be friends, when I am a little more mature. That will be something new and valuable too. I feel now, especially as we go farther and farther south, that life is full of all kinds of possibilities. I do hope I shall manage with the Italian! *Oh forgive me, Bradley, forgive me.* I expect by now you just feel that you have had an odd dream. I hope it has been a good dream. Mine was. Oh I do feel so unhappy though, I feel all topsy turvy. I don't know when I've cried so much. I have been so stupid and thoughtless. *I love you with real love.* It was a revelation. I don't unsay anything. But it wasn't part of any life we could have lived.

I can't end this letter, I feel I haven't said anything properly, and there's something else I should say. (Like sort of 'thank you for having me' or something!) (Sorry I didn't mean that awful pun.) I really can't concentrate, there's a lot of noise. A Frenchman is staring at me, they do stare so. Bradley, I hope we can be real friends later on, that would be so valuable. And we couldn't have managed, we really couldn't. It wasn't anything special. Just that we couldn't have. But I am so glad that you told me of your love. (I will *not* put it all into my novel, which

I expect you are thinking!) I expect you feel relieved and set free though. Thank you. And don't be sad at all. And forgive me for being young and dilly and making muddles. Oh I can't end this letter, but I must. Oh my sear, my dear, good-bye, and lots and lots and lots of love.

Julian

'Brad, may I come in?'

I was dressing.

'Is it good news, Brad?'

'She's in Italy,' I said. 'I'm going after her. She's in Venice.'

The letter had, of course, been written for Arnold's eye. The bit about his 'providing the stamp' made that plain. The girl was being supervised, virtually a prisoner. Of course she couldn't, as she said, 'explain clearly'. She had continued writing a vague repetitive effusion, in the hope of being able to put in a real message at the last moment, hence the references to 'not being able to end'. That had proved impossible. Doubtless Arnold arrived, read the letter and told her to complete it. Then he took it away and posted it. He would see to it that she had no money to buy stamps herself. However she had managed to tell me that she was writing under duress. She had also managed to convey her destination. 'Snow and ice', to which she had drawn attention, patently meant Venice. The Italian for 'snow' is 'neve', and together with the reference to 'Italian words', the anagram was obvious. And in 'topsy turvy' language a little place in the mountains clearly meant a large place by the sea. And Arnold had mentioned Venice, though then to mislead me. Names are not uttered at random.

'Are you going to Venice today?' said Francis, as I was getting into my trousers.

'Yes. At once.'

'Do you know where she is?'

'No. The letter's in code. She's staying with a fan of Arnold's, I don't know who.'

'What can I do, Brad? I say, may I come with you? I could help, I could search and hold forts and so on. Let me come, sort of as your Sancho Panza!'

I thought for a moment. 'All right. You might be useful.'

'Oh good! Shall I go now and get the tickets! You should

stay here, you know. She might telephone or you might get a message or something.'

'All right.' That made sense. I sat down on the bed. I was feeling rather faint again.

'And – I say, Brad, shall I do some detective work? I could go to Arnold's publisher and find out who his Venice admirer is.'

'How?' I said. The flashing lights were coming back and I saw Francis's face, all plumped out with eagerness, surrounded by a cascade of stars, like a divine visitation in a picture.

'I'll pretend to be writing a book about how different nationalities see Arnold's work. I'll ask if they can put me in touch with his Italian admirers. They might have the address, it's worth trying.'

'It's a brainwave,' I said. 'It's an idea of genius.'

'And Brad, I'll need some money. I'll book us to Venice then.'

'There may be no direct flight at once, if there isn't book us through Milan.'

'And I'll get some maps and guide books, we'll need a map of the city, won't we?'

'Yes, yes.'

'Make me a cheque then, Brad. Here's your cheque book. Make it out to "bearer" and I can take it to your bank. Make it a big one, Brad, so I can book us the best way. And, Brad, would you mind, I haven't any clothes, it'll be hot there, won't it, do you mind if I buy some summer clothes, I haven't a thing?'

'Yes. Buy anything. Buy the guides and a map, that's a good idea. And go to the publisher. Yes, yes.'

'Can I buy you some things, you know, a sunhat or a dictionary or anything?'

'No. Go quickly. Here.' I gave him a large cheque.

'Oh thanks, Brad! You stay here and rest. I'll be back. Oh how exciting! Brad, do you know, I've never been to Italy, ever at all!'

When he had gone I went into the sitting-room. I had a blessed purpose now, an objective, a place in the world where she might be. I ought to be packing a suitcase. I felt incapable of doing so. Francis would pack my case. I felt faint with longing for Julian. I still held her letter in my hand.

In the bureau bookcase opposite to me were the love poems of Dante. I pulled them out. And as I touched the book I felt, so strange is the chemistry of love, that my embroiled heart was furthering its history. I felt love now in the form of a sort of divine anger. What I was suffering for that girl. Of course I would love my pain. But there is a rich anger which is bred so, and which is of the purest stuff that love is ever made of. Dante, who spoke his name so often and suffered so at his hands, knew that.

> S'io avessi le belle trecce prese,
> che fatte son per me scudiscio e ferza,
> pigliandole anzi terza,
> con esse passerei vespero e squille:
> e non sarei pietoso nè cortese,
> anzi farei com'orso quando scherza;
> e se Amor me ne sferza,
> io mi vendicherei di più di mille.
> Ancor ne li occhi, ond' escon le faville
> che m'infiammono il cor, ch'io porto anciso,
> guarderei presso e fiso,
> per vendicar lo fuggir che mi face:
> e poi le renderei con amor pace.

I was lying face downwards on the floor, holding Julian's letter and the *Rime* together against my heart, when the telephone rang. I staggered up amid black constellations and got to the instrument. I heard Julian's voice.

No, it was not her voice, it was Rachel's. Only Rachel's voice, in emotion, horribly recalling that of her daughter.

'Oh' – I said, 'Oh –', holding the telephone away from me. I saw Julian in that second in a jagged explosion of vision, in her black tights and her black jerkin and her white shirt, holding the sheep's skull up before my face.

'What is it, Rachel, I can't hear.'

'Bradley, could you come round at once.'

'I'm just leaving London.'

'Please could you come round at once, it's very, very urgent.'

'Can't you come here!'

'No. Bradley, you must come, I beg you. Please come, it's something about Julian.'

374

'Rachel, she is in Venice, isn't she? Do you know her address? I've had a letter from her. She's staying with a fan of Arnold's. Do you know? Have you got an address book of Arnold's you could look it up in?'

'Bradley, come round here at once. It's very – important. I'll tell you everything – you want to know – only come –'

'What is it, Rachel? Rachel, is Julian all right? You haven't heard anything awful? Oh God, have they had a car accident?'

'I'll tell you everything. Just come here. Come, come, at once, in a taxi, every moment matters.'

'Rachel, *is Julian all right*?'

'Yes, yes, yes, just come –'

I paid the taxi with trembling hands, dropping the money all over the place, and ran up the path and began banging on the knocker. Rachel opened the door at once.

I hardly recognized her. Or rather, I recognized her as a portentous *revenant*, the weeping distraught figure of the beginning of the story, her face grossly swollen with tears and, it seemed, again bruised, or perhaps just dirtied as a child's may be after much rubbing away of tears.

'Rachel, there's been a car accident, they've telephoned, she's hurt? What's happened, what's happened?'

Rachel sat down on a chair in the hall and began to moan, uttering great terrible ringing moans, swaying herself to and fro.

'Rachel – something terrible has happened to Julian – what is it? Oh God, what has happened?'

Rachel got up after a moment or two, still moaning and supporting herself against the wall. Her hair was a thick tangled frizzy mass, like the hair of the insane, torn at and dragged across her brow and eyes. Her mouth, all wet, was open and shuddering. Her eyes, oozing great tears, were slits between the swollen lids. Laboriously, like an animal, she pushed past me, still leaning with one hand on the wall, and made her way towards the door of the drawing-room. She pushed it open and made a gesture forward. I followed her into the doorway.

Arnold was lying on the floor near to the window. The sun was shining in from the garden, lighting up the brown tweed of

375

his trousers, but his head was in shadow. My eyes strained and blinked, as if trying to see into another dimension. Arnold's head was lying on something strange on the floor, rather like a tray. His head was lying in a red wet stain which had soaked the carpet round about it. I went closer and leaned over.

Arnold lay sideways, his knees up, one hand palm upwards extended towards my foot. His eyes were half closed, showing a glint of white eye-ball, his teeth were gritted together and the lips slightly withdrawn from them as if in a snarl. There was blood caking his pale tossed hair and dried in marbled patterns on his cheek and neck. I could see that the skull was appallingly dinted at the side, the darkened hair descending into the depression, as if Arnold's head had been made of wax and someone had pressed strong fingers hard in. A vein at the temple still oozed a little.

A large poker was lying on the carpet where the blood was. The blood was red and sticky, the consistency of custard, skinning a little on the surface. I touched, then held, Arnold's tweedy shoulder, warm with the sun, trying to stir him a little, but he seemed as weighty as lead, bolted to the floor, or else my trembling limbs had no strength. I stepped back with blood upon my shoes, and trod upon Arnold's glasses which were lying just beyond the circle of blood.

'Oh God – you did that – with the poker –'

She whispered, 'He's dead – he must be – is he?'

'I don't know – Oh God – '

'He's dead, he's dead,' she whispered.

'Have you sent for the – Oh Christ – what happened –'

'I hit him – we were shouting – I didn't mean – then he started screaming with pain – I couldn't bear to hear him screaming like that – I hit him again to stop him screaming –'

'We must hide the poker – you must say it was an accident – Oh what shall we do – He can't be dead, he can't be –'

'I kept calling him and calling him and calling him, but he wouldn't move.' Rachel was still whispering, standing in the doorway of the room. She had stopped crying and her staring eyes seemed larger and wider, she kept rubbing her hands rhythmically upon her dress.

376

'He may be all right,' I said. 'Don't worry. Did you ring the doctor?'

'He's dead.'

'Did you ring the doctor?'

'No.'

'I'll get the doctor – And the police – I suppose – And an ambulance – Tell them he fell and hit his head or something – Oh Christ – I'll take the poker away anyhow – Better say he hit you and –'

I picked up the poker. I stared for a moment at Arnold's face. The sightless eye-glint was terrible. I felt sick urgent panic, the desire to hand this nightmare over as quickly as possible to somebody else. As I moved towards the door I saw something on the floor near Rachel's feet. A screwed-up ball of paper. Arnold's writing. I picked it up and brushed past her where she still stood leaning in the doorway. I went out into the kitchen and put the poker down on the table. The ball of paper was Arnold's letter to me about Christian. I took out a box of matches and began to burn the letter in the sink. It kept falling into a basin of water since my hands would not obey me. When at last I had reduced it to ashes I turned the tap on it. Then I started washing the poker. Some of Arnold's hair was stuck to it with blood. I dried it and put it away in a cupboard.

'Rachel, I'm going to telephone. Shall I telephone just a doctor or the police as well? What are you going to *say*?'

'It's no good –' She turned back into the hall, and we stood there together in the dim light beside the stained glass panel of the front door.

'You mean it's no good not telling the truth?'

'No good –'

'But you must tell them it was an accident – that he hit you first – that it was self-defence – Rachel, shall I telephone the police? Oh do please try to *think* –'

She murmured something.

'What?'

'Dobbin. Dobbin. My darling –'

I realized, as she now turned away, that this must be her pet name for Arnold which in all the years I had known them I had never heard her utter. Arnold's secret name. She turned away from me and went into the dining-room, where I heard her fall, on to the floor or perhaps into a chair. I heard her begin to lament once more, a short cry, then a shuddering 'fa-fa-fa-' then the cry again. I went back into the drawing-room to see if Arnold had moved. I almost feared to see him opening accusing eyes, wriggling with the pain which Rachel had found so unendurable. He had not moved. His position seemed now as inevitable as that of a statue. Already he did not look like himself any more, his grimacing expression that of a complete stranger, expressing, like a chinaman, some quite strange and unrecognizable emotion. His sharp nose was red with blood, and there was a little puddle of blood in his ear. The white eye glinted, the pained mouth snarled. As I turned from him I noticed his small feet, which I had always found so characteristic and so annoying, clad in immaculately polished brown shoes, lying neatly together as if comforting each other. And as I moved to the door I now saw little smears of blood everywhere, on the chairs, on the wall, on the tiles of the fireplace, where in some unimaginable scene in some quite other region of the world he had reeled about; and saw upon the carpet the shadowy marks of bloody footprints, his, Rachel's, mine.

I got to the telephone in the hall. Rachel's cries were softening into little almost dreamy wails. I dialled 999 and got a hospital and said there had been a bad accident and asked for an ambulance. 'A man has hurt his head. His skull cracked, I think. Yes.' Then after a moment's hesitation I rang the police and said the same things. My own fear of the police made any other course unthinkable. Rachel was right, concealment was not possible, better to reveal all at once, anything was better than the horror of being 'found out'. It was no good saying Arnold had fallen downstairs. Rachel was in no condition to be taught a cover story. She would blurt out the truth in any case.

I went into the dining-room and looked at her. She was sitting on the floor with her mouth wide open and her two hands squeezing either side of her face. I saw her mouth as a round O, she looked subhuman and damned, her face without features, her flesh drained and blue, like those who live underground.

378

'Rachel. Don't worry. They're coming.'

'Dobbin. Dobbin. Dobbin.'

I went out and sat on the stairs and found that I was saying 'Oh – oh – oh – oh –' and could not stop.

The police arrived first. I let them in and pointed to the back room. Through the open front door I saw the sunny street and cars coming, an ambulance. I heard somebody say, 'He's dead.'

'What happened?'

'Ask Mrs Baffin. In there.'

'Who are you?'

Men in dark clothes were coming in, then men in white clothes. The dining-room was shut. I was explaining who Arnold was, who I was, how I came to be there.

'Cracked his skull like an egg shell.'

Rachel screamed behind a closed door.

'Come with us, please.'

I sat in a police car between two men. I started explaining again. I said, 'He hit her, I think. It was an accident. It wasn't murder.'

At the police station I told them all over again who I was. I sat with several men in a small room.

'Why did you do it?'

'Do what?'

'Why did you kill Arnold Baffin?'

'I didn't kill Arnold Baffin.'

'What did you hit him with?'

'I didn't hit him.'

'Why did you do it? Why did you do it? Why did you kill him?'

'I didn't kill him.'

'Why did you do it?'

Postscript by Bradley Pearson

How little in fact any human being understands about anything the practice of the arts soon teaches one. An inch away from the world one is accustomed to there are other worlds in which one is a complete stranger. Nature normally heals with oblivious forgetfulness those who are rudely hustled by circumstance from one into another. But if after reflection and with deliberation one attempts with words to create bridges and to open vistas one soon finds out how puny is one's power to describe or to connect. Art is a kind of artificial memory and the pain which attends all serious art is a sense of that factitiousness. Most artists are the minor poets of their little world, who have only one voice and can sing only one song.

I had the experience of having, as it were, a new character created on me, or to me, in a space of hours. I do not mean the rather pathetic monster which the newspapers invented. I cut a poor figure at the trial. For a short time I was the most unpopular hero in England. *Writer Slays His Friend out of Envy, Resentment of Success Led to Writers' Quarrel,* and so on. All that vulgarity passed me by, or rather was transmuted by my consciousness into much longer and more significant shadows. It was like going through a glass and finding oneself inside a picture by Goya. I even began to look different, older, hook-nosed, more grotesque. One paper described me as 'a failed bitter old man'. I hardly recognized photographs of myself. And I had to live the new being which, as if ready made, had been popped over me like a horrible Goyaesque ass's head.

The first days were a maelstrom of confusion, misunderstandings, incredulity. Not only could I not believe what had happened, I could not conceptualize it. However, I am not going to tell anything more of this as a story. The story is over. And what it is the story of I shall attempt in a little while to say. As the time went on I tried various attitudes, said various things, changed my mind, told the truth, then lied, then broke down, was impassive, then devious, then abject. None of this helped at the trial. Rachel in black was a touching figure. Everyone deferred and was sympathetic. The judge had a special inclination of the shoulders and a special grave smile. I do not think anything was planned in cold blood. It occurred to me later that of course the police themselves had decided what had happened, they suggested it to Rachel, they told her what it was all about. She may even have tried to be, at the start, incoherently truthful. But the story was so impossible. The poker, wiped clean of her fingerprints and liberally covered with my own, was soon found. The whole thing was obvious. All Rachel had to do was scream. I for my part acted as guiltily as any man could. Perhaps at moments I almost believed that I had killed him, just as at moments perhaps she almost believed that she had not.

I was about to write down 'I do not blame her', but this would be misleading. It is not exactly, on the other hand, that I blame her. What she did was terrible, both her actions were wicked, the murder and the lie. And I suppose I owe it to her as a kind of duty to see what she did, to look at it and to try to understand it. 'Hell hath no fury like a woman scorned.' In a way I might have been flattered. In a way there was something almost to admire, a great spirit, a great will. For of course I did not envisage her as moved by any mere petty pusillanimous desire to preserve herself. What did she feel during the trial and afterwards? Perhaps she thought that I would somehow get off. Perhaps she only settled very gradually with many self-preserving vaguenesses into her final dreadful role.

There was even a sort of perfection about it. She had taken such a perfect revenge upon the two men in her life. Some women never forgive. 'I would not give him my hair for a bowstring at the end. I would not raise a finger to save him dying.' Christian had joined Arnold in France, as I learnt much later. But no doubt the will that powered that hammer-blow had been forged much earlier. When I glimpsed it at the start of my narration it was already steely strong. There was, almost, no surprise here. What did surprise me was the strength of Rachel's feeling for myself. There must have been, to create such a great hate, a very considerable degree of love. I had simply not *noticed* that Rachel loved me. She must have cared deeply to be able, in order to destroy me, to lie so hugely and so consistently. I ought to have been moved to reverence. Later perhaps I was. No, I do not exactly 'blame', though neither do I 'condone'. I am not sure what 'forgiveness' means. I have cut attachments, I have 'let her off', I feel no thrilling connection of resentment between us. In some blank way I even wish her well. Forgiveness is often thought of as an emotion. It is not that. It is rather a certain kind of cessation of emotion. So perhaps I do indeed forgive. It matters little what words one uses here. In fact she was an instrument which did me a very great service.

I did at times accuse her, then withdrew my accusations. It is not altogether easy to save oneself at the expense of another, even justly. I felt at times, it is hard to describe this, almost mad with guilt, with a sort of general guilt about my whole life. Put any man in the dock and he will feel guilty. I rolled in my guilt, in the very filth of it. Some newspapers said I seemed to enjoy my trial. I did not enjoy it, but I experienced it very intently and fully. My ability to do this was dependent upon the fact that capital punishment had by this time been abolished in England. I could not have faced the hangman with equanimity. The vague prospect of prison affected me, in my enhanced and vivid new consciousness, comparatively little. (It is in fact impossible to imagine beforehand what prolonged imprisonment is like.) I had been forcibly presented with a new mode of being and I was anxious to explore it. I had been confronted (at last) with a sizeable *ordeal* labelled with my name. This was not something to be wasted. I had never felt more alert and alive in my life, and from the vantage point of my new consciousness I looked back upon what I had been: a timid incomplete resentful man.

My counsel wished me to plead guilty, and if I had done so a verdict of manslaughter might conceivably have been achieved. (Perhaps Rachel expected this.) I insisted on pleading not guilty, but refused also to offer any coherent account of myself or of what had happened. I did in fact at one point tell the whole truth in court, but my truth was by then so surrounded by my own prevarications and lies that it was never seen to stand out with its own self-guaranteeing clarity. (And it was greeted with such vociferous cries of disgust that the public gallery had to be cleared.) I had decided that I could not accuse myself, but I would not accuse anyone else either. This proved to be, from the point of view of telling any plausible story, an impossible position. In any case, everyone, the judge, the jury, the lawyers, including my own counsel, the press and the public had all made up their minds before the trial even began. The evidence against me was overwhelming. My threatening letter to Arnold was produced and the most damning part of it, which contained an explicit reference to a blunt instrument, was read out with a blood-curdling intonation. But I think what impressed the jury most of all was my having torn up all Arnold's books. The fragments were actually brought into court in a tea chest. After that I was done for.

Hartbourne and Francis, in their different ways, did what they could for me. Hartbourne's line, worked out after discussions with my lawyer, was that I was insane. ('That cock won't fight, old man!' I shouted to him across the court room.) His evidence for this view was rather slender. It appeared that I frequently cancelled appointments. ('Then are we all mad?' said the prosecuting counsel.) I had forgotten to attend a party which had been arranged in my honour. I was moody and eccentric and absentminded. I imagined myself to be a writer. ('But he *is* a writer!' said the prosecuting counsel. I applauded.) My apparently calm reaction to my sister's death, which the insanity lobby also tried to use, was later taken over by the prosecution as a proof of my callousness. The climax and *raison d'être* of the theory was that I had killed Arnold in a brain storm and then forgotten all about it! And if I had displayed uncertainty and clutched my head more often this idea might have been at least worth entertaining. As it was, I appeared as a liar but not as a lunatic. I calmly and lucidly denied that I was mad, and the judge and the jury agreed with me. Hartbourne believed me guilty of course.

Francis alone did not believe me guilty. However, he was able to render little assistance. He marred his evidence by crying all

384

the way through, which made a bad impression on the jury. And as a 'character witness' he was not exactly a felicitous performer. The prosecutor sneered at him openly. And he told so many simple-minded lies and half-lies in his anxiety to defend me that he became in the end something of a figure of fun, even to my own side. The judge treated him with heavy irony. It was, to say the least, unfortunate for me that Francis had not been with me when Rachel telephoned. Francis, latching on to this, soon started saying that he had been: but was then quite unable to give any account of what had happened which could stand up to the simplest queries from the prosecution. The jury clearly believed that Francis was my 'creature' and that I had somehow 'put him up to it'. And the prosecution soon tied him in a knot. 'Why then did you not accompany the accused to Ealing?' 'I had to go out to buy tickets for Venice.' 'For *Venice*?' 'Yes, he and I were just going to go to Venice together.' (Laughter.) In fact, all that Francis managed (quite involuntarily) to contribute to the argument was another sinister theory about my motives, to the effect that I was a homosexual, madly in love with Arnold, and that I had killed him out of jealousy! Some of the lewder newspapers ran this idea for a while. However the judge, probably out of consideration for Rachel's feelings, did not highlight it in his final summing up.

Christian was one of the stars of the case. She always dressed with great care, wearing, as the papers soon noticed, a different ensemble every day. 'A smart rich woman' was just what the journalists wanted, and she even achieved during the days of the trial a kind of fame which stood her in good stead later when she decided to set up in business in *haute couture*. In fact she probably developed the idea at this very time. She was very concerned about me. (She too quite evidently believed me guilty.) But she just could not help enjoying the trial. She was in all appearance a 'good witness'. She spoke clearly and firmly and lucidly, and the judge, who patently found her attractive, complimented her on her evidence. The jury liked her too, there were several men who always exchanged glances when she appeared. However, in the hands of a clever public prosecutor she was easily made to damage my case without even noticing. Questioned about our marriage, she was made to convey the impression that I was a thoroughly unstable person if not indeed a 'nasty bit of work'. ('You would describe your former husband as an intense man?' 'Oh awfully intense!') At one point her sheer idiotic self-satisfaction moved me so much that I shouted out 'Good old Chris!' The judge reacted as to a molester of virtuous womanhood. A Sunday paper offered her a large sum of money for her 'story', but she refused.

Rachel, for whom everyone felt such lively sympathy, was not made to appear very much. When she did there was a sort of sigh of reverent appreciation. And the odd thing is that I too, even then, felt a kind of reverence for her as if she were the instrument of a god. At the time I thought that this feeling was an aspect of some frivolous sense of guilt. Later on I saw it differently. There was something magnificent about Rachel. She did not avoid my eye or act in the mechanical or dreamlike way which might have been expected. She behaved with a modest simplicity and an air of gentle quiet exact truthfulness which moved everybody, myself included. I remember when she had said: There is fire in me, *fire*. I had not then conceived how fiercely and purely that fire could burn.

It never entered anyone's head that she could have had a motive for killing her husband. Marriage is a very private place. I had myself destroyed the only piece of solid evidence for such a view. (Arnold's letter about Christian.) The excellence of her marriage, assumed by all, was piously touched upon by some witnesses. It was unnecessary to stress it. Equally, it was never suggested that I had any designs upon my victim's wife. Delicacy, everywhere so manifest in this model trial, forbade any such notion, though it might have seemed obvious enough as a speculation. Even the newspapers, so far as I know, did not pursue it, possibly because the idea that it was Arnold whom I loved was more amusing. And delicacy, as it so often does, usurped the place of truth.

More felicitously, as a result of a spontaneous conspiracy of silence, Julian's name was simply not mentioned at all. No one had any reason to bring her in since, on the one hand, I was in bad enough trouble anyway, and, on the other, that story could only do me harm. So Julian vanished. It was as if the whole fantastic scene in the Old Bailey court room, the robed and wigged celebrants, the sober yet histrionic witnesses, the quiet gleeful public, were all part of a machinery of magic designed to dematerialize her and make her as if she had never been. Yet at moments her paramount reality in that scene was such that I wanted to shout out her name again and again. However I did not. This silence at least which was enjoined was also achieved. Those who know will understand how in a curious way I was almost relieved to think how she had now been made perfect by being removed into the sphere of the impossible. This idea indeed provided a focus of contemplation which alleviated the awful sufferings of that time.

In a purely technical sense I was condemned for having murdered Arnold. (The jury were out of the room for less than half an hour. Counsel did not even bother to leave their seats.) In a more extended sense, and this too provided fruit for meditation, I was condemned for being a certain awful kind of person. I aroused horror and aversion in the bosom of the judge and in the bosoms of the honest citizens of the jury and the sturdy watchdogs of the press. I was heartily hated. In sentencing me to life imprisonment the judge gave general satisfaction. It was a mean crime of an unusually pure kind: to kill one's friend out of envy of his talents. And poor Priscilla, risen from the grave, seemed to point her finger at me too. I had failed as a friend and I had failed as a brother. My insensibility to my sister's plight and then to her death was attested by several. The defence, as I said, did their best to use this as proof of mental unbalance. But the general view was simply that it proved me a monster.

It is not, however, my purpose here to describe the trial, or even to attempt in any detail to describe my state of mind. On the latter subject a few words will suffice. Anyone who is quite suddenly on public trial for a murder he has not committed is likely to be in a disturbed state. Of course I protested my innocence. But I did not (and this too may have influenced the jury) protest it with quite the frenzied passion which might have been expected from an innocent person. Why? The notion of actually *assuming* Arnold's death (and 'confessing') did occur to me an aesthetic possibility. If I *had* killed him there would have been a certain beauty in it. And to an ironical man what could be prettier than to have the aesthetic satisfaction of having 'committed' murder, without actually having had to commit it? However truth and justice alike forbade this course. And (as ought to have been obvious to the judge and jury) it is psychologically impossible for a man of my temperament to lie in a moment of crisis. Of course it was partly that I felt I was guilty of *something* wicked. This picturesque explanation certainly had some force, perhaps simply because of the appeal of the picturesqueness to my literary mind. I had not willed Arnold's death but I had envied him and (sometimes at least) detested him. I had failed Rachel and abandoned her. I had neglected Priscilla. Dreadful things had happened for which I was in part responsible. During the trial I was accused of being unconcerned that two people had died. (At some moments, as the defence pointed out, the prosecution seemed to be accusing me of *two* murders.) The court saw me as a callous fantasy-ridden man. In fact I meditated profoundly upon my responsibility. But guilt is a form of energy and because of it my head lifted and my eyes glowed. There are perhaps moments in any man's life when there is no substitute for the discipline of guilt. Much later, my dearest friend, it was you who pointed out to me that, without realizing it, I surrendered myself to the trial as to a final exorcism of guilt from my life.

I gave myself up to the course of events with a certain resignation and without screams of protest, for another and deeper reason too, which had to do with Julian. Or perhaps there were two reasons here, one lying above the other. Or perhaps three. What did I believe that Julian thought about what had happened? In a strange way I was almost entirely agnostic about what Julian thought. I did not imagine that she saw me as a murderer. But neither did I expect her to defend me by accusing her mother. My love for Julian had somehow brought about this death. (This piece of causality I was quite clear about.) And my responsibility for it I was prepared to lodge for ever in the mystery of my love for Julian and her love for me. That was part of it. But I also felt something like this, that the emergence of my life out of quietness into public drama and horror was a necessary and in some deep sense natural outcome of the visitation with which I had been honoured. Sometimes I thought of it as a punishment for the failure of my vow of silence. Sometimes, shifting the same idea only very slightly, it seemed more like a reward. Because I loved Julian something huge had happened to me. I had been given the privilege of an ordeal. That I suffered through her and for her was, in addition, a delightful, almost frivolous comfort.

The court saw me, as I have said, as a fantastical man. Little did they know how fantastical I was, though not in their crude sense. It is the literal truth that the image of Julian was not absent from my mind for a single second during the waking hours of those terrible days. I apprehended at the same time her absolute presence and her absolute absence. There were moments when I felt as if I were being literally torn to pieces by love. (What must it be like to be eaten by a large animal? I felt I knew.) This pain, from which I almost fainted, once or twice came upon me when I was addressing the court, and abruptly stopped my utterance, thereby giving comfort to the insanity lobby. Perhaps the only thing which made me survive this period of thinking about Julian was the complete absence of hope. A grain of hope present at that time would have killed me.

The psyche, desperate for its survival, discovers deep things. How little most so-called psychologists seem to know about its shifts and its burrowings. At some point in a black vision I apprehended the future. I saw this book, which I have written, I saw my dearest friend P.L., I saw myself a new man, altered out of recognition. I saw beyond and beyond. The book had to come into being because of Julian, and because of the book Julian had to be. It was not, though indeed time matters little to the unconscious mind, that the book was the frame which she came to fill, nor was she the frame which the book filled. She somehow was and is the book, the story of herself. This is her deification and incidentally her immortality. It is my gift to her and my final possession of her. From this embrace she can never now escape. But, and this is not to belittle my darling, I saw much more than this in the black glass of the future. And this is, if I can express it, the deepest reason why I accepted the unjust judgement of the court.

I felt that every single thing that was happening to me was not just predestined but somehow actively at the moment of its occurrence *thought* by a divine power which held me in its talons. At times I felt almost as if I were holding my breath in case some tiny movement of my own should interfere with the course of this divine possession. Though in the same thought I also knew that I could not now, by the most frenzied struggling, ever escape my fate. The court room and the judge and the condemnation for life were mere shadows of a much huger and more real drama of which I was the hero and the victim. Human love is the gateway to all knowledge, as Plato understood. And through the door that Julian opened my being passed into another world.

When I thought earlier that my ability to love her *was* my ability to write, my ability to exist at last as the artist I had disciplined my life to be, I was in the truth, but knew it only darkly. All great truths are mysteries, all morality is ultimately mysticism, all real religions are mystery religions, all great gods have many names. This little book is important to me and I have written it as simply and as truthfully as I can. How good it is I do not know and in a sublime sense I do not care. It has come into being as true art comes, with absolute necessity and with absolute ease. That it is not great art I daresay I am aware. What kind of thing it is is dark to me as I am dark to myself. The mechanical aspects of our humanity remain obscure to us until divine power has refined them absolutely, and then there is no anxious knower any more and nothing to be known. Every man is tiny and comic to his neighbour. And when he seeks an idea of himself he seeks a false idea. No doubt we need these ideas, we may have to live by them, and the last ones that we will abandon are these of dignity, tragedy and redemptive suffering. Every artist is a masochist to his own muse, that pleasure at least belongs to him intimately. And indeed our highest moments may find us still the hero of such conceptions. But they are false conceptions all the same. And the black Eros whom I loved and feared was but an insubstantial shadow of a greater and more terrible godhead.

About these things, my dear fellow, we in our seclusion have often spoken, in our times of quietness together, with words whose meaning glowed out of an ineffable understanding, like flames upon dark water. So friends, so spirits, ultimately converse. It was for this that Plato, in his wisdom, forbade the artist. Socrates wrote nothing, neither did Christ. Almost all speech which is not so illumined is a deformation of the truth. And yet: I am writing these words and others whom I do not know will read them. With and by this paradox I have lived, dear friend, in our sequestered peace. Perhaps it will always be for some an unavoidable paradox, but one which is only truly lived when it is also a martyrdom.

I do not know whether I shall see the 'outside world' again. (A curious phrase. The world is, in reality, all outside, all inside.) The question is of no interest to me. A truthful vision finds the fullness of reality everywhere and the whole extended universe in a little room. That old brick wall which we have so often contemplated together, my dear friend and teacher: how could I find words to express its glowing beauty, lovelier and more sublime than the beauty of hills and waterfalls and unfolding flowers? These are indeed vulgarisms, commonplaces. What we have seen together is a beauty and a glory beyond words, the world transfigured, found. It was this, which in the bliss of quietness I now enjoy, which I glimpsed prefigured in madness in the watercolour-blue eyes of Julian Baffin. She images it for me still in my dreams, as the icons of childhood still haunt the visions of the ageing sage. May it be always so, for nothing is lost, and even at the end we are ever at the beginning.

And I found you, my friend, the crown of my quest. Could you not have existed, could you not have been waiting for me in this monastery which we have inhabited together? That is impossible, my dear. Were you there by accident? No, no, I should have had to invent you, and by the power which you yourself bestow I should have been able to. Now indeed I can see my life as a quest and an ascesis, but lost until the end in ignorance and dark. I was seeking you, I was seeking him, and the knowledge beyond all persons which has no name at all. So I sought you long and in sorrow, and in the end you consoled me for my life-long deprivation of you by suffering with me. And the suffering became joy.

So we live on together here in our quiet monastery, as we are pleased to call it. And so I come to the end of this book. I do not know if I shall write another. You have taught me to live in the present and to forswear the fruitless anxious pain which binds to past and to future our miserable local arc of the great wheel of desire. Art is a vain and hollow show, a toy of gross illusion, unless it points beyond itself and moves ever whither it points. You who are a musician have shown me this, in the wordless ultimate regions of your art, where form and substance hover upon the brink of silence, and where articulate forms negate themselves and vanish into ecstasy. Whether words can travel that path, through truth, absurdity, simplicity, to silence I do not know, nor what that path can be like. I may write again. Or may at last abjure what you have made me see to be but a rough magic.

This book has been in some way the story of my life. But it has also been I hope an honest tale, a simple love story. And I would not wish it to seem at the end that I have, in my own sequestered happiness, somehow forgotten the real being of those who have figured as my characters. I will mention two. Priscilla. May I never in my thought knit up the precise and random detail of her wretchedness so as to forget that her death was not a necessity. And Julian. I do not, my darling girl, however passionately and intensely my thought has worked upon your being, really imagine that I invented you. Eternally you escape my embrace. Art cannot assimilate you nor thought digest you. I do not now know, or want to know, anything about your life. For me, you have gone into the dark. Yet elsewhere I realize, and I meditate upon this knowledge, that you laugh, you cry, you read books and cook meals and yawn and lie perhaps in someone's arms. This knowledge too may I never deny, and may I never forget how in the humble hard time-ridden reality of my life I loved you. That love remains, Julian, not diminished though changing, a love with a very clear and a very faithful memory. It causes me on the whole remarkably little pain. Only sometimes at night when I think that you live now and are somewhere, I shed tears.

Four Postscripts by
DRAMATIS PERSONAE

Postscript by Christian

Mr Loxias has kindly shown me the manuscript written by my former husband and has asked me if I wish to make any comments on it, these to be published with the book itself. I do not think I have many comments except that the whole book seems to me to be sort of off key. I think many things are in the eye of the beholder. I was not at all 'self-satisfied' during the trial, but very upset indeed, for instance. It would have been very heartless to be self-satisfied then. Bradley has a way of seeing everything in his own way and making it all fit together in his own picture. Perhaps we all do that, but we do not write it down in a book. He does not give a very fair picture at all of the time of our marriage. I do not want to be nasty to him, I am very sorry for him indeed. It must be very depressing to be in prison, though he is putting a brave face on it I must say. (It is rather funny that he calls it a monastery. Some monastery.) In fact I cannot imagine anything more awful, and I think it is a great achievement that he has managed to write this book at all. I can say nothing about its value, I am not a literary critic, I mean its value as a novel or whatever it is. But that it is not a very true picture of the bits I know about it is all I can say. Bradley never hated me during our marriage. I think he never really hated me at all, but because I left him (which he does not say in the book) he had to pretend that he did. He describes how I dominated him or stole him from himself or something, these are very eloquent parts of the book and very well written I dare say. But it was not at all like that in real life. The trouble with our marriage was that I was young and wanted more fun and happiness than Bradley was able to give me. Because he is quite witty sometimes in the book and makes things funny (sometimes he makes things funny which are not really) a reader might think that he was an amusing person to be with, but this is not so, even when he was young. There was no sort of battle between us at all as he tells in the book, I just got very depressed and so did he, and I decided to leave him though he begged me and begged me to stay, which he does not tell us. Our marriage had been a mistake. I was much happier in my second marriage. I did not say the horrible things about my second husband that Bradley says, though I may have made a joke about him. Bradley has never been very good at seeing when things are jokes. He says somewhere in his book, I cannot now find it, that he is a puritan and that I think is the truth. He could never understand women. And I think he was jealous of my second marriage, people never like to think their wife was happier with someone else. Of course he is quite wrong when he thinks that after I came back to London at the beginning of his 'novel' I was really interested in coming together with him again. I was not. I came to see him because he was about the only person I still knew in London and also because I was curious to see what had happened to him in the between time. I was cheerful and happy and I just wanted to look him over, so I stopped by. I did not need him!! But it was jolly clear at once that he needed me, and this bit he did not tell at all properly. He was after me at once. And when I told him I just wanted to be friends in a friendly casual sort of a way, he was pretty furious and put out and then I expect he wrote those things about hating me and about my being so awful like a sort of female spider as a kind of revenge because I was not friendly enough to him when I came back to London. Really it is obvious I think from the book that he was in love with me again, or had always been in love with me. It was a great shock to him when I came back and when he found that I rejected him a second time. I think it was this that finally unsettled his reason and brought on the kind of insanity which my husband was so anxious to prove at the trial. Both his sister and his mother were very unbalanced and neurotic, incidentally, they could have done with analysis, all the family. I do believe that Bradley was really mad when he killed Arnold Baffin, it was a brain storm, and he forgot about it all afterwards as if it had been a dream. Those sleeping pills he took make people forget things. I think the death of his sister upset him terribly too, though he

394

did not seem to be very upset, and he certainly abandoned her though he must have seen what a state she was in, and left her to me to be looked after, which he was glad enough to do. Perhaps it was something to do with money, he was always a bit of a mean man. And what he says in the postscript of his book about his sister does not seem to me to be real feeling, but rather that he was feeling guilty, which he so often did, though it does not seem that it made him behave any better. As for the part about Miss Baffin, that must embarrass her a lot, as it was obviously mostly in his mind. I am rather surprised that the book is to be published. I think all that story was to veil his loving me. Anyway, people never fall in love suddenly like that except in novels. I think the trouble with Bradley was that he never really got over his background. He is always going on about 'the shop', and I think he felt ashamed of his parents and of not having had a proper education, I think that is the key to a lot. I am afraid he is a bit of a snob, which does not help anything. My husband thinks Bradley is not really a writer at all, but should have been a philosopher, only he was not educated enough. Bradley is wrong too to say that the idea of *haute couture* only came to me during the trial, I do not know why he says that. I was never going to take on women's underwear with Mr Baffin, and had planned my existing salon even before I arrived back in London. He is right about one thing though, that I am good at business, as witness the fabulous success of the salon in a few years. My husband too has taken to business like a duck to water and his knowing about tax is so useful, so one good thing came out of that trial, though as I said at the begining I was very unhappy indeed and very sorry indeed for poor Bradley. (And for Mr Baffin too of course.) I would like to say to Bradley now if he ever sees this piece that I am very sorry for him and think of him with affection. There is no point in writing him letters any more. That poor Bradley is still quite mad is shown by the postscript to his story, where he seems to think that he has become a mystic or something. That part was rather creepy I thought and really like what mad people write. And why all this fuss about art anyway, we can live without art I should think. What about social workers and people who work on famine relief and so on, or

are they all supposed to be failures or not all there? Art isn't
everything, but of course Bradley would think what he's taken
up with is the only important thing. At any rate he is getting
another publication out at last. I think by now everyone must
know that 'Mr Loxias' is really a well-known publisher who hopes
to make a lot of money out of publishing Bradley's memoirs,
which I hope that he will. The Sunday papers will publish them
too I am told. I do not know if people in prison can draw royal-
ties at all. So the person Bradley talks of as his 'teacher' and so
on and whom he seems to think so much of must be somebody
else, or else that bit is probably made up as is obviously much else
in the story. I would like to say again, how sorry I am for Bradley
and how I hope that he is not too unhappy in prison. Perhaps
being a bit out of your mind is a merciful thing if it makes you
think that you are happy when you are not.

Christian Hartbourne

Postscript by Francis

It is my pleasure and privilege to add a critical epilogue to this unusual 'autobiography'. I do so gladly as homage to my old friend, still languishing in 'durance vile', and I do so dutifully as a service to the cause of science. This remarkable piece of self-analysis from a talented pen deserves a thoroughly detailed commentary, for which, the publisher tells me, there is unfortunately no space in this volume. I intend however to publish in due course a lengthy book, upon which I have now been at work for some time, about the case of Bradley Pearson, and in this work the 'autobiography', a prime piece of evidence in this *cause célèbre*, will of course be fully treated. What follows here is merely a digest of a few concise points.

Not to skirt the obvious Bradley Pearson presents, I need hardly say, the classical symptoms of the Oedipus complex. To say so is perhaps banal. Most men love their mothers and hate their fathers. Many men, because this is so, hate and fear all women in adult life. (Adored mama is never alas forgiven for going to bed with detested papa!) Such was the case with Bradley. What a vocabulary of physical disgust he uses to conjure up 'the ladies' of his tale! Many men, often without consciousness thereof, see women as unclean. The idea of menstruation is sickening and appalling. Women smell. The female principle is what is messy, smelly, and soft. The male principle is what is clear, clean, and hard. So with our Bradley. We find him gloating (I fear there is no other word) over the physical discomfiture, the uncleanliness, the ailments of his women. In the case of his sister his sense of disgust at her symptoms of age and mental decay led him to thrust her out of his sight in an unkind and unseemly way, while at the same time protesting his duty to her and even his affection. There is no doubt that she had the misfortune to represent to him also *the shop*, that stale interior, symbolic of the rejected womb of a socially inferior mother. Alas how readily these symbols assemble themselves in this our human life, forming great daisy chains of cause and effect from which we escape never! The physical, moreover, figures the moral. Women are liars, traitors, cowards. In contrast Bradley himself appears as a self-confessed puritan, an ascetic, a tall thin man, a sort of human Post Office Tower, erect and steely. By this means, without the necessity of actual sexual prowess, our hero can see himself as 'an imaginary Don Juan'. (A touching give-away this!)

It is also of course clear from the most casual scrutiny that our subject is homosexual. He has the typical narcissism of the breed. (Consider his description of himself at the beginning of the tale.) His masochism (of which more below), his eager professions of virility, his confessed lack of identity, his attitude (already mentioned) to women, the evidence of his parental relationship patterns, all these point in the same direction. And indeed his rather surprising 'unconvincingness' at the trial may be laid at the same door. He did not believe in himself and so could hardly expect the judge and jury to lend him credence. Bradley Pearson connected this absence of any sense of self with his mode of existence as an artist. But here, as so many of the uninstructed, he mistook cause and symptom. Most artists are homosexual. This tender appreciative tribe, bereft of sturdy self-assertion as either man or woman, is best enabled thus to body forth the world and give it houseroom in their souls.

That 'Bradley Pearson's story' is the tale of a man in love with a woman need cause little embarrassment to our theory. Bradley himself gives us all the clues that we are in need of. When he first (in the story) catches sight of his young lady he mistakes her for a boy. He falls in love with her when he imagines her as a man. He achieves sexual intercourse with her when she has dressed up as a prince. (And who incidentally is Bradley Pearson's favourite author? The greatest homosexual of them all. What sends Bradley Pearson's fantasy soaring as high as the Post Office Tower? The idea of boys pretending to be girls pretending to be boys!) Further: who in reality is this girl? (Father-fixated of course and taking Bradley as a father-substitute, no mystery there.) The daughter of Bradley's protégé, rival, idol, gadfly, friend, enemy, *alter ego*, Arnold Baffin. Science proclaims that this cannot be the work of accident. And science is right.

When I say that Bradley Pearson was in love with Arnold Baffin I would not be understood to be making any crude statement. We are dealing with the psychology of a complicated and refined person. Bradley's more simple, more human, affection bore perhaps upon another object. But Arnold symbolized the focus of passion and the goal of love to this unfortunate self-darkened victim. It was Arnold whom he loved and Arnold whom he hated, Arnold his own distorted image in the stream over which Narcissus leans eternally anxious, eternally enraptured. He admits, significant word, that there is something 'demonic' in Arnold and also in himself. The 'character' of Arnold is in a literary sense markedly 'weak', as any critic would point out. Why indeed is the whole story oddly 'unconvincing' as if it were somehow hollow? Why do we feel that something is missing from it? Because Bradley does not 'come clean'. He often *says* that he is attached to Arnold or that he is envious of Arnold or that he is obsessed by Arnold, but he does not, he dare not, body these feelings forth in the narrative. And because of this omission the tale, which should feel very hot, feels in fact very cold.

This classical misplacement is not however the chief item of interest. The case is interesting mainly because Bradley Pearson is an artist and because, before our very eyes, he is ingeniously (and often disingenuously) reflecting about his art. As he says, the psyche desperate for its survival invents deep things. That he often does not realize the significance of his reflections can make his work, with suitable expert exposition, yet more fascinating and instructive to us. That Bradley is a masochist is here a banality of criticism. (That all artists are is a further truism.) How readily recognizable to the expert eye is obsession in literature! Even the greatest cannot cover their tracks, conceal their little vices, altogether moderate the note of glee! For *this* the artist labours, to get *this* scene in, to savour *this* secret symbol of his secret love. But let him be never so cunning, he cannot evade the eye of science. (This is one reason why artists always fear and denigrate scientists.) Bradley is cunning, particularly in his misleading celebration of a simple heterosexual subject, but how can we not notice that what he really *enjoys* is being discomfited by Arnold Baffin?

Of course Arnold Baffin is a father-figure. Why is it a *writer* on whom Bradley fixes his love and his hate? And why is it a *writer* that he himself so obsessively dreams of being? The choice of the art is itself significant. Bradley tells us in so many words that his parents kept a *paper* shop. (Paper: papa.) The 'crime' of soiling paper (defaecation) is a natural image of the revolt against the father. It is here that we must seek the source of that paranoia whose symptoms Bradley, with characteristic unawareness, so clearly exhibits in his story. (Consider his 'interpretation' of his lady-love's letter!) Why does Bradley gloatingly idolize 'grand' stationers' shops? Father never got *this* far! The ubiquitous gilt snuff box makes the same point. This is a 'gift' far beyond the humble resources of the original shop. (And of course gilt: guilt.) On this comparatively simple aspect of the case see my paper shortly to be published, *Further to Freud's Experience on the Acropolis.*

Of greater interest, as psychology if not as literature, is Bradley's more poetic and more conscious embroidery upon his own theme. The mysterious title of the book, ambiguous in I cannot readily say how many senses, is, though somewhat obscurely, 'explained' for us by its author. Bradley speaks of 'the black Eros'. He also mentions some yet more arcane source of inspiration. What he means, taken at its face value, may be highly significant or may be pretentious rubbish. There can be no doubt however of the psychological 'weight' of such a conception. It is surely more natural for a man to picture the force of love as a woman, and for a woman to picture it as a man. (It is true that both Eros and Aphrodite are the invention of men, but it is important that the former is the child of the latter.) Yet Bradley shamelessly delights in the conception of the huge black bully (like an enormous blackamoor) who has, as he conceives it, come to discipline his life, as artist and as man. Moreover (and what do we need more to complete our theory?) should we wish to inquire further concerning the identity of this monster we have only to consider the two initial letters of his name. (Black

Prince. Bradley Pearson.) As for the alleged Mr Loxias, he too is soon seen to be our friend in a thin disguise. There is even a marked similarity of literary style. The narcissism of the deviant eats up all other characters and will tolerate only one: himself. Bradley invents Mr Loxias so as to present *himself* to the world with a flourish of alleged objectivity. He says of P. Loxias 'I could have invented him'. In fact he did!

I hope that my old friend, when his sapient eye alights upon these pages, will look indulgently (I can imagine him smiling with that familiar self-conscious irony) upon the observations of a mere scientist. They are prompted, let me assure him, not just by a chill love for truth, but by a lively affection for a very lovable human being, to whom the author of this note feels recognition and gratitude. I have hinted earlier that Bradley was blessed with another more mundane and more 'real' attachment, another much simpler and less tormenting focus of emotion. I would not, and indeed need not, use his ill-concealed love for me as evidence of his perverted tendencies. (The transparent attempt to belittle the love-object is again typical.) I cannot however close this very miniature monograph without saying this to him: I knew of his feelings and, I trust he will believe me, I valued them highly.

Francis Marloe
Psychological Consultant

A subscription list for my forthcoming work, *Bradley Pearson, the Paranoiac from the Paper Shop* is now open c/o the publisher. Letters to my consulting rooms will be forwarded from the same address.

Postscript by Rachel

I have been asked by a 'Mr Loxias' for my comments on a piece of fantastic writing by the murderer of my husband. I was inclined at first simply to ignore the request. I also considered resorting to legal action to prevent publication. However, there has already been, and I am sure not accidentally, a good deal of publicity about the matter, and to stifle this 'outpouring' might give it the interest of a secret document without in the end concealing what it said. Frankness is better and compassion is better. For we must, I think, feel or attempt to feel pity and compassion for the author of this fantasy. It is sad that when provided with the 'seclusion' which he professes always to have wanted, what Pearson produces is a sort of mad adolescent dream and not the serious work of art of which he imagined himself capable and of which he so incessantly told us.

I have certainly no wish to be unkind. The revived publicity about this hideous tragedy has caused me great suffering. That my own life has been 'ruined' is a fact with which I have to live. I hope and believe that unhappiness has not made me bitter. I do not want to hurt anybody. And I do not believe that my frankness now can possibly hurt Bradley Pearson, who seems to be invincibly wrapped up in his own fantastic conceptions of what happened and of what he himself is like.

About his account of events there is little to be said. It is in its main outline clearly a 'dream' such as might interest a psychologist. And let me say here that I do not and cannot judge Bradley Pearson's motives in writing it. (Of Mr Loxias's motives I will speak below.) Perhaps the kindest thing to say is that he wanted to write a novel but found himself incapable of producing anything except his own immediate fantasies. I expect many novelists rewrite their own recent histories 'nearer to the heart's desire',

402

but they have at least the decency to change the names. B.P. (as I shall shorten his name henceforth) alleges that in prison he has found God (or Truth or Religion or something). Perhaps all men in prison think they have found God, and have to in order to survive. I feel no vendetta-like resentment against him now, or any particular desire that he should suffer. His suffering cannot repair my loss. His new 'creed' may be sincerely believed in or may be, as the whole story may be, a smoke screen to conceal his unrepentant malice. If his tale is indeed prompted by malice we have to do with a person so wicked that ordinary judgement of him is baffled. If, as is much more likely, B.P. has come to believe or half-believe both in his 'salvation' and in his story, then we have to do with one whose mind has given way under continued strain. (He was certainly not insane at the time of the murder.) And then he must be, as I said earlier, an object of pity. This is how I prefer to view him, though really I cannot know, and indeed do not want to know, what is in fact the case. When B.P. went through the gates of the prison I felt as if he had died and I wanted to concern myself with him no more. To think about him, for instance with anger and rage, would have caused too much misery, besides being fruitless and immoral.

I spoke advisedly of an 'adolescent' fantasy. B.P. is what might be called a 'Peter Pan' type. He does not in his story describe his extensive past life, except for hinting that there were romances with women. He is the sort of man who likes both to hint at a past and to behave as if he were eternally twenty-five. (He speaks of himself as an ageing Don Juan, as if there were only a trivial difference between real and imagined conquests! I doubt if there were really many women in his life.) A psychiatrist would probably find him 'retarded'. His tastes in literature were juvenile. He speaks grandly of Shakespeare and of Homer, but I doubt if he had read the former since schooldays or the latter ever. His constant reading, which of course he nowhere admits, was mediocre adventure stories by authors such as Forester and Stevenson and Mulford. He really liked boys' stories, tales of crude adventure with no love interest, where he could identify himself with some princely hero, a man with a sword or such. My husband often commented to me about this, and once tackled B.P. directly.

B.P. was upset and I can recall him actually blushing very much at the charge.

His general picture of himself really could not have been more false. He pictures himself as ironical and sardonic and restrained and idealistic. To admit to being 'puritanical' sounds like self-criticism, but is just another way of asserting that he was a high-principled man. In reality he was a person quite without dignity. His appearance was absurd. (And no one could possibly have taken him for being younger than his age.) He was a stiff, awkward man, very timid and shy, and yet at the same time he could be quite pushing. He was often, to put it bluntly, rather a bore. The pretence of being an artist was psychologically necessary to him. I am told this is so with a lot of unsuccessful people. He pretends he wrote things and tore them up, and he goes on and on about how he waited and waited and was a perfectionist. I am sure he never tore anything up in his life. (Except my husband's books.) He was print-mad. He desperately wanted what my husband had, fame. He wanted just to be published at any price and was always going round the publishers with his stuff, he would have published anything. He even asked my husband to intercede for him with his publisher. He was not a stoical and ascetic sort of person at all, but remained like an eager boy who wants to get his little piece into the school magazine. It was quite touching in an elderly man.

B.P. was of course a person painfully conscious of inferiority. He was an unhappy disappointed man, ashamed of his social origin and his illiteracy, and stupidly ashamed of his job which he imagined made him a figure of fun. In fact he was, though not for that reason, a figure of fun to all of us. No one, before the tragedy, could mention him without smiling a little. He must have realized this. I suppose it is possible, and it is a shocking thought, that a man might commit a serious crime just in order to stop people from laughing at him. That B.P. was a man who hated being laughed at is pretty clear throughout the story. The rather pompous self-mocking style is a defence and a sort of meeting people half-way if they decide to laugh.

Of course he turns everything topsy-turvy in his account of his relations with our family. He says rather coyly that we needed him. The truth was that he needed us and was a sort of parasite, an awful nuisance sometimes. He was very lonely and we all felt sorry for him. And I can remember occasions too when we made absurd excuses when he wanted to see us or hid when he rang the door bell. His relations with my husband were crucial of course. His claim to have 'discovered' my husband is ridiculous. My husband was already quite famous when B.P. after much begging, persuaded an editor to let him review one of my husband's books, and after that he made himself known to us and became, as I think my daughter once put it, 'the family pussy cat'.

B.P. cannot even in his dream-story conceal that he was very envious of my husband's success. I think this envy was an absolute obsession with him, he was eaten up by it. He knew also that my husband, though friendly and kind to him, despised him a little and laughed at him. The idea of this caused him *torment*. Sometimes I felt that he thought about nothing else. He naïvely himself admits that he had to be friends with Arnold, and so somehow identify with him and 'take credit' for his writing, so as not to be driven mad with envy and hate. If an accuser is needed B.P. is his own. He admits too in a moment of candour that his picture of Arnold is prejudiced. This is putting it mildly. (He admits further to a general hatred of the human race!) Of course he never 'helped' Arnold, but Arnold often helped him. His relation to myself and my husband was virtually that of a child to its parents. This too might interest a psychiatrist. But I do not want to enlarge any more upon matters which are obvious and which came into the open at the trial.

His allegations about my daughter are of course absurd, both as to his feelings and as to hers. My daughter always regarded him as a sort of 'funny uncle' and there is no doubt that she was very sorry for him, and pity can be mistaken for fondness and can even *be* a sort of fondness, and in this sort of way perhaps she was fond of him. His great 'passion' for her is a typical dream-up. (I will explain what I think about its origin and motives in a moment.) I believe that unfulfilled frustrated people probably spend a lot of their lives in pure fantasy-dreaming. This can I am sure be a great source of consolation though not always harmless. And a 'good' fantasy-dream might be to pick on some person whom you know slightly and imagine they are in love with you and picture a great love-relationship and its drama. B.P., being probably some sort of sadomasochist, of course imagines an unhappy ending, an eternal separation, terrible suffering for love, and so on. His one published novel (he implies he published more than one, but he only published one in fact) is a story of disappointed romantic love quite remarkably like this one.

The same sort of sadomasochistic fantasizing has produced the (of course quite imaginary) scene at the beginning of his story where he alleges that he came round to our house and found me lying upstairs on my bed with a black eye, etc, etc. I noticed more than once that B.P. liked to pretend to both my husband and myself that of course he knew that we had domestic differences. We laughed together about this foible of his, not then seeing it as sinister. It may be that with the naïvety of the bachelor (which in essence he always remained) he did genuinely mistake occasional light arguments for serious disagreements. It is alas more likely that half-consciously he invented the idea of our dissensions out of pure 'wishful thinking'. He did not want 'papa and mama' to be at peace with each other. He wished in his mind thus to belittle us both, and to attach each of us more closely to himself.

There is, I feel I must now frankly admit, yet a further aspect to the matter, and one which for various reasons, many of them obvious, was glossed over at the trial. Bradley Pearson was of course in love with me. This fact had been known to me and to my husband for a number of years and was also a subject for amusement. B.P.'s fantasies of making love to me make sad reading. This unhappy love of his also explains his fiction of a passion for my daughter. This fiction is of course a smoke-screen. It is also partly a 'substitute-idea' and partly I am afraid a pure revenge. (It may also be relevant that the strong attachment between father and daughter, not admitted in the story, may well have preyed upon B.P. and made him feel again, as so often, miserably excluded.) How far B.P.'s love for me led him to perform that terrible deed is not for me to say. I am afraid that envy and jealousy were inextricably mixed up inside the bosom of that wicked and unhappy man. Of these matters, of which I would not have spoken if not forced to by confrontation with this farrago of lies, I say no more.

It may be imagined how profoundly this document distresses me. I do not in fact blame B.P. for its proposed disgraceful publication. It is at least understandable that he should have written out this dreamy-fantasy-nonsense to console himself in a place of grimness and to distract himself from serious remorse or the effort of repentance. For the crime of publication I blame the self-styled Mr Loxias (or 'Luxius' as I believe he sometimes calls himself). As several newspapers have hinted, this is a *nom de guerre* of a fellow-prisoner upon whom the unfortunate B.P. seems to have become distressingly fixated. The name conceals the identity of a notorious rapist and murderer, a well-known musical virtuoso, whose murder, by a peculiarly horrible method, of a successful fellow-musician made the headlines some considerable time ago. Possibly the similarity of their crime drew these two unhappy men together. Artists are notoriously an envious race.

I would like to say this at the end, and I am sure I speak also for my daughter, with whom I am temporarily out of touch, now of course herself a well-known writer and living abroad. I bear him no malice and, in so far as he must be regarded as seriously unbalanced if not actually mad, I feel sincere pity for his undoubted sufferings.

Rachel Baffin

Postscript by Julian

I have read the story. I have also seen the other postscripts, which I believe the other postscript writers have not. Mr Loxias allowed me this privilege. (For several reasons which I can guess.) However I have little to say.

It is a sad story full of real pain. It was a dreadful time for me and I have forgotten much of it. I loved my father very dearly. This is perhaps the chief fact which I have to offer. I loved him. His violent death drove me nearly mad. I was nearly mad during Pearson's trial. I cannot recall that period of my life except as patches in a haze, as scenes. There is a mercy in oblivion. Human beings forget much more than is usually recognized, especially when there is a shock.

Not so many years have passed since these events. Yet in the life of a young person these are long years. Centuries separate me from these events. I see them diminished and myself there as a child. It is the story of an old man and a child. I say this, treating it as literature. Yet I acknowledge that it concerns myself. Are we what we were as children? What stuff is that which persists? I was a child: I acknowledge myself: yet also I cannot recognize myself.

A letter for instance is quoted. Did I write this letter? (Did he keep it?) It seems inconceivable. And the things that I said. (Supposedly.) Surely they are the invention of another mind. Sometimes the reactions of the child are too childish. I think I am 'clever' now. Could clever me have been that child? Sometimes too there are thoughts which I could not possibly have thought. Thoughts which have leaked in from the author's mind. (I am not a very convincing 'character'.) Was I not muddled and frightened and without precedents? It seems like literature, yes.

My father was quite right not to encourage me to write. And

Pearson was wrong to encourage me. I see that now. It is profitless to write early, one understands nothing. One has no craft and one is the slave of emotion. Time of young days is better spent in learning. Pearson implies that my father thought little of my abilities. The contrary is the case. My father was a man who often said the opposite of what he thought. Out of modesty or fear of destiny. This is not uncommon.

Dr Marloe describes the book as 'cold', and one understands him. There is a lot of theory in this book. Yet also it is a very 'hot' book (too hot), full of unstudied personal emotions. And of immediate judgements, sometimes not good ones. Perhaps it needs, like a poem, to be again and again reflected? Perhaps any novel needs further reflection and a truly great writer would write only one novel. (Flaubert?) My mother refers to me rightly as a writer but wrongly as well known. (I am a poet.)

So I am careful and sparing with words. There is a ring in what Pearson says about silence. That part I liked. He may be right that an experience is richest not talked of. As between two people talk to an outsider destroys. Art is secret secret secret. But it has some speech or it would not be. Art is public public public. (But only when it is good.) Art is brief. (Not in a temporal sense.) It is not science or love or power or service. But it is the only true voice of these. It is their truth. It delves and chatters not.

Pearson always hated music. I can remember that. I can remember his brusquely switching off my father's record player. (A violent act.) I was a small child then. I see the scene. He hated it. Mr Loxias must be a good teacher. (Indeed I know he is: if teacher is the word.) But is there not an irony? Pearson worked hard at writing all his life. I saw his notebooks. They looked like work. There were a great many words there. Now there is music and no more words perhaps. Now there is music and beyond it silence. Why?

I confess that I never read the books that Pearson wrote. I think there is more than one. My mother is wrong here. I did not think he was a very good critic either. I think he understood only the vulgar side of Shakespeare. But I admired what I thought of as his life. He seemed an example: a lifetime at trying and failing.

It seemed remarkable to go on trying. (Sometimes it seemed stupid however.) Naturally I admired my father too. There was no conflict. Perhaps some prescient instinct made me love the idea of a small publication. (A poet who is a novelist's child must deplore the parent's verbosity.) The idea of the secret worker making little things. But it was only an idea. Pearson published as much as he could. If my father was the carpenter, Pearson was certainly the walrus.

This is not a personal statement. Words are for concealment, art is concealment. Truth emerges from secrecy and laconic discipline. I want to argue about a general matter. Pearson seems to me merely sentimental when he concludes that music is the highest art. Does he believe it? He is parroting. No doubt Mr Loxias has influenced him. Music is an art and also a symbol of all art. Its most universal symbol. But the highest art is poetry because words are spirit at its most refined: its ultimate matrix. Excuse me, Mr Loxias.

Most important of all. Pearson was wrong to identify his Eros with the source of art. Even though he says one is a 'mere' shadow of the other. Indeed it is the hotness of the book that I feel, not its coldness. True art is very very cold. Especially when it portrays passion. For only so can passion be portrayed. Pearson has muddied the waters. Erotic love never inspires art. Or only bad art. To be more precise. Soul-energy may be *called* sex down to the bottom. (Or up to the top.) That concerns me not. The deep springs of human love are not the springs of art. The demon of love is not the demon of art. Love is concerned with possession and vindication of self. Art with neither. To mix up art with Eros, however black, is the most subtle and corrupting mistake an artist can commit. Art cannot muddle with love any more than it can muddle with politics. Art is concerned neither with comfort nor with the possible. It is concerned with truth in its least pleasant and useful and therefore most truthful form. (Is it not so, you who listen?) Pearson was not cool enough. Neither was my father.

Even this does not explain. Pearson said that every artist is a masochist to his muse. Though by now perhaps he has seen the falseness of this. (It is possibly the key to his own failure.)

Nothing could be false. The worshipping attitude concentrates on self. The worshipper kneels as Narcissus kneels to gaze into the water. Dr Marloe says artists give houseroom to the universe. Yes. But then they cannot be narcissists. And of course not all artists are homosexuals. (What nonsense!) Art is not religion or worship or the acting out of obsessions. Good art is not. The artist has no master. No, none.

Julian Belling

Mr Loxias who has read the above tells me I have not said whether I endorse Pearson or my mother. I have not seen or communicated with either for several years. Naturally I endorse (roughly) what my mother says. However what Pearson has to say is true in its way. As for Mr Loxias, about whom there has been speculation: I think I know who he is. He will understand when I say that I have mixed feelings about him. What does truth mean to him, I wonder?

I feel I should in fairness add something else. I think the child I was loved the man Pearson was. But this was a love which words cannot describe. Certainly his words do not. A literary failure.

Editor's Postscript

Since the foregoing documents were collected my dear friend Bradley Pearson has died. He died in prison of a quick-growing cancer, which developed soon after he finished his book. I was his only mourner.

There is after all little for me to say. I had thought, as editor, to have written a long essay, criticizing and drawing morals. I had looked forward with some pleasure to having the last word. But Bradley's death has made a lengthy commentary seem otiose. Death cannot silence art, but it can suggest spaces and pauses. So I have little to say. The reader will recognize the voice of truth when he hears it. If he does not, so much the worse for him.

I cannot forbear to make a few remarks, most of them obvious, about the postscripts. Mrs Belling says, in part rightly, that words are for concealment. How little the postscript-writers have been able to avail themselves of this decency. These people are indeed on display. Each lady, for instance, asserts (or implies) that Bradley was in love with her. Even the gentleman asserts it. Touching. However this is a small matter and to be expected. Equally to be expected are the lies. Mrs Baffin lies to protect herself, Mrs Belling to protect Mrs Baffin. How conveniently hazy Mrs Belling's memory has now become! This is an understandable piety, although mother and daughter have long broken off all relations. 'Dr' Marloe, who told the truth at the trial, pusillanimously fails to repeat it now. I am told he has been threatened by Mrs Baffin's solicitors. 'Dr' Marloe is no hero. For this we must forgive him. Bradley, who never saw these sad 'postscripts' to his work, would have done so.

Whatever Bradley himself would have thought or done, it is difficult not to exclaim at the small-mindedness of these writers.

412

Each piece is self-advertisement, ranging from the vulgar to the subtle. Mrs Hartbourne advertises her salon, 'Dr' Marloe his pseudo-science, his 'consulting rooms', his book. Mrs Baffin polishes the already much publicized image of herself as a suffering widow. (Here words of comment fail.) She is at least sincere in saying that when Bradley went to prison she dismissed him from her mind. Mrs Belling advertises herself as a writer. With her carefully written little essay I will concern myself in a minute. (Would she admit that her literary style was influenced by Bradley? This too she is trying hard to conceal!) Perhaps the living can always seem to outwit the dead. But theirs is a hollow victory. The work of art laughs last.

My intention in publishing these papers was originally twofold. First, to give to the public a work of literature. I am by nature an impresario, and this is not the first time I have been thus instrumental. Secondly, I wished to vindicate the honour of my dear friend, to clear him, briefly, of the charge of murder. That I have not been assisted in this task by either Mrs Belling or 'Dr' Marloe is, as I say, not surprising, though it is saddening. I have seen much of human beings over a long period, and I have learnt how little good to expect from them. In pursuance of my second objective, I had intended to write a long analysis of my own, rather like a detective's final summing up, pointing out discrepancies, making inferences, drawing conclusions. This I have decided to omit. Partly because Bradley is dead. And death always seems to commit truth to some wider and larger court. And partly because, rereading Bradley Pearson's story, I feel that it speaks for itself.

Two things remain. One to give some brief account of Bradley Pearson's last days. The other to take issue (on a theoretical point only: I leave the facts to her conscience) with Mrs Belling. The latter I will do first, also briefly. Art, my dear Mrs Belling, is a very much tougher and coarser plant than you seem to be imagining in your very *literary* piece. Your eloquence, which verges I fear on the romantic, even the sentimental, is that of a young person. When you are older in art you will understand better. (You may even then be privileged to understand Shakespeare's vulgarity.) About the soul we speak always in metaphors:

metaphors which are best used briefly and then thrown away. About the soul perhaps we can only converse directly with our intimates. This makes moral philosophy vain. And there is no science of these things. There is no depth to which you, Mrs Belling, or any other human being, can see where you can make final distinctions about what does and what does not essentially nourish art. Why are you so anxious to divide that great blackamoor in two, what are you afraid of? (The answer to this question could tell you much.) To say that great art can be as vulgar and as pornographic as it pleases is to say but little. Art is to do with joy and play and the absurd. Mrs Baffin says that Bradley was a figure of fun. All human beings are figures of fun. Art celebrates this. Art is adventure stories. (Why do you deride adventure stories, Mrs Baffin?) Of course it is to do with truth, it makes truth. But to that anything can open its eyes. Erotic love can. Bradley's synthesis may seem naïve; perhaps it is. Behind his unity there may be distinctions, but behind the distinctions there is unity and how far into that vista can a human being see and how far does an artist need to see? Art has its own austerity to it reserved. At an austere philosophy it can only mock.

As for music, which Mrs Belling acutely says is the image of all the arts but not their king: I am not disposed to disagree. In fact I am well placed to appreciate her argument. Known as a musician, I am in fact interested in all the arts. Music relates sound and time and so pictures the ultimate edges of human communication. But the arts form not a pyramid but a circle. They are the defensive outer barriers of language, whose elaboration is a condition of all simpler modes of communication. Without these defences men sink to beasts. That music points to silence is again an image, which Bradley used. All artists dream of a silence which they must enter, as some creatures return to the sea to spawn. The creator of form must suffer formlessness. Even risk dying of it. What would Bradley Pearson have done if he had lived? Would he have written another book, a great one? Perhaps. The human soul is full of surprises.

Bradley died well, tenderly, gently, as a man should. I so clearly recall the look upon his face of simple vulnerable surprise when

(I was present) the doctor told him the worst. He looked as he had looked once when he dropped a capacious teapot and saw it break. He said 'Oh!' and turned to me. The rest was fast. He soon took to his bed. The hand of death modelled him speedily, soon made his head a skull. He did not try to write. He talked with me, asked me to explain things, holding my hand. We listened to music together.

On the morning of the last day he said to me, 'My dear fellow, I'm sorry – to be still here – so boring.' Then he said, 'Don't make a fuss, will you?' – 'What about?' – 'My innocence. It isn't worth it. It doesn't matter now.' We listened to some Mozart on Bradley's transistor. Later he said, 'I wish I'd written *Treasure Island*.' Towards evening he was much weaker and could hardly speak. 'My dear, tell me –' 'What?' 'That opera –' 'Which?' – '*Rosenkavalier*.' After that he was silent for a while. Then, 'How did it end? That young fellow – what was his name –?' 'Octavian.' 'Did he stay with the Marschallin or did he leave her and find a young girl of his own age?' 'He found a young girl of his own age and left the Marschallin.' 'Well, that was right, wasn't it.' Then after a while he turned, still holding my hand, and snuggled down as if to sleep. And slept.

I am glad to think how much I comforted his last days. I felt as if he had suffered the lack of me throughout his life; and at the end I suffered with him and suffered, at last, his mortality. I needed him too. He added a dimension to my being.

As for my own identity: I can scarcely, 'Dr' Marloe, be an invention of Bradley's, since I have survived him. Falstaff, it is true, survived Shakespeare, but did not edit his plays. Nor am I, let me assure Mrs Hartbourne, in the publishing trade, though more than one publisher has reason to be grateful to me. I hear it has even been suggested that Bradley Pearson and myself are both simply fictions, the invention of a minor novelist. Fear will inspire any hypothesis. No, no. I exist. Perhaps Mrs Baffin, though her ideas are quite implausibly crude, is nearer to the truth. And Bradley existed. Here upon the desk as I write these words stands the little bronze of the buffalo lady. (The buffalo's leg has been repaired.) Also a gilt snuff box inscribed *A Friend's Gift*. And Bradley Pearson's story, which I made him tell, remains too, a kind of thing more durable than these. Art is not cosy and it is not mocked. Art tells the only truth that ultimately matters. It is the light by which human things can be mended. And after art there is, let me assure you all, nothing.

P. A. Loxias